Juli Flintoff is an English artist from West Yorkshire. Initially studying drama, she obtained a Bachelor of Arts from Sunderland University in Fine Art. For several years, Juli was a successful community arts development worker facilitating workshops throughout the Bradford, Calderdale, Leeds, Wakefield and Kirklees areas. After exhibiting five large banners at Bradford's International Youth Event attended by delegates from all over the world, she became involved with projects for young offenders. This led her to train as a prison officer and later a drugs dog handler. In 2010, she began caring for her elderly father and since his passing in 2011, she has dedicated her life to supporting, caring and advocating on behalf of her mother, who lives with dementia. 'Dear Diary' is Juli's fourth publication and is preceded by 'The Daisy Chain', a psychological thriller of murder and intrigue detailing the effects of early childhood trauma; 'Blame, Shame & Guilt' is a heartbreaking tale of child abuse and 'The Secret Back Door' is an inspiring book depicting the struggles of living with dementia.

Juli Flintoff

DEAR DIARY

To Tina
with much love &
appreciation my friend

AUSTIN MACAULEY PUBLISHERS®

LONDON ∗ CAMBRIDGE ∗ NEW YORK ∗ SHARJAH

A CIP catalogue record for this title is available from the British Library.

ISBN 9781035892358 (Paperback)
ISBN 9781035892365 (ePub e-book)

www.austinmacauley.com

First Published 2025
Austin Macauley Publishers Ltd®
1 Canada Square
Canary Wharf
London
E14 5AA

Thank you to the editorial team at Austin Macauley Publishers for their inspirational depiction of '*Dear Diary*', detailing it as being '*once again an immersive and informative read.*' I was humbled by the excerpts you chose to highlight, along with mentioning the poems between each chapter and therefore hold such gratitude that you deemed my work as being of a '*high quality*'. Thank you for affirming its potential in such a positive light and for everyone's continued support, guidance and expertise on the road to publication.

Thank you as always to Coban Flintoff and Corai Flintoff, who, without your love, support, encouragement and help, particularly with Grandma's care duties, I would not have had the freedom nor time to focus and immerse myself in such a dedicated manner. Love you guys abundantly!

Thank you to Gwen Bill, a beautiful Christian lady whose faith, loyalty to God and resolute spirit have been both an inspiration in writing this book and also a personal guide of love, friendship and moral values. It is an honour to call you my friend.

Thank you to the Well Women Centre, Wakefield, who do a fantastic job in providing a 'holistic, non-medical approach to helping improve women's mental health and emotional well-being' through a variety of bespoke, supportive measures tailored to the individual.

A shout out to Linda Seel, MBACP, the counsellor who supported me through my own personal road to recovery; boy, was it a ride and a half. Keep doing God's work, lovely lady; His hand is upon you in your restorative ministry.

Thank you to Ian Blackwood and your amazing family, especially Auntie Ann (Stevenson), Uncle Bill (Stevenson), Cousin Jo Lamb and her partner, Martin, who kept me sane during a very difficult time whilst writing this book. Your continued inclusion, unconditional love, acceptance and kindness towards me propelled me to keep writing. You guys totally rock!

Thank you to Susan Whiteley for your dedication and literary expertise in assisting me to ensure the finished article is the best it could possibly be. Your guidance, advice and attention to detail has been inspirational.

Lastly, many thanks to Barry Newton, a very dear gentleman and computer restorer who kindly loaned me a laptop to kickstart the writing process until I was able to replace my old one. Your thoughtfulness and generosity of spirit have been very much appreciated and quite overwhelming.

Table of Contents

Prologue
2018

In the midst of the burning confusion and overwhelming depths of despair, I take my seat. The one at the table facing out onto the rolling hills of the Baztan Valley in the stunning area of northern Spain. The terracotta tiled floor had scatterings of the palm fruit awaiting yet another sweep. It will have to wait until after the weekend when the tree surgeon has completed his removal of the bulbous bunches of cascading berries.

I glance around my environment to visually breathe in the beauty that envelops me. How I wish I felt a measure of this vision radiating from within me. I don't. I breathe deeply, holding it a tad too long before the pressure forces me to sigh it out with almost a splutter.

The Jamaican Ska drums that I have heard every day of my 2-week holiday begin their rhythmic dance from some small cortigo at the foot of the valley. It must be 17:15 hours, the exact same time it has danced its way along the air towards me each day. The sun tries to push through the heavily clouded, overcast sky, but it is only successful for barely a minute. I pull the grey fleecy blanket with its thin white stripe closer to me to stave off the need to go back indoors, I prefer the open expanse of the hillside with its quiet, tranquil stillness.

There is a dog barking from some property in the distance. For once, it isn't Franco, the black-and-white mutt who has persistently disturbed both my sleep and wakeful hours. A black car takes my attention as it makes its way along the dusty track at the very top of one of the roving hills opposite before disappearing over its pinnacle and then suddenly dropping out of sight.

A child can be heard coughing from the apartment below, and when I concentrate long enough, I can hear a bird not too far away sharing its song with me. I breathe in the stillness of everyday life in this beautiful village set in the mountains. I can feel my shoulders suddenly relax, having been unaware I had been holding myself rigid, again—a habit I had become accustomed to whenever he was around me.

I make a mental note to watch out for any future involuntary high-alert reactions that have become my natural fight-or-flight response. I remind myself that I am free, I managed to escape, and he cannot hurt me anymore. I assure myself that I have got this, though it is a statement I will need to work on as it doesn't sound very convincing yet.

The same photographic memories start to simultaneously reveal themselves like a projector screen of exhibits firing out from their secret hidden chamber within my brain. My eyes snap open, but it is too early for me to face the truth of dancing with the devil himself.

I feel relieved that the silence is momentarily disturbed by a man from the apartments above and behind me talking very loudly in his native Spanish tongue. I have been learning the language for some time but am still unable to decipher what is being said, as each word seemingly dribbles into the next—another skill I have tried but which seems to escape my ability.

If I had one wish before I died, it would be to master the language once and for all, but it's too late now. I don't know it yet, but I will be the person they find lying face down in the pool later tonight as the fireworks light up the night sky. If only I had more time. If only I had known what my fate would be, perhaps I could have prevented it. But I didn't, so I am sitting here in ignorant bliss, ironically believing that I am safe, unable to change this new course of events.

This will be one of my last moments sitting out here on the terrace, drinking in the sights, sounds and tranquillity of my environment. My mobile pings—it's a notification to alert me that a message has been delivered. As I use my finger to tap it open, I suddenly realise that dusk is beginning to fall, and I wonder just how long I have been sitting out here when the church bells start to ring. Counting the prominent dull tones, I am surprised to find it is now 7 pm.

I smiled a warm, glowing smile when I realised who the sender was—my first true sense of love for an exceptionally long time—was Asher. I had sent a group message to Asher, Eden, Darla & Eloise earlier, telling them of my success. Eden's reply was short, as usual—a simple 'Well done!' was sufficient. Asher, my first love, was completely different. It began:

'I came straight to the toilet to read this.'

What an image this could have projected—it's a good job I knew he meant it was so he could read my message in privacy.

'I'm so happy and proud to see your work being recognised, and to say that you are 3 for 3 with no misses is insane,' he continued, talking about a recent literary acceptance.

'You should be undoubtedly proud of yourself. Congratulations! I can just picture your grin of joy, the sense of relief for a job well done and the knowing of all that hard work and determination coming to fruition. xx.'

I was glad he couldn't see my face because there was no 'grin of joy'—just a tear-stained sadness of my personal circumstances debilitating me into submission, relinquishing any true sense of accomplishment. I am sure that I was undoubtedly thrilled; I just couldn't feel it, as there were so many other negative emotions overriding it.

My inability to be able to speak to Asher right now was due to the grief I was experiencing, and maybe this contributed to the overwhelming disbelief that my work could have been recognised so highly. As always, this was more of a humbling gratitude that my God had not forsaken me than any pride in myself at achieving a 'job well done.'

As I sat alone, dreading my return to civilisation and all that came with it, I decided to leave the safety of my little patio to take an evening dip in the pool. I collected my pre-organised swim bag from the back of one of the dining room chairs and made that one fatal mistake—I left the security of my impenetrable apartment. Within the next hour, my life would resemble an Etch A Sketch; one swift move and my picture would soon be erased forever.

Part 1
The Present

Broken

My heart is as big as a human fist,
But hurts whenever you see the red mist.
The impact creates a hollow crunch,
Your words, they score every single punch.
The pumping blood spills from my head,
As I lay gurgling, left for dead.
The beat is slowing and soon will stop,
But from your mouth, the lies will drop.
You stole my heart; I wanted it back,
But emotional intelligence is what you lacked.
The heart once given will never be whole,
Be careful, it holds the desires of the soul.

(Juli Flintoff)

Chapter 1
A Split Second

Karen Blakely was just pulling into her drive after a long 14-hour shift at the hospital to find Bob's car was already parked there. Her heart sank down to the bottom of her aching feet. The only thought that had propelled her through the last two hours had been the desperate longing for a soothing, hot soak in the bath, followed by the spicy chicken with vegetables and pasta she had waiting in her fridge. Every traffic light stop along her route home had been exasperating, as the pull to get back seemed to snag progression like the catch of a fisherman's line. She just wanted to physically wash the day from her tired bones, fill her stomach, and then collapse between the clean sheets of her king-size bed—alone!

Karen's tyres crunched heavily along the gravel drive as she reversed in alongside Bob's battered old Civic. With the outside light now activated, Karen knew that she would only have a matter of minutes before the kitchen light would flicker alive. She shifted the gear into neutral and, without even cutting the engine, she scrambled for her phone to ring Marcus needing to talk to her friend to express her disappointment. She knew he would be able to give her the strength and encouragement to face Bob and make him leave. She hurriedly communicated her thoughts whilst being careful to keep her eyes peeled on the kitchen window in case the light came on to alert her of his presence.

And there it was. She could see him through the window slipping his trainers on and knew that any moment now there would be no time to escape.

Karen suddenly felt the urge to throw the car into first gear to leave before he had time to emerge, but it was too late. The door opened to reveal him standing there. Karen observed that he was wearing the same black cargo pants along with his red polo top that he had been wearing for the last 3 days. She felt a wave of repulsion mixed with despair and dread at having to tolerate him tonight. She did love Bob, but it sickened her that this man just wouldn't hear her needs or abide by the boundaries that she continually fought to uphold. This was her house, and surely, she deserved the right to come home and do her own thing without either him having to be there or her having to explain why she wanted to spend time alone.

When they had first become romantically involved, everything had obviously been new and ultimately it had felt exciting, so naturally, they had wanted to spend all their spare time together. However, as it had since developed into a more committed relationship, she felt secure and comfortable enough to move into the sphere of healthy time apart. He, on the other hand, was not au fait with this concept and struggled to understand why she would not want to spend every waking hour with him, as he did with her.

As Karen sat in her car, the irritation at his presence in her house despite her specifically stating to him that she wanted 'to be alone tonight' was beginning to manifest into anger.

Karen hurriedly disconnected the call with Marcus and pretended to grapple with her bag in the passenger seat in the hope of biding herself some more time by keeping her back to the house. When she then heard him tap on her window and she turned to find his sickly-sweet smile, the anger intensified so much that she simply slid down the window rather than get out straight away.

'Hi, darling. I thought I would call round to surprise you, how was your day?' Bob enquired, grabbing for her through the window before she had any chance to even open the car.

'It's been a really long day, Bob; hence I said I wanted to come back for a long soak,' Karen said through gritted teeth.

'Good job I am here then to give you a foot massage,' Bob tried.

'Bob, you are missing the point, again!' Karen stressed.

'Why are you being so hostile? None of my friends would put up with the way you treat me. Most women would love their partners to be as considerate as I am,' he said, trying to emotionally guilt-trip her.

She hated the way he continually ignored the healthy boundaries she tried to install—boundaries that were important for her to manage her own self-care. Here he was again, not just turning up unannounced as he usually did but actually entering her property in her absence and without her consent. This was not something she either welcomed or needed right now, especially after dealing with two attempted suicides, a fatal road traffic accident and numerous other emergencies. Why did he always make her feel like she had to justify her need for time to herself? This neediness in him was becoming so unattractive to the point that she was beginning to feel suffocated.

'I thought I could run you a bath, get you a glass of wine and put some candles out for you to make it all romantic,' Bob said innocently.

'I don't need a night in on my own to be romantic, Bob. I just want to have a soak, get some food and go to bed,' Karen delivered as bluntly as she could before raising her window and finally killing the engine. Her annoyance at him intensified when he didn't even give her a chance to reach for the door handle before he swung it wide open.

Karen glared at him as she removed herself and made her way past him, crossed the drive and entered through the kitchen door. She really wished she could be as thick-skinned as Bob, or at least if she were a tad more selfish, she might have just locked the door behind her to further demonstrate she didn't want him there. But she didn't. She allowed him to walk all over her like he did every other day.

'That wasn't a very nice welcome,' Bob told her as he followed her into the kitchen.

'Sorry, but it is about as much as I can muster at this moment through my genuine disappointment at finding you have let yourself into my home and are monopolising my time, again,' Karen delivered without any due care.

'Wow! So, shoot me for putting you first and thinking whilst you are having your bath I could go get us a Chinese and we could eat together,' Bob said innocently, trying to appeal to her good nature along with feigning the usual *I'm a good guy* act, of which she should undoubtedly think herself lucky to have him.

'That's very kind of you, Bob, but we both know you are only interested in meeting your own needs,' Karen began as she made her way over to the fridge to take out her pre-prepared spicy chicken with vegetables and pasta meal.

'It is not really my desire to have a Chinese as I have been looking forward to this all day.' Karen smirked, but as she prised the lid off the unusually light container, she stared at the contents—or lack of them—in dismay.

'Oh sorry,' Bob said. 'I got a bit hungry whilst I was waiting for you. I didn't know how long it had been there, so I thought I would use it up.'

'Are you for real?' she asked him.

'What? I did say I would go and get us a Chinese. To be honest, it wasn't that good,' he lied, opening up the tea towel drawer to select the allotted takeaway menu

'Bob, I don't want a bloody Chinese. I wanted my spicy chicken with vegetables and pasta. My priorities were to come home and take a bath in the comfort of my own home, alone, as you know,' she spelt out. 'Just how long have you been here waiting for me?'

'I came straight after work,' he told her, believing she would be pleased that being with her had taken precedence.

'I thought you were finishing early today?' she queried, trying to find the underlying cause of exactly how long he had waited in her home.

'I did, I left around 3 pm to pick something up for you, then came straight here. I cannot wait for you to see it,' he gushed.

'So exactly what time did you get here, Bob?' she asked directly.

'It was about 4:45, but don't worry, I took a shower to ensure I was a clean boy for when you got here,' he beamed.

'So, not only are you at my home uninvited, but you have let yourself in, taken a shower, put your dirty clothes back on, eaten my tea and now you actually expect me to be grateful?' she asked in complete despair.

'Don't be like that I have missed you so much today, and I just wanted to see you, where is the crime in that?' he guilt-tripped her. 'And you are wrong I have not put my dirty clothes back on. By getting here early, I have had time to throw them in the wash and then dry them too.'

'Oh, this just gets better. So, I go to work, but you're here using my water, running up my electric bill, eating my food and also doing your laundry!' Karen was flabbergasted at his bare-faced cheek.

'Karen, everything I do is to make life easier for you. I have been waiting all night for you to get back so you can see your surprise. And like I said, I have really missed you today,' Bob pleaded his case.

'You may have missed me, Bob, but you show no consideration for my needs or the fact that I told you I just wanted to come home and relax. You turning up regardless is a gross invasion of my personal space, not to mention just letting yourself into my home. Where are you respecting my rights and choices here? You're not, you are railroading me into accepting what you want at the expense of what I need tonight, and after such a busy shift,' she said.

'That's why I thought I would get us a Chinese to take some of the pressure off you,' Bob told her.

'The only pressure on me is accepting your constant presence when I want some alone time. Bob, I can't keep doing this, seriously, your neediness is suffocating me I've got to have some space, surely you can understand how unhealthy your behaviour is?' Karen implored.

'Needy? I don't know why you keep throwing that at me I am not needy I just love spending time with you,' Bob pleaded.

'It is one thing spending quality time with someone but a whole new ballgame when it's my every waking minute,' Karen let rip.

'I think you're being a bit dramatic there it's hardly every waking minute, I haven't seen you all day,' Bob whined.

'No, Bob, but I have had seven texts, three phone calls, been tannoyed to the front desk to pick up a random sandwich that you apparently delivered, and now I have returned home to find you in my house,' she threw at him.

'I only phoned because you didn't reply to my texts,' he tried.

'I didn't reply to you because I was busy dealing with emergencies at work, for goodness' sake,' she shrieked.

'That's why I dropped you a sandwich in—because you were obviously really busy,' he persisted.

'No, Bob. You dropped me a sandwich in, not out of the goodness of your heart but because you hadn't had a response from me. You couldn't cope without your daily fix, so went to the extreme of coming down to my place of work— again. This has got to stop it is not normal behaviour,' Karen told him. no longer managing to stay civil.

'You're making it sound like I have got some problem when it is not like that at all,' he spat at her.

'Whether you can see it or not is irrelevant. Your constant pursuant to dominate my every waking hour along with your attempts to control everything I do is making me ill. I just want you to go!' she finally stated, filling the kettle and flicking the switch on before turning round to face him.

As soon as she realised the little 'hurt boy' routine had been triggered, she knew word for word the next defensive speech that would emanate from his defeated mouth.

'If you don't want me here, I will leave. I would never want to be anywhere that I am not welcome,' he said pitifully.

She wanted to say, *Hallelujah, he finally gets it,* but the experience reminded her how quickly things could escalate with him from one extreme to the next so she decided on self-control, 'I think that would be best at least for tonight.'

'I don't need to go just right now though, do I? I mean, we could have the Chinese first,' he pressured her again.

'Enough!' she bellowed. 'Bob, will you just sod off, go home and leave me alone! You're literally like a leech sucking the very lifeblood out of me. It's like you're attached to me,' she said, holding her arm out in front of her, flicking it as though ridding it of excess drips of water, 'and I cannot get you off me!'

'Is that it then, is it over between us?' came his next predictable and defeated blow.

'Why is it that I have to fight to be heard? All I wanted was a night to myself. Why is that so hard for you to accept? I don't know why meeting my needs is such a battle that always results in you catastrophising the situation. Just go. I have had enough,' Karen said, her energy completely depleted.

'Just tell me you're not breaking up with me, and I will gladly go,' Bob implored.

'Bob, please, I am exhausted, and I cannot take this mind-bending tete-a-tete with you right now, please just go, I have had enough,' Karen pleaded, turning back to the now fully boiled kettle to pour herself a drink, not wanting him to see the tears of desperation filling her eyes.

'Can I at least have a hug before I go?' Bob continued.

Much against her better judgement, Karen allowed him to take her into his arms in the hope he would finally leave, and she could lock the door behind him.

'I knew you didn't mean it. You're just tired. You go have a bath, and I will get the Chinese, then we can cuddle up together,' he said, totally void of her desperation.

'Bob, I am sick of going through this same charade. Go home and don't come back! I have tried, boy have I tried, but I seriously can't do this anymore. Enough is enough,' she said, trying to pull away from his grip. 'Bob, get your hands off of me and go home,' she said, trying to pull herself free.

Reluctantly, he loosened his grip but only sufficiently to allow him to free his hand. Then, in a split second, he had grabbed her by the throat. He smiled at her confusion, then took a moment to absorb the terror of her searching, widening eyes before whipping her head down hard upon the granite work surface. The crack was immediate, like the breaking of an egg against a glass bowl, though far more solid. The sound pleased him immensely, so he smashed her face against the granite too, just for good measure, before he was ready to release his vice-like grip on her scrawny little neck.

Robert Day Jr had snapped. He hadn't wanted to, but she had pushed him too far this time. Who the heck did she think she was, dismissing him like he was a piece of crap stuck to the bottom of her shoe? The last woman to have spoken to him like that was his mother. He smiled at the memory of silencing her too.

The surprise on her face as he had snatched up the pool trophy his brother had won a zillion years before, when they were kids. The trophy that had collected dust as it took centre stage on his mother's mantelpiece. He wasn't oblivious to the fact that his mum had wanted to encourage Craig, but it was a pool competition at their local youth club, for goodness' sake. So what? It wasn't as though it was world champion stardom level or anything, yet there it had stood like a Belisha beacon, crying out in that prime position for almost 15 years. Robert didn't know what was worse: the fact that she idolised it or that it had sat there staring him in the face every time he had entered that damn room.

His lip began to curl as he recalled how his mum had gushed with pride the day Craig had returned home with it. He, Robert, had gladly stepped back to allow his brother the glory, knowing full well that due to his limited abilities, he may not get many more future opportunities. Craig was probably the only person that Robert had ever really cared about, maybe because he too had been stuck with this pathetic excuse of a mother.

It wasn't that she was a bad person; she was just mentally challenging with her controlling, overprotective interference in their lives. No matter what friends the brothers made, she tried to integrate herself like she was one of the gang, it had been both cringey and embarrassing.

Bob recalled times of her coming down to the basement, which had been set up as their 'chill-out' zone, plonking herself down on one of the settees and making pointless conversation to join in. He had seen the look of discomfort on his pals' faces and knew that come Monday morning, he would be the laughingstock at school—again.

He had no idea why she persistently infiltrated their space it was like she couldn't bear for them to develop other meaningful relationships that didn't include her. Even when they had made a notice for the basement door stating, 'Friends Only! No Entry', she would still barge in on them with the excuse of taking them a tray of drinks or snacks. Their late father had created this dedicated space just for them, acknowledging that a man needs his own 'man cave.'

Maybe that was his mother's issue. She had clung to them because she had missed their father, but at the end of the day, it was not a reason to stunt their growth and ability to form important relationships with their peers. In fact, when Robert thought about it, he couldn't recall his mother ever having any age-appropriate friendships.

Robert looked down at the woman's lifeless body in front of him, watching the blood pooling beneath her head. There were no feelings, no sense of remorse and definitely no regrets. He studied the scene for a couple of moments but could just have easily been gazing at a blank sheet of paper.

His thoughts returned to that stupid trophy again. In the grand scheme of things, winning that trophy should have been one of life's insignificant incidents. However, their mother had chosen it as the embodiment of elevating little Craig onto what would become an ever-ascending pedestal.

It was impossible to recall the number of times Bob had wanted to smash Craig's triumphant icon to rid it from his childhood and early adulthood. Instead, he had chosen to quietly absorb the countless moments his mother had told the same story of Craig's achievement to family, friends and anyone else who would listen for that matter. The pride with which she spoke was as though she was reliving the exact moment over and over again—but for the first time. It was delivered with the same words, the same emotions and even the same intake of breath, followed by the finale of her hand raising up to her mouth as her breath caught in her throat.

Robert had begun reciting the speech word for word in his own brain, mocking her at first as she went along, but then it had become more of an aide to help him get through it. Was this really the measure of her pride in her boys—a sodding two-bit trophy that meant absolutely nothing?

To him, this piece of metal junk mounted on its square plastic plinth had basically become his mother's idol, of which Robert always seemed to come up short in comparison and continually felt the sacrifice for.

He grinned to himself now as he pictured the day, he had finally destroyed the damn thing, especially as it had not been in any of the previous ways he had imagined. He recalled the surprise on his mother's face as he had caught her off guard, spinning around and connecting it to the side of her head. The speed at which he had moved hadn't given her enough time to even raise her hands to protect herself.

In that split second though, he was convinced he had witnessed the recognition of fear prominently written across her face like the title of a good horror movie. The only thing missing was the accompaniment of some eerie music. Robert had held her look of terror in a folder titled 'sweet delight', safely stored in his memory banks ever since.

He looked at the woman on the floor again. There was no care, compassion or concern—just the same disdain as he'd had for his mother all those years before—and he felt triumphant.

'Another bitch bites the dust,' he smiled.

Chapter 2
Setting the Scene

Robert was a highly intelligent man; he knew he would have to play the scene to be believed, which is why he had asked for a cuddle. He carefully retraced his steps away from the body, then, using the edges of his sleeve, he selected some disinfectant wipes and a carrier bag out of a drawer, removed his clothing and popped them inside. He wiped his hands, face and any exposed skin, threw it all in the bag and then placed it by the door before going upstairs to the bathroom. There, he put the plug into the bath and slightly turned on the taps. He poured in a good measure of bubble bath, dipping his hand into the water to agitate the gel to create a light foam before sprinkling the petals he had already prepared into the tub.

Robert then made his way to the master bedroom, lit the candles he had placed in small tea light glass holders around the room, smiled at the heart-shaped ring of petals upon the bed, then took the ring out of his pocket and skilfully placed it at the side of the bed. He slipped on a fresh polo shirt, jeans and the new boxed trainers Karen was buying him for his birthday. Well, there was no point in them going to waste, he reasoned. Then, on his way out of the bedroom, he dimmed the lights before stopping to examine the scene. His only thought was that he would miss this room where he'd had his needs met—well, mostly. Never mind, there were plenty more fish in the sea.

Once on the landing, he closed his eyes, took a few deep breaths, then shook out his arms and legs like a sprinter going into a race. Murmuring incoherently, he gave himself a little pep talk. Finally, in character, he was ready.

Robert knew that every fine detail would be scrutinised, so he made a point of first shouting out Karen's name with an element of concern in his voice, just in case the neighbours were questioned. For added effect, he ran down the stairs, continuing to shout her name, opening and slamming the front door on his way past. On entering the kitchen, he let rip a guttural, animal-like howl—just like the one he had heard his mother release when she had received news of her father's passing. Pleased with his efforts to set the scene, only then did he take out his mobile phone to ring 999.

'Hello, you are through to 999. What emergency service do you require?' the operator enquired.

'I'm not sure,' Robert said, confused. 'I don't know if I need an ambulance or the police.'

'Is there a medical emergency?' the operator enquired.

'Yes, I have just found my partner on the floor. There is blood everywhere,' Robert stated in a panic.

'I will put you through to the ambulance service. Please stay on the line,' and then the phone began to ring again.

'Hello ambulance service,' was the quick response.

'I have just found my partner on the floor. There is a pool of blood around her head. Please come—you need to help her,' Robert said, trying to sound panicked and out of his depth.

'Is the patient breathing?' the operator asked.

'I don't know. Her face is to the side in the blood. Oh my goodness, I hope so,' Robert reacted, as though in despair at the very thought that she may be dead.

'What address are you calling from?'

'It's 357 St Michael's Mount, Walton, Wakefield.'

'What is the number you are calling from, just in case we get cut off?' she asked.

'It's 01924 579 432!' Robert said clearly.

'What is the casualty's name?' she asked.

'Karen, Karen Blakely,' he said, breaking into fake sobs as though it was all too much to part with even her name.

'What is your name?' she asked finally.

'It is Robert, Robert Day Jr,' he informed her.

Armed with basic details, along with an ambulance in pursuit of the property, the operator was finally able to concentrate upon the emergency at hand.

'Robert, can you check to see if Karen is breathing?' she guided.

'How? I can't see her face. Oh my goodness, what am I going to do?' Robert stressed.

'Robert, you need to calm down so we can help Karen,' the operator said firmly. 'Can you see if she is breathing? Look at her chest to see if it is rising and falling.'

'She doesn't look like she is, and her eyes are wide open,' he told the operator.

'Place both your index and middle fingers at the inner part of her wrist to see if you can feel a pulse,' the operator urged.

Robert pretended to follow the woman's directions whilst simply leaning back against the kitchen surface, careful not to disturb the pool of blood. 'I can't find it. There is nothing there—she doesn't have one,' he feigned despair.

'Robert, you said there was a pool of blood around her head. How was this caused?' she questioned.

'I don't know she had just got in from work, and I had gone upstairs to run her a bath. She was downstairs making a cup of tea and looking through the Chinese menu. I thought I'd heard a thud downstairs, and then I heard it again, so I called out to her. As I ran down calling 'Karen,' I heard the outside door slam shut. I thought she had gone out to her car or something, so I looked outside first, but she wasn't on the drive,' he lied. 'When I came back in, I found her on the floor behind the kitchen island.'

'So do you think there has been an intruder in the house?' she asked.

'Hold on, the ambulance is here,' Robert said, leaving the possibility of an intruder in the air.

He knew full well that the police would listen to this call, so he wanted them to also come to the same conclusion.

'She's in here,' Robert stated just to get off the phone.

'I'm sorry I have to go,' and he hung up.

It was a few more minutes before the crew arrived, giving him just enough time to knot the top of the carrier bag containing the clothes, which he flattened and secreted in the wing arch above the tyre of his battered Honda Civic. He returned to his position by the kitchen door, awaiting the paramedics' arrival.

For the sake of continuity, as soon as they were parked up and getting out of their vehicle, he raced outside with his phone pressed to his ear.

'The ambulance is here,' Robert repeated, pleased with himself for his quick thinking. 'She's in here. I'm sorry, I have to go.'

The driver was a young man in his mid-20s, with an athletic build, with short, dark well cropped hair. His passenger was a middle-aged woman in her late 30s to early 40s, slightly overweight, blonde and very calm under the circumstances.

Carrying their heavy equipment, they bustled themselves through the inner porch into the kitchen. Robert noted how the large, squared equipment bag caught the door frame as the woman passed through, jarring her shoulder. He smiled—Karen often told him off for being careless in scraping the woodwork.

Robert decided to hold back from also entering the kitchen, just to give the added effect that he couldn't bear to see the love of his life in that state. He stood leaning at the porch windowsill, his chin to his chest and shoulders slumped—a stance of defeat—waiting to be told what he already knew.

It was the woman whose face appeared around the door. 'I am sorry, love, but there is nothing we can do,' she told him.

Trying to mask his elation for devastation, he broke down, expelling the same guttural howl he had practised earlier. He would later congratulate himself on his ingenuity of buckling at the knees.

'This cannot be happening,' he mumbled in disbelief.

'The severity of the blunt force trauma that her skull sustained has caused such significant injuries it is not possible to perform CPR. I am sorry, but there are no signs of life. Can I get you a drink whilst my colleague arranges for police attendance?' she asked kindly.

Chapter 3
First Impressions

Robert Day Jr was sitting on a small wooden bench that stood to the left-hand side of the entrance to Karen Blakely's house when the first police car pulled up just past the driveway. He deliberately took no notice of their arrival. Instead, he was concentrating on perfecting the glazed stare he had seen so many actors display to represent being in shock.

At his right beside him on the bench was an untouched cup of coffee that the female paramedic had placed beside him. Despite being parched, he had purposely left it to go cold. He reasoned that under the circumstances, a normal person would not be thinking about their own needs and would remain in a trance-like state.

Two men got out of the police car and made their way down the drive towards him. He stayed rigid, focusing his stare on the three wheelie bins stood against the perimeter wall opposite him.

'Hello, how are you, sir?' the first officer tried, but he got no response.

'I am Detective Inspector Jenson Parker,' the second officer tried, but there was still no response.

The first officer stepped into the visual sight projection of Robert Day Jr's stare on the off chance he may be deaf, but he still did not move. It was only when Jenson Parker reached out and touched the man's shoulder that he jumped into life, sending the cup beside him crashing to the floor.

'Hello, sir, I am Detective Inspector Dion Jacobi, and this is my partner, Detective Inspector Jenson Parker. Can you tell me your name, please?' Jacobi asked.

'It's Robert, Robert Day Jr,' he croaked.

'Is it OK to call you by your first name, Robert?' Parker asked. The man nodded, so the officer continued. 'Robert, we understand there has been a serious incident, but before we take any details, my partner is going to have a look inside to assess the situation, and then we will take it from there. Does that sound OK to you?'

Again, Robert just nodded, staring down at the broken cup on the floor, trying hard to think of a time he'd had a real reaction that had caused him to cry. He kicked himself for not being able to muster up a few tears and made a mental note that he must practise. He knew it would be necessary to master the technique for the coming days and weeks ahead, but for now, shock would have to do.

When Jacobi entered the property, Parker did his best to make small talk, but Robert's ears had already tuned him out. All Robert could hear was the drone of something in the background whilst he busily contemplated the Chinese menu. He couldn't quite remember if it was the Green Dragon or the Lotus that did the best crispy duck pancakes followed by the Chinese Kung Pao chicken.

'Maybe the paramedics should give him a quick once-over?' he heard one of the coppers saying.

'Robert, Susie is going to sit you in the back of the ambulance just to make sure you don't need any medical attention. Is that alright?' Parker enquired.

Robert glanced in their direction, giving the impression he was staring straight through them and not actually seeing them. Robert was beginning to love the attention the officers were giving him, so he simply stood up, allowing himself to be guided towards the back of the ambulance, all the time maintaining an award-winning act. At least he would be able to use her professional evaluation of his current condition to his advantage should they later consider him a suspect.

As the doors closed behind him, an unmarked police car pulled up outside the house and stationed itself right across the gateway.

'So, what have we got, guys?' Shona Williams asked her detectives.

'To be honest, we haven't got that far, Shona. Paramedics were dispatched at 20:55 hours after receiving a 999 call from our chap, Robert Day, who is getting the once-over from paramedics.' Jacobi nodded over at the ambulance to indicate Robert Day's presence.

Taking the hint, Shona moved closer to the house and observed the smashed cup beside the bench. She looked quizzically towards her detectives.

'Day was sitting here when we arrived. The cup,' he pointed at it, 'had been on the bench next to him but fell when we startled him,' Parker explained.

'Startled him?' Shona asked, puzzled.

'Yes, our man Day is in a pretty bad state of shock,' Parker continued.

'What is your impression of Day?' Shona asked, getting straight back to business.

'He seems genuinely freaked out by what's happened and is in total shock,' Jacobi was first to state.

'Yes, it is one thing to get the news of a loved one passing in such a brutal attack, but to have been in the house at the time, it is seriously going to mess with his head!' Parker offered.

'Could he be faking it?' Shona was not the kind of detective to take anything at face value.

'If he is, I will eat my hat!' Parker declared.

'Apart from the ambulance crew, only two of them, there has only been me and Day who have entered the property,' Jacobi stated.

'Well done, Jacobi. It seems like the detective college will be making you an honorary member this year,' Shona said wryly.

'Does this mean I will get the "top of the class award for staying outside?" Parker joined in on the sarcastic banter.'

'OK then, so let's get into the house. Parker, will you keep eyes on Day and ensure no one passes the threshold before I have conducted my preliminaries, please?' Shona requested. Then, as an afterthought, she threw him her keys. 'Just in case it needs moving.'

'No problem, boss, and I will get the paperwork out ready to document footfall,' Parker said, referring to the records kept of all personnel associated with the crime scene.

Shona pulled her hair back into a tight ponytail, slipped on a white pair of shoe protectors, and donned a pair of latex gloves before entering the house via the kitchen door.

One of Jacobi's favourite aspects of the job was to stand back and observe Shona Williams's initial primary survey of a scene. She reminded him of a bloodhound as she methodically and intently sought out potential evidence, her eyes scanning every inch of an area like a searchlight.

As soon as Shona had set foot inside, Jacobi knew she was no longer aware he existed. Well, that was until water started pouring through the ceiling from the room above where they were standing.

'Jacobi, stop that water!' Shona screamed. The last thing she wanted was for her crime scene to be compromised.

Despite his age and size, Jacobi was off on his heel like a cat on a hot tin roof, negotiating his bulk up the stairways and towards the offending overspill, quicker than even he thought possible.

'For goodness' sake,' he berated himself, why hadn't he checked the house? No more 'honorary member of the detective college' for him.

When he arrived back downstairs, he tentatively opened the kitchen door, expecting a dressing down from a soaked Shona Williams. To his relief, neither was true. Shona was busy sketching out the position of the body in relation to the rest of the room to ascertain a detailed diagram for her later reflection. She noted that the blinds were up, so not only would Karen Blakely have been able to see out, but anyone passing by would have been able to see in.

The kettle was still warm, and the milk that stood beside it was still ice cold, which suggested that Karen was potentially in the process of making herself a drink. If that had been the case, it was possible she had not anticipated the attack which had cost Karen her life. Shona could not see evidence that a struggle had taken place, as other than Karen Blakely, nothing else was on the floor. Just to be on the safe side, she made a note to ensure Karen's hands got bagged in case there was any evidence beneath her fingernails.

'Dion, can you test the light switches to find which one turns these on?' Shona asked, indicating the two bulbous cream shades hanging over the kitchen's centre island.

The first switch Dion tried illuminated the kickboard beneath the kitchen units. The second revealed cabinet lighting above a chopping board, and the third bathed the island. As Shona examined the area more closely, it disclosed that not only was there blood upon the island's work surface, but that it was also present along the strip of its outer edge.

Shona crouched down to observe the injuries to Karen Blakely, which revealed not only the more obvious cracked skull wound but also an imprint of the edge of the marble work surface mapped out right across Karen's face, just under her nose above her top lip. Shona Williams felt woozy at the thought of the force to which Karen Blakely's face had hit the granite surface.

One thing Shona knew for certain was that whoever had committed this savage attack had only one intention, and that was to ensure Karen Blakely did not survive. Shona made a few more notes of the scene, including the blood pooling around Karen's head and splatter marks on the front of the island drawers. She then informed Parker she was doing a quick inspection of the house and to not allow anyone entry until she had finished. The need to preserve the area was her primary concern, and she did not want Robert Day Jr or anyone else being allowed in until she had finished.

On quick inspection, she found the source of the water leakage had been an overfull bath. Floating precariously upon its surface were two rose petals; the rest were now on the sodden linoleum floor. Behind one door on the landing was what appeared to be a spare room containing the basic furniture of a bed, side table and wardrobe. The curtains were drawn, there was no real character or comfort within the room, but there was a whole host of dust.

There was only one other door on the landing, so she had to assume it was the master bedroom shared by the victim and her partner. Here, she found about a dozen tea light candles that had been neatly placed in little dishes around the room, their tiny flames creating flickering shadows upon the walls. In the dimly lit room, they appeared more like miniature dancers moving gracefully to some inaudible tune.

Shona took in the scene for a moment, envisaging Karen and her partner's expectancy of enjoying a romantic evening together. Then in contrast, the image of the brutality of the scene downstairs became emblazoned across her mind.

As Shona turned to leave the room, a tiny sparkle caught her eye from the left side of the huge king-size bed. Then she saw it—the diamond ring sat neatly in its box. Her heart sank. What should have been a wonderful, joyous occasion of them celebrating their future hopes and dreams for both Karen Blakely and her partner had abruptly ended. Despondent, Shona made her way back down the stairs.

'You OK, boss?' Jacobi asked.

'No, Dion, but I will be when I catch the callous swine who has taken this woman's life and ruined that of her partner who's sitting outside in the ambulance,' she said, 'and I will take great pleasure in throwing away the key.'

Chapter 4
Shock

When Shona and Jacobi exited the house, Parker informed them that Robert Day Jr had been transported to the hospital just as a precautionary measure due to the severity of his shock.

'Apparently, Susie said he was having trouble recalling information and that, although this is not uncommon, she wanted to be certain he hadn't sustained any hidden injuries they weren't aware of,' Parker concluded.

Neither Shona nor Jacobi had time to react to this little snippet of information before they were suddenly greeted by the arrival of a whole host of police personnel.

'Dion, can you hot hoof it up to the hospital whilst I process the scene? I do not want to waste any time having to locate Robert Day Jr should he be discharged before we get there,' Shona urged him.

Dion initially stood back and marvelled at Shona's ability to click straight back into investigator mode before jumping in his designated car and leaving for the hospital.

Shona instructed Parker to log the names, ranks and speciality of each person entering the house along with their times in and out. She then focused her attention on managing the multidisciplined team, expertly directing them in exactly how she wanted the scene processed. She indicated firstly what evidence was the most crucial, then how she required it to be preserved, the list of photographs she expected, and the other rooms she wanted included.

Shona was well known for her attention to detail—fingerprinting of obscure areas, minute particles observed, her extensive note-taking at crime scenes and her acutely analytical mind. Shona Williams loved drinking in a crime scene to identify what was relevant and to sift through what was unimportant or were potential red herrings. She had the ability to take a mass of information and sift through it quickly to identify the relevant facts to assist her in finding the perpetrators of serious crimes.

Shona had been recognised for her problem-solving techniques and had quickly moved her way up through the ranks, being both admired and respected. Solving serious crimes to give loved ones peace of mind and putting bad people away is what energised her, and today's crime would be no exception.

Shona Williams was fastidious in her work, ensuring that the body, along with the areas around it, was left untouched whilst being certain to record everything and anything to ensure nothing was missed.

Whenever she was processing a scene, she always bore in mind two quotes. One was by Henry David Thoreau: 'It's not what you look at that matters, it's what you see.' This was why Shona Williams would excavate everything she could from a scene so that she could analyse it over and over again to really see what had happened. The second quote she lived by was by Euripides: 'Leave no stone unturned.'

It was her dogged determination to find answers and bring the guilty to justice that had gained her the reputation of being like a dog with a bone. It didn't matter to Shona how long the process took—whether it was interviewing suspects, walking a crime scene or delving deeper—she simply would not give up until she had answers.

The Karen Blakely house was no different, so when she had finally informed the medical examiner, that they could remove the body, it was early the next morning.

Jenson Parker had been relieved of his duties to collect drinks and breakfast sandwiches for the crew—a mark of thanks from Shona for a job well done. As he arrived back, ready to tuck into his bacon, egg and spam sandwich, the yolk dripping between his fingers, the blacked-out coroner's van pulled up outside.

He quickly replaced it back inside its white paper bag and took up his folder, ready to note the name of the medical examiner along with the time the body left the building. Shona was the first to approach the driver's door, expecting to welcome Sallyanne Peters, but it was a young, thin guy in his mid to late 20s whom she had not seen before.

'Oh, hello,' Shona said, unable to keep the surprise out of her voice.

The young man had earbuds secreted in the orifice of his ear canal, so ultimately did not hear Shona's greeting and swung the door wide, catching her off guard.

'Oh, my goodness, I am so sorry,' he said, removing the earbuds. 'I didn't realise you were there—I had these in.'

Apparently, you had your eyes closed too!' Shona delivered sharply.

'I am so sorry! I have come to collect the body,' he pointlessly stated.

'No shit, Sherlock, the van kind of gives it away,' Shona continued. 'I do hope someone else less careless is on their way.'

'Yes, Sallyanne will be with us shortly. It was her wedding anniversary yesterday, so she was staying at a hotel across town. She thought it would be quicker for her to get a taxi and meet me here,' he nervously explained.

Two minutes later, a black Uber pulled up in front of Karen Blakely's house, and the thick ginger mop of Sallyanne's hair with her trademark headband emerged from the back of the cab.

Sallyanne was a lovely lady in her late 50s. She was an astute woman, who was dedicated to the complexities of her work and loved nothing more than deciphering the mystery of a cadaver. Unlike a few other people in her profession, Sallyanne was very pleasant. She was always willing to prioritise where necessary and was responsive, reliable and very thorough.

She loved to talk about her work, but not everyone was a willing recipient. It made her smile when she met people and they would casually ask what she did for a living—their facial expressions never ceased to amaze her. However, there was one time at her sister's engagement party when she was talking to her new fiancé that she uncharacteristically felt creeped out by him. This guy seemed to be a little too interested in the procedures of conducting a postmortem and the weighing of the internal organs. Luckily, her sister never ended up marrying him. God rest her soul.

'This is a nice welcoming committee,' Sallyanne said as she made her way onto the drive.

Having had the pleasure of working with Sallyanne many times in the past, Shona was relieved to see that she had been assigned to this particular case, especially after her initial disappointment with 'earbud' boy.

After preliminary greetings, introductions and updates, Sallyanne and 'earbud' boy took out latex gloves, and protective Tyvek suits, tucked them into their white Wellington boots, put on a mask and pulled up the hood. They entered the property together, followed at a safe distance by Shona Williams.

'Visually speaking, an injury resulting in that amount of blood loss would definitely cause subdural haematoma and subarachnoid haemorrhage,' Sallyanne stated.

'In English, please, Sallyanne,' Shona said, perplexed.

'Obviously, we can see from the exposure of the brain that the cranium has sustained an immense blow right here across the top of the forehead.' Sallyanne pointed to the injury with her pen. 'A head injury can cause the formation of a blood clot between the surface of the brain called a subdural haematoma. In a severe injury like this one, the brain would quickly fill with blood, literally compressing the brain's tissue. A subarachnoid haemorrhage is the bleeding between the space of your brain and the membrane layer around it. Inevitably, I am visually speaking, but I would expect to find these results when I conduct further examination of the internal structures.'

'What else can you tell me at this point, Sallyanne?' Shona pushed.

'I don't want to say too much yet, Shona, but the muscle stiffness generally peaks between 7–12 hours. At this point, the muscles then start to loosen again, which is what has started here. As it is now 08:30, I would loosely estimate the time of death to be around 20:30 to 21:30 but don't quote me yet until I have completed the full postmortem examination,' Sallyanne stated.

Satisfied with a general guide, Shona made her way back outside to allow Sallyanne and 'earbud' boy to complete their examination of the scene and prepare the removal of the body. When she got back outside, she suddenly felt drained her adrenalin finally expelling its surge.

Jenson Parker was still stationed at the door, his breakfast sandwich now devoured according to the yolk stain on his tie.

'I take it you enjoyed your butty?' Shona asked.

'Yes, thank you, boss,' Parker said and wiped his mouth, mistakenly thinking Shona was referring to visible remnants on his face.

'No,' she said, pointing to the drip mark just beneath the knot of his tie.

When Parker looked down, Shona couldn't help herself from playfully flicking the end of his nose, just as her dad had always done to her.

'Sorry,' she said and walked to the bench at the left side of the door that Robert Day Jr had been sitting on hours before.

'Are you OK, boss?' Parker asked, sensing her sudden sadness.

'All in a day's work,' she lied. There were certain times in Shona Williams's life when her father would slip into her thoughts, and every time, the sadness of losing him hit her all over again. This was one of those moments.

When the door to Karen Blakely's house opened again, it was so she could leave her home for the very last time. Only hours earlier, she had returned from work expecting to enjoy a romantic evening with her soon-to-be fiancé. However, Karen Blakely did not make it to that status because Robert Day Jr hadn't been given the time to propose before she had been callously murdered in her own kitchen.

Today she would return to the same hospital, though not to do her rostered shift but instead, to lay in a cold, metal crate in its basement mortuary. As the metal gurney was wheeled out by both Sallyanne and 'earbud' boy, Shona stood to her feet in a final mark of respect for the woman whose life had been cut drastically short.

Jacobi was unsure how long he would have to hang around, so once he had pulled onto the hospital grounds, he followed the signs for the allocated visitor's car park. Having gone straight on at the first roundabout and right at the second, he came upon a small zebra crossing where he noticed a paying booth. It was still only early, so he was able to drive straight up to the barrier without queuing, where he opened the driver's window, took the automatically dispensed ticket and proceeded straight through.

The car park was controlled by a weird one-way system where he was forced to bypass the first row. He then drove down the next row, took a right at the bottom and came back on himself to the space he had seen on entry. He reversed the car into the space in preparation for his exit, envisaging he would want to get out of there as soon as possible.

Dion Jacobi did not like hospitals ever since his father had been rushed in 4 years ago with a suspected heart attack. Jacobi had raced to be at his father's side, but Harold Jacobi had promptly passed away before Jacobi had even had the chance to arrive.

Dion secured the handbrake and shut off the engine before releasing his seatbelt and stepping out of the vehicle. As he walked away, he clicked the remote central locking, then for some reason stopped, turned around and clicked it again just to double-check it was secure.

Dion shook his head at himself—he was obviously too tired, or maybe the stress of actually going into the hospital had increased too much along the journey. He hated the stark lighting, the blank, dull walls, the long corridors and the number of people aimlessly wandering around following signs or colours along the floor.

Although very patient in his role as an investigator he hated being in crowded places, especially hospitals. It was an environment where people didn't really talk to one another, they were fixed on what they were there for and finding their particular departments. Perhaps Dion had watched one too many scary movies, but he also couldn't help wondering if there were people's souls wandering the corridors, who hadn't realised they had passed. One of which could be his dad.

Outside the main entrance was the same sign found at every other NHS premises stating that it was a 'Smoke-free zone' and requesting people not to smoke on either the 'premises or grounds.'

It was about as visible to smokers as the invisible man is to the rest of us. Not only were there visitors hanging around or sat on grass verges inhaling a crafty fag, but patients in wheelchairs and others stood with drips on stands right at the entrance. Dion considered the irony of what a fantastic advert for health it was, seeing so many selfish people at every other visitor's expense, filling the foyer with smoke. Perhaps it irked him more because he was an ex-smoker, and he had developed a hatred for the smell of what he now considered a disgusting habit.

Once inside the humongous reception area, with its open-plan cafe and healthy farmers stalls, he made his way to the reception desk to locate the whereabouts of Robert Day Jr. He approached one of the two members of staff, introduced himself and explained his dilemma without giving too much information.

'Do you have any ID on you, sir?' A lady in her late 40s enquired. Dion produced his official warrant card, giving the woman his winning smile.

'Thank you, sir. As you will appreciate, due to confidentiality under normal circumstances, I wouldn't be able to facilitate your request,' the lady informed him.

'I understand perfectly,' Dion responded, and on seeing her name tag included, 'Margaret.'

It was now Margaret's turn to smile, but only fleetingly.

'According to the system, he is still in A&E waiting to see the doctor. If you follow the yellow lines along that corridor,' she said, pointing diagonally towards two fire doors, 'you will arrive at the A&E department. If he came in by ambulance, he should be somewhere in bays 1 to 9.'

'Thank you,' Dion said, striding off in the direction he had been pointed in.

The A&E department was smaller than he had expected, and although there were only about fifteen people sitting, there was an estimated waiting time of 2 ½ hours. There was no way Dion could force himself to sit here for that length of time, so if it meant him pulling a few strings, he instantly made up his mind that he would be doing just that.

He glanced around the segregated areas until he found where bays 1–9 were housed and approached the tiny receptionist desk. A young man with a sandwich in one hand was busy chewing as he typed away with the other.

'Excuse me, can you help me please?' Dion ventured. When the lad didn't even look up, Dion coughed and repeated his request.

The lad, who was around 25/26, had blond, loose curly hair and sported a lip ring, glanced up disinterestedly and just stared at Dion.

'A murder suspect was brought in today. It is vital that I apprehend him before any of your staff are put at risk,' Dion stated, staring intently back at the lad.

Lip boy nearly choked on his sandwich and was suddenly very alert and willing to assist, to the point he didn't even ask Dion for proof of his identity. That made Dion smile, and although Shona would have been pissed with him, she too would have found the situation amusing.

'The name is Robert Day Jr,' Dion stated.

'Cubicle 7,' the lad stuttered, pointing Dion in the appropriate direction.

Dion walked away, chuckling to himself, not giving a hoot about the misinformation and feeling quite proud of himself for jeering the jumped-up little shit into action.

When he got to Cubicle 7, he peered around the curtain to find a very relaxed Robert Day Jr laid back, enjoying a cup of tea. Within seconds of locating Day, a doctor arrived to declare Mr Day immediately fit for discharge. Dion smiled again at his ingenuity in exaggerating the situation to bring about such a purposeful and pleasant result.

Day genuinely seemed surprised to be getting released so quickly, and upon recognising the presence of DI Jacobi as the officer on scene at Karen Blakely's, he suddenly seemed quite tense.

'Hello, Mr Day. Remember me? I am Detective Inspector Dion Jacobi. We met earlier at Ms Blakely's residence,' Jacobi enquired.

'Yes, of course,' Day said uncomfortably, having hoped to have had a little more time to prepare and compose himself.

'If you wouldn't mind accompanying me to the station, there are a few questions about last night's events that we need to go over,' Jacobi told him.

'Surely, Mr Jacobi, this can wait until tomorrow. I am finding it all a little hard to process,' Day tried.

'I can appreciate the effects upon finding your partner's body. I mean, you ended up here at the hospital, after all,' Jacobi sympathised.

'Exactly. I need to take a day or two to come round, I think, then I will happily answer any questions you may have for me,' Day said, playing for time.

'Ordinarily, I would agree, but luckily the doctor has fitted you for discharge, and I am sure you wouldn't want to delay the prospect of finding the person who has committed such an appalling crime,' Jacobi delivered pointedly to counteract and supersede Day's seemingly feeble objections.

'Yes, yes, of course. What was I thinking? Obviously, the only reasonable action would be to assist you as fully as I can,' Day readily agreed.

Jacobi's head cocked slightly as he considered Day's statement, 'The only reasonable action would be to assist,' as though he was sharing his thoughts, but who was he trying to convince? Jacobi wondered.

Jacobi observed Day as he slid himself off the bed, suspicious of whether the unsteadiness, he displayed was real or for his benefit. Once Day had replaced his shoes and jacket, Jacobi escorted him through the hospital corridors, retracing his steps along the yellow trail to the large atrium of the reception area.

They fought their way through the smoke-filled entrance, side stepped the tab-littered footpath and made their way towards the car parking area. Jacobi remembered to stop at the paying booth, inserting his ticket, black strip up, as instructed, into the metal slot. He paid the allotted fee and requested a receipt in order to claim his expenses on his return to the station and then guided Day to his awaiting car.

Jacobi was glad he had followed his instincts to reverse the car into the space, as he had correctly predicted his desire to leave quickly. He pulled out of the space, turning left out of the space and followed the one-way circuit to the very top end of the car park to the barrier. He inserted his prepaid ticket and was rewarded with the barrier automatically rising to allow him to pull away quickly.

He joined the road at the first roundabout he had entered on his arrival at the hospital, turned left and then proceeded to the main road at the bottom, and then out towards the direction of Normanton Police Station. It was a 7-mile drive along the outskirts of the city and took around 15 minutes, most of which was conducted in general chitchat. Jacobi knew he would need to put Day at ease if he was going to get the best out of him once at the station, and a huge part of that was building up a genuine rapport with an interviewee.

When they finally arrived at their destination, Jacobi pulled up to some huge automatic gates and waited patiently for them to open. He noticed Day seemed a little nervous.

'There is nothing to worry about, Mr Day,' Jacobi tried to reassure him. 'Police officers are not permitted to use the front car park, as we are required to enter through the back of the station for security reasons, especially if we have a prisoner in tow.'

Only when the gates had fully opened did Jacobi proceed, and once the car had cleared the ingress, he stopped, applied the handbrake and waited until the heavy metal gates had fully sealed. Jacobi noted Day swallow hard as the gates clanked shut behind them and of him glancing quickly into his wing mirror, as though he suddenly felt very uncomfortable.

'Interesting,' he thought. 'Could this be the sign of a guilty man?' he considered.

Chapter 5
All the World's a Stage

Jacobi pulled into the nearest space he could find to the back door entrance, which was only four cars away. He got out of the car, opening the rear door to encourage Day to get out too, and he willingly obliged. When Jacobi approached the back door, he ensured he kept a good distance between them, using his body to conceal the combination code he entered onto the outer lock for them to gain entry. He held the door open wide, inviting Day to walk in first.

It was at that moment that Jacobi thought there was a flicker of uncertainty across the man's face and a distinct hesitation, as though he was contemplating his choices. Jacobi let the silence between them hang in the air as he contemplated the man's position, could he really have had anything to do with his partner's murder? Or did he just dislike police stations the way Jacobi hated hospitals?

It was fair to say that going into a place like this for the purpose of being interviewed was like giving evidence in court, all eyes were on you, and every word would be dissected. Day instantly composed himself, smiled and stepped through the doorway, but the clenching of his jaw told Jacobi he was anything but relaxed. The desk sergeant put his hand up on their way past as he busily inputted information into the computer he was utilising. Jacobi nodded in response, keeping his eyes firmly locked upon Day's every movement.

Jacobi led Day down a corridor to his right, and at the end, he used his ID badge to gain access through some doors on the left. 'This way,' he told him, then, as an afterthought, enquired, 'I assume we are alright to take the stairs? You are not feeling too unsteady after your ordeal, are you?'

'Thank you, Officer Jacobi, for your thoughtfulness at the situation, but I think I can manage the stairs,' Day gushed.

Jacobi noticed the way the other man seemed delighted at having his needs considered and noted this as a possible weakness if he needed to get him on his side, or indeed exploit it at a later date should the need arise. Jacobi took his time up the stairs, remaining slightly back, allowing Day to move towards the closed door first when they arrived at the top. Almost every person in his vast 30-year+ career whom Jacobi had led this route stopped at the top and waited for the officer to proceed first. Jacobi correctly surmised that uncertainty about what was at the other side of the door, along with the authoritarian environment and possible seriousness of a visit, played a key factor in this decision.

However, in all the cases where the perpetrator was masquerading as the victim, they were either a psychopath, narcissist or sadist and they had all proceeded confidently. Day swung that door open with such ease and self-assurance, a complete contrast to his initial conduct at the outside door. It felt to Jacobi as though his first hesitation was a subconscious act manifesting from hidden guilt, but once inside, as Jacobi had pampered to his ego, he was now revealing his true self. Again, another note to add to his mental hard drive.

'Please take a seat. Can I get you a drink, Mr Day, whilst I locate a free interview room?' Jacobi asked, noting the jaw clench again. He added, 'To take your statement.'

Day smiled and sat down on one of the two comfy brown settees to the right of the door. There was a small, cheap wooden coffee table between them that had seen better days. 'Yes, I would love a latte if you had one?'

It was now Jacobi's turn to smile. Not a coffee or a tea, but a latte. This man was obviously used to having his needs met that he didn't realise just how much he was giving away.

When Jacobi had removed himself, only then did Day begin to look around the room he was now in. The partial sitting area led into an open-plan workstation that was flanked by brown partitioning stands sectioning off areas that contained individual desks and chairs. At the far end of the room were three offices, each with blinds covering their windows. Day assumed that, like every police drama, it was so the boss could maintain his privacy or watch his subordinates. Day turned the word over in his mind. 'Subordinates,' he liked it. It gave him the essence of superiority, 'them and me,' of people who were inferior, of lower rank to him. Yes, he loved the word 'subordinate.' That is what they all were—of little importance and of no true meaning to him.

Around 10 minutes later, a young woman brought him his drink, but as she put it down on the table in front of him, he could see it was not a latte. That did not please him.

'I am sorry, we only have instant. Hope that is OK. The public purse won't stretch to the extravagance of speciality drinks,' she said, devoid of any sympathy, before walking off without waiting for his reply.

How rude, Day thought. *What was the point of asking someone what they would like to drink if you had no intention of actually delivering it?*

He closed his eyes and made a mental note of her face. Should he come in contact with her in the future, he would make sure she would regret treating him so dismissively. Before he could delve deeper into how he would like to teach the young woman a lesson, Jacobi reappeared with another woman. This one had mousy shoulder-length hair, a pair of Deirdre Barlow spectacles that were far too big for her small round face, and sported a black fitted skirt with a white blouse.

Day couldn't help but notice how neatly her ID lanyard with its 'police' insignia sat neatly between her cleavage. He quickly stood, averting his eyes to welcome her into his presence.

'This is Mr Robert Day Jr, the gentleman who found his partner brutally attacked in her own house,' Jacobi said, introducing the two.

He had purposely raised his voice ever so slightly as though questioning the words 'gentleman' and 'found,' whereas he emphasised 'partner' to see if it provoked a reaction in Day. It did not. He was too focused on the woman in front of him. Ordinarily, this would not have set off any red flags. However, when you considered only hours before this man had supposedly witnessed the death of a loved one, his behaviour came across as odd to Jacobi. As he continued to observe Day, he was certain he was flirting with his colleague.

'And you are?' Day asked, extending his hand.

'Detective Collins, I will be sitting in with you and DI Jacobi here to extract your statement,' she told him. Then as an afterthought, she added, 'I am very sorry for your loss.'

Jacobi noted again how Day seemed to respond warmly with not only the attention Collins was giving him but, more importantly, that she was acknowledging both him and his feelings. Jacobi knew most people responded well to positive praise and affirmation, but this was something altogether different. It felt like it strangely energised him. The policeman's side of Jacobi made him want to know more about Day—who he was, what his background was, his childhood and if he had a good relationship with his parents. He was sure that a psychologist would have a field day with this particular individual, but for now, he had to remain impartial and professional in order to conduct a non-judgemental interview.

Chapter 6
The Interview

'Mr Day?' Jacobi said again. 'The interview room is this way.'

'Sorry,' Day said, finding it very difficult to peel his eyes off the delicate yet very tasty Collins. He observed her with the pleasures of a carnivore salivating the thrill of a meat feast that was so tender it was falling from the bone. He could literally feel the pulsation of her past abuse, the draw of her insecurities ripe for the exploiting and the smell of her desperation, coupled with a longing to be loved. Oh yes, she was so ripe for the picking—what a delight for his palette to savour and utterly devour.

Collins had waited for Day to follow Jacobi so that she could fall in behind him. This was the usual adopted formation; however, his continued hesitation—not to mention the way he was glaring at her—suddenly made her feel very uncomfortable. She was just about to lead the way when something stopped her. There was something about this man that communicated his intention of trying to intimidate her to feel inferior. So, she stood her ground and insisted he bend to her. This was not a place where he was in control or could exert any power. And then a wry smile flashed across his face as though he had actually been able to read her thoughts. But Collins was determined; she would rather have him in front of her than sizing her up from behind.

Jacobi was standing at the doorway of interview room 2, wondering what was keeping them when Day appeared and walked into the room. Jacobi shared a puzzled look with Collins. Interview room 2 was slightly larger than the others, with a table to the right, and two regular chairs, but there were two much comfier seats too.

The hard seats were more like the ones that you found stacked on top of one another at the side of a community hall—the hard, plastic bucket type upon metal frames. The ones in interview room 2 were worn and dirty, with discoloration.

The comfier seats were the blue, sponge-filled fabric ones—a little dog-eared and not much better, to say the least.

Jacobi observed Day as he made a beeline for the comfier option and unashamedly took his seat. Dion smiled to himself in congratulations that Day had not disappointed him and knew full well that he had this chap summed up. So, why would he have expected any less?

Both Collins and Jacobi elected to sit on the hard chairs. Not because they wanted to be uncomfortable, but because they wanted to be sitting slightly higher than Day. They had got him exactly where they wanted him and felt sure he would talk openly.

'So, Mr Day, sorry, I mean Robert, if we are still okay to call you Robert?' Jacobi enquired.

'Yes, yes, of course. That's not a problem at all,' Day reassured him.

'Right then, Robert, just so you know, for our benefit, we're going to be taping the interview. This is to make sure that everything is recorded accurately. We always find in investigations that there are instances when we will need to revisit what has been said in interviews, where something which appeared to be a small and insignificant piece of information ended up being the vital clue to helping us find a killer,' Jacobi continued.

'And we want to be able to find the person responsible for killing your partner, Karen,' Collins interjected.

'Yes, I can understand that, and honestly, I intend to do everything I can to help you achieve this. You have my full cooperation,' Day assured them.

Jacobi was always sceptical when people used the word 'honestly.' It was a way to reassure the other person they were being open and upfront, but his years of experience had taught him it usually meant quite the opposite. Jacobi paid close attention to Day, observing the slight backward movement of his shoulders, the puffing out of his chest and the smirk to his face as Collins addressed him. It was almost flirtatious—another red flag!

Jacobi sat for a moment, noticing Day's eyes penetrating Collins's upper body like he had x-ray vision. The tension and discomfort Jacobi was beginning to feel about this man, especially at being in such a confined space with him, intensified ten-fold. Day, on the other hand, dwelt in his delight seemingly unaware that Jacobi was even in the room, never mind watching him.

'So,' Jacobi began, to snap Day out of it, 'as I said earlier, we will need to record the interview. But for the purpose of the statement, we will be using a

50

method called 'speech to text,' helping us to significantly speed up the statement process.'

'It is very helpful in situations like today for extracting the information, as it enables friends and families of victims to run through the process more quickly without causing them further undue stress or anxiety,' Collins interjected.

'Thank you for your consideration; it is most welcome,' Day gushed.

'It just saves a great deal of time from me having to hand write a statement and keep having to verify with you that I have recorded it correctly,' she reiterated.

'PC Collins will be utilising her phone for the transcription, and just so you know, this is a work phone—it's not a personal phone, and it will only be used for the purpose of retrieving your statement. The information will then be printed out, and given to you to examine, once you are satisfied it is a true and a consistent reflection of what you have said, we will ask you to sign and date the document. Is that okay, Robert?' Jacobi enquired.

'Yeah, that's absolutely fine,' Day responded.

'Right, Constable Collins, if you can produce the consent forms, please?'

Collins took out a form from her briefcase and placed it on a clipboard. She then passed it to Day before pointing out where he was required to endorse his signature and the date. Again, Jacobi scrutinised the man as he took his time to read through the entire document before being willing to sign on the dotted line. Collins replaced the signed sheet within her briefcase before taking out her phone and selecting the live 'Speech to text' app. She then placed it, face up, centrally upon the table. A large dormant icon of a microphone was exhibited on the screen, waiting to be activated for the task to commence.

'Thank you Mr...' Collins paused. 'Robert, sorry. Thank you, Robert,' Collins said.

It was there again—the slight backward movement of his shoulders, the puffing out of his chest and the smirk on his face. It was unmistakable as soon as Collins addressed him, and if Jacobi wasn't mistaken, he looked smitten. Either this guy was a womaniser, an actor or he had an elevated opinion of himself. Like every interview, Jacobi had wanted to conduct this one from a non-biased approach, but he had to admit—if only to himself—that he did not get a good feel about Robert Day Jr. In fact, his gut was telling him that maybe Parker might have to 'eat his hat' after all.

'Right, Robert, I think we are ready to proceed with your account of last night's events. So, for the purpose of the recordings, we will establish who is present first,' Jacobi announced, interrupting Day's connection with Collins. Day's jaw clenched fleetingly, followed by a slow upward shift of his brow. 'It is currently 01:35 on Saturday, 6 July 2024. I am Detective Inspector Dion Jacobi,' he stated before pointing at Collins for her to give her details.

'I am Police Constable Anita Collins,' she responded, and then they waited for Day to add his details.

After a long pause, Day finally responded, 'I am Robert Day Jr.'

'Mr Day has already agreed that it is permissible to address him by his first name of Robert, so Robert, can you explain to us in your own words what happened earlier on tonight?' Jacobi guided him, before correcting himself, 'Sorry, the evening of Friday, 5 July 2024.'

'I'm sorry, I just feel so wiped out. It must be from the shock,' Day said. 'It all happened so fast. One minute, I was welcoming her home, we had spoken briefly in the kitchen before I went upstairs to run her a bath, and then…' He trailed off.

'Take your time, Robert. I can appreciate that this is a very difficult time for you,' Collins sympathised.

'We were just so happy and looking forward to spending an evening together,' he paused. 'And then, the next minute, she was gone,' Day said.

There was an exaggeratedly long pause that Jacobi was unsure if it had been administered for effect, but either way, he didn't feel a need to fill it. It usually helped the interviewee to relax and open up more if they were allowed to continue at their own pace and without interruption. If he was honest, he wanted to draw Day into a false sense of security so he would open up and tell them everything they needed to know. Besides, Jacobi was sure that Day would enjoy having the spotlight, especially if he was allowed to take the lead. It also may give them the opportunity to trip him up with it at a later date. Day took up the gauntlet.

'Karen was supposed to finish work around 6 pm, I believe but she ended up staying behind because the department was so short-staffed. She didn't arrive home until around 8:30 pm. I knew that she'd be exhausted after doing an almost 12-hour shift, so I decided to spoil her. I picked up a couple of Chinese menus because I knew she wouldn't want to cook, and she would be desperate for a long hot soak. So, I got her some flowers, bubble bath and candles to prepare a little spa for her return,' he recalled.

Day took a deep breath as though he was trying to compose himself, then let it out, slowly. He swallowed hard.

'I know this is really difficult for you, Robert, but if you could try and give us every little detail that you can think of, it will help us in the long run,' Jacobi smiled encouragingly.

'Yes, yes, sorry. I just got a flashback of her lying on the floor,' Day revealed.

'So, what happened as soon as she arrived home?' Collins asked, ignoring Day's statement.

Day snapped out of his trance-like stare. He glanced towards her and smiled, picking up the story again. 'I was just closing the curtains in our bedroom when I saw the lights of her car reversing into the drive,' he lied. In reality, he had been in the laundry room removing his clothes from the tumble dryer and was in the process of getting dressed.

'I was thrilled to see her, so I raced downstairs, entered the kitchen, switched the light on and—' he began, unable to finish his sentence.

'Why did you need to switch the lights on? Surely, at 8:30 pm during summertime, you wouldn't require any lights on?' Collins asked reasonably.

'It is an old house, so gets quite dull in there, and besides, when Karen has been in the hospital all day with its stark lighting, she finds it oppressive,' he stated unwaveringly.

'What had you been doing when you were upstairs, Robert? Apart from pulling on the curtains,' Jacobi interjected.

'I'd been upstairs, uh, preparing things,' he told him.

'When you say preparing things, what do you mean, Robert? What were you planning?' Jacobi enquired, as if he hadn't got a clue.

Day's breath caught in the back of his throat as if catching him unaware, but he held himself together, biting his lower lip to stop himself from crying. Jacobi and Collins glanced at one another and waited.

'I was planning to ask her to marry me,' he said solemnly before the tears came thick and fast.

'I'm so sorry, Robert. I didn't realise. How horrendous for you,' Collins responded appropriately.

'It's okay,' Day spluttered. 'How could you have possibly known?' He took a couple of minutes to compose himself before continuing. 'So, I'd been upstairs to arrange the perfect proposal scene for her. I had carefully placed the box at the side of the bed, so it was open with the ring exposed in it,' Day explained.

'I know this will sound like a daft question in the grand scheme of things, but at which side of the bed was the box?' Jacobi enquired. He was asking for this minute detail to test Day's ability to recount the fine details.

'I placed it to the left of the bed, if you were stood at the door looking at it,' Day responded easily.

Jacobi noted how Day reeled the answer off without having to pause to consider it. Ordinarily, when interviewing a witness immediately after experiencing such a brutal encounter, they would be knocked off balance by such a futile question. It would generally cause them to hesitate briefly as they focused on a seemingly unimportant detail. This alone would cause them to falter, stop in their tracks, engage their brain, search for the information, then physically demonstrate a position using a hand gesture. Day immediately answered without having to break his flow, like it was a preplanned, pre-prepared script.

'I had bought Karen two dozen red roses, half of which I had stripped the petals from and that I had used to form a heart-shaped display in the centre of the bed. I'd got her lots of tea light candles at Christmas, but she had never had the time to use them, so I put them in glasses, which I arranged around the bedroom. I took the excess petals into the bathroom and sprinkled them along the bottom of the bath so that once I added the water, they would float on the top. I opened the window in the bathroom ready for the steam to go out once it was time to run the bath, and thought I'd heard a car, but wasn't aware that it was Karen's until I walked into the bedroom. As I said earlier, I was closing the curtains when I saw the lights of her car as she reversed into the drive. Once I knew she was home, I quickly pulled on the curtains, ran downstairs and went into the kitchen, where I turned the light on, and I put my shoes on to go out to greet her. When I opened the side door, Karen's car was stationary next to mine, and it looked like she was gathering her bag and things from the passenger seat. I didn't know how much stuff she had to carry in, so I went out to see if she needed any help.' He stopped abruptly, bowing his head down so his chin touched his chest.

'Are you alright, Robert? Do you need to take a break?' Collins asked, genuinely concerned.

'I went up to the window,' he smiled, as if remembering her face.

'And how did Karen seem?' Jacobi asked.

'She turned around and jumped at first, not expecting me to be standing right there, but then she quickly got out of the car and jumped into my arms. She was as thrilled to see me as I was to see her,' Day informed them.

'Did she say if anything unusual had happened at work or if she'd had any altercations with anyone?' Jacobi enquired.

'No, she just said that it had been a really long day as there had been quite a few casualties and that she was really tired and glad to be home,' Day said.

'How was her mood?' Collins queried.

'She was really happy, told me I was a sight for sore eyes after such a long shift and she was looking forward to getting in, having some food, a bath and cuddling up,' Day lied. 'Then she rushed inside as she needed the toilet,' Day congratulated himself on his quick thinking, just in case the nosey parker next door had been observing them and seen Karen's cold reception towards him.

'So, you followed her in?' Jacobi asked.

'Yes, why is that relevant?' Day wondered.

'I was just wondering if you had heard or noticed whether another car had pulled up after Karen's, or looking back now, if you had seen anyone hanging around?' Jacobi asked.

'I am sorry, I don't recall anything like that, but I was only focusing on Karen being home and the excitement of being about to ask her to marry me,' Day stated. 'Are you thinking that something happened at work and that maybe someone followed her home as a result of it?'

'We have to look at every possibility, Robert, and we cannot rule anything out at the moment,' Collins told him.

Jacobi could see how the cogs were working in Day's eyes at the introduction of his insinuation that someone may have followed her home. This little red herring was a decoy to see if Day would use it to create a scenario to point them in an altogether different direction and suspect other than himself. Jacobi had used this technique many times before and found that the guilty always jumped on the red herring to divert attention from themselves, whereas innocent people refused to entertain false statements.

'So, what happened once the two of you had entered the house, and after Karen had used the toilet?' Collins asked, getting the interview back on track.

'I had laid the Chinese menus on the island and was busy looking at them when she came up behind me, so I turned round to give her a welcome-home kiss,' Day said, pausing as he remembered her screaming at him about the messages, phone calls and annoyance at having been tannoyed to collect the sandwich he had dropped in.

'I asked how she was feeling because she hadn't felt well before setting off for work that morning, especially as she had stayed an extra couple of hours after her shift had ended. I had tried to get her to stay home, but she was so committed and went in because they were so short-staffed. I messaged her a couple of times throughout the day or rang her to offer support and tell her I was thinking about her. Just to make sure she was okay,' Day explained.

'And was she OK?' Collins asked.

'She tried to placate the situation, but I could tell she was stressed. Then she revealed it had been that busy, she hadn't even had time to eat lunch, so asked if I wouldn't mind dropping her a sandwich in. Which I did, and they called her to the desk to come and collect it,' Day answered.

'Did you see her or get to speak to her?' Jacobi asked.

'No, I didn't hang around. She was busy and at work, so I dropped the sandwich in as asked and left,' Day stated, drifting off into some crevice of his mind.

'Are you OK, Robert?' Collins asked again.

'Sorry, I'm just remembering the beauty of her face as she killed the engine and turned round to see me standing there. This all just feels like I am on the outside, looking in, watching a video playing back, as I'm sat here talking to you,' Day told them, looking for sympathy.

Jacobi and Collins nodded their understanding and sat quietly, allowing Day the time to pick it up again when he was ready.

After a few moments, Jacobi attempted to propel him on. 'So, she appears fine, you have the menus, you have welcomed her home, and then what?'

'She hung her bag up on the length of coat hooks and sat on the shoe box to remove her trainers, as we don't wear shoes in the house due to the new carpets. That's when I noticed her flinch. I was always telling her to wear more appropriate footwear to support her feet as she did miles up and down the hospital corridors, but she preferred her trainers.'

'So, I knelt in front of her, rested one foot upon my thigh, took the other in my hands, and began giving it a relaxing massage as we talked about what we were going to do for the evening. I suggested I make us something nice whilst she had a bath, but she was starving, didn't fancy anything we had in, and decided she wanted something from the Chinese menus.'

'After I had given her feet a quick massage, I left her to make a cup of tea and gave her the time to decide what dish she wanted whilst I went upstairs to prepare her bath,' Day told them.

The pause that Day executed now was intense to the point both Jacobi and Collins desperately wanted to fill the silence to urge him to continue, but instead, they waited.

After a few moments, Day continued of his own free will.

'So, I went upstairs. I went into the bathroom first, setting the taps going really slowly, because I knew that, although it takes a good 10 minutes or so to fill it before needing the cold water, Karen was desperate for a cuppa first. I poured some bubble bath under the flow of the water and put my hands in to agitate the bubbles to make it as luxurious as I could. A few of the petals I had placed in earlier were stuck to the bottom of the bath, so I went into the bedroom to take a few more off the stemmed flowers. I then sprinkled them into the water to ensure they would be floating on the surface when Karen saw them.'

'I then went into the bedroom to light all the candles. I hadn't wanted to light them any earlier as they burn far too quickly, and I wanted to enjoy the atmosphere with her later, if you know what I mean?' he said coyly. 'I then opened the ring box to expose the diamond, set it at the side of the bed—the left side,' he stressed to Jacobi, 'walked to the door, visibly checked it over. I found it pleasing, so I dimmed the lights.'

'You found it 'pleasing'?' Jacobi repeated, as he thought it an odd choice of word.

'Yes, everything looked just perfect, exactly how I had pictured it would,' Day beamed.

'Would you say you are a man who pays close attention to the details?' Jacobi asked.

'Yes, I wanted it to be just perfect,' he stated. 'But then I heard a thud which stopped me in my tracks, and I stood and listened carefully, unsure whether it was coming from outside or inside the house. When I heard it for a second time, I was sure it was from downstairs, so I shouted out Karen's name, but there was no response, and everything was silent. I shouted her name again as I set off to run downstairs, continuing to call, 'Karen!' I didn't know if she'd fainted due to her feeling unwell or over-exertion, so my first thought was to get to her as soon as possible.

'That's when I heard the door slam shut so, at first, I felt relieved, thinking she must have gone outside to her car or something?' Day explained.

'So, what course of action did you take?' Jacobi asked.

I didn't see her in the kitchen immediately, as typically I would have expected her to be standing up with a cup of tea in her hand if she had been in there. At first glance, nothing seemed out of place. So, I looked out onto the drive and walked up to look down the side of the cars, along the front of the house, and across to next door, but I couldn't see her anywhere. I was really perplexed, and I couldn't understand where she could have gone because I had definitely heard the door slam shut,' Day explained.

'How can you be so sure it was the door slamming? After all, you had been upstairs and heard two loud thuds that you couldn't distinguish,' Jacobi enquired.

'We had new doors fitted 3 months ago—the type where you have to depress the handle down to shut properly. They both have a five-point multi-locking system, making it difficult for the mechanism to slip into the frame otherwise. It will, but you would need to slam hard to achieve it, which happened this week when Karen was out the back hanging clothes out and had both doors opened at the same time. It was the same noise,' Day said.

Jacobi was beginning to think that Day had an answer for everything, and either this was due to his forte for attention to detail or he had a gift for the gab. 'Did you check anywhere else?' Jacobi enquired.

'Yes, at that point I had exhausted all options. So, I went to the gate—I don't know why, because I wasn't really expecting her to be outside the gate. But I just couldn't understand where else she could be. Then I came back inside. I noticed her shoes on the floor where she had taken them off, and then I was really confused, about where she could be.'

'That's when I saw her foot sticking out by the side of the island.' Day suddenly went quiet, the corner of his lip trembling, his forehead rapidly rising up and down to display a thick set of creases. He stared off into the distance, and then his head suddenly fell forward into his awaiting hands. His breathing became quite heavy, which manifested into a mild panic attack borne out of his inner distress.

Jacobi remained silent but nodded to Collins, indicating she should take the floor.

'I know this is very distressing for you, Robert, but it is really crucial for you to cast your mind back, picture the scene and think—was there anything different from when you'd left her making a cuppa?' Collins asked.

'No, no, there was nothing. Just Karen on the floor!' he said, his voice taking a slightly higher pitch.

'Robert, I want you to take your time, as even the smallest clue could be very important. I know it is hard, but we need as much detail as we possibly can if we are going to find Karen's killer,' Collins said earnestly.

'Honestly, I can't think of anything. The only thing I heard were the 2 thuds and the door slamming. I didn't hear anybody's voice. I didn't see anybody outside, and I didn't see anybody inside.'

Day paused, and then a glimpse of recognition crossed his face.

Collins looked at Jacobi, hopeful, 'What is it, Robert?'

'This is going to sound crazy, but there was a smell. I didn't really take any notice of it, but it was like a body odour type of smell—you know what I mean—not very pleasant. Like someone had been working all day and had perspired profusely, though not somebody who lived on the streets. To be honest, it had a mix of body odour with a clinical tinge to it as well, but I just put it down to being from Karen's uniform,' Day told them.

'But Karen was not dressed in her hospital garments,' Jacobi reminded Day.

'No, you're right. She wasn't, was she?' Day answered, puzzled but inwardly congratulating himself at remembering Marcus—the guy at work who had been sniffing around Karen for months. Robert was sure Karen had mentioned him being on the day shift with her. Well, there it was, a lead for the police to pick up on and misdirect them from him.

He hated Marcus—with his tall, rugged, square-jawed, athletic look—the typical kind of doctor that you would get on one of those American TV shows. You know the one, that all the nurses swoon over and the patients automatically gravitate towards. He had met his type before. They used their charm, appearance and good looks to manipulate those around them, especially women who hung on to their every word, vying for attention.

Yes, he had seen how women ate out of the hands of these predators. Well, of course, he had—he saw himself through the same lens. He had been aware of Marcus' presence and had carefully monitored its effect upon Karen in recent months. But he wasn't going to allow him to steal her away from him. Why else would he have been going to ask her to marry him? It was the only way to ensure he stayed the prominent leader of the pack, to deter Karen's heart from being stolen from under his nose.

Perhaps Marcus was the reason Karen's attitude had changed so dramatically towards him recently, but he was not going to risk a repeat performance like the one he'd had with Josie Bellamy. How on earth had she managed to outwit him, to pull the rug so successfully from under his feet when he was on the home stretch? Just a few more months and he would have had her exactly where he had wanted her. The painstaking months of coercive manipulation, false representation and conditioning had been for nothing.

Didn't these women understand the time, effort and dedication it took out of him, day after day, month after month, to rewire their stupid little brains? No, he had not wanted Karen Blakely's investment to be wasted in the same way. Yet, in the end, she had chosen to push him too far. It wasn't his fault that he had needed to teach her a lesson, she should have kept her mouth shut, and then things would have continued happily on. The trouble is, she had now created a situation where he would have to start all over again from scratch.

A nuisance yes, and a delay to his plans, but he had to admit—if only to himself—that he did enjoy those first few months of fun and new experiences. He actually didn't even mind devoting his time, if he was honest, because it was well spent if he could ingratiate himself quickly to brainwash them to give him what he wanted in the long run. And he was always able to fully control, direct and influence their behaviour patterns to create compliance.

It wasn't his problem if they were so willing to not only believe but actually hold onto those early false representations as fact, instead of opening their eyes to the truth. It was always there—literally staring them in the face. It would be like an artist having a lion in front of them but painting a picture of a tabby cat. Just because the artist had interpreted the lion as a tabby cat it didn't make it any less of a lion.

These stupid women only wanted to see what the magician allowed because they were focused on believing in the magic of true love, of their prince charming arriving to save them from the mundanity of everyday life. So yes, he enjoyed those months of make-believe moments—weekends away, trips abroad, festivals, fancy restaurants, socialising and seeing bands at the local pubs. It was humorous to Day that by investing in these things for his long-term goals, they actually believed their lives had permanently changed for the better.

Their naivety to believe that it should actually cost them nothing was the very reason he had no qualms that it would eventually cost them everything. If they were prepared to willingly be showered unsparingly in those early days, taking all that he kindly offered, then he was prepared to unconditionally drain them of all their resources, period. By failing to keep watch, failing to discern his character, and choosing to hold on to the image of what they wanted to see rather than what was real, then they were ripe for his picking.

Middle-aged women with kids were always the best. Let's face it—in broken Britain, they were ten a penny, so no harm done. He would just have to go out and find himself another one, and soon. For now, Day would have to settle with misdirecting the police and giving Marcus to them on a platter. He was the ideal person to frame.

'Do you know of any disagreements or altercations that Karen may have had with anyone?' Collins enquired.

'No, she's never said anything,' Day replied honestly.

'Do you know anybody that could have stirred up any bad feelings, like within her family, her friends or anybody at work?' Collins tried to stimulate Day's memory bank.

'No. I am sorry; I really can't think of anybody.' Day shrugged hopelessly.

'What kind of a person was Karen? How would you describe her?' Jacobi asked.

'She was an intelligent woman who knew what she wanted. She was dedicated to her work and loved helping other people, so had a kind and nurturing disposition. I know it sounds corny, and everyone always says it when people die, but she lit a room up when she walked into it, and when she smiled, you felt alive—like her light was reaching down deep within you too,' Day recited from some film he had watched recently, remembering to sniffle on cue just as the actor had done.

'Do you need a break, Robert?' Collins enquired.

As if caught in his own thoughts, Day totally ignored the offer.

'You know, seeing that light and her ability to touch people in such a special way tells you everything about her innate goodness. She would do everything she could for anybody who asked, always going out of her way for them—even strangers. I never heard her say a bad word about anyone, but neither would anyone have anything bad to say about her. I absolutely adored her, and we loved spending time together.' He looked from Jacobi to Collins and, giving his head a theatrical nod that appeared more patronising, he finished, 'Her light will continue to shine on in many of us.'

'Didn't you say she worked up at the hospital?' Collins asked.

'Yeah,' Day succinctly replied, getting a bit fed up with their questions now. How much longer did he have to keep going over this?

'Did she mention having any issues with staff members or if there was one in particular?' Collins tried again.

'Nobody that would have wanted to cave her head in. After all, she works in an environment that treats people's injuries. They are not the kind of people who would cause them. What she sustained was horrific and heartless,' Day mindfully compared.

'Yes, I agree with you, but somebody who works in that environment would also be used to seeing those kinds of injuries and perhaps be desensitised to the brutality. No one can say for sure, which is why we need to look at every aspect of her life and discount nothing at this time,' Jacobi rightfully stated.

On cue, Day immediately exposed his awarding-winning look of a light bulb moment across his face, and boom—as soon as it flashed, Collins dived straight in.

'What is it Robert? What have you remembered?' Collins asked, her excitement unmistakable as her spine straightened and she slightly leant in further towards him.

'There was one person at work, a guy who worked with Karen. I think his name was Marcus. Sorry, I don't know his last name, but I do remember Karen saying that he was constantly sniffing around her. That she would go out of her way to try to avoid him if he came into her department,' Day said, thrilled she was taking the bait.

'Is there anything else you can tell us about Marcus? For instance, more specifically, why she felt she had to keep out of his way? Were there any inappropriate advances, innuendos, touching or him segregating her?' Jacobi asked, pinpointing what issues they were seeking.

'Not that I am aware of. I just know he was a bit of a hit with the ladies, and according to Karen, everybody fancies him. But because Karen and I were solid, she didn't want to ride the same bandwagon as everyone else. Whether he saw her detachment and disinterest as some kind of a challenge, I really couldn't say. But I cannot think of anybody else in Karen's world who had a grudge against her,' Day said.

'So, as far as you're concerned, she got on well with everybody. She did everything that she could for those around her. She was a really kind person, had a lovely aura about her, and there is no one else other than this Marcus guy from work you could pinpoint as having a potential motive to hurt her? Does that fairly sum up what you have told us so far, Robert?' Collins put it concisely.

'Yes, that is what I am saying. I really cannot think of anybody else who would want to hurt Karen,' Day agreed.

'Thank you,' Jacob said. 'I think we will leave it there for now, Robert.'

'Thank you, I would appreciate that,' Robert said. 'I do feel quite exhausted. It has been quite a strenuous night.'

'We can see just how difficult it has been for you, Robert, and I would personally like to thank you for your commitment to helping us with our investigation. Your input has been invaluable,' Collins assured him.

'As I said, if there is anything that I can do to help catch this person, I'm more than willing to do whatever I can,' he stipulated, gushing at Collins's appraisal of his performance.

'That's great,' Jacobi interrupted. 'Where is it that you will be staying now that Karen's house is a crime scene, just in case we need to get hold of you *when* we need to speak to you again?'

Jacobi was too long in the tooth to mistake an act when he saw one. So, with an infused determination, he decided this may have been Day's opening night, but he would be bringing the curtain down on his performance.

'I have a house at the top of Edge Lane, also in Walton,' Day began, then on recognition, 'Oh my gosh, yes, I guess, I will have to go back there now. What about all my stuff? Will I not even be able to go back and pack the things that I have at Karen's house?'

'No, I'm afraid not, as it is now a crime scene,' Jacobi informed him.

'The bath! Oh my goodness, I didn't turn the bath off,' Day replicated panic as though it had just occurred to him.

'It is all right, Robert. I actually turned the taps off myself before it affected the crime scene,' Jacobi stated.

'So, what happens now?' Day enquired.

'The crime scene will need to be thoroughly processed by a multitude of personnel, including the body, to see if there were any fibres from the perpetrator's clothing, any DNA under her fingernails like skin or blood, and of course, the coroner will need to perform a postmortem examination to determine the official cause of death,' Jacobi informed him.

'Yes, after securing the site, we collate as much physical evidence as we can from the scene itself. Then, over the next few days, whilst this evidence is being processed, we have procedures we have to follow. Inevitably, talking to yourself was one of our main priorities, as you are the closest person, we have to a witness, despite you not actually seeing anyone leaving the crime scene. What you have told us, Robert, I am sure will prove to be vital in the long run,' Collins told him.

Jacobi saw the man's ego raise itself again, as though it was a secondary spirit within him, as soon as Collins told him he was a 'main priority' and again with how his information was 'vital.'

'We will now look at gaining as much additional information as possible from other sources, such as whether any neighbours saw anyone lurking around either last night or leading up to it, in case there was anyone observing the property beforehand. We will look to see what intelligence we can find, like camera footage, known criminal activity in the area,' Collins gave him a brief rundown.

'Yes, and of course, we will be speaking to Karen's colleagues and interviewing this guy Marcus that you have told us about,' Jacobi did a Robert Day Jr pause for effect, 'to collaborate on what you are telling us. Inevitably, we cannot dismiss what you have told us, but equally, we cannot take it as gospel either.'

Jacobi smiled at the irritation written across Day's face. Did he really think he was going to walk into a police station and that they would so easily fall for his act? Collins shot him a look of disapproval; apparently, one of them was Team Day.

'Did Karen have any cameras at her property?'

'No, I'm sorry. I did offer to get them installed for her, but she was adamant she wouldn't have them. She said it was bad enough being monitored all day long on the cameras at work without having them at home as well,' Day told them.

'That's a shame, although no one could ever have predicted that this could have happened,' Collins said, saddened.

'So how long have you and Karen been together?'

'It's only been a year, but it feels like forever when you meet the one,' Day said easily.

'And yet, you were going to ask her to marry you?' Jacobi said, unable to keep the surprise out of his voice.

'Yes, as soon as Karen and I got together, we clicked instantly. I'd never felt like that about anybody at all, and Karen said exactly the same. You see we loved the same bands, restaurants, exploring different countries, walking, and films. She was my soulmate, and I was hers. So, yeah, it might have only been a year, but it felt like we had known each other all our lives because we were mirror versions of the other and had been waiting for this our entire lives. So, we didn't want to waste time waiting any longer to make a formal commitment,' Day explained.

'So, you only bought the ring yesterday. How can you be so sure she was going to actually say yes if you hadn't had the opportunity to ask her?' Jacobi played devil's advocate.

'Obviously, we had discussed our plans. I wasn't going to railroad her into it; she just did not know the exact time I was going to surprise her,' Day said, getting a bit agitated at the scrutiny of his intention.

'Where did you purchase the ring from?' Jacobi enquired.

'From the little jewellers shop on the precinct in Wakefield next to the bank. It's called Dysons,' Day stated.

'At approximately what time did you go into the jeweller's?' Jacobi continued.

'It would have been around 3:00 to 3:15, I would say. Obviously, with it being a jeweller's shop, they will have CCTV, so they will definitely be able to place me there,' Day smirked.

'Thank you.' Jacobi smiled. Day may think he was clever, but it was more about what he wasn't saying than the information he was offering up that gave him an alibi.

'Didn't you say you had also bought 2 dozen red roses that you had used to strip the petals from? Where were they purchased from?' Jacobi enquired.

'I got them from The Little Flower Shop,' Day announced, 'down the side of the ginnel by the Co-op.'

'What is the little flower shop called?' Jacobi asked.

'The Little Flower Shop,' Day said, confused.

'Yes, the little flower shop?' Jacobi repeated, wondering if Day was stalling for time.

'No,' said Collins, 'the shop is called *The Little Flower Shop*!'

'Ah, sorry. I didn't realise. The last time I bought flowers, it was called Blooms, but that was about five years ago. If you don't have further questions, Collins, I think we can wrap up the interview here,' Jacobi declared.

'No, I think we have everything we need for now. I will get the speech-to-text extracted and accurately transcribed for you. I will get it printed out straight away and ready for you to sign. If you wouldn't mind waiting here for a few more minutes, then we can have you on your way. Can I get you another drink, a cup of tea or anything?' Collins offered.

'Could I have a cappuccino, please?' Day asked hopefully.

'Sorry, Robert, we only have instant coffee, which is marginally better than the cheap teabags in the canteen,' Jacobi scoffed.

'Fair enough,' Day said, unable to hide his disdain. 'Strong instant coffee it is then. Thank you.'

As Collins left to sort out the transcription and drink for Day, Jacobi nonchalantly enquired, 'Do you have any questions for us, Robert?'

'No, I'm sorry. I can't think of anything at the moment. Everything just seems unreal,' Day told him. 'When you said that Karen's house is now a crime scene, does that mean I cannot get my things? I'm just wondering about my car. You see it is still parked on the drive, but I am going to need it for work—not to mention having to sort some groceries out now I am going back to my house. Will I at least be able to retrieve it from the drive as it doesn't form part of the actual crime scene?'

'I shouldn't think that would be a problem, but I will have to get authority from Detective Chief Inspector Shona Williams as she is heading up the investigation. When PC Collins returns, I will put a call in to get permission for its removal,' Jacobi said.

At that moment, the door opened, and a young female officer entered the room with a small cup of coffee set into a saucer, handing it directly to Robert Day Jr. Jacobi paid close attention to Day's repulsion at the meagre offering and then how his face changed when his eyes hit the woman holding the cup. As he longingly looked her up and down, Jacobi couldn't help but notice the intensity of Day's stare as he examined the young woman, who was old enough to be his daughter.

Clearly, this man had no boundaries or any understanding of what was right or wrong—all the more unnerving when Jacobi considered that the partner he was about to get engaged to only a matter of hours earlier had just been murdered. Jacobi excused himself to make the call to Shona Williams, following the young woman out of the interview room. He suddenly needed to take a break from this man to breathe some cleaner air.

Once the statement had been prepared and printed out, Collins reconnected with Jacobi so they could return to the interview room together. As they opened the door, they were stunned to find Day sitting with his head resting on his arms on the table, fast asleep. Jacobi lightly tapped on the door to alert Day that they had re-entered the room.

Day startled awake before exaggerating a loud yawn. 'Sorry,' he began. 'I am just so exhausted. This whole experience has knocked it out of me.'

Jacobi glanced at the full cup, which had been left untouched on the table— *a mark of Day's disgust,* he thought. Jacobi pushed it aside as he and Collins retook their seats. Collins removed the sheets of the printed transcript from her clipboard, turned it around to face the correct way up for Day to observe, and laid it on the table in front of Day.

'If you could take your time to carefully read through the whole statement, double checking that everything we have talked about, and more importantly, the answers you have provided, are correct. If there is anything that isn't correct, please let me know, and we will delete it. Equally, as you read, if it stimulates further information, speak up so this can be added to give the fullest picture, we can obtain the better. Only when you are happy that it is a full and clear representation of last night's events do I want you to sign, date it and also add the time if you wouldn't mind,' Collins explained fully.

The room suddenly went silent as though the air had been sucked out of it whilst Day poured over the written paperwork, intently examining every word, absorbing it, understanding it. He turned over page after page, reading each side, and only when he was absolutely Satisfied, did he pick up the pen to endorse it as directed.

Once he had declared it was a true representation of the facts, he looked up and addressed them.

'If that's everything, I'd really like to get home and get some sleep now.'

'Not a problem, Robert. I will let them know we have done here,' Jacobi said, leading Day back out towards the chill-out area of the integral offices.

He took out his mobile phone to inform the staff on the ground at the scene they were on their way when Jacobi was given some new instructions.

'You are just in time. We were about to release him,' Jacobi said, alerting Day.

'Is there a problem?' Day asked irritably.

'No not a problem as such, just a slight delay. The boss has requested that we take some swabs, including under your fingernails, along with retaining the clothes that you are wearing,' Jacobi announced.

'Am I a suspect?' Day asked, stunned.

'It is just procedure to help us eliminate you from our enquiries, Robert. So, if you would like to follow me this way,' Jacobi said expectantly. Without even waiting for an answer, he turned and walked back in the direction of the interview rooms.

Day followed Jacobi to a private area where he was then expected to strip his clothes which were handled by latex-gloved personnel and watched them then being bagged for testing. He was then given a disposable, white, zip-up the front suit to put on.

'Really?' he said. 'This is most unreasonable and inconvenient.'

'I am sorry you feel that way, Mr Day,' Jacobi said, intentionally reverting back to a more formal address, 'but as you said yourself, you want to help in any way you can to catch your late partner's killer.'

Seething, Day allowed them to photograph his hands, take swabs from his hands and mouth, then scrape the underpart of his fingernails. The pressure he was feeling, coupled with being treated like a criminal and having had no sleep was mounting.

Jacobi detected his irritation rising. The twitch to his forehead had become more prominent, his jaw was set, his breathing heavier and his fists were clenching and unclenching. Jacobi thought he was going to have a fit when he declared that they would also need to take his fingerprints rather than disturb him at a later date.

'There, Mr Day, now that wasn't so bad, was it?' Jacobi said nonchalantly, returning him back towards the chill-out area, but Day chose not to comment.

Jacobi held open the doors to let Day through and followed him back down the stairwell, through the corridor and out of the back of the building. He let Day into his car and negotiated his way through the automatic gates before driving back along the road to Karen Blakley's house on St Michael's Mount.

Inevitably, the scene wasn't as chaotic as when they'd left it only a few hours earlier. The ambulance was long gone, but the odd patrol car was still there.

The first thing that Robert Day Jr noticed when Jacobi's car came to a standstill directly opposite Karen Blakely's gate was the 'Crime Scene Do Not Cross' tape flapping across the length of the gateway. Normally, either he or Karen would close the gate each evening to maintain some semblance of security, regardless of how minor that might have seemed.

He grinned at both the fact it had been left open all night and the irony.

How's that working for you now, Karen? he thought callously.

Stationed outside the gate and at the entrance to the house were two static policemen with clipboards to record the details of any individuals attending the scene—their times of arrival/leaving, their departments and job titles.

'If you wouldn't mind waiting in the car for a moment, Mr Day, whilst I make arrangements. Thank you,' Jacobi said, immediately getting out of the car and heavily slamming the door shut—without even waiting for him to answer.

Jacobi approached Constable Betts, who was now tasked with guarding the gateway, to ask, 'How is it going?' Then, as an afterthought, 'Is DCI Williams still around?'

'Yes, sir, she is. Can you sign in please?' the young officer asked, handing him the clipboard with the pen attached.

He signed in, ensuring he underlined the date to highlight that he was back on the scene and that it was different from last night's.

He was more than aware, that at first glance, an auditor or administrator could easily assume that he had been on scene all night like DCI Williams, so he always made a habit to underline it. As he ducked under the tape and approached the door where Davis was standing, Shona came outside with a surprised expression upon her face to find that Jacobi had managed to arrive so quickly.

'How did it go at the hospital?' Shona asked Jacobi.

'I got there just in time. Day was being released almost immediately as I arrived, so I transported him straight down to the station. I had Collins in with me whilst I interviewed him, and we extracted a statement,' Jacobi informed his boss.

'How did he present himself?' Shona queried.

'I haven't made my mind up about the guy yet, but I'll tell you this—he is a strange man. I don't think he was genuinely in shock; he seems non-plussed at seeing his partner in the state he supposedly found her in, and he was positively flirting with any female going,' Jacobi stated. 'It seemed like it was all just a show he was putting on for our benefit.'

'Jacobi, I know that look, what's going on?' Shona enquired.

'I don't know. There's something off about him that just seems to be lying under the surface, and I can't quite put my finger on it.' Jacobi puzzled.

'So, do you think he had something to do with Karen's murder, whether directly or indirectly?' Shona wondered.

'I am not sure yet whether he had anything to do with it, if he knows who's done it, if it was planned or not——I am not quite ready to make that call. But there is something with this guy that, doesn't quite sit right,' Jacobi stated.

'Is that your copper's intellect, your gut instinct—'I don't know but there is something off about him'?' Shona laughed. She was far too tired to interpret Jacobi's description at the moment, but she was sure if he felt something was off then he was right.

'Time will tell. Anyway, like I said on the phone, he wants to pick his car up, so I've got him here waiting,' Jacobi said with a tilt of his head towards his car. 'Inevitably, he had left it here yesterday preparing to ask Karen Blakely to marry him, so he's going to need it to get to work. Is he still alright to take it?'

She looked over to the two cars that sat on the drive.

'Which one is his?'

'The old battered Civic, apparently,' Jacobi replied.

'Fair enough. I can see no reason for it to stay here, so yeah, you can have him move it. It will give our guys the room to remove Karen Blakely's car for forensics. Get Betts to document the car's removal and that the line has been broken,' Shona said.

As Jacobi turned away to approach Betts, Shona suddenly asked, 'Does he have his keys on him, or are they somewhere in the house?'

'Oh, I don't know. I never thought to ask him. Give me a minute, and I'll just double-check,' Jacobi said, going back to the car.

When Jacobi proceeded towards his car, he could see that Day had certainly made himself very comfortable. He had sought to reposition the passenger seat so that he was now sat at a more severe obtuse angle, with his head rested back, relaxing like he hadn't got a care in the world.

Again, under the circumstances, this did not seem appropriate behaviour, although Jacobi was trying to stay impartial and hoped that perhaps Day was just stealing himself to go back into the place where his partner had just been brutally murdered. And, of course, it could just have been a sign of exhaustion, but it was also a possibility that he was an uncaring, sadistic murderer.

Either way, Jacobi was surprised to find that he did look exceptionally peaceful under the circumstances. Jacobi tapped lightly upon the passenger window to get the man's attention before opening the door.

'I just want to check if you have your car keys on you, or are they in the house?' Jacobi enquired.

'I've got them here,' Day began, taking them out of his pocket and holding them up in front of him.

'Fair enough,' Jacobi began, then did a double take on the keys. 'We will need your key to Karen's house before you remove your car, Mr Day,' Jacobi said, congratulating himself for noticing a lone key on a separate keyring with Karen's photograph attached to the bunch.

It seemed logical to Jacobi that the Yale key was for a house, and it was as equally likely to be for Karen's house as it was for anywhere else so, he thought he would give it a stab in the dark and see if it drew blood.

Day reluctantly removed the key, taking his time as though he was having trouble taking it off. But now Jacobi knew it was for the crime scene, he was glad to have retrieved it, so he would wait regardless of how long it took him.

Once he had detached it from the bunch, Jacobi held his hand out, and Day pressed it a little too firmly into the palm of his hand as though it was a cattle branding iron. Jacobi decided to overlook the man's action and noted his annoyance at having his choice and control taken away from him.

'Alright, Mr Day if you would like to follow me, DCI Williams has given permission for you to remove the car, but you will have to give your details to the officer on guard so that we can identify the time the car was removed and by whom,' Jacobi informed him.

As Day got out, he made sure he locked his car.

The men walked together across the road and adhered to the procedures for Day to be allowed to cross the outer threshold of the scene. Jacobi kept his eyes on Day as he ducked under the tape and made his way across the gravel drive.

Not once did Day falter in his steps. He was direct and resolute as he made his way determinedly towards his car without a look nor sideways glance towards the house—not once.

It was as though this man had already detached himself from the house. He was no longer connected with the woman he had bought flowers and an engagement ring for the day before, whose feet he had massaged and whom he had seen with her head bashed in.

Jacobi shook his head in disbelief. Then he made a vital mistake.

Instead of continuing his close observations of Day, he began dislodging the tape to remove it, to allow Day to reverse his car out. In focusing his attention on the tape and the officer posted at the gate, he failed to notice Robert Day Jr's swift movement to retrieve the bag secreted in the wheel arch at the top of the tyre.

As he slid into his seat, he made a quick glance in his rear-view mirror before quickly securing it beneath his seat. He clicked his seatbelt into place, turned the key in the ignition, slapped the car into reverse, then gradually eased it out of the drive, slowly passing the two police officers.

'Fools' he said to himself through a gritted smile before continuing on to the end of the street.

Once he had turned the corner, he accelerated—and then he was gone.

Chapter 7
Chewing the Fat

At 11:30 that morning, Shona Williams was finally able to secure Karen Blakely's property before seeing her team of forensic personnel into their vehicles. She arranged to meet with Jacobi back at the police station, to re-confer about what they had so far to assist her with which direction she wanted to proceed.

Sometimes Shona enjoyed the solitude of this process in the quiet of her office with just herself, the whiteboard, a clean sheet of paper and a couple of felt tip markers. Today, though, she was ready to welcome the interaction of Jacobi to get his thoughts on both the scene and the witness to establish their combined efforts before jotting them down.

Shona and Jacobi made a very unlikely team. He was her senior by 15 years and was happy to maintain his Detective Inspector title without the need to progress any further through the ranks. He was a typical middle-aged man who enjoyed going home after work, putting his feet up and cracking a beer. Shona, on the other, had been fit, flighty, constantly on the go—a high achiever who was flying through the ranks and making a name for herself.

The things they did have in common were their dry sense of humour and a love of locking up criminals. Their key to working so cohesively together was their shared determination to never take anything for granted, to stay alert, their commitment to communicate and bounce ideas off each other, and to trust their instincts.

They both had a tendency for stubborn persistence when it came to ascertaining the facts, seeking credible evidence and their attention to the minutest of details. The most important similarity was their respect and support for one another—they didn't just have each other's backs, they were the other's backbone. Due to this, they also shared a typical understanding of how the other one thought.

'So, what have we got?' Shona asked.

'At this moment, we haven't got anything. The victim has been described as a person everyone loves, she hasn't got any known enemies, there doesn't appear to be any motive, and a random intruder allegedly entered the property, killed her and made his escape without being seen,' Jacobi surmised.

'Is that strictly true though, Dion?' Shona began. 'We cannot say we haven't got any witnesses before we canvas the area, nor can we say we don't have a motive before we find one. Also, let's not forget we may have been led to believe there was an intruder, but unless we can prove one exists, we don't know whether this is true.'

'OK, the key facts are: there were two people in the house at the time of Karen Blakely's murder. One is dead, the other one is not, but he claims to have not seen anyone,' Jacobi stated.

'Is there anything to suggest that Day could be lying or that he committed murder? I know you said there was something odd about him, but can you elaborate on that for me?' Shona asked.

'There isn't anything concrete to suggest he is lying. It just felt like a performance, and he showed no care or concern about Karen or what had happened to her. He was all about how the situation was affecting him. The other key fact is that there is no sign of a robbery, and he has offered little explanation other than to implicate one of Karen's work colleagues,' Jacobi offered.

'He has offered up a work colleague, now that has pricked my attention,' Shona replied.

'Day was adamant Karen Blakely was a model citizen, and he couldn't think of a single person who would want to harm her. Then he happened to mention something about a guy called Marcus. Apparently, he was a bit of a ladies' man. With regards to my feeling Day was a bit off, I found it really difficult being in his company,' Jacobi admitted.

'How so?' Shona asked.

'He may have accused Marcus of being a bit of a ladies' man, but to be honest, the way he was drooling over Anita Collins and a young officer who brought him a coffee was embarrassing. It felt like he was literally undressing them with his eyes one minute, and then the next, we were being rewarded with a performance fit for the West End stage,' Jacobi told her.

'Hold on a minute—his partner has just been murdered, he has been taken to hospital suffering from shock, and he is openly eyeing up other women within a matter of hours? Really?' Shona said incredulously.

'Yes, that's what I mean about him being off. When asked questions, he acted—and that is the correct word to use—he acted the part of a trauma victim, but his true character was evident whenever the questions ceased. He was flirting with Collins right in front of me from the moment he set eyes upon her. It was also weird how he seemed to gush each time he perceived she had paid him the merest of compliments,' Jacobi said.

'In what way? How did Anita respond?' Shona asked.

'I don't think Anita was even aware. She was handling the situation in a professional manner, just demonstrating understanding for his circumstances and displaying empathy,' Jacobi explained.

'Interesting observation, Sherlock. So, we could interpret this as Day cannot help but reveal his character traits when there is a woman present. I have to say I am quite intrigued now, and I will definitely look forward to teasing out more of Mr Day's personality as time goes on—in the most professional capacity, you understand.'

'Like I said, there is something really odd about the guy. He finds his partner's lifeless body on the floor, having been savagely attacked, then hours later he is sucking up to the officer interviewing him about it,' Jacobi said in disbelief.

'What was the rest of his demeanour like?' Shona asked.

'I could be wrong, but I did not get the impression he was genuinely upset about her death or the conditions in which this had occurred. In fact, thinking about it, when I arrived at the hospital, he was in a jovial mood as he interacted with the female nurses. Well, that was until he saw me, and then a more sombre expression hit his face—as though this was what he considered appropriate to display to me,' Jacobi said, confused.

'Jacobi, I don't think I have ever heard you say that before,' Shona said seriously.

'You have never heard me say what?' Jacobi asked, perplexed.

'I could be wrong but…' Shona said, lightening the mood.

'Funny! I just find it hard to fathom that this poor woman had come home from work, was attacked but life just carries on for her partner as though nothing has happened. He made it feel like her life wasn't important. She was the victim, yet he was devaluing her further—not only with his behaviour but his lack of grief. The impression I got, was he was just playing a character, the words were coming out of his mouth, but there were no feelings behind them,' Jacobi said remorsefully.

'Alright, so let's get this Marcus guy in and see what he has to say for himself and where he was between 8–9 pm. It will be good to place him at the scene or eradicate him as a suspect.'

'Whilst we get him in for questioning, we will have a couple of officers make some preliminary enquiries at the hospital—both about Marcus and his behaviour at work. Let's see if there is any truth in the allegations of him being a potential suspect whilst also finding out about our victim.'

'Let's enquire about whether she had any issues with her work colleagues and exactly what her relationship was like with this Marcus. For all we know, she could have been having an affair and Day found out.'

'We need to establish if it was a targeted hit on Karen Blakely and, if so, why—or whether it was an uncontrolled crime of passion. Let's also bear in mind that she had just arrived home from work, so was there any altercation during her last shift? Is it possible that some random with a grudge simply followed her home and attacked her?' Shona said.

'And what about Day?' Jacobi asked.

'I thought we could give him a little bit of rope and let him think he is in the clear whilst we look into other avenues. Then we can knock on his door again and ask him out to play,' Shona said, meaning she was intent on doing the next interview with him.

'So, for the time being, we put a great big question mark over Day's head. I like it,' Jacobi stated.

'Our guys processing the scene will soon establish if there was anyone else in that kitchen. But in the meantime, whilst you and I get some rest, I will organise officers to start by questioning neighbours.'

'Let's see if we can pinpoint anybody in the area between the times of eight and nine. Maybe somebody saw her arrive home. If so, did they witness anyone else hanging around beforehand, or a car pull up immediately after she arrived home?'

'Also, let's take a look for any CCTV footage—not just around the vicinity of the house but tracking Karen Blakely from the hospital to her final destination,' Shona planned.

'I noticed there were two principal windows that faced directly onto Karen's drive from the neighbours to the right of the house. Maybe that would be a good place for them to start,' Jacobi stated.

'Going back to Day for a minute, how long did you say they were in a relationship for, just so I have it clear in my mind?' Shona enquired.

'He said it was for about a year,' Jacobi answered.

'Yet he was going to ask her to marry him?' Shona said, astonished. The very idea of marriage did not appeal to her, but it astounded her why people would contemplate giving over the rest of their lives to someone they couldn't possibly know in such a short period of time.

'Day describes them as having a solid relationship, which they may well have had, but equally, we only have his say on this—so again, we cannot jump the gun,' Jacobi highlighted.

'What else did he give you that we can work on behind the scenes?' asked Shona.

'He did mention that the jewellers where he bought the ring from was called Dyson's, and the flowers came from a shop called *The Little Flower Shop*, so it will be easy enough to verify the information,' Jacobi replied.

'I will have a couple of P.Cs drop by both shops to establish the exact times he was there, but we hold off on everything else,' she said with a grin.

'What is going on in that little head of yours, DCI Williams?' Jacobi asked coyly.

'If he is the slippery, egotistical womaniser that you have painted him as, then I would rather discount everyone else around him first—especially if he is looking to point the finger at others. I would much prefer our guy to be the last man standing whilst the firing squad, namely you and I, carefully take our aim,' Shona smiled.

'I like you're thinking, DCI Williams—as long as I get to play 'shotgun',' Jacobi said, laughing at his own pun.

'I don't know about you, Dion, but I'm absolutely wrecked, so I think we should leave it there for now. I'll get in contact with Damien Clark, Chief of Special Basic Command, and give him the run down so he can relay everything to the troops. He can delegate the jobs whilst the evidence from the scene is being processed and we are catching up on some sleep. I will see you back here tomorrow morning,' Shona said.

'Alright, boss, I will see you in the morning,' Jacobi said, making his way towards the office door before turning back. 'Don't stay too late, Shona.'

'I don't know what you mean,' she said innocently.

'I know you. You may be sending me home, but there will be all manner of loose information running around your brain. Just remember it doesn't all need tying up today. Go home and get your rest too, so we can catch this guy!' Jacobi said firmly.

'Aye, aye, Captain,' Shona said, giving him a mock salute.

Chapter 8
Pondering the Facts

As Jacobi closed the office door behind him, Shona made herself comfortable at her desk. There was no way she could go home just yet, whether sleep was beckoning her or not. Instead, she began reviewing the points that she and Jacobi had made to see if there was anything she may have overlooked.

The main point of interest, as with every other case, was to establish a motive, as this would ultimately take her to the most direct route to finding the murderer. Inevitably, the first point was the necessity to identify whether or not there had actually been an intruder. Hence, she needed to get the newbies door knocking in the area and checking CCTV to investigate whether anyone had been seen lurking around; this was a primary factor. At the moment, the only word they had for a third-party suspect was from the mouth of the only other person on the scene.

Shona was not the type of woman to take anything for granted, nor to believe everything that a witness chose to tell her. Until she could find the specific evidence to suggest that what Day was stating was in fact true, she would inadvertently discard it as a lie. This way, she could never have the wool pulled over her eyes, and boy, many had tried. She stood up, walked around her desk and perched on the end of it, gazing at the whiteboard, scanning over it. Her brain was suffering from fatigue, so she was finding it hard to absorb the information.

She decided that, firstly, she would request a copy of the recorded call Day had made to the emergency services and, if necessary, have it analysed. She decided to ask Damien to put the newest recruits in the team on the streets to conduct the old-fashioned face-to-face with neighbours. Everything nowadays was tracked via the immense network of CCTV around the towns and city; however, for a crime of this nature, she wanted to assure the public that they were doing everything they could to catch the culprit. Besides, they could offer vital information leading up to the attack, the victim, her partner and the status of their relationship. An outsider's perspective on an internal relationship could be very revealing, and with a case like this, it often loosened the lips of the neighbouring busybodies.

She was particularly interested to find out if they were really as happy as Day was leading them to believe. After all, Jacobi had informed her, they had only been together for a year, yet on the night she is brutally murdered he is about to ask her to marry him. Is it possible that he was far more invested than she was? Did she say no? Or could she have been seeing this Marcus guy from work, and Day snapped with the old phrase, 'If I can't have you, then nobody is going to have you'?

It was a possibility she couldn't disregard so early on in the investigation, but first, she needed to know more about who the victim and Day were, both as a couple and as individuals. It always amazed Shona how anyone would want to throw their whole life in by committing to a relationship in such a short period of time. Shona remembered reading something online about it only taking something like 3 months for the honeymoon period to begin to subside, and that by 6 months, you would know whether they were the one. What utter claptrap, she had thought. How anyone could really know another person when they were only showing their best version of themselves?

Give it a couple of years down the line when they couldn't keep up the act anymore, and then maybe you could say if you were willing to invest in that person. But dating for 6 months is ridiculous. Her thoughts refocused on the victim and Day, and she considered: they had only dated for 12 months? Was it long enough to decide whether you wanted to spend the rest of your life with them? Obviously, it was for Day, because he had been out that afternoon to buy her an engagement ring. But how had that sat with Karen Blakely?

It was times like this that Shona wished she could ask the victim directly for their insight, but of course, she couldn't. Shona decided to allocate an initial 2-mile radius of the property, within a 2-hour time frame on either side of the time of death, to the CCTV department to see what it raised. This would give her time to make other preliminary enquiries, and If need be, she could always extend both the time and area of the search.

Shona hated being called to investigations that took her through the entire night, as it meant she had to have the following day off when, in reality, all she just wanted to do was get stuck into the investigation. Shona Williams was stubbornly persistent when it came to a case; she followed her own proven five-point mode of practice: observe, analyse, deduce, prove and prosecute. Her gut instinct was always on par and had never let her down yet. So, despite both her and her right-hand man Jacobi having to be out of the office for the day, she would delegate the workload, primarily looking into Day and Karen Blakely's relationship.

As she scribbled her notes down, she wondered whether Karen Blakely had any life insurance, and if so, who the potential beneficiary might be. Inevitably, there hadn't been any attempt to cover up the brutality of the attack, which did seem a crime of passion as opposed to a random attack. She made a note of the appropriate searches for any insurance details and whether there had been any adjustments, although she found it most unlikely. Inevitably, she would create a search of both Day's and Karen Blakely's financial records to ascertain whether there were any debts or large unsubstantiated debits and to further collaborate with Day's purchasers on the day of the murder timeline.

She would specifically allocate Jenson Parker to have a chat with any personnel or colleagues of Karen Blakely and to ascertain who the unidentified Marcus guy was. However, she would save any further talks for her and Jacobi to conduct, as she wanted to get a full picture of what she was dealing with so no stone could be left unturned. Hopefully, pulling all the information together whilst she and Jacobi were absent from the office would establish a few unanswered questions, or at least narrow down the playing field a little. The telephone interrupted her thought process.

'Good morning, this is Detective Chief Inspector Shona Williams, Wakefield Police Incident Room. How can I help you,' Shona said breezily, despite feeling frazzled.

'Morning, Shona. I hear there was a murder in Walton last night. What's the news?' Superintendent of the Criminal Investigation Unit, Gary Morgan, asked.

'Good morning, Superintendent. Yes, it was a residence, 357 St Michael's Mount, Walton. Our victim is a 35-year-old woman called Karen Blakely. She was a nurse up at the hospital and had just arrived home after her shift when she had her face brutally smashed on the work surface of her kitchen,' Shona briefed him.

'Have we got a suspect in custody, or is the perpetrator unknown?' Morgan asked.

'At the moment, we do not have any motive, although there was one other occupant in the house at the time. He was upstairs and apparently saw no intruder, although he did hear the door slam shut. I did all preliminary checks, along with organising an immediate peripheral search by the dog section of the whole area, but it produced nothing,' Shona told him.

'There was a second occupant, whom you say was upstairs, who heard a door slam but who saw nothing?' the Super asked in disbelief.

'Yes, I know. It piqued my suspicion too. He was transferred to the hospital in shock, so Jacobi met him there and brought him in for an initial statement,' Shona informed him.

'What did Jacobi relay back to you about him?' the Super queried.

'Initially, his shock seemed genuine, and Parker also saw him at the scene, who was also keen to agree. However, when Jacobi met with him later, he did feel that there was something really off about him and that he may have been acting. So, we are keeping him in mind, but concentrating on our victim at the moment,' Shona stated.

'OK, can you walk through the process, plan your route and deliver it this morning to the team?' he asked as he always did.

'Already on it, sir,' she responded as she always told him too.

'Good, good. I didn't expect any less. Designate roles and execute them, and we can have a catch-up at the end of the day,' he concluded, then, as usual, he rang off before she even had a chance to respond.

The morning meeting was like every other update about all ongoing investigations, new leads that needed to be followed up, and the sharing of information before the floor was opened up. Shona informed the group of officers about the murder, that forensics had been up throughout the night gathering evidence, and that it would be processed over the following days. She highlighted the point about a possible intruder and therefore the importance of gaining information as to whether this was true, along with whether anybody in the vicinity had seen anything suspicious.

She ascertained whose schedule was full of other investigations and then delegated her list of responsibilities to available officers. Before dismissing them, she informed them that an officer was posted outside the residence to ensure that should someone return, they were not able to gain unlawful access.

Chapter 9
Taking a Little Time

Unlike Jacobi, who didn't need telling twice to go home—having got in, he dropped his pants and jumped straight into bed—Shona needed to go for a drive. She made her way out into the private car park to her gleaming red 2-seater MR2, the only guilty pleasure in life that she allowed herself. She loved its sleek dashboard with the 2 pop-up concealed compartments, its small neat, smooth steering wheel, the soft leather seats and its swift change gearbox.

On a day like today, where the shift had been mentally taxing, she required the open road, so she popped the lid, slid into the driver's seat and started the engine. She gave the MR2 a couple of revs to let her know that, this morning, she meant business, and then she slid it into gear and carefully manoeuvred her way out onto the open road. Shona chose to take the dual carriageway so she could instantly fly through the gears to enjoy the cool wind blasting through her hair along the open countryside.

Once over the Heath, she decided to turn left at the lights before taking a sharp right towards Walton, just so she could pass by the crime scene at 357 Saint Michael's Mount. This was the format Shona would always follow once a case had begun: she would process the scene, then take a step back to analyse the facts, then have a brainstorm with Jacobi to look at what routes forward it determined. Once she had delivered the information to the group, she would then take some time alone with her thoughts to allow it to wash over her. The only trouble was Shona continually lived the scene, mentally walking it over and over again, trying to imagine every conceivable possibility of what could have happened. Today was no different.

Shona pulled up outside a small shop on the opposite side of the road to 357 St Michael's Mount. It was a small, old, stone detached building with a little drive to the right and its own little wall around it, with overgrown trees down the left-hand side. The grass didn't look like it had been cut in months and the roof wasn't in a particularly good state of repair. The house gave more of a cottage vibe that looked like it had been stood for 100 years. The gravel drive didn't seem in keeping with the rest of the style of the home, but perhaps it had been a conscious decision to alert the homeowners when people were on the property. Maybe it was just for ease of maintenance; after all, Karen Blakely worked long hours. But then again, wouldn't Robert Day Jr have helped keep it tidy if he had been there all the time?

Shona glanced at the neighbouring house, and Jacobi was right: their principal windows did look straight on to Karen's driveway, which could be very helpful indeed. Shona stared intently at the house, trying to imagine Karen Blakely driving up the street, exhausted from work and then pulling into the gateway, not knowing that it would be for the very last time. Not only did she not know she would never execute that manoeuvre ever again, but her life was going to be stolen from her within minutes of entering the house that should have been her safe haven.

Shona was so focused on trying to imagine what had happened, how, why and whether somebody had been lying in wait for her, that she didn't see the officer approaching her car. She was abruptly returned to the present by a hollow tapping on her window. She looked up to find the officer peering in at her through the open roof.

'Sorry, DCI Williams, I hadn't recognised you from across the street. It's just that we have been told to keep a watchful eye for any suspicious activity, especially an intruder returning to the scene,' Josie Petroni informed her.

'It's OK, Josie, have you just taken the next shift outside?' Shona queried.

'Yes, it's all been quiet, apart from the parents on their way back from the afternoon nursery run, trying to get information on what's happened,' Josie told her.

'There will be a few of the newbies out in the next couple of hours to do some preliminaries, so I am sure it will satisfy our morbid bystanders. I just need to have a few minutes alone with my thoughts before I go home, and then I can get some rest,' Shona said.

'No worries, I will leave you to it,' Josie said, turning back to her post.

'By the way, Josie,' Shona called, 'well done for spotting my car and coming over to check it out.'

As soon as Josie had gone, Shona immediately turned her thoughts back to her puzzling questions: How did you get in? Did you jump over the wall or boldly walk through the gate? Were you already here or did you follow her home?

She did a quick scan of the houses to see if there were any cameras in close proximity, but she couldn't see anything prominent straight away. The tape that was attached across the gate flapped in the slight breeze, briefly taking her attention. She shook her head and glanced away. On the outer wall of Karen's house was the sign for the name of the street, St Michael's Mount. Shona was sure that it had some meaning or something. She was unsure whether she had got it mixed up. Was she thinking of Saint Christopher, who represented courage and strength, along with the offering of protection to travellers or those pursuing their dreams?

No, she was sure that Saint Michael's also had a meaning for something, so knowing she wouldn't settle, despite how insignificant this was to her case, she took out her phone to research it.

As Shona read the words of St Michael, being the most powerful of all angels and the one who will defeat evil, she felt sad that this hadn't been Karen Blakely's reality.

Shona wasn't sure how long she'd sat there, imagining all the different scenarios of where an intruder could have gained access. Had they concealed themselves by the overgrown trees, or had they come from the back of the property? She wondered from what angle had they approached the house and which direction had they come from: down the street or up this way.

Shona deduced that it wasn't really possible that anybody would have really been able to maintain any cover because the wall was so short and, therefore, she was sure there would have been mud in the house. The street that the house was situated on also seemed quite wide and open, although at this time in the early afternoon, there weren't very many cars around.

She guessed it was possible that, at nighttime, the people living in these houses perhaps did leave their cars along the road. Shona decided to do a walk up and down the street and found the reason that there were not so many cars was because most houses had their own drives.

So, it was highly unlikely that somebody could openly walk down this street without being seen, especially as it was still light at 20:30–21:30. Inevitably, there would be dog walkers in the area, people attending the public house further along the street, cars passing by people potentially coming home from work. After all, Karen Blackley had just finished her shift.

She, therefore, felt sure that no one had been hiding in the bushes and was able to dismiss the theory because the police handler and his dog hadn't picked any scent up in these areas either. Shona thought about that for a while. The dogs had not been able to track any scent at all, which suggested there couldn't possibly have been an intruder; however, she would still go through the motions of enquiries. If Jacobi had been correct about Robert Day Jr, then she did want to eliminate every possibility before she hit him with their thoughts. At this particular moment, she was happy to let him think he had committed the perfect crime, for now.

She made some notes of enquiries she wanted to pursue with regards to asking Karen's colleagues about the possible route that she might have driven home, just to ensure she hadn't been followed. It was a possibility that somebody could have pulled up outside, seen Day turn the light on upstairs, observed her through the kitchen on her own making a coffee, and taken the opportunity to run in.

She decided she wanted to know as much as she could about the victim and her relationship with Day to establish if he could have committed this crime, because she felt that this was a crime of passion. It had been a quick, direct, determined and forceful blow. If it had been just a random opportunist criminal, then she felt sure he would have probably been surprised by Karen's presence.

Perhaps he had seen her arrive home alone in the car before the light was switched on upstairs and assumed she was up there. If someone had cased the place for a few nights and had seen her generally go in on her own before going straight upstairs, then they could have been surprised to find her in the kitchen. Maybe they could have just reacted, but in this scenario, she was sure they would have just run back out again, not wanting to get caught. Therefore, there was no reason to smash her face on the counter, kill her, yet take nothing.

The other point was the kitchen blind had been open, so an intruder would surely have seen Karen before entering, it just did not seem a viable theory at all.

Shona knew she was going to keep driving down the route of endless scenarios until she had a lead, which was a lot like doing a jigsaw puzzle: you empty the box out onto the table with all the pieces available, but you just don't know where to start.

Shona knew that her colleagues would be arriving shortly, so reluctantly, for now, she would have to put her gruelling thought process on hold until she could sift through what information they were able to raise today that she would be able to go through tomorrow. Shona needed to take her car for more of a run rather than going straight home, so she drove through Walton and cut towards Sandal before taking Durkar Road past Asda. At the roundabout, she picked up speed along the dual carriageway back across to Wakefield and Thornes Park, where her humble abode sat in a small block of flats. She pulled into parking lot 34 and flicked the switch to reinstall the car roof, whilst glancing in the rear-view mirror at the mess the wind had made of her hair.

Shona loved the coolness of the breeze, even though there were times it did make her scalp feel quite cold. Yet, it was a feeling that she really enjoyed; it was as satisfying as taking a cold drink on a hot summer's day. For Shona, it seemed to stimulate both her scalp and her mind, but today the tiredness was overwhelming as her brain had been working like a steam engine, puffing away. Right now, after being up all night without food and very little to drink, she was exhausted, so she slid out of the car, secured it and made her way towards the lift.

Whilst waiting to reach the third floor, where her flat was situated, she had to make a concerted effort, not to glance into the full-length mirror in the lift. The last time she had been in here, she was hurriedly applying some makeup as she rushed out to get to the crime scene. Feeling dishevelled and unkempt after a long night, the last thing she wanted to see was what she looked like now, so settled for how she felt, and that was bad enough. When the doors opened, she was automatically stepping out before she realised that she was on the wrong floor, having to retreat to allow a gentleman she'd never seen before to get in.

Finally, when the lift had settled on the floor above and the doors had opened, she exited, walked down the stark corridor to number 34 and pulled out her key. Shona sighed at trying to fumble with the lock. It was one of those keys that did not have the regular vertical locks; these were horizontal, which she struggled to utilise when this exhausted. Once unlocked, she thankfully stepped into her beautiful apartment that she never got tired of being welcomed home by. Unlike the complication of her thought process here, everything was in order, perfectly positioned, set in its place exactly how she'd left it. The pristine cleanness and order greeted her, inviting her to come in and relax.

She placed her shoes to the right on the vintage shoe rack and decided to immediately pop a Bud (As in Budweiser). She took a long, thirsty swig from the bottle before placing it on the counter, and satisfied by its gassy effect, she belched loudly before making her way into the shower. Uncharacteristically, Shona dropped her clothing straight down onto the floor rather than placing them directly into her clothes basket. She then selected a hotter temperature in the shower than the cold one she had needed earlier to wake up. Her head stung immediately as she acclimatised from the coldness of having the car roof down to the intense heat of the water. The rhythmic pelting of the power shower was like being hit with 1000's of pebbles, yet it was all part of Shona's normal routine and the therapeutic massage treatment her body loved after a long, hard night.

Once she had allowed the water to wash away the thoughts and stresses of the day, she gave herself a soothing, cleansing scrub all over before drying herself, wrapping it neatly around her body just underneath her arms and then tucking one corner into the top at her cleavage. She selected a small hand towel from the ladder-style shelving unit, bent her head downwards, wrapped it around her wet hair, pulled it back up at the top of her head and secured it like a turban. She then went back into the lounge to finish her bottle of Bud.

Shona was about to do what she did every time she entered her property, and that was to select her favourite tunes on her Wurlitzer Jukebox, but today, she just needed the silence. Inside her head resembled the static of a TV when you used to turn it off at the end of the night in the 1980s: just black-and-white moving static. When she closed her eyes, it actually felt that, without the music, she could hear a slight whistling noise as though she was standing outside in a field under an electric pylon. She focused every effort to concentrate on herself breathing, finding the in and out motion soothing as she watched the towel on her chest, moving up and down.

It wasn't long before the intrusive images of Karen Blakely's body began to force their way into her brain: the stillness, the coldness and greying of her body as Sallyanne began the removal process. Her face smashed under her nose; the congealed blood that was left behind on the floor. Despite the work that Shona performed, she would never understand how anyone could do that to another human being. Shona had never become desensitised to such scenes, and nor did she ever want to, as it helped her to humanise the victim, and it motivated her to catch the killers and seek justice.

She found it hard to fathom how it was termed a civilised society when there were those who walked amongst us committing such barbaric acts. In her mind's eye, she stared into Karen Blakely's face, knowing that it was an image she wouldn't be able to forget for a long time. She tried to picture Karen in the moments before her death, as she was making herself a cup of tea, about to turn around her eyes latching on to the person behind her. Had she been aware of their presence? Did she hear or see them when she turned around? Did they panic and instantly grab hold of her, or was it somebody she knew? Did either of them speak, or was she silenced by their surprised intrusion? Would she have asked what they were doing there? Surely, she would have screamed, whether she would have known them or not, because they were obviously there with the intention of harming her.

Shona gave her head a wobble. It was no good; there were far too many questions and at the moment, the pieces felt like they were all over the place. The number of uncontrolled thoughts floating around in her head reminded her of the golden buzzer moment on Britain's Got Talent when thousands of golden strips haphazardly filled the open space, fluttering down. Shona always found the start of the investigation frustrating, as nothing fitted together at this point, so she desperately hoped that when she returned to work, there would be some lead in order to be able to move things forward. She wanted this for herself, but she needed it for Karen Blakely, and then she thought of the victim's mother and father, or her brothers or sisters if she had any. How were they feeling today, going about their daily routines without a care in the world, unaware that their lives were about to be turned upside down?

This was a job for the family liaison officers, but she would also ensure that either she or Jacobi would be on hand to deliver the horrendous news that would change their lives forever. Shona got up from her designer grey settee and crossed the room to look out of the window. She suddenly began to feel claustrophobic, yearning for the escape of the park, but for now, she would have to make do with observing life from a distance, as though under a microscope. She was the scientist, looking down, inspecting, dissecting and separating the particles to discover the answers.

Exhausted from the multitude of differing thought patterns, came the overwhelming pull of sleep, so she took herself off to the bedroom. She slipped the damp towel over the radiator and selected a tiny pair of bed shorts and a matching vest top before sliding between the sheets. With her hair still wet, she decided to keep the towel loosely on her head to ensure her pillowcase remained dry. Then she returned to the exercise of concentrating on her breath. She breathed in deeply, exhaling slowly, repeating the pattern over and over again, methodically in and out, whilst fending off any unwanted thoughts that were trying to invade her mind. In her mind's eye, she was physically blowing the thoughts away, as though they were clouds being moved along, not allowing them to interrupt nor change the course of her destination, which was sleep. And then, just as Robert Day Jr had done physically earlier in the morning, she was gone mentally.

Chapter 10
Spaghetti Junction

When Shona Williams fluttered into life, her first thoughts were that she needed to get into the shower, grab a bowl of cereals and then get out into the fresh air. She slid from her bed, removed the screwed-up towel from her pillow, grabbed her bath towel from the radiator on the way out of the bedroom and made her way directly to the bathroom.

Whilst the water regulated itself to its allotted temperature, she began detangling her hair. Having left it wrapped in a towel overnight, it was now a scrunched-up mess. She took a wide tooth comb to the matted mass and gently eased it through the lengths of the strands of her hair. She tried hard not to drag the comb, but her impatience against the resistant ball resulted in follicles surrendering their desire to keep hold. When she finally got it to some semblance of normality, she grabbed a scrunchie and tied it back despite the soreness of her scalp, ensuring there were no loose ends escaping.

She stepped into the shower to adjust the directional flow of the water rather than it hitting the glass screen, where she had carelessly left the shower head after washing her hair the night before. Once she had adjusted the nozzle to a less harsh flow, she placed it more centrally within its metal fitment. Then she dropped her bed shorts and removed the vest top before stepping into the cascading water.

Mindful of not wanting to get her hair wet, she tilted her head back, holding her face directly beneath the water flow, allowing the tiny speckles of water to gently massage her face. It was perfectly refreshing. She decided to adjust the pressure flow on the shower head so that her back and neck could be massaged before pivoting around to fully enjoy its pulsating treatment.

Having been in a car accident two years earlier, Shona seemed to hold her body's tension in her neck and shoulder blades, particularly her right one, and at the beginning of a case was when it seemed to prick the most. She stood for a few minutes, allowing the heat and the pressure to minister to her aching body before readjusting the shower head again for it to return to its natural spray.

She wet her exfoliating sponge and lavishly doused it in gel, rubbing it in to create a slight froth before smothering her body from top to toe with a foaming mass of soapy bubbles, the aroma hitting her sensors thoroughly enjoying the meditative experience of feeling every inch of her skin. Shona thoroughly rinsed the suds from her body, sprayed some extra water down the shower screen to stop it from leaving scum marks behind, then used the squeegee to clear the water so it wouldn't leave drip marks. Next, she washed away the excess soapy water from the shower base before turning the water off.

She reached for her towel, drying herself from head downwards before stepping out onto the shower mat after drying each foot—she hated the look and damp smell left behind by footprints. Shona loved nothing more after a shower than to enjoy the sense of smooth, silky skin, so she applied a scoop of body lotion, taking the time to allow her skin to fully absorb the thick, rich cream. Feeling well-pampered, invigorated, fresh and alive once more, she was now ready to start the day.

Shona glided along to her bedroom, where she selected some white pants and a matching bra, a short-sleeved fitted polo shirt and cropped jeans. Although it was warm outside, she didn't feel it was hot enough for shorts, and besides, she generally kept those for when she was on holiday and less likely to bump into anyone she knew. Although her legs weren't too bad, they were not her favourite aspect of her body.

Next, having applied a pair of trainer socks, she chose her cerise Dr Marten trainers—the ones with the webbed fabric to keep the feet ventilated and their hallmark yellow stitching. She then popped in her earbuds, arranged a playlist on her phone from all the different tune selections she had downloaded, connected them through the Bluetooth, slipped the phone into her pocket and was out of the door.

Today, she chose to avoid the lift, so once she had gone down the corridor outside her apartment, she took a left through the fire door and swiftly descended the stairs two at a time. Once in the lobby, she headed for the front door into the communal courtyard, out onto the street and across the road into the park.

She loved being so close to this open expanse, with its mini train, children's playground area, sports field and tree-lined road running at the far end of it. This was where she headed so she could jog along the footpaths to the little road, where she followed it up past the old college building and into the woodland at the top, over the brow of the hill and down towards the little Gate Cafe.

Without missing a beat, she took a left between the mini pitch-and-putt golfing area and tennis courts, taking herself the entire route through the car park and behind the bandstand. As she continued along the path, she was a little dismayed to see the events field—where only a week ago a vibrant fair had stood—was now littered with debris from overflowing waste bins.

Shona soon came upon the destination she was making for—her favourite bench, the one that overlooked the expanse of the greenery. The one that was positioned perfectly to sit upon to watch the day roll by. The one with the gold-coloured plaque positioned in the centre of the top backrest slat, dedicated to her father, was the only place she was able to find solace and solitude.

There were a few people meandering around—the odd couple walking hand in hand, some young guys sitting upon the amphitheatre-style steps and people pushing prams through the tree-lined paths beyond.

Shona soon became mesmerised with a guy whacking a ball with a tennis racket, sending his Weimaraner dog galloping across the field to retrieve it before it doubled back—only for the owner to take another one out of his pocket to whack again. She smiled to herself at the owner's ingenuity in ensuring that the dog dropped the ball from its mouth and, in using the tennis racket, minimising his effort and shoulder strain.

For as long as the dog possessed his interest and will to keep pounding back and forth, the man kept hitting the ball for him. Shona watched as he persistently changed his directions, hardly giving the dog a chance to slow down or drop the ball before he swung the bat, swapping between north, east, south and west.

Shona studied this concept and pondered on the similarity of managing an investigation, where if you weren't careful, you could end up running out of steam, incessantly following leads that basically turned out to be a misdirection. She made an instant decision that, in the murder case of Karen Blakely, she was going to be precise in the directions she took. It was important to get the preliminaries out of the way to ascertain the facts whilst the evidence was being processed, but she was not going to get stuck down a rabbit hole, not knowing which route to take.

If there was no evidence to suggest that an intruder had been present, then she had every intention of pursuing the possibility that Robert Day Jr was her culprit, and she would not stop until she had justice for Karen Blakely. Like the dog owner, she would focus her energies where they were needed most to get the best results—and woe betide Day if he was responsible for Karen Blakely's death because, like that ball, there would be far-reaching consequences.

So deep in her thoughts was Shona that she had failed to notice a young mother with a baby in a pushchair walking up the path towards her. She became momentarily startled as she furiously tried to get her younger son to hurry up so that she could get the baby for its feed. The baby began to scream in reaction to the hunger pains within its tummy, whilst the mum battled in vain with the young boy, torn between making him walk quicker and soothing her crying baby.

Shona could see the stress building in the mother as she continued to struggle with her predicament along the path and out through the main gate. Again, Shona's thought rested once more upon how stressful an investigation could become—especially in juggling so many avenues, departments, staff and interviews where time continued to run, but she never seemed to have enough hours in a day.

As she sat in the calmness of the park, she contemplated how different both she and Jacobi dealt with stress. He would stay calm and methodically address each task, whereas she tended to plough on full steam ahead and then she ended up burnt out. The most impactful case she'd dealt with had been the apparent suicide of a young woman called Cassandra Matthews and the subsequent effect this had had upon her child.

It had turned out to be quite a shocking case that had taken many twists and turns along the way—and one she would forever reference to evaluate her performance. This one had taken her on many winding roads that, at times, it had felt like she was persistently rotating around the famous Gravelly Hill Interchange in Birmingham, famously termed Spaghetti Junction.

Shona contemplated how the stress of getting to the truth had swarmed her brain, particularly during her downtime periods, resulting in difficulties with processing her thought patterns. At points, it had felt to Shona that she had been immersed in water, the distortion of sound penetrating her brain. The effect had caused a restriction to her wavelength of thoughts, preventing any structure to formulate plans or for connections to occur to bring about any conclusion.

Therefore, by recognising the effects the stress had had upon her, she had become less susceptible to its effects by implementing strategies to manage herself sitting on her favourite bench in the park, jogging, engaging in a methodical pampering of her personal care, taking regular breaks, bouncing ideas with Jacobi rather than pinballing in her own mind, and taking control of the investigation rather than letting it control her.

She returned to the present time and the murder of Karen Blakely, noting her aim was to discount everyone else and see who was left standing. The last thing she wanted was to represent the Weimaraner chasing the ball in one direction, to return to the start only to be compelled to chase leads running in another direction.

The facts were Karen Blakely's murder appeared to be a response to an emotion, as it was delivered in an instantaneously swift and determined action—which suggested to Shona that she knew the killer. She was absolutely certain it was a crime of passion. But was it Robert Day Jr, this unidentified Marcus guy, or someone else who was as yet unknown to them?

Either way, she was sure the blow had been administered in the heat of the moment by someone who had not been able to exercise any self-control. So, she was looking for someone who perhaps didn't think through their decisions, who was emotionally reactive, and perhaps unable to process the seriousness or consequences of their actions.

Shona was unsure how long she had been sitting on the bench, but she was suddenly aware of the heat radiating along her arms, chest and down the top of each thigh. Equally, the exposure of her ankles due to her cropped jeans were specifically heating up. She had no idea of the exact temperature, but it had definitely grown hotter since she had been sitting there.

She tilted her head slightly backward and closed her eyes whilst she set her face towards the sun. As she focused on the thin layer of skin behind her eyelids, she could see the colours changing from yellow to a pinkish-orange colour, then a burning orangey-red fireball as the heat bore down on her face.

She lost herself in her meditative state until she became aware that there was somebody crunching leaves as they were walking. She could feel a delicate, almost non-existent breeze gently sweep across her ankles and listened intently to see if it was strong enough to rattle through the trees. It wasn't.

Close to the bench was a derelict building whose roof had been stripped, and where the council had constructed a metal fence around to ensure it was not accessible from either trespassers or prying eyes. Despite its vacancy, the abandoned and dilapidated old building groaned to itself as the exposed timbers creaked in the warmth of the sun's rays.

Shona relaxed intently as she revelled in the peace, quiet and absolute solitude that only her favourite bench in this area of the park afforded her.

'I thought I might find you here,' Jacobi said, startling Shona into full consciousness.

'What on Earth are you doing here?' she asked, surprised.

'We need to get back to the station,' he informed her.

'Why? What's wrong?' Shona asked, puzzled and now on full alert.

'I'll tell you enroute,' Jacobi said.

'Oh, okay,' she began. 'Give me a chance to collect some stuff though first.'

She stood automatically turning towards her right with the intention of returning to her apartment when Jacobi said, 'No, the car is this way,' and took off to the left, making his way out through the gate, nearest to the bench.

Shona followed Jacobi, wondering what on earth could be so important that he'd had to track her down to her place of perfect peace only to disturb her and bring her back to the station—especially as she wasn't due there until the morning.

Once she'd slipped into the car and fastened her seatbelt, she said, 'OK, so you have my undivided attention. Spill it, what's going on?'

'Well,' Jacobi began, 'this guy Marcus that Day put in the frame does seem like he has got form, and a couple of the women at the hospital had actually put in a complaint about him. Apparently, he was given a warning about his usage of sexual innuendos, stalking characteristics and inappropriate contact with the nurses.'

'Was Karen Blakely one of the two women who submitted a complaint?' asked Shona.

'No, Jenson Parker said there was nothing to suggest there was any inappropriate behaviour between the two. In fact, most members of staff seemed to think they were really good friends and got on fairly well,' Jacobi informed her.

'Not to mention Karen Blakely was in a serious relationship with someone else, so maybe he respected this as her not being fair game,' Shona pointed out.

'The chances are, though, it could still be our guy,' Jacobi stipulated.

'What makes you think that?' Shona enquired, not wanting to be misdirected down the rabbit hole she was hoping to avoid with this investigation.

'Because whilst Parker was making his enquiries today and requested a word with Marcus St John, he ran,' Jacobi smugly stated, 'like a pizza boy making his delivery with seconds to spare before the food became free.'

'Oh, right!' Shona said, her interest piquing.

'Yeah. He tried to slip out down the backstairs when Parker called out to him, so he had the receptionist call security to the lobby to stop him from making his escape,' Jacobi informed her.

'Well done, Parker, for his quick thinking,' Shona said, impressed. 'So, I take it we have got him then?'

'Yeah. That's why I've just come to get you because we've been tasked with interviewing him. He is back at the nick awaiting our arrival and apparently, he is shaking like a first-time rider on a rollercoaster.'

'Goody, goody, then let's hit it,' Shona said, initiating the blues and twos with a grin plastered across her face.

Jacobi gladly responded, increasing his pressure upon the accelerator pedal before swiftly negotiating the traffic as he sped along the most direct route through town towards the Heath, along the dual carriageway back towards the police station.

They pulled through the security gates, drove around the back of the station, parked the car, entered the building and made their way through to where the desk sergeant was busy booking someone in. Damien Clark had seen them arriving from his upstairs office window, so had taken the time to go down to greet them.

'Sorry for calling you back in, guys, but I felt sure you would like to conduct this interview yourselves,' Damien told them.

'You got that right,' Shona said.

'We've got a live wire here. Apparently, he wouldn't go down without a fight and skipped reception before being stopped on his way out of the back door of the hospital. They actually had to physically restrain him as he was adamant he was leaving, and the security was not going to stop him,' Damien briefed them.

'What has he been like since he arrived?' Jacobi enquired.

'A bit more subdued, but he is literally shaking like a jelly on top of a washing machine's fast spin cycle,' Damien said.

'So, what actually happened at the hospital?' Shona enquired.

'Jenson Parker had taken Danny Driver up to the hospital with him. Danny had entered the unit that Marcus was working on, but before he could talk to him, he had sneaked out the other side of the ward. However, he made the mistake of entering the unit next door, possibly to wait unit Driver moved on, but Parker had been on there making enquiries, so a nurse pointed him out. Before Parker had a chance to turn round to get eyes on him, he was off,' Damien told them.

'You mean they weren't working together to keep the area covered?' Shona asked, dismayed.

'It's a hospital. We don't have that much manpower, Shona. Besides, they had no reason to think that he was going to do a runner,' Damien backed up his staff.

'Fair enough,' Shona accepted. 'I presume that's when Parker telephoned the security staff to stop him.'

It wasn't lost on Shona the fact that Parker had not only used his initiative but that he was demonstrating her strategy of reserving his own energies yet still accomplishing his goal.

'The security held him until Parker and Driver caught up with him, and then they arrested him for obstruction and brought him back here for questioning. That is where you two come in now, so he is all yours,' Damien said.

Jacobi looked at Shona for a response, and when he didn't get one, he said, 'I think it's fair to say we are not dealing with a very intelligent criminal then.'

'See, for yourself,' Damien said.

'Whereabouts is he?' asked Jacobi.

'Interview room one,' Damien said with a grin, turning away and retracing his steps back along the corridor.

'Ooh,' said Jacobi. 'Interview room one. Is he shackled as well?'

'Yes, of course. He is an unknown risk, and Collins is in with him at the moment awaiting your arrival,' Damien said over his shoulder before opening the fire door at the end of the corridor and making his way back upstairs towards his office.

'We must have a bit of a wildfire,' Shona predicted.

'Oh, goody, goody,' said Jacobi. Will I play good cop or bad cop?'

'Sometimes, Dion, you are insufferable. Come on, let's see what we can get out of our man Marcus.'

Shona politely knocked on the door of interview room 1 before opening it, mainly to alert Collins of their presence. She found that it usually unsettled the arrested person as they expected the police to come in hitting hard, especially if they were shackled in interview room one.

It also helped to arouse the person if they had inadvertently fallen asleep. Shona felt that a little bit of respect was the introduction to being treated with respect and showed consideration despite the surroundings.

This was ultimately the premise from which she started the interview, but how the person who sat behind the door behaved afterwards would define the course of the rest.

After a few seconds, Shona opened the door wide. She momentarily observed the man before stepping inside, with Jacobi following close behind. Prior to uttering a word, they both took their seats.

'I'm Detective Chief Inspector Shona Williams, and this is my colleague Detective Inspector Dion Jacobi. Apparently, you were Usain Bolt this morning?'

Marcus looked up puzzled. 'What?' And then he got it. 'You mean because I ran.'

'Yeah.' Shona smiled.

'I haven't done anything wrong,' Marcus said pitifully.

'So, if you haven't done anything wrong, mate, what are you running from the police for?' Jacobi asked.

'I just got really scared when I heard the cop on the unit specifically asking for me. I knew that something had happened to Karen last night because there was a lot of chatter going around about it,' Marcus said.

'Am I missing something here? Because I cannot see a reason there for you to bolt off the ward and try to get out of the hospital,' Shona said.

'When somebody was on the ward asking about me, I knew you would look at me, but I hadn't done anything. I promise you, honestly, I didn't do anything at all. I really liked Karen. I really, really liked her,' he said, shakily.

Shona and Jacobi looked at each other and then back to Marcus.

'Before you say anything else, we need to read you your rights with regards to resisting police, so: You do not have to say anything. But it may harm your defence if you do not mention when questioned something that you later rely on in court. Anything you do say may be given in evidence,' Shona delivered.

'Do you understand your rights, Marcus?' Jacobi asked.

'I don't understand it. Why do I need to be arrested for running away just because I was scared? And why do I have to have these cuffs on?' he said, slightly lifting his hands.

'You don't now we are here, but just so you know, if you start playing up, they will go straight back on,' Shona said as Jacobi stood to remove them.

'Do you understand your right not to speak to us? Are you happy to talk to us now and get this mess sorted out?' Shona asked as Jacobi retook his seat.

'Yes, of course I understand, and I am more than happy to talk to you,' Marcus began, rubbing at his wrists. 'I have done nothing, absolutely nothing wrong.'

Jacobi found it very difficult to visualise the man in front of him as being in a professional job at the hospital, where self-control, working under pressure, being decisive and having the responsibility of caring for others were paramount. He appeared very vulnerable and childlike.

'I'm sorry, but my ex used to do this to me. She used to want to cuff me, and I hated it. I felt humiliated, but she seemed to love the discomfort it caused me. Then one day, she went off and just left me there cuffed to the radiator. I had to stay there all day until she came home from work. She thought it was hilarious. So, you see I just panicked at the thought of being arrested and cuffed. I am sorry. I promise I'm not going to do anything.' Marcus revealed, his lip beginning to quiver as his eyes filled with tears at the memory.

Both Shona and Jacobi had instant compassion for the gentleman in front of them, and neither were convinced that he was the man that could have savagely attacked Karen Blakely, nor had the dispassion to leave her to die.

'When the officers came to the hospital today, they were looking for information and just wanted to ask you a few questions. There's nothing to worry about, especially if you haven't done anything wrong. So, shall we start again to get this matter cleared up and then you can be on your way?' Shona assured him.

'Yes, please,' Marcus said, looking from one to the other, hopeful to be able to tell them what they wanted to know and then he could get out of there.

'Can you tell us what your relationship with Karen Blakely was like?' Jacobi enquired.

'She was a colleague—one that I admired and really looked up to. She was so caring to her patients; and other staff, and she stood out to me because she always seemed to go the extra mile,' Marcus told them.

'We are still trying to get to know Karen. In what way did she go the extra mile?' asked Shona.

'There was this little old lady that had been admitted after she'd sustained a fall. She didn't have any family or anybody to visit to simply check in on her,

100

but Karen made time to sit with her and hold her hand. She would assist her to eat and drink and drop by to give her some chocolate or a newspaper because she didn't want her to feel sad when everyone else had visitors.

'There was also a little girl in the paediatric ward who was really scared because she had never been in hospital before. Karen stayed after her shift, reading her stories until she fell asleep. And after her operation, she sat through the night with her so she would see a friendly face the moment her eyes opened. She also took her a doll to give her comfort when she couldn't be around.'

'Karen cared—like really cared—with such compassion, as though that elderly lady was her mother, and that child was her daughter.' He started to tear up, the loss suddenly overwhelming his heart. 'She put herself in other people's situations to understand what they were going through, to be able to connect with them in order to alleviate their stress. That way, she was able to fully help them to heal and to overcome their fear.'

'I know you said that you admired Karen and looked up to her, but had you developed other feelings for Karen?' Jacobi asked.

'No, not in a romantic way,' Marcus stated.

'What other way did you have feelings for her, apart from looking up to her and admiring her?' Jacobi pushed.

'As a friend. Karen and I got on really well together, so we would be relieved when we were on the same shift. They could be long days, so if we were working together, it made it all the more bearable—especially if you were dealing with emergencies. I knew the way Karen did things and vice versa, so we worked in sync with one another,' Marcus explained.

'The problem we have, Marcus, is that we were informed concerns were raised about some inappropriate behaviour towards two of your female colleagues, which resulted in disciplinary action,' Shona threw in.

'Who has told you that?' Marcus asked.

Ignoring the question, Shona continued, 'The phrases used to describe you were the usage of sexual innuendos, that you had stalking characteristics and inappropriate contact with nurses.'

'I admit I like to have a laugh, but I would never take it too far.'

'But these women who took it to their managers and put in formal complaints obviously thought you had taken it too far and felt uncomfortable working with you. Isn't that why you were moved departments?' Jacobi cut in.

'It is true they did put complaints in. I was moved departments, given a verbal warning and put on probation for 6 months. However, those women only put those allegations in when I had to question their handling of an elderly gentleman who kept shouting out through the night.'

'They had both made inappropriate comments about being annoyed by him and failed to adequately make the night checks they were supposed to conduct. They actually pulled his curtains around the bed so they wouldn't have to look at him. So, when the elderly man fell out of bed trying to get someone's attention, it went unnoticed. He lay on the floor for over two hours shouting for help, but they ignored him. It was another patient who brought it to my attention when I came on duty, so I reported the incident.'

'Inevitably, they denied it but retaliated by making false allegations. So, what the report will also state is that I voluntarily moved departments because the two women in question began a character assassination campaign, and I wasn't having my good name dragged through the mud,' Marcus eloquently described.

'So, are you denying making any inappropriate comments or of making any sexual advances towards them, including stalking, touching, giving them gifts or anything of this nature?' Jacobi queried.

'Absolutely,' he stated. 'In fact, I suggested the six months of probation to prove my innocence, so it was merely a formality along with the verbal warning, as my manager had to discuss it with me.'

'So, you wouldn't consider yourself as being a ladies' man?' Jacobi pushed further.

'Seriously, nothing happened. They were literally pissed at me for questioning their professional conduct—nothing more, nothing less,' Marcus stated adamantly.

'The thing is, we are not really interested in the problems at the hospital— just whether this type of behaviour is connected to the murder of Karen Blakely,' Shona directed straight at him, whilst staring into his eyes. She wanted to see his reaction as she quickly changed track to the real reason he was sitting in front of them.

'Can you understand how this could be perceived to have been an escalation of those behaviours and why we would need to speak to you first?' Jacobi asked him.

'I understand what you are saying,' Marcus began, unable to remove the panic out of his voice. 'But what I am telling you is the truth. Karen and I were really good friends,' Marcus reiterated.

'The problem we have, Marcus, is that we only have you here alleging this about your relationship—as the other person, namely Karen, is in the morgue,' Jacobi said insensitively.

'I can show you the long list of messages on my phone that will demonstrate our friendship, the camaraderie we had, our similarities, how she confided in me—especially about her relationship. She was really unhappy with him; she was getting to the point that she didn't want to be with him anymore,' Marcus told them, much to Shona and Jacobi's inner surprise.

'What makes you say that, Marcus?' Shona enquired.

'He was so demanding, and she just felt that he took up all of her time, like she no longer had a life that didn't include him. There were so many other things that she wanted to do, like to go out with friends, take a short trip, drive to the seaside to watch the sunrise—countries she wanted to visit—but it wasn't permissible without him,' Marcus stipulated.

'When you say 'him,' who are you exactly talking about, Marcus?' Shona asked.

'The guy that she was seeing—Robert. She didn't feel like she had a life anymore because everything had to revolve around him. She couldn't do anything, couldn't go anywhere, because he seemed to be there the whole time, so she just didn't feel like she had room to breathe.'

'She had been frustrated about the situation for months because it was as though he couldn't function without being close to her, but she couldn't function being smothered. It had become harder lately due to the long shifts at work that we were having to pick up, as there were a lot of staff on sick. When she went home, all she wanted to do was have a soak, eat and go to sleep, but he wouldn't allow it because he had missed her and wanted to be in her company.'

'She found it invasive that he would just turn up despite her objections. She was beginning to feel like she was losing herself, but she couldn't seem to end things because he wouldn't let go. I had seen a massive change in Karen over the past few months—she was no longer happy, her eyes weren't sparkling, and her spirit seemed drained,' Marcus said sadly.

'Did Karen talk to anyone else about her feelings regarding the relationship, do you know?' Shona asked.

'I'm not sure if she confided in anyone else. You see, since she got with Robert, she wasn't really allowed to socialise with any of us anymore. Although there was the Christmas party,' Marcus remembered.

'Can you tell us what happened at the Christmas party that may clarify more about their relationship?' Shona asked.

'He was basically glued to her the entire time. He wouldn't leave her alone for a minute, and if anybody walked in their direction, he would turn her around and walk her away. She couldn't enjoy herself because she couldn't relax and basically was forced to baby-mind him and his insecurities the whole time. I remember seeing her breakaway to go use the toilet when somebody took the opportunity to speak to her midway, within seconds he was straight over to redirect her to the toilet and then waited outside the door to retrieve her the moment she came out. I felt so sorry for her. This was our Christmas do—she had been looking forward to it for months and was keen to show off her new boyfriend—but she ended up acting as his comfort blanket,' Marcus said sadly, remembering his friend's difficulty.

'What was Karen usually like at these kinds of events?' Jacobi asked.

'She was an amazing social butterfly that radiated the room as soon as she entered it, everybody looked forward to her arrival because she had this ability to make you feel truly loved. When she got with Robert, everyone was pleased for her, especially as they seemed to fall in love so quickly. Then she started making excuses for not turning up at functions until she completely stopped meeting up with friends, and then her light seemed to diminish bit by bit due to the way he suppressed her right to be herself.'

'I was worried about her, but inevitably you cannot get involved in other people's relationships. It was her choice to be with him and no one's right to interfere. Then I started seeing a drastic difference in her at the end of the shift when she knew she had to go home, and she didn't seem to want to. That was when I kind of came alongside her to make sure that she was alright. At first, she was closed down and would pass it off a bit like when you want to make a doctor's appointment, but you cannot get past the receptionist. I wasn't going to give in because I cared about her so much, but with no longer seeing her outside work, I had to make sure life at work was good for her,' Marcus told them.

'What was your life like at work with Karen?' Asked Shona.

'We used to sit and have our lunch together, giggling and laughing about what we had done that morning. I tried to keep it light and relaxed, so she knew

I was there if ever she needed anyone. I loved the way that her nostrils flared every time she giggled about something or the way she would look at a bright light when she was about to sneeze to stop herself. She liked to smile, and her laugh was so infectious. She had this deep belly laugh that came from her heart. Wherever we sat—whether it was in the canteen, the coffee shop or outside on the grass—there would soon be a group of people joining us,' Marcus spoke from his heart.

'It sounds like you really cared about her, Marcus,' Shona offered tenderly.

'I do. I mean, I did,' he said, beginning to sob. 'She was a beautiful person— a beautiful friend—who had a brilliant mind and encouraged me to follow my dreams because she felt he was a parasite who was draining her of the dreams and motivation she'd had for hers.'

'How can you be so sure it was that bad, Marcus, if she wasn't opening up to you?' Jacobi enquired.

'During the past three weeks, she has described how she has tried to end it with him, but he won't allow it,' Marcus said.

'Won't allow it?' Shona jumped in.

'That's a strange choice of words, Marcus. If she wanted to end the relationship, she is well within her right to walk away,' Jacobi pointed out.

'Despite telling him it was over, he would kick up a fuss because he wanted it to carry on. Then he would badger her to change her mind. But apparently, this had happened many times before—only this time, she wasn't budging. She told me it had taken her ages to get him to leave her home and that he had applied all kinds of emotional and manipulative tools to pressure her to change her mind. When he finally did leave, she was so relieved because she believed that was it and she had got rid of him. But a couple of minutes later, she received a text message saying it had been lovely seeing her that evening,' Marcus told them.

Both Jacobi and Shona had to hold back from making any comment, as neither would have been very professional.

Marcus continued, 'She would have been more than happy to be on her own. She didn't really want another relationship; she just wanted the space to be able to live her own life her way—to be able to make firm choices and decisions for herself instead of having these persistently taken away from her. I loved Karen— truly loved her as a whole person—but he stole her joy and seemed infatuated with the idea of this perfect romance, without any consideration for who she was or what she wanted,' Marcus finished.

Then, as if a dam had suddenly cracked, he burst into tears, his whole body beginning to shake. His chest, rising and falling, was getting heavier as the sobs grew louder. Shona and Jacobi sat in silence, unwilling to interrupt the unleashing of grief and pain that Marcus was expelling as the tears poured down his face and dripped off the end of his chin.

What Shona and Jacobi were witnessing was a heart of pure love for a friend he both respected, admired and would forever miss. Shona passed the tissues across to Marcus and stood up at that point, indicating to Jacobi she needed a word with a nod of the head towards the door.

'Marcus, we will just be outside to give you the space and respect to grieve. I will get you a coffee and come back in a few moments,' Shona informed him.

Once they had shut the door and given it a wide enough birth out of his earshot, Shona asked, 'So, what do you make of that?'

'Well, that's obviously not our man,' Jacobi answered simply.

'No, the pain and grief he has just displayed cannot be faked, and besides, no one who loves that deeply could ever have hurt Karen Blakely in such a vicious and inhumane way. Besides, he is a giver of life, not a taker. He is compassionate and caring, not heartless and murderous,' Shona agreed.

'And may I point out,' Jacobi began, 'Robert Day Jr's interview, in comparison, was dispassionate, uncaring, flirtatious, non-descriptive, self-adulating and unemotional. So, what does that tell us?'

Shona shook her head as she made Marcus a coffee with extra sugar, as she felt he needed it right now, along with a plate of biscuits.

As they re-entered the interview room, Marcus's tears were beginning to subside, and at the clinking of the cup and saucer upon the table, Marcus looked up. His eyes were red and swollen, his face stained and blotchy the loss of a dear friend etched on every inch of his face—though he managed to smile weakly in gratitude.

It was Shona who broke the silence first. 'I am sorry I didn't even ask if you take sugar, but I thought you could do with some, so I have put two in.'

'That's great, thanks,' Marcus said. 'I do appreciate your care.'

'It's fine,' said Shona. 'I am just sorry that we are meeting under such difficult situations.'

'And I am sorry that I panicked and ran. Please believe me, I did really love her with all my heart, and today was the worst news that I have ever received,'

Marcus sniffed. 'If only I'd done something—if only I had helped her break free.'

Jacobi said, 'Marcus, this is not your fault. How could you have ever known this would happen?'

'Because I felt that there was something off about him. The way that he was controlling her and how he was making her feel as though everything that she did was wrong. She would talk to me and tell me about something that had happened, but then the next day, it was as though her version was wrong, and he had made the situation out to be something completely different. Nothing was ever his fault—it was either him reacting to something she had done, or he made her believe that her perception of events was completely wrong and made her feel guilty for judging his intentions. He had her examining everything she said and did to the point she was riding in circles on a hamster wheel of worrying and wondering. This is why she wanted to get away from him—because she feared he would tip her over the edge. Hence, after her shift, she wanted to just go home, relax, have a bath, get some food and go to bed,' Marcus informed them.

'Marcus, what do you mean she wanted to go home and just relax? Do you mean in general after a shift or last night?' Shona asked.

'That's what she said when she left last night because she was so exhausted after a full 12 hours. She told me that her feet were really aching and all she wanted to do was get into a hot bath. In fact, she had preplanned what she was going to do because I remember her saying that she had already made herself some tea that morning, so all she had to do was warm it up and then get tucked up in bed with a book,' Marcus relayed.

Jacobi and Shona looked at each other again, but this time Marcus didn't miss it.

'What did I do? Did I say something wrong?' Marcus wondered.

'No,' said Jacobi. 'You've actually mentioned something that we need to check out. Thank you, Marcus.'

'Take your time finishing your coffee. Then, when you're done, I'll escort you out. Marcus, thanks again for your time and my deepest condolences,' Shona smiled.

'Before we go, do you have any questions for us?' Jacobi enquired.

'Will you need to confiscate my phone?' Marcus asked innocently.

'Confiscate your phone? Why would you think that, Marcus?' Shona asked.

'To look at the texts and the other conversations we shared to prove what I am saying is true,' Marcus said before adding, 'and the evidence of the call she made to me last night when she arrived home.'

'Sorry,' Jacobi and Shona said in unison.

'Karen rang me as soon as she arrived home last night, disturbed at the fact Robert's car was on the drive of her property. She had made it very clear to him that she hadn't wanted to see him, but as usual, he had ignored her and just let himself into her property,' Marcus told them.

'Do you know at what point she had rung you, or the exact time?' Jacobi asked.

'Yes, it was around 8:30, and she was still sitting outside in the car because I could hear the engine running,' Marcus recalled.

'What did she say to you on the phone, Marcus?' Shona asked.

'As soon as her call connected, she just said, 'I cannot believe it, he is at my house again.' She reiterated that she had told him she didn't want him there, that as she was working a late shift the next day, she wanted the house to herself to recuperate. Then she saw a light go on in the house, and the despair in her voice rose at the fact he'd had the audacity to not only turn up but let himself in. She was very close to tears as she described her space and boundaries as being persistently violated. Then she freaked out he might have seen her on the phone with me, so she cut the call,' Marcus informed them.

'Do you have your phone on you now, Marcus?' Jacobi enquired.

'No, I am sorry, but we cannot have it on us at work, so I leave it in my locker until the end of my shift,' Marcus apologised.

'Can you provide us with your mobile number? I will send you a link for you to screenshot me the details of the time Karen placed that call and the number of minutes you were connected. Is that OK?' Shona asked.

'Yes, of course it is. I will happily send you it if you think it will help in some way,' Marcus said, confused.

'Oh, it will help us, Marcus. Can you have a look through for anything else that Karen has told you about her relationship with Robert as well, please?' Shona clarified.

'Yes,' Marcus said, then shock flashed across his face. 'Oh no, you don't think he had anything to do with Karen's murder, do you?'

'That is something we need to investigate. Marcus, in the meantime, please keep the details of our interview confidential. We do not want anything to jeopardise catching our killer. Is that clear?' Shona stressed.

'Loud and clear. I want this son-of-a-bitch caught just as much as you do!' Marcus stated.

Shona and Jacobi led Marcus out to the front of the police station, thanking him for his cooperation and assuring him no further action would be taken against him regarding his arrest for resisting a police officer.

'So, what do you make of that?' Jacobi asked in surprise once they had shut the doors and were walking back along the corridors.

'Well, I think we can safely say that Marcus is not our man, but I can bet we've both got somebody else in mind that we need to turn our attention to,' Shona answered.

'Yes, that was my thoughts too. I think it's time to talk to Robert Day Jr again,' Jacobi agreed.

'I think I am going to enjoy rattling his feathers,' Shona concluded.

Chapter 11
Who Is Robert Day Jr?

Shona Williams strode into her office, closely followed by Jacobi. Only when she had heard the door close did she swing around to face him.

'Well, that was a turn-up for the books,' she said, perching on the end of her desk.

'You're not kidding!' Jacobi stated.

'When you said our man Marcus had done a runner as soon as he saw the cops, I felt sure we were on to something,' Shona said.

'Well, we are on to something, but I don't think it was quite what either of us was expecting,' Jacobi said, slouching down into the chair opposite her.

'I told you there was something off about Robert Day Jr, and if Marcus is telling us the truth, then everything he told Collins and me was a pack of lies,' Jacobi said in disbelief.

'So, according to Day, he and Karen had a strong bond, a loving relationship and he was about to ask her to marry him,' Shona said.

'Yes, but according to Marcus, that was not how Karen portrayed their relationship. She was fed up with his controlling behaviour, she felt suffocated and wanted out,' Jacobi reminded her.

'Marcus said Karen had rung him and was annoyed at the fact that Robert Day Jr had not only turned up despite the fact she had specifically asked him not to when she needed some space but that he had also let himself into her home,' Shona threw in.

'Whereas Day told Collins and I that they had planned to enjoy a night in, have a Chinese and basically cuddle up,' Jacobi said.

'Yes, the Chinese story. But Marcus stipulated that Karen had told him she had pre-made a meal for herself that morning so she could save herself messing about when she got in because she knew she would be tired. There was a Chinese menu on the counter surface in the kitchen, but Day could have picked that up or brought it with him,' Shona contemplated.

'Or, if they did eat takeout on a regular basis, then they would have had a menu in a drawer somewhere,' Jacobi reasoned.

'Interestingly, I never thought to look in the fridge, but I think it may be worth checking if there was a pre-made meal awaiting Karen's return. If there was, we will definitively know who is telling the truth,' Shona said.

'I know who my money is on,' Jacobi said.

'So, who is Robert Day Jr?' Shona mused.

'That, boss, is the pertinent question,' Jacobi told her.

'Well, you interviewed him. What is your take on it?' Shona asked him.

'As I said at the start, I felt there was something off with him. It was almost as though he was revelling in the attention, and the interview became the Robert Day Jr show. I did not feel he was being authentic in any capacity. His emotions seemed orchestrated, his speech was flat and matter-of-fact, and there was the uncomfortable sense that he was actually flirting with Collins. He was the same with the nurses when I arrived at the hospital. His mood was jovial and light-hearted—not the picture of a man who had just found his partner savagely attacked. There was no genuine emotion either then or throughout the interview, and I felt like I was dealing with a character who was just delivering his lines. It was all very bizarre, to say the least,' Jacobi puzzled.

'So, is there a disconnection from reality and his emotions? Are you thinking along the lines of this being some sort of depersonalisation/derealisation disorder?' Shona enquired.

'No, because that would mean he is experiencing some type of out-of-body experience or that he perceived the things around him weren't real. He was more than aware of what had happened. He was able to discuss it, had no problem relaying things in detail—there were just no feelings towards what had happened to Karen Blakely,' Jacobi highlighted.

'So, he is unable to demonstrate empathy, and according to Marcus, he was controlling—not allowing Karen to have any other friendships that took the focus away from him. He inappropriately dominated her time and wouldn't take no for an answer, actually turning up despite her expressed desire to be home alone. There was talk of her wanting to end the relationship, but she felt like she couldn't get out because he would ignore her and wasn't ready to let go. His solution was to go into town, select a ring from the jewellers and plan a surprise

'Will you marry me.' The man clearly has no respect for other people's choices or boundaries. He just wants his own way, even if it is at a huge expense to her,' Shona itemised.

'She must have felt quite helpless, having no say or control over her life. It must have been exhausting, especially as she was working long hours too,' Jacobi said in sympathy.

'Maybe it was due to her exhaustion that she finally decided to put her foot down, insisting he leave, and he didn't like being told no,' Shona surmised.

'But it didn't warrant smashing her head against the granite worktop, killing her,' Jacobi said, outraged.

'Nothing warranted that, Dion,' Shona stressed.

'Or maybe Day didn't like what he was hearing and knew that Karen had a friendship with Marcus despite his attempts to cut her off. Maybe he was paranoid that something was going on between them?' Jacobi wondered.

'The thing is, Dion, I don't know about you, but I certainly didn't get that impression from Marcus, did you?' Shona queried.

'It's not about whether I got that impression, but more of if Day had. This could be the motive for killing her and for throwing him under the bus as a distraction,' Dion suggested.

'I think we might have our hands full with this one. As you said, there is something odd about him, so we need to find out more information about who Robert Day Jr is. If he is capable of committing murder then behave with the lack of compassion you described in the interview, then you can bet your bottom dollar this isn't the first time,' Shona stipulated.

'I think this is going to be a case of slowly, slowly catchy monkey,' Jacobi stated.

'Yes, we are going to have to put our detective skills to the test in order to stay one step ahead. Maybe by bringing him in to ruffle a few feathers, we can test his ability to stay calm under pressure,' Shona said.

'Then we had better do our homework first and find out who Day really is,' he said.

Chapter 12
The Briefing

The next morning, both Jacobi and Shona were in bright and early, itching to hear what information officers had found out on their community outreach. After much debate and several cups of coffee, followed by trips to the toilet, they heard staff making their way to the briefing room.

'Looks like it's time to get the show on the road,' Shona said gleefully.

'Aye, aye, Captain,' Jacobi playfully said.

As they made their way down the corridor, Shona was still focused on Robert Day Jr. Was he a cold-blooded killer who had so swiftly thrown Marcus under the bus? Shona let her mind wander down the path of who was Robert Day Jr? She contemplated the traits Jacobi had told her he had displayed up to press, and she couldn't help feeling intrigued to sit in front of him and witness this for herself.

She put herself in Karen Blakely's shoes, and what it must have been like trying to function whilst unwillingly being in a relationship with such a person. Shona knew that when she had finished a long shift, all she wanted to do was pop the lid on the MR2, fly down the dual carriageway with the wind in her hair and get back to her pristine, highly desirable apartment. She needed the luxury of solitude, the comfort of her own private surroundings and the blasting of her favourite indie music whilst kicking off her shoes and enjoying a cold Bud.

It made sense to Shona that, considering the pressures of Karen Blakely's career choice, she would indeed need the same isolation. In that case, it was highly likely that Marcus had received a call from Karen depicting her angst at returning home to find her space had been occupied without permission. Also, if Karen was trying to leave the relationship and he wasn't taking no for an answer, she must have felt suffocated and powerless.

There were numerous avenues beginning to build upon her 'to-do' list, so as she entered the briefing room, she took her seat and began quickly running through them whilst waiting for Damien Clarke, the Chief Inspector of Basic Command, to arrive.

'Right chaps and lasses, let's get this show on the road,' Damien Clarke, Chief Inspector of Basic Command, said, addressing the crowd. 'I know you will want to jump straight on it, Shona, so let's get stuck into your investigation first. The night before last we were called to a house at 357, St Michael's Mount, Walton, is that right, Shona?'

'Yes, that's the correct address,' she confirmed.

'Our guys processed the scene throughout the night, and I am aware that there are a few loose ends to tie up, but as usual, we won't know any results for a few days yet. At this stage, the investigation is in its infancy, so we are unaware of the circumstances resulting in the death.'

'Who is the victim, Chief?' an officer shouted out.

'Maybe you could pick it up from here, Shona,' he began as he glanced towards her. 'For any of you that don't know her, this is Detective Chief Inspector Shona Williams, who works directly with Detective Inspector Dion Jacobi.'

'And DI Jenson Parker,' Shona reminded him.

'Oh yes, sorry—and DI Jenson Parker,' The Chief corrected himself, much to Parker's embarrassment but also pleasure at finally being recognised after 20 years in the field.

Jenson Parker had begun to lose his passion for his job, having been passed over so many times over the years to sift through the crap. His motivation had dwindled down to counting off the monthly paydays to retirement. After the resurrection of the Cassandra Matthews case, his creative juices had begun to flow again. As a result, he was given more responsibility and, subsequently, the opportunity to invest in his pension pot through promotion.

Parker glanced in Shona's direction and returned the smile she was offering, knowing full well of her intention to elevate his sense of pride and self-worth. He had always admired Shona Williams from the moment he met her when she was a new recruit. She'd had a demeanour about her that resonated with calmness, respect and integrity—not like some of the newbies that came through with their cocky, need to show off self-inflated egos.

Shona was always polite, yet there had been an intensity about her to want to delve deeper to ascertain the facts. He found her style, abilities, methods and career path admirable, so when she had encouraged the pursuit of his promotion, he had willingly obliged. He watched Shona as she took her place at the front of the crowded room, confident and self-assured.

'Our victim is a 35-year-old nurse called Karen Blakely. according to sources, she was very well respected by her colleagues and a caring, considerate and compassionate lady. She had a partner called Robert Day Jr, who was at the scene when Karen was murdered,' Shona told them.

'Is he a suspect?' Davies shouted out.

Chief Inspector Damien Clarke shook his head, dismayed that this question still arose but refrained from telling them his usual phrase that 'everyone was a suspect until you could positively discount them.' Jenson saw his annoyance and smiled to himself.

'We are looking into him, but his account was that he was upstairs at the time of the murder, his attention alerted to a possible intruder after hearing a door slam shut. He subsequently went down to the lower floor to investigate and found his partner's body on the floor. She'd had her head smashed against the work surface at least twice. He ended up at the hospital being treated for shock,' Shona concluded.

'But he is still a suspect?' Davies queried again.

Damien Clarke could not resist the bait a second time. 'How many times do I need to say it? Everyone is a suspect until we eliminate them, lad. Didn't they teach you anything at the police academy?' Damien Clarke asked in utter despair, much to everyone else's amusement.

'Yes, he is still a suspect,' Shona said wearily. 'A source has come forward to suggest the relationship was not all it was cracked up to be. We have reason to believe that our victim had tried to end it on several occasions but was emotionally bound to it. Jacobi and…'

Shona visually searched the room but she was unable to find her target. 'Collins,' she finished, 'interviewed Mr Day after he was discharged from hospital. I don't want to say too much about him before we have had a chance to delve a little deeper.'

'I take it they are not married, then?' Josie Petroni innocently dared to ask.

'What gave it away—the different surnames?' an older, more experienced officer sniggered.

'Some women are known to prefer their own name. I mean, if you were called Teresa, you wouldn't want to marry Simon Green?' Josie stated, holding her ground.

'What?' declared the older officer, confused at the seemingly immaterial direction of the conversation, before simultaneously realising his mistake. He groaned loudly both at her reference and his own stupidity at being drawn in, especially as the rest of the group sniggered at his expense.

'Come on, chaps and girls,' the Chief ordered. 'Let's leave the frivolities for the youth club. We have a different playground to deal with here.'

'In answer to your question, Josie, no, they were not married,' Shona said to stay on point.

'Was the postal address hers or the partner's?' asked Betts.

'She was the resident, but we are unaware whether she was the owner or just renting the house. Maybe you could look into that, Officer Betts, and find out who the owner is. Because if it was rented, they will need to be aware of the situation. Don't contact them yet. We will hold off until we are done with the crime scene—there is no need to add any unnecessary problems,' Shona requested.

'OK, thanks,' agreed Betts, happy to have been delegated a specific role.

'What about her partner, where is he staying?' Damien asked.

'He has a house at the top of Edge Lane, also in Walton,' Shona informed him before re-addressing the group. 'As the Chief stated, we are still awaiting news from forensics, which should be in the next few days,' Shona continued.

'Which Medical Examiner is conducting the postmortem examination, Shona?' Damien asked.

'We have the lovely Sallyanne Peters, and she has scheduled it for 11 am today, so hopefully I will get the results by the end of the day. If not, it will be first thing tomorrow,' Shona told him. She knew Sallyanne personally and, having worked with her on numerous cases, always found her to be efficient with a timely turnaround.

'Right, before I designate any other roles, can you update me on what we have so far? Who went out into the neighbourhood?' Shona asked.

'We did,' a small group of officers at the back of the room piped up to Shona's right.

'The neighbour whose property overlooks the victim's said she was emptying her trash into her wheelie bin when Karen Blakely returned home. She confirmed it was around 20:30 hours. Apparently, the soap *EastEnders* had just finished, and she had gone into the kitchen to make a cup of tea, realising the bin needed emptying when she threw the teabag in,' PC Gregory Marsh said.

'Does this neighbour have a name in case we need to speak to her again, and did she say whether our victim had spoken to her?' Shona asked.

'Sorry, her name was, eh, Paula Stanley, and no, they didn't speak. She actually stated that after emptying the bins, she had then secured her gate and put her car in the garage, but Karen was still sitting in the car. This made her approach the wall between them to see if she was all right but had noticed she was on the phone, so went back inside,' Marsh emphasised.

'Interesting,' Shona said, looking at Jacobi.

'The rest of us canvassed the area with no further information to report regarding anything or anyone suspicious in the area,' PC Jonathon Bennett offered.

'What about CCTV?' Shona asked.

'There was one house backing onto our victim's property, but it was more of a camera to capture wildlife at night than CCTV footage,' Davies stated.

'Any doorbell cameras in the area or neighbourhood watch schemes being operated?' Shona enquired.

'There were plenty of these, but absolutely nothing has been recorded to suggest any evidence that there has been anyone lurking around,' Michael Jones said.

'Oh, the old chap who lives in the bungalow at the other side of 357, called Kenneth Potter, was adamant nobody was lurking around that night,' Bennet chirped back in.

'Pray tell,' said Damien Clarke, intrigued. 'How an old chap who could be potentially hard of hearing was so adamant no one was lurking around?'

'He has a two-year-old, very reactive German Shepherd dog who, apparently at the slightest of sounds, alerts the whole neighbourhood!' Bennett delivered triumphantly.

'Excellent, lad,' Damien commended.

'He also said that, with it being summer, the dog predominantly lives in the backyard, where he was only too pleased to show me the setup. It was quite ingenious, really—the back fence had been replicated across the full width of the garden by the depth of two fence panels. This secure and unobservable area was paved, had a huge walk-in kennel that some of our dog handlers would admire, and the dog was freely able to wander. The access was via one of the panel partitions with the latch at the top of the inner side. Therefore, to anyone, including myself, you could easily mistake the false fence for being the end of his garden. On Friday, the dog had spent most of its time outside; therefore, had an intruder been hanging around, he was adamant the dog would have reacted. He was as quiet as a mouse all day; hence, the old chap was adamant there could not have been an intruder!' Bennett relayed.

'Good work, PC Bennett. That's what we like to see good old-fashioned police work out in the field, sifting through the chaff to get to the wheat,' Damien Clarke commended him, whilst Shona and Jacobi shared a knowing look.

'What did we find out about Dyson's, the jewellers, and *The Little Flower Shop*?' Shona enquired.

'Davidson and I were tasked with those enquiries, boss,' Taylor piped up.

'Yes, it was pretty run of the mill. The lady in the jewellery store remembered Robert Day, not just because she had only sold one engagement ring that day, but she said he was quite a handsome chap. However, her opinion of him soon changed when, unlike most promisors selecting an engagement ring, he went for a cheap zirconium option rather than a diamond,' Davidson told them.

'Wow!' Jacobi mouthed to Shona in disbelief.

'Promisors?' Shona queried.

'Yes, apparently a 'promisor' is the correct term for someone making a proposal,' said Davidson proudly.

'The cameras at Dysons showed he was there between 15:07 to 15:38.'

'What about The Flower Shop?' Shona asked.

'We know that he went there after the jewellers because he couldn't resist telling them of his plans and showing them what they thought was a very expensive diamond,' Taylor confirmed.

'Obviously, he was hoping to also con Karen Blakely into thinking it was an expensive diamond too,' Jacobi said.

'Unless he knew that there was a possibility that she was going to say no,' Shona surmised.

'The opening hours are 09:00 to 16:00, and she was just about to close. So, although there were no cameras at The Flower Shop, she estimated it to be 15:55. The precincts CCTV caught him going in at precisely 15:47 and leaving at 16:05,' Taylor clarified.

'Did we secure the operator's 999 call made by Robert Day Jr reporting the attack?' Shona asked into the room but to no one in particular.

'Yes, the IT co-ordinator has liaised with our CCTV guys, who should be here any minute,' Damien Clarke suggested as the door opened.

'CCTV operators?' Shona addressed them.

'Yes, I am Tony, and this is Charlotte,' he said, a little overwhelmed to be addressed as soon as he opened the door to a crowded room.

'Please come in and join us,' Damien Clarke suggested, standing up to make his presence known. 'I guess you guys are very busy, so if you'd like to jump straight in and update DCI Williams on what you have found out, I am happy for you to get straight back to your duties.'

'So, we were tasked with trying to establish if there had been any suspects within a two-mile radius of 357 St Michael's Mount on the evening of Friday 5th July 2024. Other than some youths climbing on top of one of the old bus shelters along Benton Road, which sits adjacent to St Michael's Mount, it was a typically quiet night. There was the odd drunk wobbling home later that night and a couple of youths hanging around outside The Wheatsheaf pub, but that was it,' Tony said.

'We did see the victim pull into the drive at exactly 20:28 hours, so rather than guess which way she had travelled home from the hospital, we decided to rewind her journey. Once we had her back at the starting point, leaving the building at 20:07, we went back to 19:45 to see if there had been anybody waiting for her prior to leaving work. There was no evidence of anybody either already in the car park, following her out of the building, pursuing her as she left the hospital grounds, or tracking her along the route home,' Charlotte delivered.

'I was also asked to inform you by the IT department that she has sent you a recording of the 999 call that you requested,' Tony concluded.

'Thanks, guys,' Shona said as both Tony and Charlotte promptly made their way back towards the door.

'So, what have we found out about Karen Blakely from her work colleagues?' Shona enquired.

'You allocated that role to me, and I took PC Danny Driver up to the hospital with me,' said Parker. 'The general consensus of opinion was that Karen was a very well-liked person who was admired by those around her. I didn't find anyone saying anything to the contrary. In fact, the compliments just kept on flowing. With regards to her relationship with Marcus, it was purely platonic.

The two made a good team professionally, generally ate lunch together, they would always be seen laughing and had never had a cross word.'

He looked over at Danny Driver to see if there was anything he had missed, but he looked nervous to input any information.

'Was anything offered about her relationship with Robert Day Jr?' Shona asked hopefully.

'Interestingly, this was a bit of a mixed bag,' Parker revealed.

'How so?' Shona enquired.

'Well, the female nurses thought he was quite dishy and sweet, especially when he would drop her some lunch in. The male staff felt he was really weird, and on a couple of occasions, he had actually been seen hanging around the car park when Karen was on duty. On Friday, the 5th, the day she died, Paul Peters—' he paused and checked his notebook, '—sorry, Paul Spencer was on the unit with Karen when reception rang for her to attend at the front desk. Apparently, when she found out it was to pick a sandwich up that he had dropped in, she was furious. Her verbal response was, quote, 'Why can't he just get the message and leave me alone',' Parker concluded.

'Did she say anything else?' asked Shona.

'No. Paul Spencer said her whole demeanour instantly changed. She became quite rigid, her facial expressions turned to stone, and she seemed irritated and annoyed.' Parker explained.

'Some of the people I spoke to described a change in Karen over the past few months. She had always been the life and soul of things, but she had become more withdrawn. There were concerns raised with regard to her partner's effect upon her after witnessing his control, separation and exclusion from being allowed to socialise with other staff. This had been evident at last year's Christmas party, but according to staff, when Karen had complained, Day's behaviour intensified—especially over the last few months,' Driver offered.

'Oh, I also spoke to Marcus St Johns' manager, Patrick Nevilles. He actually said that the allegations made against him were down to two nurses trying to cause conflict. Marcus chose to move departments for the sake of his colleagues and patients. The complaint was subsequently withdrawn, and the two nurses reprimanded,' Parker remembered.

'I also looked into what life insurance both parties had invested in, and surprisingly neither one had any,' Driver said.

'Anything else, anyone?' Shona threw open.

After a short pause, Driver said, 'I did enquire whether Karen had ever had an altercation with any patients, and none could be recalled. To be on the safe side, I did request hospital security to check with members of their team and to provide any appropriate CCTV footage. I hope that was alright,' Driver said nervously.

'Alright, lad, that's what I call great initiative. Well done, everyone!' Damien Clarke said, giving a solitary round of applause.

'Okay, I will chase Sallyanne Peters primarily for the official identification along with the postmortem examination results. But in the meantime, PCs Davidson and Taylor, can you locate Karen Blakely's next of kin? It would be helpful to learn some background information—does she have children, any brothers or sisters and whether her parents are still alive?' Shona said.

'Yes, boss,' Taylor and Davidson said in unison.

'Parker, can you take our door canvases to cover background checks on both Karen Blakely and Robert Day Jr, including their financial records? Let's see just how equally matched these two were on paper, and then we can look at how solid they were as a couple. Can you do a follow-up with Marcus and remind him to send me the evidence of their call on the night of Friday, the 5th, and anything else that might help us with our investigation?' Shona requested.

'No problem, boss,' he said, turning around to face the room. 'Jones, Davies, Bennett and Marsh—you're with me.' They nodded in agreement.

'Where's Anita Collins?' Shona asked, looking around the room again.

'She is back in on a late shift this afternoon,' Damien Clarke informed her.

'Can you assign her to take the social media route? I want to know what Day and Karen Blakely were saying about their relationships. What little nuggets of information have they been putting out there that we need to be aware of? Jacobi, I want you to take Driver back up to the hospital and have a word with Patrick Nevilles. He may have collaborated with what Marcus has told us, but see if Karen Blakely ever spoke to him about her personal details. Driver, I want you to follow up on your request for further information with both security and the CCTV guys. Any questions?' Shona asked as PCs Marsh and Bennett put their hands up.

'What about us?' Taylor and Davidson asked.

'We know that Day did purchase things from Dyson's and The Little Flower Shop last Friday, and we also have the times. But see if you can secure the evidence. Get me the footage and then find out his whereabouts for the rest of the day. When did he finish work? Where did he go? What time did he arrive at Karen's? That kind of thing. The information is out there, people—we just need to find it,' Shona stated before sitting back down.

'What about getting on to the land register to find out who owns 357 St Michael's Mount to update them about what is happening to their house before someone else does?' Damien Clarke suggested.

'At the moment, Chief, I want to hold off until we have official identification from Sallyanne. Although everything points to it being Karen Blakely, there was no passport or driving licence available. I know we have other means at our disposal, but I am biding my time at the moment as I don't really want a neurotic homeowner thrown into the mix just yet,' Shona explained.

'Fair enough,' began the Chief, 'but ensure that either you, Jacobi or Parker accompanies Police Liaison when her next of kin are told—and sooner rather than later.'

'Right, any questions?' There were none.

'Good, let's get to it,' Damien said as usual.

Chapter 13
Getting to Know You

Over the next few days, whilst each team were tending to their respective duties, Shona Williams worked alone in the background. She wanted to know more about Robert Day Jr before she got him in for questioning, so she reviewed his 999 call along with his earlier taped interview. It was a wonder the disc hadn't worn out, the number of times she had carefully dissected every word.

Today, she was now ready to follow the same practice that she always did at the start of the investigation, and that was to revisit the crime scene. She took out some protective garments, acknowledged Samuels—the officer tasked to stand guard—before signing into the register, then she adjusted her body camera and entered the property.

As she stood at the door, she took a moment to scan the kitchen, trying to refrain from looking at the markings on the floor where Karen's body had lain. Her automatic response took over, with her eyes involuntarily resting upon that very spot. Shona took a few paces into the room before stopping, looking at the door with bated breath as though she was expecting the owner to come walking in.

She replayed the moment Karen Blakely arrived home from work, trying to imagine her tiredness after such a long shift. Her aching body longed for a bath. What her mood might have been like to find Day unwantedly inhabiting her home? What would she have done first—gone straight to the fridge, put the kettle on, sat down to remove her shoes, hung her coat up, what?

She envisioned Karen entering first, with Day hot on her heel. Would she have gone through to the laundry to achieve a quick distance from him? Shona stood for a moment, trying to remember what items were where before forensics had removed and bagged them for analysis. She could see intermittent areas of black granular residue that had been left behind where latent prints had been removed. Mostly, alternate light source methods had been used, but in some parts, they'd had to resort to the old-fashioned method for securing the evidence.

She decided to satisfy her curiosity and made her way to the fridge, grabbed the door and tugged it open. Taken aback by the sourness of an open jug of milk and the rotting of a cucumber and some vegetables, she instinctively re-shut the door. It was too late. Despite the mask that she was wearing, it wasn't able to protect her from the stench.

She moved five feet back before taking in two quick breaths and then one big gulp, before grabbing the handle, scanning the contents, and then disappointedly moving away. There was no pre-made food.

Shona decided to do a full walkthrough—something she always felt compelled to do once the scene had been processed. The silence and solitude in the aftermath of the team's business allowed her to focus her thoughts, to imagine what had happened and to sense the owner's presence.

She noticed that the lead of the washing machine was exposed above the machine itself and still turned on at the plug. Instinctively, she wanted to turn it off but then decided she would check whether prints had been lifted. There was nothing in the machine, and if Karen had been doing a 12-hour shift, she would have turned it off prior to leaving for work.

Maybe Karen had used the toilet, plugged the machine in ready to take off her uniform and then throw it in—but no, she couldn't have because she was not wearing it. Shona noticed a rattan laundry basket at the side of a small chest of drawers, so she lifted the lid and peered in, but the uniform wasn't in there either.

Shona had to conclude that perhaps Karen had left the uniform in her work locker, as some people do, preferring it not to be contaminated by anything outside the hospital. There was nothing else of importance in there.

She moved her way through the lounge, the silence almost deafening and with the curtains drawn from prying eyes, she felt like a thief in the night. She was careful not to touch the newel post at the bottom of the stairs whilst scanning the banister and every spindle as she softly moved up each step.

Her pace was slow, her footing precise, keeping to the edges of the carpet nearest to the wall without scraping against it. She glanced upwards, almost expecting a sleepy face to have been looking down at her, asking what she was doing—but of course, no one resided there anymore.

She stood at the bathroom door, peering in, The water, now cold, the petals shrivelled, had darkened slightly in colour. She was sure there was something, but nothing was speaking to her, so she made her way to the master bedroom.

Immediately, she felt as though something was screaming out at her—maybe Karen Blakely trying to tell her to pay attention to the details. This is where Shona was at her best: scrutinising the details. Her eyes covered every inch of the room like a microscopic searchlight, but nothing was forthcoming.

'Come on, Karen, what are you trying to tell me?' she uttered to herself.

Despondent, as though she was letting her imaginary friend down, her eyes fell to the carpet, and something stirred. She knelt down, straining her eyes to obtain a clearer view, and she was sure she could just make out the faint imprints of the soles of a shoe.

Robert Day Jr had specifically said that they did not wear shoes in the house due to the new carpets. What if he had killed her, then prepped the upstairs to mimic a romantic night in? Or perhaps he had planned for that kind of evening, but due to her tiredness, Karen Blakely was having none of it.

The footprints were only to the right of the door, insinuating that the person had not fully walked around the room. Therefore, Day could not have had his shoes on around the house prior to Karen's return home. She needed to get forensics to do a copy of the shoe's imprint to see if it matched the ones Day had been wearing.

Thank goodness she had told Jacobi to remove his clothing for evidence. Satisfied that at least her journey had not been entirely wasteful, she returned to the station.

As Shona entered her office, the first thing she saw was the infamous Medical Examiners folder sitting on her desk. Before examining the papers, Shona put a call to the Forensics lab to see if they had anything for her. They didn't, so she contacted the Chief to inform him of the new findings, hoping he would put his shoulder against the team's reluctance to move any faster.

It worked. She replaced the handset before turning her attention to the report in front of her.

Shona read and reread the data to absorb the finer details, not finding it any easier each time she poured over it. Sallyanne's examination of Karen Blakely's body found multiple fractures to her face, with microscopic fragments of granite embedded into the small tissue areas.

Her brain had shifted inside her skull as a result of the force within which her head had been propelled back and forth. The impact had caused massive internal bleeding, swelling and bruising to the brain itself. Skull fragments had intensified the tearing to the internal lining and soft tissue areas.

There was the mention of other external bruising, lacerations and contusions, but it all sounded a bit too technical for Shona. All she was interested in was the severity with which the murderer had acted. Most worryingly was the fact that the cause of her death had been a complete airway obstruction of blood.

So, not only had she suffered from a savage attack, but she had choked to death on her own blood. It also stated that she hadn't died instantly from the impact and that death had occurred several minutes afterwards.

So, if the brain injury wasn't sufficient enough to have immediately killed her, Karen Blakely may have remained conscious. That meant not only was it possible for her to have been aware she was dying, but that she was in the room with her killer and that they also did nothing to save her.

Shona rested back in her chair, feeling sickened. She may have been a homicide detective, but she would never become immune to such levels of human suffering.

She stared at the board in front of her, where she had pinned up an arrangement of photographs from the crime scene, her eyes flicking from one to the next. She moved closer to focus in on a photograph at the top left of the board, but she couldn't quite make out what she was looking at.

Shona searched through the drawers of her desk, frantically looking for her magnifying glass, and then closely examined the photograph again. Yes, she was right—a Tupperware box at the side of the hob, just above the bin. Shona couldn't see if there were any contents in the box.

She glanced through Sallyanne's report again. The contents of the stomach were reported to have been fully digested and had passed through the colon. Therefore, she had not eaten since her lunchtime meal, which was interesting as she had specifically made herself something that morning.

Day had rattled on about them planning to have a Chinese, but Marcus had stated Karen had pre-made a meal.

There was a slight tap at the door.

'Come in,' she said, still standing, pondering the photographs to see if there was anything else she had missed.

'Parker has just returned from accompanying Jennifer Reece, the Police Liaison Officer, to deliver the bad news to Karen Blakely's mum. There was only her and a younger sister called Mabel. Both were in bits and immediately wanted to arrange to see her. Parker escorted them to the mortuary but left them in the capable hands of Jennifer. He seems visibly shaken by the experience, so I have advised him to give himself a minute—none of this 'men don't cry shit',' Jacobi informed her.

'I cannot help but feel so frustrated. I have rung forensics again, trying to push for some results, but it's like everyone has been on a go-slow for the whole of this week,' Shona said, frustrated.

We will get there, boss. Anyway I was just coming to let you know the Chief has called the troops in for an update, so we need to attend the briefing room in 10,' Jacobi told her.

There was a tap at the door before it was immediately opened by Parker. Shona looked at him questioningly as both hers and Jacobi's mobiles simultaneously started to ring.

'Have you heard?' Parker asked excitedly. 'Robert Day Jr is downstairs getting booked into custody.'

'What?' Jacobi and Shona chorused.

'Two patrol officers attended a job requiring immediate response to a young lady apparently feeling threatened by an older male. When they arrived, the male was only Robert Day Jr,' Jacobi delivered.

'What happened?' Shona asked, sitting more upright.

'Apparently, he kicked up quite a fuss. He certainly wasn't the meek-mannered, grief-stricken guy who was suffering from shock the last time we saw him,' Parker told them.

'So, he is actually here in custody?' Shona clarified.

'Yes, I just saw him on my way up,' Parker confirmed.

'So, it seems Cinderella,' Jacobi said, addressing Shona, 'you will go to the ball a little sooner than anticipated—just as long as you know I am riding shotgun,' Jacobi stated.

'Right, before we interview him, let's get to this meeting and pull together all the information that we have so far.'

Chapter 14
The Update

As Jacobi, Parker and Shona entered the briefing room, everyone else had taken their seats or were mulling around, leaning against walls. The Chief raised his eyes at them to communicate his annoyance. Without breaking her stride, Shona marched straight up to him and whispered in his ear, which got everyone's immediate attention. Something was going on, and they wanted to know exactly what that was. The Chief displayed a look of surprise, nodded and graciously stepped aside.

'Okay, everyone, I need to quickly ascertain what we have so far in the Karen Blakely case, as Day has just been arrested and is currently downstairs in custody,' Shona delivered.

A mumbling of whispers shot around the room but died down quickly when the Chief ordered silence.

'Dion, can you take notes, please? Taylor, Davidson, I understand that the next of kin was Karen's mother. Do we have a name for her?' Shona asked.

'Yes, Diana Blakely. She had one sister called Mabel, her father is deceased, and she left no children,' Taylor stated.

'Ok, thanks. Driver, I believe you went with Jacobi up to the hospital to retrieve any CCTV footage and to question the security was there anything to report?' Shona asked.

Driver hesitated and looked towards Jacobi, hoping he would conduct the update, but Jacobi shrugged his shoulders and lifted his pen and paper to demonstrate he was busy.

'Security confirmed that they had never been asked to attend nor assist in any altercations pertaining to Karen Blakely. They were, however, called to check sightings of a man loitering in or around the hospital grounds. I conducted a photo line-up with two of the security guards, and both picked out Day as being the offender on multiple occasions,' Driver said.

'Well done, lad, for obtaining a positive I.D,' Damien Clarke said, impressed.

'Thank you, sir,' Driver mumbled before continuing, 'We then sat in the CCTV hub where I was shown incidents based on the time and dates the security staff had noted the sightings.'

'Can we get a copy of those?' Damien Clarke asked.

'Already requested, sir. They should be in DCI Williams's inbox as we speak,' Driver told him.

'Good work,' Damien Clarke said, nodding, impressed.

'Anything else?' Shona asked, getting irritated by the Chief's interruptions.

'Yes, I remembered that Patrick Nevilles had been questioned about the allegations from the two women about Marcus St John. So, as Nevilles was St John's Manager who worked with Karen Blakely, I thought it was safe to assume he was probably her manager too. Therefore, when I saw him in the cafeteria, I took the opportunity to enquire whether Karen had ever spoken to him privately about her relationship,' Driver said, with all eyes on him.

'And did she?' Shona asked with bated breath.

'No,' he began, Shona instantly disappointed, 'but he advised me to talk to Charmaine Westbury, who Karen generally picked up extra shifts for. She hasn't been in all week—something to do with her daughter being off sick from school. Anyway, I was able to anchor her down this morning. She made it perfectly clear that Karen not only wanted to get away from Robert Day Jr but that recently she had divulged that she was scared for her safety.'

'Give me some specifics. What had happened to suddenly shift the dynamics?' Shona pressed.

Charmaine just said that Karen had stipulated that she didn't love him, didn't want to be with him and hated being alone with him in her house. Apparently, since trying to pull away from him, he had held on, had become more demanding—especially sexually—and she didn't feel safe around him. As early as two weeks prior to her death, she had woken up to find that he had let himself into her home despite her never giving him a key. She had then been startled awake to him inappropriately touching her, sexually,' Driver concluded.

'Wow,' exclaimed Jacobi, suddenly looking up from his notebook to see Shona's reaction.

'Well, that certainly changes the perimeters of the ballpark,' Damien Clarke stated.

'Parker, you and the team were looking into his background, tackling the financial checks. Where are you with that?' Shona asked.

'I will jump straight into it,' Parker began. 'There was no information to delve into with regards to their life insurance because neither one had any. With regards to Karen's financial status, she had amassed savings of around £33,000 give or take. The house at 357 St Michael's Mount in Walton was owned, not rented. To say that Karen was relatively young, she had almost paid her mortgage off, she had never been married and left no children. She had worked as a nurse for 14 years, she saved a set amount each month, paid into a private pension along with her work pension, and everything screamed of textbook stability. Marsh and Bennett, do you want to discuss what you found out about Day?'

'Day was a completely different story. He had amassed £235,000 in debt,' Bennett paused for effect, whilst there were expressions of great surprise around the room.

'Settle down,' said Damien Clarke.

'Carry on,' advised Shona.

'These were accumulated through years of spending beyond his means. He had several credit cards that had been used to the max, his house had been remortgaged twice and he had gambling debts,' Bennett told them.

'Gambling debts?' Shona asked.

'Yes,' Bennett confirmed, 'online gambling debts.'

'He was also subject to an Individual Voluntary Agreement, probably to get the creditors off his back and cease the constant accumulation of the interest,' Marsh added.

'The interest would have been huge at that level,' Jacobi threw in.

'Do we know what has contributed to such high levels of debt?' asked Shona.

'Looks like it was a case of plain old living beyond his means—just slap it on the never, never whilst I indulge myself at everyone else's expense. He had bought cars, two static caravans, and enjoyed lavish holidays there was no expense spared as long as it wasn't directly coming out of his funds. As I said, he made an IVA to get the debt wiped out,' Marsh told them,

'Apparently, the creditors had been sending him demands for payments, but he was refusing to even entertain them. They had tried to negotiate a lower sum by slashing thousands off his debt, but he ignored them, sitting it out, hoping they would reduce it even further,' Bennett said disgusted.

'What does that tell you about our man Day?' Parker asked.

'That he is a self-obsessed, egotistical, overindulgent, irresponsible, self-centred user?' said Jacobi, unable to hold back.

'Now, now let's keep it professional, Jacobi,' Damien Clarke said.

'Sorry, sir. Did I actually say that out loud?' Jacobi said, rolling his eyes.

Shona threw him her best Paddington Bear stare, indicating she was none too pleased with him either.

'What else?' She asked.

'A part of the debt was also down to fiddling his tax credits. He had made false statements, so they inevitably wanted to recover what he had not been entitled to,' Bennett interjected.

'Yes,' said Marsh, 'but unlike the creditors, this is one debt he could not get out of—like his income tax.'

'Oh, this gets better and better!' said Shona in disbelief.

'In the last tax year, 2022–2023, he made false tax returns and ended up with an overpayment of over £5,000. This was seen hitting his bank and leaving it within three days, but there is no evidence of it being deposited anywhere else. Inevitably, HMRC pursued him for the recovery of that debt, along with filing a case for fraudulent evasion of income tax,' Bennett explained.

'He is quite a slippery character, isn't it?' said Damien Clarke.

'Yes, it makes you wonder why women swoon at his feet?' Jacobi commented, having witnessed it for himself.

'Maybe, because he feeds them a pack of lies,' Shona said, sticking up for all the women out there. 'Please tell me we are up to date.'

'Not yet. Do you want to share your little titbits, PCs Jones and Davies?' Parker said as Shona took a deep breath to steal herself.

'Well, we were looking more into his working background, and I have to say it was just as colourful,' Jones began.

'Day worked for approximately 25 years for a package distribution company in Halifax, where he had the freedom to negotiate new contracts and manage existing ones. Anyway, when the company was handed down to the owners' sons, a new accountant raised red flags concerning Day. It was discovered that Day had been falsifying his travel expenses throughout his career with the company,' Davies said.

'For 25 years!' Shona exclaimed.

'It doesn't end there,' said Jones. 'They hired a financial fraud investigator who found out that Day had also been adding substantial overpayments to all new contracts. He was siphoning this money off to his own account on a monthly basis. He had over 70 customers.'

'Please tell me they took legal action or at least reported him,' Shona urged.

'Unfortunately not. Michael the son that we met with, felt it would kill their father to know how Day had deceived him because he had looked upon him as a son figure. Besides, they didn't want the company being brought into disrepute, nor did they want to lose the confidence of customers and suppliers,' Jones finished.

'To make matters worse, he stole a list of all their client base and has unashamedly continued to be a thorn in their side, undercutting quotes to steal contracts ever since,' Davies added.

'Cut-throat and cold, with a serious lack of remorse, comes to mind,' Shona expressed. Then, seeing Damien Clarke's disapproving look, she said, 'Oh please, that was the edited, polite professional version.'

'Anything else?' Shona asked Jones and Davies.

'Wasn't that enough?' Davies said wryly, with a smirk.

'Talyor and Davidson, what did you find out about Day's whereabouts on the 5th?' Shona asked.

'Well, we were going to pick it up from when he left work to focus in on the hours leading up to Karen's death, so we first had to look at his National Insurance number to find who was paying him. We couldn't understand why it initially came up with no recent payments until we retrieved his bank details. The last payment from Finch & Bird Packaging was over 5 months ago, and they confirmed he had been sacked from there for also making fraudulent claims on his expenses,' Taylor told her.

'Sounds like a pattern where our boy's only motivation is money,' Shona let slip.

'So,' Davidson took over, 'we knew he wasn't working, so we asked Tony and Charlotte, the CCTV technicians, to backtrack his movements from when he arrived at Dyson's, the jewellers. Interestingly, we found out that his journey had started and finished from Karen Blakely's house. Just to be sure, Taylor and I paid Paula Stanley a visit.'

'Paula Stanley?' she questioned. 'Remind me who she is.'

'Karen Blakely's immediate next-door neighbour—the one whose windows look directly over Karen's property. Anyway, she had been sitting out in the garden sunning herself when Day appeared. She described a short conversation of expecting him to have been at work and him mentioning he had the day off etc. She said he appeared a bit uncomfortable but had put it down to him being in a bit of a rush because he seemed relieved when her mobile rang. She showed us the exact time that he had left, which was 14:28. Tony then assisted us in tracking his journey from Walton to Wakefield along the Barnsley Road route and into the town, where he parked in the multi-storey car park at the shopping mall. He had a cursory look in a couple of other jewellers' windows before entering Dyson's. After picking up the flowers, he returned to Walton, calling in at the petrol station en route and arrived back at Karen's at approximately 16:45,' Davidson updated her.

'It appears that he remained there for the duration of the evening until Karen Blakely arrived home at 20:28 hours, and the rest, as they say, is history,' Taylor concluded.

'Is that everything?' Shona asked, looking around the room, and when no one offered anything else, she finished, 'Thank you, everyone. There are some excellent examples of police work and strategies used. Well done, team!'

She glanced at Damien Clarke.

'It's okay. Go on, go,' Damien said before addressing the room. 'Right, moving on—where are we with the Marion Stark case?'

Shona made her way to the back of the room and exited out into the corridor with Jacobi and Parker in tow. She informed them about her recent walkthrough of the crime scene and asked Parker to have the body cam footage downloaded. She also requested he obtain digital clarification of the unidentified box at the side of the hob. She asked him to contact the lab to see if they had any results, along with arranging for someone to go out and lift the shoe print from the bedroom carpet.

'Right, Jacobi, shall we go see how Mr Day wants to play this one?' she asked.

'Oh let's. Do I get to play too?' he asked in fun.

'Yes. We will swing him around a bit, spin him on the roundabout until he is dizzy, and then take him straight down the slide,' Shona said.

Chapter 15
A Hard Nut to Crack

Shona Williams rang custody to arrange for Day to be moved from the holding cell he was waiting in to an interview room before her, and Jacobi made their way downstairs. On their arrival, the custody sergeant looked up midway from what he was writing and said, 'Room 4.'

'Is he in there ready?' she asked.

'Yes, ready and waiting,' the desk sergeant grinned. Shona stood back to allow Dion to enter the room first and immediately heard Day's welcome.

'And about time, do you know how long I have been made to sit waiting for someone to explain to me what the heck is going on?' Day bellowed.

'If you would like to take your seat, Mr Day, I will be happy to discuss the matter with you,' Jacobi said calmly.

'What if I don't want…' he began until he saw the divine creature following Jacobi into the room. Then his whole posture, facial expressions and voice softened. 'Yes, I will happily take a seat if you wouldn't mind explaining.'

'Thank you,' said Jacobi. 'So, my understanding is that a lone female made a call to the police as she felt threatened by your behaviour. The police arrived, and you became aggressive and argumentative.'

'No, I wasn't aggressive or argumentative. I thought her action was totally ridiculous, and I have a right to put my view forward. The officers at the scene,' Day stated, then turned to Shona, 'no offence, but they were bigoted and had already taken her side without listening to my account.'

Shona felt it appropriate to smile at him to give him a false sense that she sympathised and may even be on his side. He immediately responded by flashing a toothy grin back at her. *Sucker!* Shona thought.

'The lady in question had made a complaint, so the officers are obliged to take any action that they deem appropriate to secure her safety. This starts with ascertaining the facts,' Jacob tried to explain.

'That is what I was trying to explain. How she interpreted the situation was bore from poor judgement; that is not my fault,' Day stressed.

'The problem is, Mr Day, we are all accountable for our words, actions and behaviour. It is possible that what may offend one person may not offend another that doesn't mean the offended person is wrong or more sensitive; just that we all have different experiences,' Jacobi tried.

'But that is ridiculous. My intentions were not to cause harm, so I am not culpable,' Day dismissed.

'It is very easy to slope shoulders, insinuating it wasn't your intention, so therefore you don't need to own your actions, but you have caused the problem. For instance, you may think a white person should not be offended by a racial slur, but what if she was offended on behalf of her black boyfriend?' Jacobi gave an example.

'Now you're expecting people to be mind readers,' Day persisted.

'What if I employed you to come to my house to cut my hedges but made it clear I didn't want you to touch my prize fir tree? I leave you to do the work, but when I come back, the tree has accidentally been cut down. Whose fault is it?' Jacobi played devil's advocate.

'Nobody's, it was an accident,' Day said quickly.

'But I communicated well, I was clear what I wanted from you, and I specifically set out my boundaries. You ignored everything and did the one thing I asked you not to do,' Jacobi said.

'But if it was an accident, it wasn't intentional. Therefore, I am not to blame,' Day said.

'You didn't do what I wanted, so I am refusing to pay,' said Jacobi.

'You can't, because I still did the areas you wanted me to do, so you have to pay,' he said adamantly.

'Is that what you felt about Karen Blakely?' Shona jumped in.

'Sorry,' Day said, genuinely confused.

'That she had to pay because you had put in so much effort with her, but she wouldn't do what you wanted?' Jacobi said.

'What has Karen got to do with the women from today?' Day spluttered.

'That is what we would like to find out,' Shona said.

'You seem to have a habit of trying to control the narrative to fit whatever story you are telling. Take our earlier interview, for instance,' Jacobi said. Day kept quiet as this change of tact had both surprised and discombobulated him, so Jacobi took advantage of the situation by swiftly continuing. 'The account you gave of your relationship with Karen Blakely was nothing more than a fabrication.'

Day had no idea what on earth was going on. One minute he was angry at the inconvenience of this stupid woman and of being arrested. The next he was answering hypothetical questions, and now he was being challenged about Karen Blakely. He sat in silence, confused and disorientated.

'The thing is, Mr Day, I have looked into the account that you gave me and, quite frankly, I would have to say it is beyond fabricated,' Jacobi stated unyielding.

'In what way?' Day said, finally finding his voice but not wanting to give anything away.

'You stated that when Karen came home, you were both looking forward to having a takeaway and relaxing together. Is that true?' he asked.

'We were,' Day insisted.

'Or do you mean you were?' Jacobi asked.

'No, we were!' he insisted.

'Are you sure about that?' Jacobi continued to press the matter.

'Yes, why wouldn't I be?' Day insisted.

'What was it that gave you the impression that was how Karen wanted to spend her evening?'

'We had already decided it, that morning, as I told you, she hadn't felt well,' Day stated.

'There you go again, using the word *we,* but in reality, it was only what you wanted, and therefore Karen would be forced to do it, whether she was compliant or not,' Jacobi hit hard.

'I am not quite sure what you are insinuating, Mr Jacobi,' Day said innocently.

'I am not insinuating anything; I am specifically telling you that Karen had made it clear to you what her intentions were and how she wanted to spend her evening, but you didn't care. It's a little like the example I just gave you about not listening to specific instructions, of overstepping boundaries and cutting down the tree,' Jacobi said cleverly.

'What boundaries did I overstep?' Day asked.

'The fact that she made it clear to you that she wanted to spend the night alone, but you had other plans, didn't you? So, despite what Karen needed, you were only interested in what you wanted, regardless of the expense to her,' Jacobi delivered.

'You didn't know Karen, so how you can sit there and tell me what she did or didn't want?' Day criticised.

'We have collected numerous statements that stipulate not only Karen's state of mind but also her intentions for that evening. Therefore, Mr Day, nothing can be insinuated, misconstrued, and words cannot be twisted nor left open to interpretation,' Jacobi stated.

'I think what my colleague is trying to tell you, Mr Day, is that we see you— like really see you—and what has been seen, cannot be unseen,' Shona said cryptically, much to Day's confusion.

'The fact is, Karen Blakely did not want you at her house. She had been telling you for months she no longer wanted to be in a relationship with you, and yet you ignored her. Again, it didn't fit the picture that you had painted, so you weren't accepting the details and continued to do exactly as you pleased. See how the guideline with the tree fits again? You didn't listen, you overstepped boundaries, and then there was a problem. Next, you will be telling me that killing Karen was also not your fault, because that too was an accident,' Jacobi said, looking at Shona.

'Was it an accident, Mr Day? Did she do something that caused you to react in the heat of the moment?' Shona asked almost empathetically.

'What do you mean? I didn't kill her. It wasn't my fault. There was an intruder, I told you I heard the door slam,' he specified, his voice rising a decibel.

'Yes, you did say that, Mr Day, but at this point, anyone in your shoes would say just about anything, wouldn't they? I know I would,' Shona finished.

'You said you heard a door slam, but there is absolutely no evidence of there being an intruder. What have you got to say about that?' Jacobi asked.

'But there was only Karen and I in the house, so there has got to have been an intruder,' Day said triumphantly.

'But has there really got to have been an intruder? As you have just stated, you were the only other person in the house, so the obvious alternative is that you killed her,' Jacobi put to him.

'I did not kill her, there was an intruder. I heard a door slam,' Day said, his jaw set rigid with the same forehead twitch dancing up and down like a polygraphs needle.

'I think that's his story and he is sticking with it,' Shona said.

'The trouble is, when we investigate, we are not in the habit of just taking a person's word for it, are we, DCI Williams?' Jacobi asked.

'No, we don't. We investigate all possibilities, look at all angles and determine from the evidence the most plausible probability,' Shona reeled off.

'What evidence?' Day homed in.

'The facts are, Karen did not want you in her home. She had tried for months to break up with you, but for some reason, you weren't budging. The more she tried to break free, the tighter you held on, to the point that on the day she died, you wanted to secure the prize by achieving the ultimate commitment,' Jacobi said.

'Asking her to marry you, but that was the last thing Karen Blakely wanted,' Shona chipped in.

'She had tried to escape you for months, so why would she want to be stuck with you for the rest of her life?' Jacobi said, trying to push his buttons.

'Was it the ultimate rejection, a sense of betrayal or the time you had invested that caused you to lash out and kill her?' Shona asked in an almost understanding manner.

'I didn't kill her, I loved her,' Day reacted.

'But did you, really?' Shona asked with a melodic, sing-song tone to her voice.

'She didn't love you, did she? And that sucks, right? But murder, because you can't get your own way, a bit drastic. don't you think?' Jacobi said patronisingly.

'She did love me,' Day stated, ignoring the accusation of murder.

'Well, Karen had made it more than clear to a number of her work colleagues that not only didn't she love you, but that she wished you would just get the message and leave,' Shona stated.

'In fact, quite a few noted the change in Karen after she had become involved with you, and it wasn't for the better,' Jacobi inserted.

'Change? I don't know what you are on about, and anyway, they are hardly qualified to make judgements about our relationship. Karen barely socialised with them,' Day hit back

'That was also brought up, the fact that you were so controlling that you had cut her off from all of her friends, and how withdrawn she had become. The truth is, Karen Blakely was absolutely miserable being with you, because the only thing that revolves around your universe is you.'

'If that was true, why would I go to the extent of buying her an expensive ring, running her a bath, planning a romantic evening and buying flowers?' he asked smarmily.

'Yes, let's talk about the engagement ring,' Shona said.

'Are we going there?' Jacobi asked Shona knowingly.

'We are now,' said Shona.

'What about it?' Day asked, confused.

'You just said it was an *expensive* ring. Exactly how much did you invest for the love of your life, who would wear it on her finger and admire it for the rest of her days?' asked Shona directly.

'Eh?' Day stumbled.

'Come on, Mr Day, how much was spending the rest of your life with Karen really worth to you? It's a simple enough question,' Jacobi enquired.

'The cost of the ring is irrelevant; it was the sentiment, and besides, if Karen had wanted a different one, we could have chosen another one together afterwards,' Day said, recovering himself.

'Would that have been at a cost to Karen, yourself or the credit card?' Shona asked, changing tact again.

'I don't see the relevance of your questioning, nor do I think it's appropriate for you to know how I would purchase it,' Day batted the question aside.

'The thing is, your credit rating is pants, isn't it? And with you not working for the past five months, cash flow has got to be a little low. Was it the £33,000 Karen had in the bank that kept you holding tightly on to her?' Shona hit him like a wave and nearly knocked him off his feet.

'As we said at the beginning, Mr Day, we investigate from all angles, so no stone is left untouched,' Jacobi informed him.

'Then surely you wouldn't have overlooked the fella at the hospital, that Marcus guy?' Day said smugly.

'You're right,' Shona paused for effect, 'we didn't overlook Marcus. In fact, he was more than helpful and provided quite a bit of key information.'

'Like what?' Day asked, intrigued and yet paranoid at the same time.

'I am sorry, but I am not at liberty to discuss that with you at present. However, I am sure that our time will come to discuss that at a later date,' Shona told him menacingly.

'Yes, we know you killed her, Mr Day, so just know, we are going to do everything we can to prove it,' Jacobi stated before shifting in his seat, a sign to Shona that he thought they had rattled Day's cage enough without overdoing it.

'So don't get too comfortable, Mr Day, because it won't be long before we turn up to feel your collar again,' Shona concluded, with both her and Jacobi getting to their feet.

'We will let the custody sergeant know that we are done with you for today; they will process you in due time,' Jacobi said over his shoulder as he followed Shona out of the room.

'All yours, Dan,' Shona called over to the custody sergeant, nodding towards the room they had just vacated.

Once Jacobi and Shona had passed through the fire doors at the end of the corridor into the privacy of the stairwell, they hit a triumphant 'High 5' in celebration.

'I enjoyed that,' said Jacobi. 'But why did you leave me to do most of the talking?'

'Did you see his face when I walked in? I figured I would initially play the dumb blonde, make him think I was the weak link, you know, that I would sympathise with his situation and be on his side,' Shona said.

'Wow, that lasted all of 10 minutes. I have to say, that was the most unsettling part of the interview. Please don't do that to me again,' Jacobi laughed before adding, 'so now that you have got to know him, what do you think of our Mr Day?'

'He seems to me to be a manipulative, cold-hearted, callous individual who will stop at nothing to get exactly what he wants,' Shona spat out.

'Perhaps if he had been taught values, and respect and understood that his actions have consequences, especially on other people, then we might not be here today, probing a murder case,' Jacobi insisted.

'For a man of his years, it's the worst case of 'the world owes me' I have ever seen. I know most teenagers go through it, but at least they grow up, come through it and grow out of it,' Shona summed it up.

'I honestly do not think there is any hope for a man who cannot acknowledge his wrongful behaviour. Using people and then discarding them when their sell-by date is up is tantamount to a lack of connection with humanity,' Jacobi shook his head in disbelief. 'I don't think he realises it is literally abhorrent to normal everyday people.'

'But that is why we do this, Jacobi, to identify these people so we can extract them from society and put them where they cannot harm innocent people,' Shona said soothingly.

'It's frightening because a man like that doesn't just get up one morning and find himself in this predicament. He has chosen to take a set path; there have been no accidental occurrences, but a pattern that he has created before it has escalated to murder,' Jacobi deduced.

'There is no doubt in my mind that you are right. This has definitely been a long time coming so, we now have to delve deeper to find the answer to bring him to justice,' Shona finished.

Chapter 16
Addressing the Troops

'So, we have interviewed our only suspect in the Karen Blakely murder just to stir his pot and see which way he swirls. There is no doubt in our minds he is one slippery character,' Shona delivered, glancing at Jacobi.

'Yes, he's as slippery as the enemy's serpent,' Jacobi agreed.

'From what we have seen of him, 'his ways are devious and dark', but we will pursue and harass him like the angels of the Lord' to get justice for Karen Blakely,' Shona said, quoting her favourite Psalm 35, verse 6 from the Bible.

'So, what now, boss?' Driver enquired.

'We need to press ahead with renewed gusto, which means getting that crucial bit of evidence to nail him. Right first thing tomorrow morning, Taylor and Davidson, I want you to go back to when he was at school. Let's find out who he was, what he was, were there any concerns? There has got to be at least one or two teachers still kicking around, or old school friends. Just get me something.'

'OK, boss,' they echoed.

'Parker, I want you to obtain the necessary permissions to get access to Day's phone and then get it downloaded as soon as possible. I know our tech guys will say they are snowed under and have a backlog waiting, but we need this guy off our streets. Try liaising with Delia Paige; she's usually pretty good at expediting info on cases like this,' Shona said.

'No problem,' Parker responded happily.

'I'll ring down to custody to get them to confiscate Day's phone now whilst he is still in custody. No point trying to chase him for it,' Jacobi said, excusing himself.

'Marsh, Bennett, Jones and Davies, if you guys can stick together, I want two of you to go through the emails, messages, photos, media—anything that will give us a foothold. I am not trying to tell you how to suck eggs; you know the drill. I just want evidence that he is our man,' Shona urged.

'Got it,' Parker stated.

'The other two, get in contact with Jennifer Reece, the Police Liaison Officer, assigned to Diana Blakely and her daughter, to get permission to access Karen's phone. I am sure that she will be forthcoming, especially if it is going to help find her daughter's killer. Then the same thing goes: scrutinise the data,' Shona directed.

'No problem,' Taylor said as Davidson sat, nodding his agreement.

'Driver, can you stay under Jacobi's wing and do some digging into Day's past relationships? Has he been married? Does he have any children? That sort of thing? If you can get anybody prepared to talk to us, I want to know immediately, understand?'

'Yes, you can count on me,' Driver affirmed.

'Taylor and Davies, have a look into his health. Does he have any diagnosis or addictions that could have contributed to him snapping? I am not saying it's an excuse, but I want to know about it before he hides behind it. Check out if he is on medications; if so, has he been collecting them? Again, let's not allow him to hide behind a non-usage flaw. Is that clear?' Shona asked.

'Crystal, boss,' they agreed.

'Also, you guys on the phone details, if you find anything that will help your team pass on the information. Let's work together,' she stressed. 'Does everyone know their role?'

There was a chorus of 'yes,' 'we got it' and 'yes, boss' as Jacobi re-entered the room.

'Great, Dion, can you and Parker pull the whiteboard from my office and bring it into here, please?' Shona asked.

Jacobi glanced at Parker, a little confused, but said, 'Yeah, sure,' and walked straight back out of the room again.

'The reason I have asked them to do that before we leave is because I want you to take a look at the Karen Blakely crime scene photos. Let's remind ourselves every day we are on this case, specifically who we are working for. The board will remain here until we have achieved justice for Karen Blakely, so familiarise yourself with her. I don't want a plea of temporary insanity or manslaughter—it is murder. There will be some evidence at the scene, I am sure of it, but as this takes time to process, we need to be the best we can be in the interim period,' Shona said as Jacobi and Jenson positioned the board as directed.

'Yes, Robert Day Jr is slick; he is as cool as a cucumber, which tells me he thinks he is untouchable, with no emotion, care or concern about Karen's loss of life just the impact on himself,' Jacobi echoed.

'Can you believe he is still being flirtatious with any woman he comes into contact with and today has actually been reported for harassing a young woman? Today, he gave no accountability; it was as though being interviewed about the death of his partner, the one he was about to ask to marry him, was a massive inconvenience,' Shona described dismally as the door suddenly burst open.

'Shona, I think I might have found something!' Anita Collins stated. 'It is a response to a post on his social media account from last year. You had better come and read it.'

The Narcissist

Women, Women everywhere,
Young or old, he doesn't care.
To be adored is what he needs,
To be ignored, makes his heart bleed.
A whining, maungy, pathetic man,
A deviant, with a secret plan.
He steals your life for his own,
Will move himself into your home.
He'll take your all, but gives nothing back;
A personality is what he lacks.
The face may smile, the lips are sweet,
But he'll turn vile if you retreat.
His manner is cold, his heart is black;
If he loses control, he will attack.

(Juli Flintoff)

Part 2
The Past

Chapter 17
Regret
(Rosina Wray)

'How did Rosina Wray feel?'

She had no idea, but that was the question her therapist had just asked her. On the outside, to everyone else, she appeared to be in control, that her life was sorted out. She was a mature lady; she had a good job, and she would go as far as to say she was attractive. She might have been a single parent, but her two grown-up boys were both doing well: one had finished college, and the other one was in his last year.

'But how do you feel?' Her therapist persisted.

That was the one question she hadn't been able to answer each time the therapist had asked it during their last three months together. She didn't know how she felt or how you were supposed to respond when a therapist asked you, 'How do you feel?' Was it a trick question? Rosina had stumbled, with being unable to give any response in case it was the wrong one, and then she would have to sit there whilst it was unpicked. She was tired; perhaps she had been thinking far too deeply, and the reality was there wasn't even a right or a wrong answer to give.

Perhaps just giving an answer, any answer would be the key to setting her free, but for some reason, he'd had such an effect upon her she analysed everything, fearing a personal attack, ridicule or having her feelings invalidated. So, she had simply replied that she 'didn't know how she felt.'

Maybe to answer the therapist meant that she would have to actually admit to herself that she felt stupid to think he could have loved her, embarrassed about how he had so easily discarded her like yesterday's newspaper, or that she struggled to sleep in fear he would turn up in her house late at night.

She had met Robert many, many years earlier when he and her childhood friend Heather had started going out together. They had quickly become serious, buying a house together when Heather had received a huge inheritance. Rosina and Heather's friendship had flourished into adulthood, supporting each other during life's ups and downs, and they'd enjoyed many evenings at the house, chatting, drinking wine and catching up as old friends do.

Obviously, Robert had always been there in the background, making a cuppa, watching TV or reminding them of how late it was, but he was never really a part of their friendship. To Rosina, Robert had just been Heather's husband. But then, one night, she died, so it kind of brought them together in their shared grief not from a romantic perspective, just in a supportive role.

Rosina only felt close to Heather whenever she was at their house. Here, both Heather and Rosina had snuggled together under blankets on the settee, watching a scary movie or wine glasses in their hands, getting ready upstairs, animated and excited about a night out. Or they had sat at the breakfast bar, grasping coffees, pain relief on the counter, nursing their hangovers.

After the funeral, she had felt lost, having no reason or excuse to go to the house anymore, and so her grief for her best friend since their schooldays had hit depths that she hadn't imagined were possible.

Rosina thought back to the journey they had shared with one another: from primary school, going through college together, their first pint, buying cigarettes, their first experience at the polling station, an 18-rated film at the cinema; they'd even gone on their first double date together. Then, at the tender age of 35, she had suddenly died—gone, just like that, without warning—which Rosina still felt was difficult to comprehend. It had started off as every other normal Friday. They had confirmed their plans, and Rosina was just leaving the office when Heather had placed the call.

'Hiya, I am just leaving the office now. I will be home in 20 minutes, so give me an extra half hour to grab my gear, a quick bit to eat, and I will be with you by 18:30,' Rosina had told Heather.

'Slight change of plan,' Heather had informed her friend.

'Oh, is everything alright?' Rosina had asked, stopping in her tracks to listen more attentively. 'We are still meeting, aren't we?'

'Definitely! But do you mind if I come to yours instead tonight and we go for food before drinks? I haven't eaten all day,' Heather had requested.

'Yeah, sure, see you soon,' Rosina had said breezily. It hadn't even crossed Rosina's mind that anything could be wrong; selfishly, she was just looking forward to seeing her friend and was relieved they were still meeting up.

As Rosina pulled up outside her house, she was surprised to see that Heather was already sitting on her doorstep awaiting her arrival.

'You, okay?' she asked, feeling the tension.

'Not really. Robert has been an arse all week and tried every trick in the book to stop me from going out tonight,' Heather confessed. When Rosina looked at her friend with a puzzled look, she continued, 'Roz, you have no idea what it is like living with him. I feel suffocated, and I am not sure how much more I can take.'

'What? I thought you were really happy; I mean, you two are my role models. I covet your relationship, waiting for my prince charming to come along,' Rosina said in disbelief.

'Roz, it is nothing like you think. He is that controlling; my wage has to be paid into the joint account, and he decides what I can and cannot have. So, because he doesn't want me to go out tonight, he is refusing me access to any of my wages. He emotionally blackmails me to get his own way, plays on my soft side, wears me down to manipulate me to get what he wants, and if that doesn't work, he would win an Oscar at his instant ability to cry,' Heather confessed.

'Heather, why haven't you said anything about this before now?' Rosina asked, flabbergasted.

'My friendship with you is the only light at the end of the tunnel. I didn't want it to come between us or to risk losing you,' Heather said.

Rosina reached out and grabbed her friend into her arms as they both began to sob.

'Why on earth would you think you would lose me? We have been through thick and thin together. I will always be there for you,' Rosina affirmed.

'Robert made me believe that he would destroy our friendship if I went against him. He is worried I will talk to you about what is going on, which is why he hovers around every time you come around to the house. But seriously, Roz, I have had enough. It is so draining!' Heather had said.

Rosina fumbled in her bag with one hand whilst maintaining her grip with the other around Heather's shoulder. She located her house door key, shoved it into the lock and then they both slipped inside which was when the whole story of who Robert Day Jr really was unfolded. They didn't end up going out that night. Instead, they ordered a curry, bought several bottles of wine because they didn't know which one they fancied, and then cuddled up on the settee, the curtains drawn just in case Robert walked past. They hadn't got drunk, but the wine had certainly helped Heather to open up and to share her deepest concerns. It may not have been the evening they had initially planned or that they had necessarily expected to have, but it was exactly what Heather had needed, and Rosina had welcomed.

Rosina remembered being shocked about some of the words that Heather had used to describe Robert, painting him as the true definition of being a narcissist with his emotionally coercive and manipulative behaviour to control her every thought and actions for his greater good. Rosina had asked Heather why she had married him if he was so bad, but it had apparently gotten so much worse once he had placed the ring on her finger.

Heather had described herself as feeling 'trapped' from that moment onwards, as he began to tighten his grip upon her like she was actually his property. Rosina had listened intently to the times she had apparently tried to leave him, only to be showered with promises of change and his undying love for it only to revolve around the same cycle of him only focusing on his wants and needs.

Since she had given birth to Belle, his selfishness had worsened, vying for her attention at the expense of their babies, like some strange competition. At one point, Rosina found out that he had actually expected Heather to leave Belle crying whilst he demanded sex. To Robert, having his needs met was his only natural and ultimate goal, regardless of what Heather wanted or whether his child required comfort, food or a nappy change.

It had decimated Rosina's heart to see her friend broken, struggling emotionally, mentally and totally exhausted.

Lost in deep conversation, focused on the sensation within their bodies of their own individual emotions and the feelings that were being generated from their thoughts, they failed to hear someone outside. The loud, continuous banging at Rosina's front door suddenly scared them both out of their wits.

'I know you're both in there,' Robert was shouting. 'Don't be a fool, Heather. It is time to come home.'

The girls sat quietly, huddled together, not daring to breathe as the banging continued.

'What are we going to do?' Rosina asked in a hushed voice.

'I am going to have to go,' Heather said dismayed.

'Stay here, he sounds far too angry for you to go home,' Rosina pleaded.

'I can't. He will use Belle as a weapon against me, and if I don't do as he says, he will hold that against me too,' Heather said, defeated.

'Heather, if it is as bad as you have told me tonight, you have to leave. Come here, both you and Belle,' Rosina had pleaded.

Heather's eyes had lit up at the prospect of not only being offered a way out but that she could stay with her friend where both she and her daughter would be safe.

'Don't say it unless you mean it, Roz, because once I walk out of that door I am never going back, and I don't know how long it will take before I'd be able to get back on my feet,' Heather stated.

'I don't care. We have been friends all our lives. You and Belle mean the world to me, so there is no way I can stand back knowing you are fighting to survive getting through each day! You are coming to live with me, and that is final,' Rosina had said, putting her foot down.

Heather had not needed any other encouragement.

'I will do it. Thank you so, so much, Roz. You don't know how relieved I am. Thank you, thank you, thank you!' Heather had said, crying tears of both joy and relief.

'I will go now so he doesn't get suspicious, but can we talk tomorrow when he isn't around to make a plan of action?' Heather had asked.

'Of course. However, you want to tackle it, I will be at your side. Just know we will get through this together,' Rosina smiled. 'Quick, lay down and pretend to be asleep,' Rosina instructed as she threw her blanket over her and went to answer the door.

'Robert, what is all the noise about? You are going to disturb the neighbours, not to mention wake Heather up?' Rosina hushed him as Robert pushed past her, not even waiting to be invited in.

Heather lazily opened her eyes, yawned, smiled and said, 'Oh, hello love. What time is it? I must have dozed off.' She faked admirably.

'It's time you were coming home to feed Belle, that is what time it is. Say goodbye to Rosina, that's a good girl,' Robert dismissed.

Rosina bit her lip as Robert basically frogmarched her friend back up the street towards their house and couldn't help wondering how he had managed to keep this side of himself hidden for so long. Or maybe she was just cross with herself for never looking deeper than the surface and allowing her friend to endure such a toxic, unhealthy relationship.

That had been the last time she had seen Heather alive. The image of him dragging her up the street against her will had been engraved upon her mind for the past 17 years, along with the questions should she have answered the door? Should she have insisted Heather stay the night with her? If she had, would she have still been alive today?

Apparently, later that night, Heather had suffered from a fatal asthma attack, which of course Rosina knew could come out of the blue, but equally, she hadn't known Heather have one since their college days. Rosina was too overcome by grief to have contemplated any wrongdoing on Robert's behalf, but there was just something about his behaviour that was off. He would not look Rosina in the eye, and he never expressed any sorrow nor demonstrated any grief at losing his wife, the mother of his child. In fact, it was for the sake of Belle that Rosina had stayed close, assisting with her care as Heather would have wanted, if only to make sure she was safe.

Rosina observed how this beautiful, wide-eyed little girl was becoming more withdrawn without her mother's light. It killed Rosina to see Belle being treated as nothing more than a nuisance, an inconvenience, an unwanted responsibility that Robert was being forced to bear. This was probably why Robert's mum had intervened to save her granddaughter from her beast of a son. No sooner was Heather's body in the ground did Robert find a mother figure for the child, by starting a relationship with a random neighbour on the pretext of being a father figure to her children. It was a double-edged sword, as it also acted as a way to keep his interfering mother at bay. In reality, all Robert wanted was a woman to lie down with on a nighttime to expel his lustful desires. The fact that it omitted Rosina and his mother from his life was a bonus.

Torn between protecting Heather's daughter and honouring her memory, Rosina had to settle with indirect contact, praying Belle would be safe with this lady and be untouched by Robert's detached, unemotional, uncaring, unsympathetic, unloving approach to everything.

So, how did Rosina Wray feel 17 years later, after succumbing to a relationship with Robert and recognising he was every bit as self-centred and uncaring as Heather had described? How could she have sullied her best friend's memory? She felt sick, she felt used, and she hated him with every fibre of her body—but not as much as she hated herself! She was still unsure how he had

154

managed to break through her armour. Maybe the passing of time had desensitised her opinion. Or maybe it was due to his charismatic disposition and fake likeable character that she had been led into a false sense of security, and therefore she had subsequently let her walls down.

Part of the appeal had been seeing Belle again, a now beautiful, elegant vision of her mother. Rosina had felt like she was back in her friend's company once more, especially with her eyes closed, listening to Belle's voice and being allowed back into the old family house. The more time she spent in Robert and Belle's company, she felt like she had been given a second chance to be close to Heather. Oh, how she had missed her friend.

When she caught Robert staring at her from across the room, smiling, she had simply smiled back, and that was the only confirmation he had required to pursue her as his prize. Of course, the first time they had slept together felt awkward, but Robert was attentive, reassuring, loving and completely unrepentant. He had actually made her believe they had Heather's blessing by stating that she had appeared to him in his dream and told him it was time to let her go. He had even compared his love for both women, that he loved Rosina more than he had ever loved Heather, just to keep her beholden to him. How had she fallen for this rubbish?

Rosina had spent the last few months unpicking her decision with Isla, her therapist, but she still did not know how she felt—maybe duped now she knew it had all been one big joke. When she looked back, she failed to understand how she could have fallen for the silver-tongued patter of his lips. She could still hear his voice laying it on thick from the start: 'How had he not realised before just how beautiful she was, both on the inside and the outside? How he was falling in love with her, showering her with love, attention, flowers and falling over himself to be all that he could for her.'

She had felt so special, it was hard not to get sucked into the vacuum of his certainty that they were made for each other, especially when he had hinted at them settling down together and making a permanent commitment.

Rosina had been on her own for several years, so she was an inexperienced participant in the dating world and had inadvertently given him control without even realising it. There again, he had made her feel safe, that he would look after her, secure that they had a future together, and loved in the way he desired her. She had quickly become putty in his hands, so the hard exterior of the strong, capable, confident woman became much softer and gentler as the walls crumbled to dust, like Joshua taking down the walls of Jericho. From that first long, lingering kiss, it had accelerated to being a full-on, intense relationship, where he had wanted to spend every waking minute with her.

However, somewhere along the line, maybe a prick of her conscience, maybe Heather somehow trying to warn her, she had decided to take a step back. When she observed it from a different viewpoint, she realised that she had become like a kid on a helter-skelter without any control. Everything they did together, everywhere they went, when and with whom, was being dictated by Robert, whereas her life had become a measure of simply fitting in with whatever he wanted.

On the outside, Robert appeared strong and decisive, but she was beginning to see a side to him that Heather had described as him being emotionally manipulative, contrasting with the needy, crying side if he couldn't immediately get his own way. Rosina knew if she didn't find a way to stop herself, and quickly, she could spiral down the helter-skelter like Heather, until she too was unrecognisable. The more she observed, the more convinced she became that Heather was right, there was something mentally imbalanced with him. Her only quandary was, how could she protect Belle?

Secure in her decision, Rosina arranged to meet with Robert at their local bar, as it was the one place she felt comfortable and knew she would be safe. The last thing she wanted was for him to put on a show or continue to press matters by making promises she knew he couldn't keep. She was glad that she was getting out virtually unscathed, as it had only lasted a few months—not like his last relationship, which had been for over a decade. Yes, Rosina was sure she had made the right decision, and she needed to do it quickly with as little fuss as possible. She was not the woman for Robert Day Jr, but more importantly, he was not the 'man' for her.

She arrived at the pub by car, as she had no intention of staying longer than to deliver her decision and then get out of there. It was done. There was no use in hanging around or prolonging things. So, she parked her car and entered through the back door of the pub to find him comfortably perched in the 'love' seat, an intimate alcove just beyond the fireplace. He stood beaming as soon as he saw her, but '*not for long*,' thought Rosina, and then he leant forward to greet her.

Rosina coldly turned her head, not giving him an inch, and whilst she allowed him the opportunity to hold her, she did not reciprocate his embrace. His face was questioning, but she refused to meet his gaze, so he shuffled up to give her room to sit down and was dumbfounded to see her pull out a buffet from under the table.

'Everything okay? You don't seem yourself tonight,' Robert queried.

'Yes, I am fine. In fact, I am more like myself tonight than I have been during the past few months,' Rosina stated.

'I don't understand,' he shrugged.

'I have decided that things aren't working out for me, Robert, so I am calling it quits,' Rosina said bluntly.

'What? Is this some kind of joke?' he asked perplexed.

'No, I just want my life back, where I make informed choices and decisions to suit what's right for me, not bob along in the ocean of 'meeting only Robert's needs',' she told him.

'That's not fair. I do everything I can to make life easier for you. If you felt I was taking over, you should have said, because that is certainly not my intention,' he said, hurt.

'The problem is I keep bringing things to your attention; you either invalidate my perception or feelings about things, or you dismiss me completely. The only reason it has got this far is because of the way you made me feel initially, but I realise that was only so I would find it harder to leave you and would always hope that you would revert back to how it was before. But I know it never will and now I have seen a side to you that I don't like, so I am getting out before it goes any further. I am sorry, but it is over,' Rosina stated, and she quickly got up and marched back out the way she had come. By the time Robert had got up from behind the table, crossed the pub and was outside of the back door, Rosina was in her car and driving away.

As Rosina drove home, deep in thought about the things he had said to her over the months, she was more and more certain his behaviour was indicative of exactly what Heather had described in the early stages of their relationship. All the stuff he had said was rubbish; he didn't feel those things at all. They were just a rouse to get her to stay with him because he just didn't want to be on his own. She thought back to what she perceived was the worst indignity, that every time they went out to their local, he was persistently staring at another woman the whole time whenever she was in. Rosina would try unsuccessfully to engage him in conversation as she normally did, but he paid no attention to her at all. He only had eyes for that one person the whole time, to the point her blood would boil yet he remained totally unaware Rosina was even present.

Nobody wants to be disrespected to that degree, but if she challenged him, he would lie through his teeth and just deny it, even though she was sitting right next to him observing him. His eyes were literally like magnets being drawn towards this woman, and even though he would try to mask it by periodically looking away, they would almost instantly spring straight back to her. It didn't matter what she was doing; he was captivated by her every move: the way she danced, listening intently if she sang, and snapping his head in her direction if he heard her laugh. It had felt to Rosina that he might be sat next to her, but his heart was with this other girl. So yes, she had done the right thing by getting out now, to save the heartache later on.

Of course, he had denied it, even made her feel insecure, as though she was seeing things that weren't there, but he couldn't hide his responses. They were natural, instinctive, and they didn't lie: he wanted her.

Rosina berated herself for actually being fooled into thinking she had ever loved him, as it was clear to her now that it had only been the image of what he had first presented her with, and this had been a fake representation of who he really was. He was like a fisherman casting his net, dangling the bait to see what he could catch to bring home. He wouldn't have cared less about who the person was; the world was merely a hunting ground for him to snare whomever he chose to trap.

She knew he had no good intentions towards her. His words were empty, simply lines cast out to reel her in, make her feel good, and safe until he had her on a tight enough line. She could then be dropped into a much smaller container to be controlled, where he would knock her semi-conscious through manipulation, coercive behaviour and mental abuse. She had been like a fish out of water, flapping to his tune, reliant on him, thankful for a few words of praise, whilst the rest of the time he had conditioned her to fall in and do his bidding. This was indicative of exactly what Heather had described, culminating in financial abuse to assert full control.

Rosina then thought back to the lady who had lived with him for over a decade and how she'd had to rely on him for every penny. He had a cold and callous heart, one that was devoid of love for any other person in favour of only himself. She didn't know it yet, but by initiating the separation she was about to find out that he would pull back much more aggressively. Robert Day Jr did not like to be told 'no,' nor would he willingly let go of a source that was meeting his needs without a fight. Now Rosina had pulled away; she would be forced to endure weeks of mental and emotional stress of him using every trick in the book: pleading, begging and lying to get her to change her mind, and then his ultimate resort of stalking.

Rosina Wray may have thought she had seen the worst of Robert Day Jr, but she hadn't seen anything yet!

Chapter 18
Fear
(Rosina Wray)

During her waking hours, Rosina Wray felt like she was literally tearing her hair out, and by night she feared closing her eyes jumping at any sound the night released. She was sleep-deprived, waking with panic attacks and on antidepressant tablets.

As a last resort, she contacted her doctor again only this time, she opened up about what was happening in her personal life too. She described being terrified in her own home by her ex, who was not just walking past the house because he lived nearby, but that she would find him standing in her garden, or at the window when she opened the curtains, watching her from across the street, staring into her windows and literally scarring the bejeebies out of her.

The doctor listened intently without interruption and then advised her to seek the help of the police before referring her for counselling.

Rosina felt like she was going mad. Maybe that's what he was trying to do, tip her over the edge, trying to weaken her resolve to induce a submission so she would give in to what he wanted at the expense of her own mental health and well-being. His behaviour demonstrated just how relentless and demanding he was, with zilch insight, care or concern for the impact upon Rosina.

As far as Robert Day Jr was concerned, he was only interested in meeting his own needs, and to him, the end justified the means—she was just collateral damage. He did not see her worthy of any consideration. To him, she was totally dispensable; she meant absolutely nothing to him and was simply available for him to use.

The mental anguish this had upon Rosina was the very reason she had ended up seeing a therapist in the end. She was too terrified to go out, scared to open the curtains, resulting in her virtually becoming a prisoner within her own home.

Rosina had not only become housebound, but she felt restricted to only using the upstairs of her home, where she would eat, watch the TV and try to relax. When she was downstairs, he still had the ability to intimidate her.

The psychological damage was probably the worst, especially when he then started turning up at her work to drop a sandwich off, expecting her to be grateful. He didn't seem to get the message that it was over, and he just wouldn't let her go. She couldn't understand what was wrong with him. Was he unable to comprehend, or did he not possess the mental capacity to recognise that crossing defined boundaries was beyond inappropriate?

Rosina began to fear that she would never get rid of him, and her thoughts turned to Heather once more and how she had been driven to utter despair too. Most people took a hint; others you had to be blunt with, but Robert Day Jr was incessant, determined not to lose his prize and unrelenting.

Then she would be bombarded with messages or voicemails (when she refused to take his calls) about her sandwich, as though he expected gratitude for his efforts, a bit like a child wanting his mother's approval. She was actually beginning to feel like she was living in some parallel world to him, where he still thought they were together or wouldn't allow himself to acknowledge they weren't. It was beyond embarrassing; it was mind-bending and very, very scary.

So, when her therapist had asked 'how she felt,' was there any wonder that she couldn't find the words to describe how she felt?

Rosina Wray had always been an astute young woman. She was stable, adept at discerning a person's character, carefree and enjoyed socialising. However, since getting mixed up with Robert Day Jr, she had become a recluse, fighting anxiety issues and had been stripped of all her confidence.

For the first time in her life, she was second-guessing every move and every decision, with her heart and head constantly battling against each other. She felt confused and totally out of sync—like she did not even align with herself, let alone with the world outside.

She was an intelligent person, so she could not understand how she had believed the lies that he had told her. Maybe she was equally to blame. Maybe he had seen a desperation within her and taken advantage of her naivety.

'Enough,' she told herself. You are still giving him control over your thoughts and emotions, and she knew he was not worth that. Besides, it was he who had been staring through her window, stalking her, following her wherever she went and just turning up in random pubs or sitting on his own looking pitiful if she was in a restaurant with friends.

No, it wasn't her—it was him. He was mentally sick to exhibit this type of psychotic behaviour, and it was nothing less than a dangerous, disturbing and uncomfortable character trait. One that she knew he had performed at least once before with Heather—and look what had happened there. It had cost her, her life.

She shuddered at the consideration that, one day, there was the potential she could wake up with him standing over her, knife in hand. His behaviour and responses were so erratic and unpredictable.

At least she was no longer jumping every time a notification sounded on her phone, telling her that a new message had been delivered. Yes, the long-lasting psychological damage he had caused had been the worst. Then, without warning, it had stopped when he had succeeded in catching the attention of the girl in the pub, whose laugh, songs and appearance he had been fixated upon.

After months of staying off the grid, Rosina had finally ventured out to meet a friend in a local bar, to find him there exhibiting the exact same behavioural patterns that he'd used with her. Rosina's anxiety levels escalated, so she'd had to quickly take a seat at the opposite side of the pub to him, hoping not to attract any unwanted attention from him.

At first, she had thought he was performing his stalking routine again, so she had quickly brought the situation to her friends' awareness. As they sat and observed him all over this girl, Rosina was both dismayed and astounded. For anyone that didn't know them, you would have thought they had been in a relationship for years.

Then, somewhere in Rosina's brain, she realised why he had been staring at her for months, because he was homing in on her, as his next target.

Rosina felt sick, not only due to the fact he had openly been doing this in front of her yet vehemently denying it, but that there was nothing she could do to warn this girl. It wasn't like she could go over and tell her to run a mile, get away before he strips you of yourself.

What could she say? *You're dealing with a narcissistic psychopath whose only intention is to use you, abuse you, make you question his intentions, doubt your own thought process, shake your mental health and completely deplete you of all your energies.*

Of course not, as she would come across as the mentally imbalanced one. But then, Robert knew Rosina's limitations, so he openly cavorted in front of her, knowing there was absolutely nothing she could do about it.

As Rosina was considering the options of how not to come across as the disgruntled ex, she suddenly realised Robert Day Jr was striding straight towards her—and there was nowhere for her to go.

Her body became rigid. Her heart quickened. Her breath felt like it had caught in her throat and was starting to create a cramping sensation, whilst her eyes grew ever wider as she waited for his assault, like a sitting duck.

'Hi, Rosina, you alright?' he said effortlessly, with what would have appeared to anyone else as a warm, hearty grin.

She sat there, stunned in utter disbelief at his seemingly disassociation with the reality of the prolonged and persistent abuse she had sustained from this man—sweeping it aside as though it had never happened.

He really was the epitome of Christina Perri's song *Jar of Hearts*. It was about a man who hopped from woman to woman, collecting women's hearts, though his remained as *cold as ice.*

'Don't worry, love, just ignore him. That was plain to see it was just for everybody else's benefit,' her friend had said wisely.

However, for poor Rosina, it just incapacitated her further, especially as the new power couple began dancing, having fun, whilst she looked on, her messed up head, trying to make sense of what was happening.

Evidently, Rosina was now a forgotten commodity, whereas he had swiftly sidestepped into something completely new without any care, understanding or accountability for the harm he had caused to her.

Whilst he immersed himself in his self-seeking, self-centred pursuit to have his needs met by anyone who was available, Rosina no longer existed—she had now become invisible.

Chapter 19
Invisible
(Rosina Wray)

'You can feel it, can't you?' asked Rosina.

'I'm not sure what you mean, Rosina. Feel what?' Isla asked.

'That I am done. Done with being disrespected. Done with sitting on the sidelines. Done with never getting invites anywhere. Done with pouring into everyone else and being left depleted,' Rosina exclaimed.

'I would say that this is a breakthrough, Rosina. You have struggled to say 'no' to others and have actively put everyone else's needs before your own. Therefore, I would call it setting healthy boundaries,' Isla taught her.

'Isn't it selfish, though?' Rosina wondered.

'Why would it be selfish, Rosina, to put your needs above people who have no problem putting their needs above yours? Didn't you tell me earlier that, despite how exhausted, ill or how busy you have been, whenever it was their birthdays, anniversaries, Christmas or Easter, you would buy gifts and almost break your back to ensure they were delivered to them on their special days? For years, you have gone above and beyond demonstrating your love, care and commitment. I appreciate these acts have sometimes stimulated an equally beneficial response. However, over the past two years, when you have stepped back to see who is in your corner and who isn't, you have clearly found your answer. So, let's just identify—how many delivered a present to you for your birthday?' Isla queried.

Rosina remained silent as the realisation began to register before saying, 'One.'

'Alright let's give them a chance. How many sent you a card?' Isla asked.

'One!' Rosina said, beginning to tear up.

'Why would it be selfish to remove the effort that you put into non-rewarding relationships and redirect it to invest in your own needs? Life is too short to waste your energies on sources that deplete you in every capacity. The relationship with Robert was exactly the same. You met his needs, but he had no intention of meeting yours and actively kept you at arm's length,' Isla pointed out.

'I just cannot understand what it is about me that is so repugnant, or why no one actually sees me—or who I actually am as a person,' Rosina said, breaking down.

'They do not see you, Rosina, because you do not see yourself!' Isla told her.

And there it was—slam dunk, straight between the eyes!

'But I really cared about these people, and I have invested donkey's years into our friendships, always being the first to make contact and bring everyone together. I just do not get why I wasn't important enough to them,' Rosina sniffed.

'You cannot hold on to people based on the history you have had with them. Sometimes, you open a new chapter, and this is when you decide who is going to turn the page with you. You informed me earlier that you had given them an extra two years, and still, nothing changed. So, maybe it is you who needs to change the story that you are writing. Who knows—perhaps there are new characters waiting to pounce out of the pages to be part of your future. But you have to be brave enough to make room for them. This is your story. Who remains in it and who is edited out is your decision—no one else's and certainly not people who are emotional vampires, draining you of your positive energy,' Isla explained.

'I suppose because I lost my best friend, everyone else in my life had become a priority to me. But I recognise now that I have never been a priority to them,' Rosina acknowledged.

'Regret is one of the harmful battering tools we use on ourselves, along with self-recrimination. But ask yourself—would you really regret leaving behind the past so that you can look forward to a brighter future? Or are you happy beating yourself up, accepting the scraps that you're thrown? No one should go through their lives carrying the baggage of old relationships, especially when they are no longer productive. You deserve so much more but without digesting that, the only person holding you back is yourself.'

'In John 15:1–2, the Bible depicts God as the gardener who cuts off every branch that does not bear fruit and prunes the ones that do, in order to produce even more fruit.'

'This tells us that we have to get rid of all that holds us back if we are to move forward in God. If there has been no effort, no care, no concern and no love shown towards you, where is the goodness in those relationships? It seems to me that the only harm is not freeing yourself from the strangleholds of non-productivity. Love is the centre of your faith and the route of all that is good in the Bible. If any relationship is not mutually respectful, equal and bound by love, then it is as useful as the dead wood of a shipwreck sat at the bottom of the ocean,' Isla told her wisely.

'I guess when you feel like you don't register on anyone else's radar—or you don't even make it onto anyone's list—then you get to the point of feeling like no one cares whether you live or die. If you are lucky, they may turn out for your funeral. They may even remember all the good stuff you did for them, the laughs you had together and be reminded about what you meant to them. But by this time, it is too late. They never told you when you were there.'

'They never picked up the phone to ask if you were alright or to enquire why they hadn't seen you in a while, or to show any level of care when they could. I don't know why it takes people until it's too late to wake up and smell the coffee. It is only when you have no more to give that they wonder why you are either shutting the door—or have ended up taking your own life?' Rosina poured out her innermost being.

'Is that what you are contemplating, Rosina, taking your own life? And was that what you meant by your phrase at the beginning of our session that you 'were done'?' Isla asked directly.

'No, not at all. I am just sick of the bullshit. People are so self-seeking, wanting to get their news out, how they are feeling and what is happening to them, but never do they ask how you are. There seems to be this unwritten rule that, because you have a history with someone, then you will continue to take that shit and actively be their doormat or emotional punchbag until the end of time. I am just sick of being invisible. Sometimes, I just feel like I am everyone's garbage disposal unit,' Rosina stated. 'I am sick of being invisible!'

'If someone's not meeting your needs despite you effectively communicating what they are, they either don't care or they're just not listening because they don't care. Either way, we are back at the beginning and the fruitlessness of those relationships. If you want a different outcome, you either have to do something differently or you have to replace the people,' Isla told her.

'I think it has all come to a head because of the situation with Robert. Seeing how he has blatantly disregarded me as a human being has highlighted how the other people in my life treat me. It goes beyond a lack of consideration and borders on contempt with an unwillingness to engage with me as a friend unless I do all the leg work. I have even been told I am part of someone's inferiority problem when they were bullied at work just because of where I lived as a child.'

'Despite being shocked and devastated by this comment, I then had to deal with their passive-aggressive behaviour towards me as a scapegoat for their own inadequacies.'

'On another occasion in a distressed state, I had tried several times to contact another lady. When she finally rang me back, I had just averted a collision, so was in a panic. Did she show understanding, care for my situation, or demonstrate empathy? No, she was too busy berating me because of the way I spoke or handled her call in the middle of driving. Her superiority complex to want to enforce boundaries of conversation rather than actually humanise the situation cost her my lifelong friendship,' Rosina offloaded.

'This is exactly what I am showing you, Rosina. If these so-called friends do not have the ability to humanise you and to actually see you, then yes, you are right—you are invisible. Hence, that is why they have failed to notice that you have slipped away. Whether it is a friendship or a romantic relationship, when you have to question your self-worth within it, it is already dead in the water. Once you see things for what they are, you cannot unsee those things. We then have to decide upon the action we are going to take. Are we going to ignore it and keep treading that stagnant water, or are we going to ride the crest of a different wave—one that will take us back to shore where we can place our feet firmly on the ground and start walking? Whatever the situation, we always have choices. The key is to decide to keep moving forward with or without them,' Isla pointed out.

'You have asked me every week how I felt, and I haven't been able to give you a solid answer, but I think it is that I feel invisible, and if truth be known, I have done since Heather died,' Rosina admitted.

'Perhaps that is why you have placed such an emphasis on your other friendships because you hoped to find one as fulfilling as you had with Heather.

The problem is we can stay in the rut of comparisons instead of allowing new ones to fully develop. So, when else have you been feeling invisible?' Isla asked.

'In my relationship with Robert,' Rosina said succinctly.

'Would you care to expand a bit, giving me some details?' Isla asked.

'I felt like I was a ghost intruding in his house when, in fact, it was him who had invited himself to live in my home. I seemed to be bending over backwards because he didn't want to feel uncomfortable about using the electricity, getting a bath when he wanted one, using the washing machine and helping himself to the food that was there. He conditioned me not to say anything, so I didn't make him feel unwelcome, but it then gave him licence to exploit me and disrespect my home until I didn't feel that it was my home anymore. If I tried to point anything out or specifically say, 'Please don't do that because this will happen', he would purposely continue,' Rosina explained.

'Which is the definition of conditioning. You request how you want things to be, he ignores your repeated requests, and he continues using the same behaviours until you give in and stop saying it. He then triumphs at winning the small battles, recognising it works upon you, and gradually plays the game, increasing the size of the wins,' Isla stated. 'Were there any specific points of destructive behaviour?'

'There were lots. He has ruined so much within the house there is no way they have all been accidental. We always used mats to protect woodwork, but he suddenly started putting wet glass bottoms on my expensive bedside furniture, a pew I had, or putting it on the floor and accidentally on purpose kicking it over.'

'I would even pick it up, replace the mat under it and he would remove it, which would inevitably cause a watermark. Then he would swear blind it wasn't him. I don't know if he actually believed what he was saying, but he could argue black was white. A similar situation would be when he turned up with a curry unexpectedly. I'd already eaten, so wasn't having any. Instead of carrying on home, he made me feel obliged to let him stay and eat it. The problem was I knew he wouldn't want to leave then, and I would be forced to let him stay, and he would push for sex,' Rosina said.

'How did it make you feel, him pushing for sex?' Isla asked.

'It felt cheap, one-sided, like he had used the curry as an excuse to get through the door and expected me to be thankful—the same way as he did when he was dropping sandwiches in at work. It was as though he saw it as his currency for sex, whereas for me, I was expecting a quiet night in on my own that he had disturbed, and then he was making unwanted advances,' Rosina told her.

'You termed it unwanted advances. Did he apply pressure upon you in any instances where you had specifically said no?' Isla asked.

'All the time. I was direct and very clear, but he would not take no for an answer. If he was sexually aroused or wanted to be, then he was going to be satisfied,' Rosina began. 'Most of the time I just wanted it to be over so I could get rid of him or go to sleep.'

'Rosina, if you're very clear that you are stating 'no', but the person does it anyway, whether you are in a relationship or not, there is only one word for it. You do know that, don't you?' Isla challenged her.

'To be honest, I just pushed it to the back of my mind. I know what word you are referring to, but I am not ready to face that side of things yet,' Rosina said honestly.

'That is a typical trauma response to allow yourself to cope in a difficult situation. It is our bodies' inbuilt survival mode to freeze which helps our mind to seek refuge elsewhere or to compartmentalise those memories, so we don't have to face what is happening. From what you have told me over the past three months, Robert's persistent manipulation, coercive behaviour gaslighting tactics have conditioned you to the point he has created indirect compliance,' Isla specified.

'I know. I think from doing the sessions with you, I have finally realised how lucky I am,' Rosina confessed.

'Lucky? Now that is an interesting word to use. Why do you feel you are lucky?' Isla asked, surprised by Rosina's choice of words.

'Lucky because not only have I got to see him for what he is—a danger to women—but I have had the freedom to be able to speak out openly and in a safe environment. I recognise there was no human element to how he treated me and that I was just a pawn to give him what he wanted. Yes, I am hurt, angry and humiliated by the acts he committed against me, but I am free. So, I am very lucky as my beautiful friend Heather was never given that opportunity,' Rosina stated.

'We are coming to the end of our last session now, Rosina, but before we do, can you sum up what you have learnt during our time together?' Isla wondered.

'I have learnt it is OK to say no. It is OK to change my mind if I do not feel up to doing something. I need to set appropriate boundaries, as they are my safety net. I know that toxic situations are not for me, and if something doesn't feel right, I have two legs to walk away. I have learnt I do not need to stay in a relationship just because that is what the other person demands or because of history.'

'I acknowledge that some people may be in the picture for only a season. I don't owe anybody anything, and it is good to let the dead wood float along at their own pace and path downstream. Above all I have learnt that I matter, and it is time to step up to put me first—to not be afraid to step out and try new things and step into what God has for me. A man may have broken my heart, but God can use my brokenness for His glory, so I can trust God to look after my every need as long as I am walking in a right relationship with Him,' Rosina delivered.

'Wow, Rosina, it really has been a pleasure to work with you during the past few months. So, thank you for putting in the time and effort because you have benefited tremendously from when you first began,' Isla told her, getting up. 'Do you give hugs?'

'Absolutely,' Rosina said before continuing, 'I will be forever grateful for our sessions, Isla. I have felt I have been heard here. I have not been judged. You have challenged me appropriately, but more importantly, I have never felt invisible, and I vow to never let anyone degrade me like that ever again!'

As Isla closed the door behind Rosina, she fought hard to hold back the tears, meditating on the transformative experience Rosina had described. Isla was certain that Rosina now had a chance of full recovery to heal from the damage that had been inflicted upon her, and she knew her work was done.

If only she could gain the same success with the other women that Rosina had aptly named this vile man's *Jar of Hearts*.

Chapter 20
Exhaustion
(Josie Bellamy)

November 2022

Josie Bellamy was beside herself, but despite the exhaustion that had consumed her over the previous six months, there was one thing she was now absolutely certain of—she wanted him gone. Gone out of her life, out of her home and the persistent torment of him swirling around inside her head, gone.

The sadness was debilitating, though she couldn't differentiate whether this was due to the acknowledgement that she had wasted three years of her life; the stupidity and humiliation she felt; the loss of her hopes and dreams for the future; or of finally seeing him for what he really was. Maybe it was a mixture of all the above!

It was so clear now how he had played her right from the beginning to the very end, and he would have continued had she not severed all connection with him. She winced at the memory of him quick to declare his wrongdoing, but only when it had been pointed out to him followed by the pleading for 'one more chance,' before professing his fake love and what she had since come to realise were also fake tears, just to manipulate her into giving him his easy life with her back.

The moment recognition had started to prevail was when she had told him for the umpteenth time, 'I cannot continue to do this anymore, Robert.'

'What do you think I can? Do you think I want to keep going round in this same circle either?' he had stated.

'What you don't seem to be getting is the reason we keep going round this same circle is because of you. Each time we are at this point, I communicate clearly what I need from you for this to be a sustainable, healthy relationship but you just agree to get back in the door and then continue regardless. Do you know what it feels like to have your feelings ignored and your boundaries persistently violated?' Josie asked him.

'I don't ignore you. I just want to be with you. What is so wrong with that?' Robert had asked defensively.

'Nothing is wrong with wanting to be together as long as there are positive times apart too,' Josie tried.

'When I go to work, I am racing around to get finished just so I can get back here to be with you. When I call to see Belle, I don't stay long because I want to be back here with you. I think about you all the time. I have never felt like this about anybody. Why is it so wrong to want to be with you?' he asked, perplexed.

'It is not wrong to love someone so deeply that you miss them when you are not with them that is beautiful and develops into a deeper love. However, it is unhealthy behaviour when it occupies your entire thought process, where everything revolves around that one person, and you are preventing them from living their own life. You are not giving me room to breathe; it is stifling and does not provide growth.' Josie tried hard to differentiate between love and obsession.

'I don't get you. All the other women I have ever gone out with would have loved me to spend more time with them, whereas with them, I did my own thing, and I didn't give a damn,' he stated, hurt.

'I think you're missing the point, Robert. It isn't about past relationships, or you making unsubstantial comparisons just to coerce me to comply with accepting your unacceptable behaviour. I am trying to communicate with you that there are two people in this relationship, and if I am meeting your needs and you are meeting your needs, who is there meeting mine?' she tried to plead her case.

'I would give you everything I have got, but it's just not enough, is it?' he said emotionally.

'Robert, it is not about doing more—it is actually about doing less and giving me the opportunity to do more of what I want to do, like spend time with my friends without you gatecrashing the scene. Or allowing me to go for a walk without you, letting me work without the constant interruptions, making yourself scarce so I can rest and recuperate at leisure. I just want to live a life that is peaceful, in a non-confrontational environment in which I can flourish. Surely you can understand that,' she said, exasperated.

'You're making me sound like I have issues when all I want to do is love you,' Robert said, refusing to take anything on board.

'Don't you see? I lose myself in your need for me. It's like having a child glued to my side or a lost puppy walking in my shadow. It is impossible for me to function appropriately, and it's mentally draining having this pressure 24/7. You consume my every waking hour. You do not allow me to breathe, you don't listen, and it is suffocating me—not just on the outside but on the inside too now,' Josie said, exasperated.

'I am sorry I am such a disappointment. Maybe you are right—we should just call it quits altogether then if I am such a disappointment,' Robert said, beginning his pity party.

'Please don't put words into my mouth. I didn't say you were a disappointment. You are a kind, thoughtful, caring man who is exceptionally generous with your time, and I appreciate you as a person, but I do need to spend time on other things. As a human being, we require many facets to thrive, so when you hold on so tightly, the result is like being a caged bird with my wings clipped. I need more so that I can be happy in my relationships—both with you and everyone else around me,' Josie said honestly.

'So, what you are saying is I am not enough for you,' Robert threw back, only hearing what he wanted to hear.

'Robert, I think we are going around in circles again. Maybe we are just at different stages in our lives or want different things—I don't know. But it feels like unless I tell you what you want to hear, you are closed off,' Josie said defeatedly.

'We are not at different stages! I love you more than I have ever loved anyone else-even my wife. It's crazy just how much, but you always push me away. Is it just your way of treating me mean so it will keep me keen?' he accused.

'Why on earth would you say that? I am trying to resolve the conflict, and throwing comments like that is so unhelpful,' Josie said confused.

'You started it?' he argued.

'Perhaps we should take a couple of days to really evaluate what we both want, what we are individually prepared to accept, and see if we can agree on a way forward,' Josie offered, not wanting it to turn into another of Robert's pity parties.

'You always do that—send me away like I am a naughty schoolboy, shoving me out and pushing me away. How are we supposed to sort anything out when you won't even talk to me? You do this every time!' Robert demanded.

'I am not doing anything of the kind. I am merely suggesting that we can take the time to calm down, reflect upon our needs and seek a potential way forward. It is not a punishment. I am trying to protect our relationship and each other from unnecessary conflict,' Josie tried to reason.

'You say that, but I bet as soon as my back is turned, you will be ringing Louise and going for a few beers with her,' he accused.

'Robert, this is one of the issues I have just stated that you don't allow me to go out with my friends. Why is it so difficult for you?' she enquired.

'Probably because you will both be having a right laugh at my expense,' he retorted.

'Is that what you really think? Seriously? If I did go and have a couple of drinks with her, it would be to put some distance between the conversation, we have just had in my home so it isn't lingering here,' Josie was losing the will to keep explaining herself.

'I will go if you want me to, I don't want to stay anywhere I am not wanted, but I am not going home,' he said childishly.

'Where you go is up to you—I respect that. But also, respect my choices and decisions too. It isn't nice when you stipulate that you wouldn't be happy with what I might choose to do in the hope it will prevent me from doing it. That is tantamount to indirect control and not conducive to us developing a healthy relationship,' Josie pointed out.

'So now I am controlling?' Robert said, alarmed at Josie's choice of words.

'Robert, you can be very controlling. Everything I do is controlled by you— who I see, where I go and even what I eat!' Josie stated.

'What you eat? That's a bit farfetched,' he scoffed.

'No, Robert, it's not. If I go shopping without you, I get to choose things I want to eat, but even then, I focus more on your needs because I know you will moan excessively if you don't get what you want. If you go shopping, you buy a whole host of stuff for yourself, but I am lucky if I even get a salad and potatoes—nothing else for a week's shop. I have to make do. If you offer to go for just one thing in particular, I know to be specific about exactly which one I want, yet you always buy the opposite regardless.'

'Inevitably, this approach conditions people to neither trust you to get it right but also to never ask, and so that's another job you don't have to have any responsibility for. Bingo, I am now doing your shopping for you. It was the same with your washing or any help around the house. You always find a way to do it badly or break something to condition me to do it for you. I am not your mother, and you're not a child, but this is the measure of our relationship, which I am persistently feeling is one-sided. Hence, I am backed into a corner by being overburdened at your lack of care for me, and if I dare to try and balance the odds, I am met with such resistance,' Josie finally unburdened herself.

Robert's forehead began to twitch up and down, his blinking becoming more rapid as he attempted to conceal the anger which was evidently seething beneath the surface. He was barely able to control himself from lashing out, so switched to the breathing exercise he had learnt from his anger management classes, whilst also clenching and opening his fists.

Josie instantly made an excuse that she needed to use the toilet, remembering Robert's divulgence of being handy with his fists as a young man.

When she returned, she was confused to find him making a cuppa and acting as though the conversation they had just engaged in hadn't happened. It disturbed Josie how Robert seemed to switch from one extreme to another so quickly and often without warning, so she decided to tread very carefully.

'Don't make me one, I am going to run a bath,' she said light-heartedly and then, as she walked out of the kitchen, 'I will see you in a couple of days.' And she let the door close behind her, hoping against hope he would just leave.

Once upstairs, she listened carefully to him banging the kettle down into its cradle and slamming the fridge door. She cracked open the bathroom window not only to allow the steam to evaporate but to also gauge the exact moment he left so she could run down and lock the door behind him.

It annoyed her that she had to continually tread on eggshells when he was around—navigating his emotions, being forced to justify her feelings, and that he made her feel so uncomfortable in her own home.

She had just wanted a loving, equal relationship in the beginning, but he wasn't capable of that, she was sure. And now, after months and months of the same rubbish, she just wanted him gone.

She silently prayed for his exit but then heard him running up the stairs, so she slid the bolt on the bathroom door into place.

'I was thinking of ordering a Chinese. Do you want me to pick you one up too?' he asked.

'No, thank you. I am going to have a bath and go straight to bed, but enjoy yours,' she said, trying to remain cordial, knowing full well he was trying his Mr Nice Guy act so that by the time he had got it and returned, she may let him stay.

Josie had been hoodwinked too many times, and the only way to deal with him was to not waiver. If he saw any chink in her armour, he was straight on it.

This had been one of hundreds of experiences she'd had the misfortune of dealing with, regarding Robert. She really could kick herself.

It was unfathomable to her how an intelligent woman like herself could have fallen for this con man who was only interested in a lifestyle that he could not provide for himself. Josie felt like she had experienced every trick in the book facilitated by Robert.

Though she knew that even when he had gone through the process of losing her, the same pattern emerged again the next time. He would plead, cry, use any attempts he could think of to emotionally blackmail her—anything to talk her around but nothing would change.

Sure, he would be on his best behaviour for a couple of days until she lowered her guard, and then it was business as usual.

She had read somewhere on Facebook that 'There is nothing more convincing than a narcissist who needs a place to live.'

What a fool she was to think he could have just loved her for her. The ease of his charm, the flattery of his words, the initial explosive 'love-bombing' techniques. How he had consumed her with his ultimate expressions of love.

Never had he 'met anyone like her before in his life.' Convincing her they were 'meant to be together,' she was his soulmate, and 'where had she been all of his life?'

Inevitably, his previous relationship had meant nothing to him, and he had only stayed with her due to them having a child together. He explained that they had only got together because his wife had passed away and, being left with a young child to bring up alone, she had presented as a care provider for the child.

Josie realised, on that admission alone, she should have run for the hills.

After all, it showed he saw women as a commodity to make his life easier. Even his mother, who had apparently bent over backwards for him and looked after Belle as though she were her own, was described as being a nuisance who interfered too much.

At the time, Josie had found his revelation quite harsh, as in these circumstances everyone just pulls together. But no, Robert hated the way she arranged her clothes, got in the way and outstayed her welcome.

He didn't want to have responsibility for Belle and actually described how he had put his partner's children before his own.

These should have been warning signs, especially as he was prepared to go on holiday with his new partner and her children, leaving someone else to look after Belle at home.

When Josie reflected on the multitude of scenarios he had described, her thoughts immediately checked into how she could support him to change those behaviours in order to give his daughter the experience of being included in a loving family atmosphere.

At one point, Josie's own son had relinquished his large bedroom space so it could be emptied, freshly painted and then a new carpet fitted so she had the opportunity to be included. However, Robert didn't want Belle to be included, as this would instigate a shift in everyone's focus away from him, and he wasn't going to risk a threat to his own security within this newfound family.

Josie had hoped that through guidance, support, advice, love and the setting of positive examples, he would ultimately respond more positively. At first, he pretended to respond, but like all true narcissists, he was unable to remain consistent.

Robert complained about everything from the food he had to buy for Belle, her personality, her responses to his unacceptable attitude towards her, that she was lazy, messy and so much more. When Josie thought back now, the list actually seemed endless.

Even when Josie had tried to appeal to his love for his wife and how she might view the way he showed disrespect for Belle, it still made no difference. All Josie could do was step in the gap for her by building her confidence, giving her a voice to develop her self-worth, acknowledging her struggles, praising her achievements and empowering her to make positive choices and decisions for her own life.

This had been particularly hard as Robert had described how his mother had continually disempowered her to the point of not allowing her to grow or even use the toilet independently. The similarities of being in a relationship with Robert were indicative of his mother's suffocating and overbearing attempts to force reliance and strip this beautiful young woman of her rights as a human being.

Josie felt sick at the systematic and lengthy attempts Robert made to overpower, consume and dominate her life—pouring in his nothingness and taking her everything until her very soul now felt polluted.

'You're the only woman who has the ability to make me incessantly angry and then defuse it instantly by reducing me to laughter,' Robert began. 'I have never given a shit about anyone, ever. I have always done what I wanted when I wanted, I didn't care; I just did my own thing. My attitude was, 'You're living in my house, so it's my rules take it or get out.' But with you, I am crazy in love with you, and yet you don't fall at my feet.'

'If that is what you are looking for, you have picked the wrong girl this time because the difference with me and all the rest is that I don't *need* you,' Josie delivered strongly.

At the time Josie had grabbed the dogs' lead and left. She'd no longer had the will to keep rotating around the same problematic wheel that bumped the same potholes over and over again.

He reminded her of the *Homer Simpson* clip where he is hanging in mid-air and there are some cans of beer next to him that Homer is desperate for. Homer reaches for them and is electrocuted. He wants the beer so much that he reaches out again and, inevitably, he is electrocuted a second time—and a third.

It was the same situation and the same action but for some reason, he thought the outcome was going to be different. His wants dominated and controlled how he behaved, and despite the pain it induced, he was unable or unwilling to seek a different action in order to change the situation.

Robert was exactly the same. These behaviours, and possibly words, had worked in his past relationships, so he was simply reproducing rather than acknowledging he was destroying their relationship. Josie did not want to be the collateral damage in his ignorance to look outside the box, as she was so exhausted mentally and emotionally.

Why couldn't he see how much she had bent to compromise instead of favouring only what he wanted—unlike him, who expected everything his own way, always at her expense?

She had tried on so many occasions to communicate with him, to educate him on what was and was not acceptable. Each time he would say all the right words but then career off like a steam train, railroading down the tracks to the non-negotiable station of 'Only Robert Matters.'

It astounded her how each time she stepped off the carousel, he would display the same level of shock, as though he couldn't have predicted the same outcome with the same behaviours.

As Josie eased herself down into the bath water, she gave that thought a little more time to sink in. Wasn't she doing exactly the same—expecting him to change—yet she wasn't doing anything differently other than wanting him to get it?

Maybe he just did not have the mental capacity, and her giving him chance after chance to wake up and simply change was beyond his capabilities.

What she needed to come to terms with was the fact that he wasn't the man for her, despite her love for him, and he simply could not give her the deep, meaningful relationship that she was after. Yes, he could talk the talk, but he had probably just watched too many romcoms, repeating the lead man's actions without having any real substance.

At the end of the day, how he was treating her was only what she was allowing, so therefore she needed to cut her losses and get out of there.

She had no idea what other people had let him get away with, but she wasn't playing this game any longer, regardless of the flannel he was giving her.

He was not what she wanted, and he was certainly not what she needed either. So today, come what may, was his last day.

Or so she thought. But Mr Right, who turned out to be Mr So Wrong, would continue his charades for a further six months—keeping his foot in the door and holding on as Mr Right Now.

Chapter 21
Devastation
(Josie Bellamy)

June 2023

Josie Bellamy no longer had the capability nor inclination to hold back the tears that flowed like the persistence of a bubbling beck. For months, she had perfected the ability to separate and individually compress the multitude of incidents that now bellowed out the truth to her. Why had she allowed herself to fragment so willingly, not wanting to attach any emotion? Was it for fear that she might, in some small way, reveal the inner depths of her own secret despair? Or was it simply the fact that she could not face the truth, which was now literally screaming into her face?

The unrelenting voice continued to mock her: *You, Josie Bellamy, have been the subject of some elaborate con.*

She tried in vain to shake it away, tormented by its hysterical laughter as the onslaught continued to taunt her fragile mind. 'Leave me alone,' she said aloud to no one in particular, worn down by her own repetitive mental self-abuse. She took a deep breath and blinked away the tears that obscured her vision, only for them to be instantly replaced.

Her shoulders began to rise as another involuntary sob forced its way out—Josie now powerless to prevent the expulsion of the pain that was beginning to overwhelm her, again. The only question that emanated was, why? Like every other victim that had ever lived, Josie continued to examine in the minutest detail every inch of the last three years in the hope that, somehow, she had been mistaken.

She wanted to believe him. She had needed to believe him. Yet she knew, beyond a shadow of a doubt, that despite her scrutiny, the truth remained: it was just about money and the lifestyle she could give him. The moment she had been able to face this fact, everything else about him had instantly slotted into place like the coins of a self-checkout.

When she took away his lying, manipulative words and false promises, she was left with the facts. It was her house he had lived in, her apartment in Spain he had lazed his days away in, her top-of-the-range car that he had driven and her pocket they had continually delved into.

Yes, she reasoned, he had bought shopping, but on examination, these were persistently things just for himself. Josie recalled his selfish behaviour of hiding food to ensure no one else but he could eat it—like hiding things in really obscure places and then going off on one if the kids had made it their mission to re-hide it elsewhere as a joke because they, too, found his behaviour ridiculous.

Josie shook her head in despair. Hadn't it been their home which he had invited himself to inhabit without actually being asked to do so? In childish, wasteful retaliation, he would then only purchase food that he knew they didn't like. *Oh well, more for me then.*

This had proved to be indicative of his whole core: as long as his needs were met, then no one else mattered, not really. How stupid and naive she had been to accept his fading, pretty-boy face, actually grateful for the miserly £26 per week he had gifted towards the household bills. Blind that she was now doing his laundry, supporting him into a successful career and a worthwhile lifestyle—all without any personal intent.

She kicked herself for not paying closer attention to these warning signs and of merely dismissing them at the time as being behavioural traits he would ditch when he had time to reflect. He didn't, Josie could now clearly see that unless he'd been gaining from a situation in some positive way, he had shown no interest.

It was hard for her to understand how she had been so gullible to fall for his 'woe is me' act, other than he had played upon her good nature. Josie meditated on those memories for a while before re-acknowledging that she would much rather be the kind, open, honest, loving and compassionate person she was any day of the week than the parasite he had turned out to be.

She recalled how she had first bumped into this man whilst he was out riding his bike with his son the epitome of father-and-son togetherness. This was one of the many guises he would hide behind: doting father, perfect partner, of being financially stable, a hard worker, provider, potential husband and stepfather.

He was none of these. Everything was just a smoke screen to attain her lifestyle one he could never provide for himself. In fact, he would soon morph himself into being her perfect partner, integrating himself masterfully within her life so effortlessly. It was all part of his expertly driven plan to make her believe he was everything she had ever wanted.

He would intentionally become indispensable, moving himself into her home without her even realising that she had been chosen because she fitted his modus operandi: a middle-aged woman who lived in a big house, was really popular, but more importantly had money.

He had nothing, no job, no prospects, no friends, was heavily in debt and was a loner. All he had to do was create the opportunity to accidentally-on-purpose bump into her.

Unlike a lot of his other targets, this had proved difficult because Josie had shown no interest and didn't succumb to his usual, proven track record attempts. The fact that she had children was a huge advantage that he could use in his favour to manipulate his doting dad's image. So, it was game on.

Josie wanted to shout out to the memory, 'Run, Josie, get away as fast as you can!' But, of course, it had been too late. Much to Josie's ignorance, his orchestrated plan had been set in motion several months prior when he had first started stalking her social media pages.

Also, unknowingly, he had secretly placed himself close by, eerily watching her every move as she danced, sang and enjoyed her friendship base. He wanted her, he was going to have her, and no one was going to stop him.

Josie felt physically sick at the thought of having her emotions so easily manipulated. How had she become so helplessly in love with what had turned out to have been created by the figment of her stimulated imagination?

How effortlessly he delivered the words that his lying lips had told to so many women before her—that *he had never met anyone like her before in his life*. How he *could not believe how they hadn't met before.* He even went to the extent of mirroring some of her life experiences for added effect, just to mimic sympathy.

He was good at that, mimicking emotions but never really having the ability to feel.

What Josie Bellamy did not know was that she was dealing with a narcissistic psychopath who was out for one thing: to have *his* needs met in any form possible.

It will take Josie Bellamy three years to recognise that this seemingly charming man, whom she thought she had waited her whole life to meet, was nothing more than a con artist.

Under the surface of his elaborate game was a mass of fake tears, controlled emotions, captivating lies and empty promises. Anything and everything would be used to his advantage. And that little boy she had first seen him riding his bike with? Well, he was just another pawn who would be discarded at will, along with anyone else if it enabled him to reach his goal. He was like a chameleon who could change depending on the company he kept.

Josie wished she hadn't been so blinded by his act of the world being his stage to play any given role. She reprimanded herself. Wasn't she supposed to be an intelligent woman? How could she have fallen hook, line and sinker for an image that he had personified? Was she really that desperate to be loved? Had he seen something in her that made her easy prey? Had her good nature—of wanting to see the best in everyone and wanting to live a peaceful life—been used against her?

As the tears continued to flow, so did Josie's thoughts, over and over again, round and round in circles. She shuddered at the memory of his hands on her body, of his tongue greedily exploring her and the staleness of his drunken breath as he lay exposed next to her.

She brought her knees up to her chest, then wrapped both her arms around the calf area, hugging herself and slightly rocking in a feeble attempt to afford herself some measure of comfort in the absence of anybody else. She contemplated the silence, which magnified her loneliness despite her so-called friend being sat inside the apartment, immune and disinterested to her grief. It had been so difficult for Josie to finally open up, to admit the truth behind her seemingly perfect relationship, to reveal the gravity of her situation to Louise.

At first, she had seemed receptive, almost caring, but maybe Josie had been mistaken and it was just her friend's shock. Time had revealed that Louise had absolutely no interest at all in Josie's sorrow and definitely did not have the capacity nor capability of extending any hand of compassion, genuine love or understanding. In fact, time would reveal huge similarities between Louise and Robert in their self-centredness and inability to connect to another human being.

Josie Bellamy could not feel any more alone than she did right at that moment at the recognition of all the people who were in her life but who had never stepped in the gap for her as she had so fearlessly for them. Here she was: the positive influencer, the embracer of inclusion, the dedicated friend, financial supporter and advisor to so many others through the ups and downs of their lives—and yet, in her worst trauma, she had absolutely no one. Abandoned, ignored and alone with her thoughts, her pain, distress and violating memories began to consume her. In her brokenness, Josie finally cried out to God, almost accusing Him of also abandoning her.

In the midst of her sorrow, a miraculous thought dropped into her mind—of that one person who had the potential to lift her spirits. In sheer desperation, she took out her phone, brushing aside her tears to see her contact list more clearly for that one specific lady's number. Josie longed to hear the elderly lady's voice, yearned to have her words of wisdom imparted into her soul—to be reminded that despite her failings, she had a God who could conquer all things.

Unable to locate the number she required, she began frantically reading through her messages, unable to logically contemplate the simplicity of highlighting the bearers' details at the top of the page. In her frenzied state to quench her desire to hear her voice, Josie decided to message another lady from church. Despite her incoherent written ramblings, Josie soon had the number she required. But now the dilemma was whether she should actually bother the older lady. After all, what would she say? How would she explain the situation? And worse still was the underlying, nagging fear of judgement and critical condemnation?

No, she was not going to let the enemy take its foothold in her mind she had to capture those negative thoughts and fix her mind on what was true. This beautiful, wise lady would surround her with the blessings of God's word to uplift and strengthen her, and this was exactly what she needed right now. Before she could talk herself out of it any longer, Josie pressed the call button and with a racing heart, she waited in anticipation.

'Hello?' said the shaky voice at the end of the line.

'Hi, Delia, it's Josie—from church,' Josie mustered, trying desperately to keep her emotions in check.

'Hello, love—oh, how wonderful to hear your voice! How is your holiday going? Are you having lovely weather? I bet it is hot, isn't it?' Delia delivered triumphantly.

There was a silence that Josie no longer felt she could fill. After a short pause, Delia spoke with such tenderness, 'Josie, are you OK, love?'

'No, Delia. It's like all hell has been let loose and I am getting battered by every spiritual attack from all directions,' Josie admitted.

'I am here to listen, love, but if you don't feel you can share the details, that's OK too. Just know I am here to support you in any way I can,' Delia offered.

'I think I just wanted to hear your voice, Delia to know I am not alone and that I can get through this,' Josie said.

'You can get through all things in Christ who strengthens you (Philippians 4:13). It may not look like it at this moment, but stand firm on Him. Take all your troubles to Him, Josie, and lay it at His feet, for his yoke is easy (Matthew 11:28). Remember, you must give your worries to the Lord and He will take care of you. He will never let good people down (Psalms 55:22),' Delia softly urged.

'Thank you, Delia. Just hearing your voice and loving words of support is enough to keep me sustained,' Josie told her.

'I thought you were in Greece with your friend, love?' Delia enquired.

'I thought I was too, but ever since we arrived, she has done nothing but sit on the end of the settee with her face in her phone. She neither speaks nor acknowledges my presence. She is locked into her phone at the expense of everything, it is mind-bending,' Josie revealed.

'Maybe you have chosen the wrong person to go with, love?' Delia queried.

'I was trying to give her a holiday and thought we could be supportive of one another, but she has basically cut all communication by using the phone as a barrier. To be honest, everyone had warned me that she could be quite ignorant, and she herself has told me she does use her phone to do this to stop people talking to her,' Josie confessed.

'I am sure she must have her reasons, love, but it seems a very cruel and unkind way to treat you especially when she is enjoying your hospitality,' Delia reminded Josie.

'To be honest, Delia, I would rather have been here on my own. At least I wouldn't feel like I was walking on eggshells, and nor would it have created this much deeper void within me,' Josie admitted. 'I literally cannot stop crying, and her disdain for me is making me feel like I don't want to be here anymore.'

'Oh, Josie, don't talk like that, love. Surely it isn't that bad?' Delia responded, alarmed.

'It is though, Delia. Without going into too much detail, I have finally told the police about what Robert has been doing. Just before we flew here, I was called into the police station at 06:30 to conduct a four-hour police interview on video. I am literally beside myself, broken and so very alone. I am exhausted and, worse still, ashamed!' Josie trailed off, her tears trickling down her already reddened, blotchy-stained face.

After a moment of silence, Delia offered the only thing, she could. 'Would you like me to pray for you, Josie?' she asked.

'Yes, please,' Josie managed to whisper through her tears.

'Jesus, I pray that you surround Josie right now. I don't profess to know what is going on, but I know that you do. God, I ask that you strengthen Josie mentally, physically and spiritually. Please restore her emotionally. We ask you to bind all things that are not of you, and I declare that we have faith that you will use all these things for Josie's greater good. I thank you that you are the God of hope, the God of peace. Be Josie's comfort in her distress and restore her in your precious, wonderful name. Amen!' Delia proclaimed.

'Thank you, my darling. I appreciate your kind words of support,' Josie told her friend.

'I will be keeping you covered in prayer, Josie. God bless, beautiful lady,' Delia finished.

Feeling the protective measure of both this lady's love and God's grace, Josie decided she needed to have a walk up to the little church along the narrow, cobbled streets of Plaka in Athens to take in the Acropolis.

When she entered the small apartment, she was not disappointed to find Louise still sitting at the corner of the settee that they had built together, with her face still on her phone. When Louise didn't even bother to look up in acknowledgement of Josie's sudden presence, a decision was made on the spot. Like Robert, this woman would never again take advantage of her goodness.

From now on, things would be on Josie's terms, and no longer would she extend the hand of kindness to this woman who so expectantly just took everything on offer but who gave nothing—not even mediocre friendship. Feeling gutted again, Josie collected her bag, gave her face a quick rinse, then heard the kettle click off, having reached its boiling point. On her return to the lounge, Josie was astounded to see Louise had helped herself to a cuppa without even enquiring if she wanted one.

Ironically, at the side of the microwave were the bundle of receipts from the shopping that Josie had paid for and was still awaiting Louise's half. Josie's lip curled in disgusted contempt for the woman she had actively supported both financially and emotionally for over two years whilst everyone else had given her a wide berth. Josie was beginning to understand why. She had been nothing less than a leech too. Did she think no one had noticed how she had perfected her ability to hold on to her pint and then quickly down it if someone else was paying, feigning surprise?

Josie had overlooked so many of Louise's negative traits in order to simply be a friend to her. However, to callously withhold the hand of friendship when Josie was in desperate need was something she couldn't ignore. Unfortunately, a Pandora's Box had been opened, exposing not only Robert and Louise's true identities but a lot of dead wood that Josie had invested too much time in for far too long. Regardless of her current situation, Josie knew she needed to embrace these changes to restore her own self-worth. So, despite how difficult things were right now, Josie maintained a heart of gratitude.

The temperature outside seemed to have risen slightly as Josie made her way across the communal courtyard with its ornately tiled fountain, terracotta tiles and central water feature. Josie took a moment to sit on one of the three stone benches that were neatly placed between the overhanging palm trees. She glanced up towards her terrace and sat observing the beige-coloured parasol protruding above the green railings. The warm breeze was titivating its edges like one of Ken Dodd's tickling sticks. She loved the effect this peaceful place had upon her when she allowed it.

No longer requiring the exercise in the 39-degrees heat, she decided to make her way towards the communal pool, hoping that everyone else would have returned to their apartments by now. Unfortunately, this was not the case, so Josie made her way down the steps to the toddler's splash pool. At least here, she could enjoy some degree of privacy. Josie had always been a social butterfly, but today she just wanted to melt into the background and to be left alone with her thoughts.

The pool was cooler than she had expected, but nevertheless, she kicked off her purple flip-flops and stepped into its inviting embrace. The water barely covered her knees, but it was enough to soothe her aching feet. She walked back and forth, silently praying to herself, cutting through the water, which caused a rippling effect like a migratory birds' V-formation as she propelled herself forward.

Oblivious to anything else around her, Josie seated herself at the edge of the pool, its rounded lip neatly supporting the crevice of her knees. Finally succumbing to her environment, she eased herself down until she was lying on the harsh stone floor, its roughness coarse to the touch. Closing her eyes and slightly tilting her head back to feel the sun, she began to relax in the heat of its rays, the large leaves of a nearby palm intermittently casting shadows across her face.

The sound of passing traffic below gave the illusion of rushing water created by the purr of their engines, so Josie was more than able to convince herself that she was by the sea. Relaxed by the tranquillity of her surroundings, she tuned in to the slight breeze gently caressing the length of her body as it persistently came across her in warm waves, as though someone was carefully motioning a giant fan back and forth.

She smiled at the thought of being some rich entrepreneur able to afford such pampering services rather than melting in the ever-increasing heat. Above her, Josie was stirred by the delightful excitement of children being thrown into the pool despite their unconvincing protests. She decided to take herself back up the steps at least she would be able to enjoy the scene, even if she would not join in.

Josie laid her towel across the scorching slabs of stone that surrounded the pool—now the only space available to her—and secretly studied the people in her midst, careful not to draw attention to herself. Two ladies were strategically propped up, facing directly towards the sun at opposite sides of the smaller-than-average pool. Another lady, in a bright yellow bikini sporting matching mirror-reflective sunglasses, leisurely rested upon a pink inflatable bed upon the surface of the pool.

How Josie hated mirror-like glasses, which had a habit of projecting piercing shards of light periodically her way whenever the woman looked in her direction. Maybe she knew that Josie was surveying her, so she quickly averted her gaze and considered the row of beds that were clothed with towels yet did not seem to have their owners in the nearby vicinity.

It mystified Josie immensely why hotels always displayed signs stating sunbeds could not be reserved and that any towels that were left would be removed—but never were. It generated the same pointless threat parents issued to misbehaving children: that if they didn't behave, then they wouldn't get any sweets.

It always made Josie want to scream, 'The reason your child is defying your command is because they know your words are simply an empty threat.' Surely parents needed to be clear and say what they meant. That way, little Jimmy would know that no meant no.

To Josie, it was plain and simple: if they were already misbehaving, they didn't deserve any sweets. Surely the adult could control their little darlings without using bargaining tools. If they acted without compromise, the child would have clear guidelines, and then there would be no pushing of boundaries because they would know where they stood.

Josie had always lived by the underwritten rule: IF you behave THEN you get a treat, and WHEN you do as you are asked THEN you can have this. No negotiation—just a simple message of who was in control and the guidelines within which to operate to keep everyone safe, happy and healthy.

Her thoughts slid towards Robert, wondering if this had been part of his early teachings, or had his parents simply allowed him to dictate what he was and was not going to do, and this was why he thought he could do what he wanted at everyone else's expense.

From what she had experienced with him, he did not respect the need for boundaries, and he viewed everything she tried to implement in this area as a rebuke. When she had requested space for just a couple of days, he had taken it so personally—like she was excluding him or that it was some sort of punishment.

Josie found it crazy that she'd had to fight for the right to be alone, to rest, recharge, to maybe spend time doing something that she enjoyed, like reading a book or going on a solitary walk, to engage in her writing, to paint or to see friends. Yet she had been continually denied these pleasures by his coercive manipulation, as though he was a barrister pleading a case.

His subsequent acts of being downtrodden, sulking or saying inappropriate things just to make her feel guilty so she would back down and make him the centre of her universe had been nothing less than draining. For instance, having finally negotiated that on a Monday he would go home for 48 hours, when the time arrived, he would behave horrendously, mocking her: 'Just look at her, so happy because she is sending me home.'

Josie found his behaviour ridiculous. So unrelenting, Josie just let him moan, giving him no springboard on which to provoke an argument. She was so determined he would not change her mind she began to tune him out until he had finally left, despite him stipulating vehemently that he would rather book into a hotel than go back to his own house. He knew damn well that Josie was a good steward with her money and hated unnecessary, wasteful expenditure. But, having used this tactic several times before to get his own way, it had lost its power.

Josie smiled as she pictured herself telling him he was the master of his own universe, who also had choices just as she did. So, she reinforced that she would see him on the Wednesday before closing the door behind him. How she had felt empowered at the time! But now, contemplating things, it did feel like his patterns of behaviour were something he had perhaps got away with as a child. Maybe if he'd had a firmer hand and better direction, he wouldn't still be using the same techniques that had gotten him exactly what he had wanted.

Josie was perplexed. This was not something that she would have accepted in her own children, so why should she be forced to be comfortable with this in a grown man, especially as she continually communicated effectively with him? Josie had noted that his responses had barely changed throughout their relationship, with him always leaning towards the emotional blackmail element—playing her feelings—and when all else failed, the tears came. The first time it had happened, she had instantly softened by his outpouring of seemingly deep emotion. She hadn't realised at the time how gullible she had been, nor how susceptible she had become to this style of his manipulation, until she had seen the smirk across his face when she had told him to put away the fake tears.

She had instantly berated herself, feeling terrible for her lack of empathy as though she had somehow been cruel, until the smirk, a tilt of the head and an immediate, complete composure. That had been the exact moment the gloves were off, and Josie vowed to put her foot down, but then he had suddenly changed tact. Apparently, he professed to love the fact that she could give him a kick up the backside, as it made him realise the only person he was hurting was himself by being excluded. Josie had wrongly believed he was praising her when, in fact, what he was telling her was he only saw things from his own perspective and how it affected him.

Robert Day Jr was incapable of understanding that how he behaved affected Josie immensely. He had hurt her to the point she was inwardly screaming, whilst the same wheels kept turning, careering her along the same route as an unstoppable cargo train rattling down the same track.

As she sat on her fluffy towel the hard surface below, she couldn't help comparing the seemingly soft exterior of Robert in contrast to the hard heart that lay below.

She dreamily watched a young couple as they playfully splashed about in the cool water before he lovingly pulled her to him. Josie sighed, saddened that the love they shared had not been a sustaining love that she could have enjoyed, as opposed to the hurt she was nursing like a newborn child. Despite her experiences with Robert, she had loved him like she had never loved anyone else before. Maybe that was why she had so readily believed his lies.

She had thought they were a perfect fit, that he was the final piece to her jigsaw when, in reality, the picture she had put together had never existed. She mused over the times she had tried to resist his control, finally developing an unwillingness to accept the unacceptable, whilst he refused to try to comprehend. Instead, he favoured the position that she was simply preventing him from getting what he wanted, rather than her trying to protect herself from the unhealthy toxicity of his control.

A new wave of longing swept across her as she contemplated the same couple who had now returned to their sunbeds, where he had wrapped her in a towel, their eyes locked together, mesmerised with one another. Oh, how she had loved to catch those moments, gazing upon Robert as they had sat with friends in a beer garden or watching him having fun and letting his hair down. She had loved his smile, the upward twitch of his forehead as he had sat in deep contemplation, working across the table from her, unaware of the warmth it created within her.

She would smile to herself as he furiously jotted down figures, pressing the pen so hard upon the paper that it indented the sheets below. She had loved to see his car reverse into the drive and watch him walk along the front of the house, where she would secretly marvel, doting upon how much he loved her and that they would be together forever, or so she had thought.

Josie had never had a love so fulfilling, so intense, consuming her every essence, and therefore she had been proud that he was hers and she was his. Josie believed she had found her one true love, her soul mate the person she had waited her entire life for. How stupid she felt now.

How could she have been so naive to have believed it had finally been her turn to have found love and to be loved, to never be alone or have to go to gatherings without a +1 again? At the time, it had amazed her that this dark, handsome fellow fancied her, and oh, how wonderful it had felt to feel desired, to be seen, to be validated and no longer invisible. Well, that was what he had demonstrated during the first 12 months because that was what he had wanted her to believe.

How deluded! She was the same insignificant, unappreciated, nothingness whose piece of the jigsaw puzzle certainly didn't fit anywhere into the puzzle that he had initially presented her with. No, unbeknown to her, he would be exposed as a silver-lipped jackal who was, as the saying goes, 'far too good to be true'.

She wondered now if it had been some deep-rooted ego that had generated a self-obsessed yearning that she might have deserved to meet her prince charming or enjoy the happy-ever-after princess stories she read from her childhood. Disheartened, she had come to realise they were just stories, and no one was going to rescue her from the mundanity of everyday life.

What was abundantly clear to her now was that Robert Day Jr was nothing more than a predatorial, self-seeking parasite that fed off the insecurities of women, like a paedophile segregating his next victim. This epiphany had made her wonder if she had been wearing her weaknesses so plainly, like a coat of armour, just ready for his exploitation.

An image perforated her brain of a wolf in sheep's clothing, slithering in beside her, his salivating serpent's tongue slipping in and out of his greedy mouth. How black and cold is the heart of the Godless child when the enemies spawn sits in wait to capture the innocent, to feed and quench the thirst of their sordid desires.

Yet the audience applauds the foolish, clumsy, funny displays of the charismatic newcomer who seems to hold court, entertaining and fitting in well. Where have they been? Where did they come from to know me so well, to be the epitome of the one I have always longed for? How laughable it must have been to be fooled by the foolish man, finding his words fruitful and his antics heart-warming, whilst all along he laughed beneath the cloak of deceit.

Josie's head was beginning to run down the same old cul-de-sac of no return, so, like the little robotic car she had once bought for Eden, she rebounded from the wall and decided to propel herself in the opposite direction by taking a swim.

The children were now huddled together enjoying a packed lunch, the loved-up couple were lying back yet still held hands, and the woman with the mirror glasses had her head in a book. Josie livened her senses with a cold shower prior to entering the pool, the sharpness of the icy droplets releasing an involuntary shriek, but no one seemed to notice. She cleared the newly cut grass clippings from her feet before stepping onto the concrete slabs and followed the path to the steps at the shallowest part of the pool. The water was pleasantly warm in contrast to the temperature of the shower, so she was able to walk straight in before slipping fully beneath the water and then pushing herself off from the bottom step.

Josie gracefully stretched out her hands in front of her, sweeping them out to the side before snapping them up in front of her chest and back out again, with her legs moving in sync. The breaststroke was her most favoured action as she liked to look ahead along with being able to see everything beside her. She cut through the water, noting the sound and feeling its pull against her hands, watching the reflection of the sun upon the tiny mountain peaks she was creating as she moved along. Once she had completed her daily twenty lengths, she spun around onto her back and positioned herself in front of one of the pools jets by the steps so that she could enjoy its powerful massage along her shoulders.

She breathed in the calmness, feeling like a boat tethered to its jetty, bobbing along the water's edge. Anyone observing her would probably think she hadn't a care in the world when, in fact, the peace she may be demonstrating had not reached the pit of vipers attacking one another in her stomach. Had she done the right thing in reporting him? What if the police didn't do anything? Worse still, what if he lied? Would she end up having to go to court and then be forced to stand alone in the witness box and tell everyone what he had done to her?

Josie closed her eyes, unable to fathom how the man she had loved hated her to such a degree that he could have committed the acts upon her that he had. Was she to blame, or had she made it clear to him that she was not a willing participant? She shook the intrusive thoughts away.

Why was she questioning herself? *Stop trying to make excuses for him, Josie. He knew full well what he was doing was wrong because you told him repeatedly, and that was why he would make excuses that he had to have you because he loved you so much. It was a lie, Josie. He didn't love you, nor did he care about how it might affect you either then or now. So, stop showing him such mercy, or worrying about how he will feel when the police arrest him. He is to blame, and he deserves all he gets.*

Josie thought of the most crucial of times she had tried to protect her mental health from his onslaught of pressure to give him what he wanted or to stop the barrage of his merciless attacks but right now, she just wanted to silence the noise within her head.

She gently wiggled her legs up and down, feeling the support of the water around her body assisting her to keep afloat. But this was physical; would she be strong enough to mentally get through what she was facing?

Perhaps if she just concentrated on taking it day by day, as she had been doing, and maintained a heart of gratitude for what she had rather than what she didn't have, it would help. Josie closed her eyes and let her head relax back into the water, muffling the environmental sounds so she could tune in to God in prayer.

'Lord, I asked you to reveal to me exactly who Robert Day Jr was, and you have most certainly done that. You may not have revealed what I had thought, which was that I was wrong about him in the confusion he had generated, but nevertheless, I am glad I have seen the unseen. I know you can use my brokenness for my good and for the good of others, so I ask that you heal me sufficiently so that I may be an instrument in your work. I thank you for this place, I thank you for the temperature of the sun, the beautiful landscape, and the people you put in my midst to help me at this time—like Delia. I pray for Louise, that she may find it within her to enjoy this place, and yes, I even pray for Robert. The path that he has chosen to walk was generated from the decisions he has made and the actions he alone has taken. Therefore, I remove my fingerprints from the situation, and I give it fully over to you so it is safely in your hands from now on. Amen.' Josie rose to a standing position and, as if the water had cleansed her through baptism, she walked back up the steps a little freer than when she had first submerged herself.

Robert Day Jr had constantly pushed her to tell him it wasn't over—well, now it was, the cord had once and for all been severed. The conditioning side of him had persistently forced her boundaries, to break down her resolve, but from this moment on, she decided she would make every effort to heal in all conceivable ways so that she could rise as the victor and emerge as the warrior woman she knew she was. No matter how long it took or the battle she would have to fight, she knew that with God on her side, no one could stand against her (Romans 8:31).

Chapter 22
Too Good to Be True
(Josie Bellamy)

April 2024

Josie Bellamy's holiday seemed like it had been a hundred years ago as she now sat in the small waiting room, nervously taking in her surroundings. There was a small glass reception window behind which four women sat chatting or tapping away at their computers. This resulted in Josie feeling both exposed and self-conscious. One laughed, igniting Josie's fight-or-flight mode of response, wondering if it was at her expense.

She shook the thought away, annoyed at herself for allowing the paranoia to raise its ugly head—another remnant left behind because of him. Josie may have felt uncomfortable, but she was determined to face these counselling sessions with gusto, as her feelings were unimportant compared with her need to heal. She refilled the plastic cup she was holding with water again and sipped greedily—it was her fourth. Nerves, stress or thirst? She couldn't be sure, but she did know that unless Isla came soon, she would have to use the toilet again. There was nothing worse than wanting the toilet at times like these when you needed to concentrate on the task at hand, but that untimely pressure on the bladder kept persisting until you relieved it.

She glanced up at the clock to the right of the glass receptionist window. Only a few more minutes to go. The noticeboard beneath it had an arrangement of flyers regarding different courses or talking therapies that were available. The walls to her left were also intermittently splattered with them. The front doorbell behind her rang, alerting the four ladies that a new client had arrived. She gave her name, her appointment time and the person she was scheduled to see, and the door was released for her entry. At least it was possible to feel safe here in this old, tired building with its host of many small rooms.

Josie shifted on the less-than-comfortable hard plastic chair and observed the newcomer as she entered, walked across to the window, signed in and then sat in one of the three other possible seats. The young woman smiled thinly, nervous and uncomfortable at being seen in her embarrassing predicament of also requiring counselling.

'Hello,' Josie said warmly. 'Is it your first time?'

The woman's head nodded furiously, but she was unable to utter a word.

'Don't worry, it's not that bad. You are doing brilliant—you came, didn't you?' Josie encouraged.

'Thank you,' she managed, but then admitted, 'I just don't know where I am going to start.'

'I would suggest you don't have any preconceived ideas. Just go in and wing it—that's what I do,' Josie said, grinning.

'Really? You can do that? But what if I don't get better?' she asked.

'The secret is to know that there is no right or wrong way with therapy. Just be open, express your feelings, but most of all, be honest with yourself. It's a piece of cake!' Josie told her.

The young woman's face lit up to achieve a warm, soft smile. Her shoulders relaxed, then she delved into her handbag and produced a small bag of boiled sweets, offering one to Josie. Politely, she selected one and thanked the young woman. The famous heavy thud of wedged heels could be traced from a back room above them, crossing the landing and hitting the stairs before appearing between the acute triangle of the roof and the stairs above them. A hand appeared on the banister before a head bobbed down, revealing the familiar face of Isla.

'Are you ready, Josie?' Isla asked, not waiting for an answer before retreating up the staircase, expecting Josie to simply follow.

Josie pursued Isla through the maze of the upstairs corridors to their allocated room. It was small but comfortable and very colourfully decorated, with a rug on the floor, cushions on the chairs and a wonderful, scented aroma. It was welcoming despite her feeling suddenly on edge.

Josie had no idea what she was going to say or how the session would progress, as she liked to live in the moment, keep it real and stay open to let things run naturally. The last thing she wanted was for this to be a space dictated by control. She'd had enough of that from him and so she remained open and honest to freely express herself. Never again would she bite her words, have her thoughts or feelings forced into a box of someone else's making, nor invest where there was no fruit to blossom. If being with Robert had taught her anything, it was that dead wood needed to be pruned regularly and paying attention to how people treated her demonstrated her place in their lives.

She may have hit rock bottom, but she was determined that there would no longer be any dead wood floating in the stream of her life. If people made no effort with her, she no longer had the inclination nor interest to fight for their presence in her life. During the last couple of years, she had been faced with some very harsh truths—mainly that she hadn't made it onto anybody's list of 'I care about you.' Therefore, the reality she'd had to face was of all the wasted years she had invested in other people's lives.

However, on a positive note, she now had so much more time available to invest in herself. Isla had made her see that meeting her needs was not selfish but vitally important for her to live a happy, fulfilling and enriched life. Josie felt freer than she had in years, resting in the knowledge that she didn't owe anybody anything but she owed herself everything.

As Josie made herself comfortable, Isla pulled out the dreaded questionnaire, which was supposed to measure her weekly progress and, at the end of their sessions, identify how far Josie had travelled during their whole journey together. Inevitably, Josie could see the benefits of this but also how dreadfully disappointing it could be if it highlighted no progression from start to finish for someone. Now that had the power to be very destructive to an individual. Josie sped through the questions about whether she had been suicidal, had angry outbursts, spoke slower/faster, was unable to sleep/slept too much, was lethargic/overdoing things, and then they could begin.

'So last time we were discussing your feelings of you having had no control over your life during your relationship with Robert, that he had robbed you of your confidence, that you felt suffocated and unable to enjoy your life. How have you been this week?' Isla asked.

'You know my primary goal is to heal as soon as possible, but to be honest, I feel that whilst he still inhabits my thoughts, I can also not eject him from my heart,' Josie stated.

'So, indirectly, are you feeling you are still allowing him a measure of control over your life?' Isla wisely pointed out. 'You do realise this is a normal response, Josie, and just because someone behaved in a disgusting manner towards you, that doesn't mean you can simply eradicate them from your heart.'

'He has. Only two weeks after speaking to the police, he just sidestepped into a new relationship, and the love he pertained to have for me was dissolved as quickly as melting snow,' Josie said despondently.

'Josie, as we have discussed, people like Robert are parasitic predators. There are no feelings in his actions. It is simply a case of you were no longer willing to meet his needs, therefore he must find someone else to fill the void and validate his pathetic existence. Don't measure your sense of self-worth by the inadequacies of a person who does not have the capacity to feel real love,' Isla told her.

'I guess it is hard to face the fact that I meant absolutely nothing to him,' Josie said.

'Yet you mean absolutely everything to a lot of people. You may feel like you have wasted three years, but can you not be thankful that you broke free? My advice would be to learn from those experiences, remember who you were before you met him, and live a life with purpose despite what has happened,' Isla challenged.

'I know what you are saying, which is why I am pushing myself to heal so that I can regain some of who I was whilst also making room for who I am now and whom I intend to become in the future,' Josie offered.

'So, what are the parts of your character you want to regain?' Isla enquired.

'My confidence, sense of fun and spontaneity. I was thinking about this after our session last month, contemplating who I used to be and what he had reduced me to, and I have to say I did feel quite angry,' Josie admitted.

'Oh dear, but wasn't your answer to my questionnaire a 'no' when I asked about anger?' Isla queried.

'Yes, because although I felt angry about the situation—and I have a right to be—I didn't let it manifest into an outburst. In fact, I took a more positive approach, one the old me would have been proud of,' Josie confessed.

'Can I ask you to share the details?' Isla enquired.

'I am at my best when I am angry,' Josie began. 'So, rather than reacting in an inwardly destructive manner, I took the positive outward perspective and booked a single return ticket to Spain,' Josie said triumphantly.

'Wow! Did this also have anything to do with your previous trip with Louise to Greece having been spoilt a few months ago?' Isla asked.

'I guess it did a little bit because, as a result of the Greek trip, I concluded I would rather have been on my own than be forced to bend and compromise myself to accommodate people who were unprepared to give anything in return. Though ultimately, it was about the progress I have been making over the past few months. I desperately needed to regain my confidence whilst shedding the cloak of self-consciousness and paranoia that he had wrapped me in. So, it was a huge step of faith to retrieve the inner core of myself that he had stolen,' Josie answered truthfully.

'That was a brave move, Josie. How did it make you feel?' Isla asked.

'Terrified at first, then a bit apprehensive about whether I had done the right thing.' I did begin to waiver, and I could have quite easily talked myself out of going through with it had I taken enough time to dwell on the situation. However, I knew that if I wanted to get my confidence back, I had to bite the bullet and just go. In my life, when I have been faced with similar quandaries, I have taken drastic action like this, and it has always worked out for me. As Franklin D. Roosevelt said to help the American people reclaim their faith in themselves as a nation, 'The only thing to fear is fear itself.'

'Besides, I had complained about never having any time for myself, so doing this re-established the importance of making this time happen. I did feel a little overwhelmed, but it wasn't as though I didn't know where I was going to end up. It was just about navigating the journey on my own and securing a car at the other end. Funnily enough, whenever I am on my own—like if I go to a bar or something—I tend to feel quite self-conscious, but I didn't have that feeling at all. I felt empowered and strong, and I would hasten to say it has enabled me to get my warrior spirit back. The one thing I have never been and will never be is a victim that allows the abuser to maintain control and to keep you pressed down.'

'I can definitely see there is a massive difference in you, Josie, and I am astounded at the journey you have propelled yourself along, each week taking great steps. How would you describe yourself from when you first started coming here and now?' Isla wondered.

'At the beginning, I was so overwhelmed by how the relationship had ended. Inevitably, I had been trying for 6 months to break free from him, but he wouldn't let go. It was during these months that I felt the most depleted. It was like the very lifeblood was slowly draining away from me, and I couldn't stop it. He obviously knew he was losing me because I no longer cared. Maybe this is why he felt so threatened and had to resort to sexual abuse to maintain some semblance of control,' Josie admitted.

'What were you actually thinking or feeling during these months, Josie?' Isla asked.

'I felt like I was helpless in a hopeless situation—that I was trapped until he chose to make the decision to end it himself. I didn't feel like I had a choice. It was as though he had a right to be in my house, a right to do what he wanted, when he wanted and however he wanted,' Josie explained.

'How did you cope in that situation?' Isla asked.

'I don't think I coped. I think I found a way to just survive by blocking out what was happening and continuing to walk on eggshells, waiting for it to stop. Maybe, by then, I had given up. I didn't love him, I didn't want him and there was very little about him that I even liked. It was as though I was on the outside looking in, just existing, not really there. Do you know the funny part of it?' Josie asked.

'What?' Isla asked.

'When I look back, I couldn't have been any clearer that I didn't want him there. I was persistently communicating it verbally, I was not initiating any physical contact or sexual touch, and I had become so withdrawn,' Josie said.

'Why is that the 'funny part' of it?' Isla asked puzzled.

'His response was, 'If you don't want me here, just say. I would never want to be anywhere that I am not wanted.' Each time I would tell him it was time for him to go that I had no more to give, I was done and that I didn't love him anymore. He used to say, 'When you have seen something, it's impossible to unsee it.' I would therefore tell him that now I had truly seen who he was, I could not unsee it, and therefore, my love had gone. I had always remained hopeful that things would change, and we would be able to rekindle what we'd had in the beginning, but that was just a fallacy. That wasn't who he really was. He used this lie to keep me hooked, kept me dangling with endless promises. But when he admitted that he had never really invested anything of his true self, the spell was broken,' Josie stated.

'How did that make you feel?' Isla enquired.

'I was gutted. I felt like I had been strung along, so that's the point I mentally exited because I knew it was hopeless and my energies were finally depleted. I was a diluted version of my former self, trying my hardest to continue to work, and continue to invest in the things around me blocking out the situation with him. Yet he still continued to be demanding. He wanted to keep me down, so he would attempt to persistently sabotage my work. When I wouldn't allow it, in my exhaustion, he began taking what he felt was rightfully his, my body,' Josie admitted sadly.

'Josie, you speak as though it were someone else's experience and not yours. It is like you go to another place, and all your emotions and feelings are severed. Yet, when we talked of your recent trip, you were full of fun and quite animated. Can you help me to understand what is going on for you at these times?' Isla tried.

'I am not sure I know what you mean,' Josie stalled.

'I guess what I am trying to ask is, what are you feeling when you talk about the two different topics?' Isla clarified.

'When I speak of the effect he had upon me, I have to detach to cope with the depth of depression that gushes underneath. I don't want to be swamped by it and to be taken under the fast-flowing undercurrent. Therefore, I have mastered the ability to instantly remove myself emotionally and mentally so that, psychologically, it doesn't continue to send uninterrupted, closed-circuit messages to my brain and heart. The pain is too much, and I guess I am fearful that I will go under and completely break down. So, before the emotion is allowed to surge through my system and overload it, it's a kind of RCD safety switch that stops the current from blowing my electrics,' Josie explained.

'That's quite an amazing and descriptive analogy. Thank you, I can see exactly what you mean. We often find that people who have experienced unthinkable trauma somehow develop the ability to switch their mind to an alternative, less painful place, to allow themselves to cope with what is happening to them,' Isla informed her.

'Do you mean like when people are in terrible accidents and say a limb has been severed, so the body numbs the area by producing endorphins?' Josie queried.

'Yes, Josie, that is a very good comparison. It is a natural response from the body to protect us from added pain,' Isla said elated. 'So, when you had 'escaped,' as you put it, and you had given your statement to the police, how did you feel then?'

'I was sickened because I'd not only had to say it out loud, and to strangers, but it was also filmed. At first, I thought it was enough for me to have found the strength to face him, to challenge his disgusting behaviour towards me, to tell him he didn't get to sexually abuse me and think that it was OK,' Josie began.

'What was his response, to being confronted with the truth?' Isla asked.

'I had told him to leave but as usual, he was attempting every trick in the book to not be ejected. First, he wanted to come into my house to use the toilet despite living a few streets away. Then to ask for a hug, I knew this was to disarm me, and psychologically, it was the most inopportune moment when he had just been challenged about being a sexual abuser. It demonstrated a total ignorance towards the damage he had done, or the effect his sordid behaviour had had upon me. Then he wanted to give me a present, next to hand me some keys it just went on. And then, believe it or not, within two weeks, he was with another woman,' Josie explained.

'How did you feel about this other lady?' Isla asked.

'I was scared for her, really scared for her, because I knew he would con her in exactly the same way. However, she must have wised up quickly because I saw him out a couple of weeks ago, and he was on his own. So there is no way they are still together, as that would never have happened unless they had split up. Two days after that, I saw him sniffing around someone else, which did really worry me as I know how vulnerable this lady is.' She paused.

'But, no doubt, he will have already conned her into believing he is the answer to all her prayers. When I spoke to her, she told me that her husband had passed away only a few months before and about the substantial amount of money she had inherited. There were other factors about her situation too that had reduced her confidence and outlook on life, so she was a prime target for him to sweep in and step into her dead husband's shoes.'

'All he would have to do is listen, convince her how caring he was, and she would soon think he was her knight in shining armour. Crazy, isn't it, that he would have another man's life given to him on a plate without having to work a minute for it? How easy is that? As soon as she opens the door for him, he will believe he has a right to everything she owns, and he will begin to live the high life at her expense. But she won't mind one bit. In fact, she will feel elated because they are planning a future together. She will be glad she is no longer walking through life single after being married for so long and she will want to show him off to everyone.'

'Of course, he will revel in the attention because it is the stage he likes to play the most—to see how many people he can charm. All her friends will be thrilled for her he will get everyone's approval, especially her children because she will seem happy again after grieving for so long. His life will merge into hers without any effort, just like a chameleon suddenly being interested in all her hobbies, desires, plans, places, bands—you name it, he will suddenly become it. He can do this because he is an empty vessel, and when he moves on, he will disengage from everything about her as though she was last night's boxershorts to make room for whoever is to become his next victim.' Josie sighed.

'Josie, you have to warn her in some way. Surely you can filter some information through a mutual friend or something?' Isla pondered.

'I can't warn her because he will have immediately set the stage to help draw her in. She will have already connected with him on an emotional level by believing he is the victim of his last relationship by the scenario he has created, despite it being a pack of lies. Naturally, her motherly instinct will kick in, so she will immediately want to protect him, shielding him from any further hurt that she thinks he has already sustained. So, the balance of the scales begins one-sided. Therefore, he will already have her hook, line and sinker.'

'Even though it may seem like very early days, she will have fallen hard, quickly because he will be love-bombing her into believing he has too. This is all just a ploy to make it harder for her to leave him later. I know because it was the same method he used on me, and on Rosina before that, and probably every other woman during his life. So, as you see, I cannot warn her because he has already convinced her he is what she has been waiting for. He is the one, and he will talk of marriage almost immediately too, as though he has waited his entire life for her.'

'He will even defile the memory of his wife by convincing her he loves her more than he ever even loved his wife, but it means nothing. It is just another ploy to keep her attached. The money and lifestyle are all he is interested in. Sadly, she is nothing more than a means to an end. As for me, I am just the jealous ex whom he needs to keep her well away from because the last thing he wants is for us to compare our experiences in case they reveal his fraudulent behaviour. He may have deleted everything about our life together, but I still have everything on my phone, despite him resetting my last two phones, a bit like he did with Rosina,' Josie explained.

'You mentioned Rosina?' Isla tentatively approached.

'Yes, sorry. She was his previous girlfriend. After we had split up, I bumped into her in town, and she just delivered the sentence, 'Now you know who he really is.' I wasn't sure if she was being sympathetic at the time or trying to rub my nose in it. However, we have since sat down and chatted, and our stories are basically identical. Apparently, he kept on stalking her, applying pressure for her to accept him back, whereas I informed the police because of the abhorrent sexual assaults and the fact he stole a large sum of money out of my safe. Even then, there was no remorse, no culpability just dismissiveness and his right to do what he wanted, when he wanted. As far as he was concerned, I would have to just wear it.'

'I felt like I was a piece of shit not just on his shoes, but these shoes were worn by the person who had disregarded me as a human being and defiled me as a woman. Only a couple of weeks earlier, he had messaged me detailing how sickened he felt for his behaviour towards me—that he had 'broken down' reading extracts of my interaction with a Rape Support Line. Confronted, he described being 'appalled at himself,' 'sickened to the core,' that he 'hated himself,' and he even told me 'I hadn't deserved what he had done' and that 'it was disgusting.'

'Apparently, he 'hated himself for what he had become' to the point he wanted to 'lock himself away so that he couldn't hurt anyone else.' He even acknowledged his 'negligence and negativity,' and that 'his behaviour had isolated me and created the toxicity.' He still attempted to connect with me further by reiterating that I 'hadn't deserved his abuse' and that I 'was the strongest person he knew with a heart of gold.' But then, bizarrely, it was as though he somehow detached from what he had done, and he checked out again. Suddenly, he was wishing me well for the future as though he realised what he had said and then wanted us to 'still be friendly' and 'hopefully get together in the future to chat.'

'When I didn't respond, he sent another message a week later to say he had voluntarily 'put some money into my account.' He had never done that before, so I think he was scared and trying to resurrect the Mr Nice Guy image. It didn't work. I absolutely despised him, and as I could see him for exactly what he was, I was finally done. I hadn't seen him since—well, not until very recently when, like I said, he was out on the prowl for his next victim. I wouldn't mind, but the one who was exceptionally vulnerable and whose life he is no doubt slipping into based on the lies he has told her—he was watching me whilst I was talking to her. Oh, how I wish I could share those messages with her. It would certainly open her eyes because no doubt he is still playing the victim,' Josie said defeatedly.

'Maybe she will come across them at some point, like on his phone—you never know,' Isla said hopefully.

'All of it will have been deleted, but luckily the police were able to intercept his phone, and they are currently waiting for it to be downloaded. However, there is such a backlog they have had it for 10 months so far,' Josie said, deflated.

'What made you speak out, Josie?' asked Isla.

'There were so many reasons,' Josie paused. 'I guess he had dismissed my thoughts, feelings and right to be treated with respect and dignity once too often. When he refused to pay back the monies he had stolen, I was forced to consider the overall cost to myself emotionally, mentally, physically, psychologically and spiritually. I knew I was worth so much more, and I was not going to be thrown out like yesterday's garbage as though I was nothing.'

'It was a very hard call to make but having told him he was 'a thief, a liar and a rapist,' I too was confronted by the truth, and I knew I had no other alternative but to inform the police. In that moment, I knew that the messages he had previously sent me were lies, and he was not remorseful at all, nor had he learnt a damn thing. I had exposed my inner self and revealed the damage he had done to me, but he didn't care, and therefore there was a huge risk of his offending being repeated. He had already told me that 'many women in his past had complained about him sexually abusing them in their sleep,' so his attitude towards me soon after the fact meant it wasn't going to stop. I therefore had to stand in the gap and report him to the police to protect the subsequent women he would encounter, in the future,' Josie stated.

'How do you feel now?' Isla enquired.

'Sickened, it doesn't leave me, ever. Both about what he has done, how he has treated me, his arrogance and my immediate disposal to replay his game with another unsuspecting victim. Sickened, but I no longer feel like I am drowning.' When I was with him, I felt suffocated, hemmed in, unable to get away. After making the report, I was then forced to face what he had specifically done to me, so I have been trying to work through an array of feelings and emotions. It wasn't something that anyone could have helped me navigate my way through, and besides, I have never made it to anyone's 'I care about you list', so it was just another solitary walk to get through it.

'Before I came here, it mostly felt like I was treading water in the middle of the ocean somewhere, surrounded by hundreds of black bin bags filled with garbage representing the toxic waste he had created. Some of it was floating around me, the bags having been snagged, polluting the dirty water all around me whilst I furiously tried to keep my head above the water. Sensing the danger of getting my legs caught in the bags or the rubbish, I desperately continued treading water for fear of getting tangled up or of being dragged under,' Josie explained.

'Josie, that sounds like an overwhelming situation to have been in,' Isla sympathised.

'This was my wakeful experience, but my sleep time was far worse,' Josie admitted.

'How could it have been worse than that?' Isla asked, shocked.

'The bed where he violated me was mine, so how do you sleep there and feel comfortable and relaxed afterwards? You can't, it's impossible. For a couple of months, I couldn't force myself to get between the sheets. I was unable to fall asleep for the memories replaying in my head and when I finally did drift off, I would startle awake within minutes. I was averaging three, maybe four, hours of sleep per night. Now, 10 months later, I am still lucky to accomplish 4–5 hours at best. I think the intensity of the fear and foreboding undercurrents within my dreamworld created such severe threats associated with being attacked that I persistently woke with anxiety in the middle of a full-blown panic attack. The nightmares always tracked the same pattern of being followed and then of being brutally harmed through some form of an attack.'

'It had a profound effect on me, literally not wanting to be alone in the house, being too scared to use the toilet during the night, and not being able to enjoy solitary walks unless it was a quick one around the block. So, regardless of whether I was asleep or awake, I lived in fear. On several occasions, the dreams were so vivid and terrifying that I am ashamed to admit I wet the bed. There was so much of who I was that no longer existed. I was always fastidious in showering morning and night, of my bed being pristinely made, being carefree, fun, loving to socialise and include others. Before counselling, I cried so much, proper heartfelt sobs of despair. I would curl up on the settee with a blanket around me and just sob. I had no one to talk to, no one to reach out to and, worse still, no one to reassure me that everything would be alright.'

'I remember at one point calling in at my friend Lynn's house as she needed some support. I was glad to feel useful as sometimes it helps to focus on someone else's problems. Anyway, on seeing me, she knew something was wrong and wanted to give me a hug but the very threat of someone in my personal space literally freaked me out. This is why I needed to access counselling sooner rather than later, because I didn't know how much longer I could last. Your services rang my doctor with concerns for my welfare and then she immediately contacted me. Between the two services, I was fast-tracked to counselling. It has been a very hard 10 months trying to come to terms with being lied to, love bombed and manipulated to believe one thing, have all my choices taken away, and then to be finally sexually abused. It has been a lot for me to contend with,' Josie drifted off.

'How would you say you are now, Josie?' Isla asked.

'I am numb. I feel stupid for believing his lies, for allowing him to continue to string me along on the belief of a hope for a better future whilst, in reality, he wasn't even applying himself at all. Sickened at his dismissive contempt and outraged that he has the audacity to still play the victim in order to snag his next target. Life just keeps on rolling for Robert. He goes from woman to woman, conditioning us, exploiting our good nature just to meet his demands, and he keeps on getting away with it. So, I would say I have massive trust issues now and therefore I just keep myself to myself without any interest in sustaining any form of relationships with anyone. He has done that to me and then discarded me, so he doesn't have to face up to the damage he has done nor take any responsibility. Hence, it is hard to believe he was ever taught the importance of his actions having consequences because he continues with the same sinful, immoral behaviour,' Josie said sadly.

Isla discreetly glanced at the clock. 'I am sorry, Josie, but we need to finish there as our time has come to an end.'

Josie Bellamy thanked Isla, collected her things and made her way back down the narrow staircase to the reception desk. She signed herself out, bid the ladies behind the glass screen 'farewell' and exited out onto the busy street. And here she would hide amongst what she called normal civilisation until the same time next week when she would be able to speak openly again. For now, she would safely bury her feelings, keep her emotions under check and lock away the memories deep in the vault termed 'Handle with Care.'

Chapter 23
Panic
(Josie Bellamy)

In the quiet of the night, he had returned. Maybe it was due to Josie being so exhausted that she had fallen into a deeper sleep than normal; she wasn't sure, but the fear was very real. One minute in her dream, she was walking along the high street, it was just becoming dusk; there was no one else on the street and the streetlights were on. As she walked past a pub, she remembered feeling confused as to why it was shut and in darkness so early, but she continued on towards her home.

The first sense that something was wrong was an awareness of a man on the opposite side of the road who had stepped out of the shadows, and then the streetlight in front of her suddenly turned off. In the eerie darkness, she quickened her step then once she had turned the corner, she ran across the road, sensing an ominous threat to her safety. Behind her, she could hear his heavy footsteps getting nearer, so she picked up her speed. However, in her haste to get away, she stumbled, tumbling to the floor. His shadow cast an elongated, almost demonic shape across her, and as she turned, raising her hands up to protect herself from his fists as they came down hard. She startled herself awake.

Josie lay rigid, not daring to move, her ears straining to see if she could detect whether someone was in the room with her. Her imagination was running wild. Was there someone standing near the door? Had she just seen a shadow moving at the bottom edge of the door? Was he on the landing? She was desperate to go to the toilet, but her heart was racing with fear, that she could not summon up the courage. A tear slid down her cheek onto the pillow as she was faced with her own helplessness. The fear was so debilitating and yet irrational, but to her, the regularity of these episodes had become too real to rationalise. She hated feeling like this; it was almost as though he held a remote control in his hand, that he was flipping to the horror channel each night her eyes closed to continue his torment.

In these early hours, when the rest of the world slept in blissful ignorance, Josie could not help but consider the danger he posed to women in general with his lack of consideration, care or empathy. There seemed to be no human element whatsoever. He just used people for his own amends. Josie thought about his disrespect within her home: putting cups on the carpet instead of the coasters provided and how they accidentally—on purpose—always seemed to spill on the carpet, especially if he hadn't got his own way with something.

Or when he would turn up unannounced to eat his takeaway late at night, when she was supposed to be having a time alone, nothing for Josie—just for him. The next morning, she would find stains on the carpet or along the settee where he had been sat. But it was never him, despite the fact he had been greedily shovelling it into his mouth like a food-aggressive dog, frightened it would be taken away at any minute.

Josie realised now why she was so terrified that he was in the room: because there had been several times he had let himself into her home, despite her never having given him a key, where her bedroom door would quietly open to reveal him standing there. Josie instantly felt sick at the memory of his presence—unwanted, uninvited—knowing full well he was there for only one thing, despite her unwillingness to engage sexually with him.

In trying to get herself back to sleep, she mentally walked herself through each room of the house, noting the areas she had specifically asked him not to touch, but he had done it anyway, intentionally causing damage. It seemed to Josie that he had some kind of psychological disorder or hero syndrome, because he was so adept at causing an accident or disaster and then wanting to revel in praise for swooping in like the hero to solve it. The trouble was, he had zilch understanding or any recognition that praise wouldn't be forthcoming because he had been at fault in the first place.

One of the main things that irked Josie was his inability to ever take any responsibility and to lie continually that he wasn't to blame, even when she had just witnessed it with her own eyes. His excuses, whenever faced with the truth, especially when she would not allow him to shirk away from it, were that because his intention did not match your accusation, then he wasn't culpable. Josie had never worn his little boy act and continually challenged his 'it wasn't me, it was my foot' mentality, often telling him if he wanted some dumb blonde who would believe his BS, then he was with the wrong person.

Josie accepted she had probably become worn down over time by his antics. It wasn't that she had ignored them or let him get away with things; it just felt pointless constantly challenging a brick wall.

There were so many incidents, like his interference with a floor being laid where he hit a nail straight through the water pipe, so the new room that had just been decorated was ruined, along with a sodden new carpet. Or the time Josie had removed articles from the bathroom windowsill so she could paint it, only to find within minutes he had gone in and put them back on to it. Or the time he was allegedly going to help out by painting the bathroom ceiling and, of course, he knew what he was doing but then he had bought the cheapest paint.

The result had been that the surface had bubbled, appearing to have a plastic coating, so it had to be fully removed, sanded down, undercoated and then repainted. It was always the same: whatever he attempted, he made a mess and caused considerable work to salvage it. He reminded Josie of the character Rodrick in 'A Diary of a Wimpy Kid,' who purposely made a mess of tasks to ensure his parents never asked him to do anything again.

The irritation of his 'I am not going to be told what I can and cannot do' attitude within her home and towards her belongings had been a long-standing issue throughout their relationship. Josie remembered having just bought a Karcher washer that she made very clear to him she did not want him to touch because he had destroyed so much of her property. She had been so specific about him not using it on her patio, yet as soon as she had gone away on holiday, he had got it out to power wash the Yorkshire stone patio.

Not only was it on the wrong setting, causing damage to the cement, but every single slab had black circular, swirly marks over the entire 30-foot-long patio. It gave the impression that hundreds of tiny cars had performed a multitude of handbrake turns, scorching circular black tyre marks over every slab. It had been so bad that, despite having travelled for 12 hours to get home, she was forced to immediately rectify it. Robert, immune to the distress and annoyance he had caused, was befuddled as to why she wasn't thrilled with his efforts and instantly treated her to the silent treatment.

That was the problem with Robert: he had no ability to connect with how other people felt. He had learnt behaviour techniques that had worked for him in the past and applied them with a willy-nilly 'one size fits all' mentality. For Josie, he was like the child who saw a button and was compelled to push it, despite being told what would happen if he did, and then he would be thoroughly surprised at the results of his actions. Although, as Josie had surmised earlier, whether the results were down to his actions or not was irrelevant in Robert's mind because that hadn't been his intention, so in his head he wasn't to blame. It had become his go-to 'get out of jail card,' hence why Josie did not want his interference under the guise he was helping as she always suffered the consequences of his actions.

The other equipment he had been irresponsible with was her brand-new Dyson cordless hoover that she had paid £600 for, and so inevitably, she had stipulated he must leave it alone because she could not afford to replace it. He broke the lid of the cylinder when choosing to empty it, caused cosmetic damage to several areas on the body, the brush roller stopped rotating and finally his refusal to listen to potential damage to the motor if used in wet areas, resulted in its failure to pick anything up. She wouldn't have minded, but her cleaning had nothing to do with him so yet again, because he had caused the damage under the guise of helping, he was unable to understand why she wasn't pleased. Equally, despite the hoover being in a new condition until he had touched it, and then afterwards broken, it had raised the same pattern: his surprise, followed by a denial of being to blame.

The worst damage had probably been to the new kitchen, where he had persistently banged the Dyson against the units until they were chipped and unsightly. As Josie lay there contemplating his attitude, she was unsure if he had just been jealous of the standard of her home in comparison to his own, which was horrendously rundown, smelt appalling and was disgustingly filthy. Hence the reason Josie hardly ever visited and had never stayed the night.

Josie tried to fathom why an individual would intentionally choose to perform the same destructive behaviours repeatedly yet expect a different outcome. It was mind-bending and indicative of why she felt her home wasn't her own, that he took away her right to make decisions and determined why she didn't want him there. The greatest disappointment had been his disregard for her top-of-the-range car that had a double sunroof and every extra upgrade available. She had been kind enough to give him sole usage for 2 ½ years, and yet when she had finally received the car back, two of the tyres were deemed illegal, with the other two termed borderline. There was a 6" knife cut to the drivers leather seat, predominant chips along his door where he had carelessly banged it multiple times, the alloys were ruined and the engine had a serious fault that he had failed to deal with. His evident right to everything that was hers, without any appreciation, care or gratitude, had sickened Josie, which was probably why she had bouts of a lack of self-worth.

Josie felt the injustice of the amount she had invested and the levels to which he had taken. Since she had finally had him removed from her life, it had amazed her the amount of people who had come forward to say how little they had liked him. *What a pity they hadn't expressed their opinions earlier,* she thought. Apart from the sexual violation, Josie had been stunned to find that Robert had also stolen £2,000 out of her safe and then tried to justify his actions by saying, 'Well, I took the car for you to sell it.'

It had astounded her that when the car was sold for £4,000, he had only relinquished half of those funds and then, almost a year later, he'd had the audacity to take it upon himself to secretly remove the other half from her safe. But, to appease his guilt, he had somehow convinced himself that it did not constitute as stealing. She had absolutely no reason whatsoever to consider that the monies would have been at any risk. But this again was just further evidence of whatever was available, he clearly thought it should benefit him and no one else.

Josie thought about all the times he had said, 'I would never ask you for money,' as though he had morals when, in reality, he was obviously indirectly asking, hoping that it would stimulate her to offer him financial assistance. There was no way she was going to be saddled with his debts, so her response every time had been very clear: 'Good, because I wouldn't give you any!'

Josie tried to picture him sneaking through the laundry with the intention of gaining access to her safe, rather than turning right and leaving her house. Of him hiding in her pantry, finding the key safe, fiddling as he tried to get it into the lock, his hands shaking at the excitement of securing his prize. The trepidation of getting caught as his hand thrust inside to grasp the envelope, before quickly sliding it into his pocket, locking the door, replacing the key to hide his indiscretion. Then, like the thief he had become, slipping back through to make his exit outside and then quickly off the property via her car.

Oh, the irony was not wasted upon her, nor the cold, callous act of the man who returned for months to share her bed, her life, her love, as though nothing had occurred. Yes, sickened was what she now felt every single time she thought of this predatory, narcissistic conman. At no point had he contemplated the disrespect he was displaying, nor stopped to consider his morally wrong actions. This was a man who arrogantly perceived that he had a right to anything he could get his hands on because she was his, and everything she had, he could use for his own amends. Josie tried to fathom where this innate belief could have originated, or the mindset to justify any actions to fit whatever narrative he wanted, without any conscience—just a selfish want at the expense of whoever crossed his path.

Josie recalled reading something about how quickly a narcissist would fall in love, especially if they needed somewhere to live. It had described Robert to a tee, along with his trait of declaring his abundance of fake love that was only borne out of self-interest. To some degree, she had wished she'd read the article sooner, but she had to admit that when she was in the situation, her eyes had not been fully opened to have been able to have identified the similarities. He had certainly mastered his art of manipulation with his flattery, little gifts and constant attention. She could see now the game he had played was just to get access to her and everything she had, whilst draining her mentally with his need for constant emotional support.

The reality was, there had been nothing genuine about Robert Day Jr; he was as fake as the replica Dr Martens she kept seeing advertised on Facebook for £30. Had she realised who he was, what his true intentions were and what he was up to, she would have obviously run a mile. However, the people who could have warned her from his past relationships were so glad to be free of him, they couldn't get away fast enough and didn't want to dance with the devil further.

Though she wouldn't have believed them in the same way she didn't see any of the red flags, even though they had been furiously flapping in the wind for all to see. So, the best she could do for her successors was to apply for Claire's Law through the police, in the hope it would be granted to save her from the heartache and devastation that erupted whenever Robert Day Jr was around. For now, she would try to get some rest and not continue to beat herself up for being fooled, whilst promising herself that next time, whoever came into her life would have to prove themselves worthy of her trust.

That was if she could get to a place of allowing anyone in ever again.

New beginnings

No one could hear the call of my heart,
Yet in my head, screams tore me apart.
He knew the lock, I could release,
So brought me begging to my knees.
The isolation, the depth of despair,
But no one around me seemed to care.
I tried to tell you, I really did,
I left you a clue, find where it's hid.
My spirit is yearning, do you hear my call?
In death, I am gone, do you miss me at all?
Secrets are buried, with me in my grave,
But I'm calling beyond, so others you'll save.
Now life goes on, as I lie all alone,
A bag of bones, as cold as stone.

(Juli Flintoff)

Part 3
12 Months Ago

Chapter 24
Removal Day

Demi Lee was like a cat on a hot tin roof as she made her way down the stairs and was about to proceed through to the kitchen when she caught sight of the massive van pulling up outside. She punched the air in absolute excitement.

Demi haphazardly fumbled with the latch to get the door open, wanting to instantly greet the removal men so they could begin. Today was the day. She could see that the postman had already been, as there was a light, white letter protruding out of the letterbox. As she rushed past, she hastily pulled the letter out briefly hearing the click as the flap immediately snapped back into place.

'Morning,' she greeted them cheerily. 'Would you like a cup of tea or coffee whilst you work?' She did not want to say 'before' you work, as she was too eager for them to get on with it.

There were two men: one in his early 50s, small and rotund, wearing a scruffy dark blue t-shirt and jeans that looked like they were screaming for their yearly machine wash. They were so bad that Demi considered whether they would make an independent break for freedom if they were given half a chance. The other guy didn't seem as bad, although she certainly would have guessed he had perhaps forgotten to shower that morning. He was in his mid-40s, tall, and slim with random tattoos dotted on his hands. They both smiled and greeted her with the gusto of men ready for a hard day's work. The thin guy swung open the giant metal doors at the rear of the van whilst the rotund driver made his way towards her.

'Good morning, Miss, I am sure you are raring to go, so Larry and I will just get on with it but—' He paused before shouting over his shoulder. 'Joel, my son, will have a tea.'

A young lad of about 19 walked around the cab of the vehicle towards them. Demi couldn't take her eyes off him, he was gorgeous. He had a white designer polo shirt on, hung loosely over straight-legged faded Levi jeans, his dark curly mop sat loosely upon the top of his head. Demi couldn't stop staring, even when he was standing in front of her, and his green, penetrative eyes bore into hers. His father grinned, having seen this reaction probably every day of the boy's life, and joined Larry at the van.

'My father and Larry always call for a breakfast sandwich before we arrive, but it's a little too early for me, so I wouldn't mind a tea with two sugars now, before I start, if you don't mind?' he said politely.

Demi just smiled and nodded, her voice somehow lost before she retreated inside, a tad embarrassed. She filled the kettle, before taking out two cups, one for her and one for Joel. *What a great start to the day,* she thought. Once she had handed the drink over, his father made his approach.

'Shall we have a walk through the house first, and then I can decide how it's best for us to proceed?' he said.

As they walked together through the house, noting the larger items, he was pleasantly surprised to see that everything was perfectly stacked in neatly labelled boxes denoting the different areas each would be going to when they got to the new house. Although she was happy to give him free rein on how he proceeded, she did ask for a priority on the kitchen areas, as this was the first she needed to establish, and it would probably be the longest to get sorted out.

'Right,' he said, 'if you want to move your car, we should be able to get cracking,' he said confidently.

Demi grabbed her bag from the coat hooks beside the door, threw it over her shoulder, stuffed the envelope inside it and collected her car keys from the dish on the windowsill. She realised that this could be the last time that she would perform this routine, so rather than rush, she stalled for a few minutes just so she could say goodbye to her home.

'Sorry, I won't be a minute. I just forgot something,' she said, not lying.

Demi rushed up the stairs to give the impression of being in a hurry, whilst the man walked back outside. She slowed at the top of the stairs to savour the moment before taking her time to pass through each room on the upper level. Quietly, she nostalgically looked out of the front window to where she had watched the fireworks display each year. She touched the groove in the door frame where they'd had to force the wardrobe through.

She held on to the post of her own bed, remembering the nights of passion spent with Stephen and the loss she had felt when he was no longer here. She thought of the long soaks she had enjoyed in the bath and the times she had bent over the toilet, puking after a boozy night out. There was a tinge of sadness as she realised, they were just memories now, with that part of her life gone. The chapter had been lived, and the page turned, so it was time to move on to something new. She mentally thanked her home for the bond they had shared and, knowing a part of herself would always remain there, she walked out into the sun with tears in her eyes.

Demi got into her car, opened the window and pulled to the edge of the drive. With a wave of her hand, she called out to the trio, 'See you at the new place' and drove out without waiting for a reply.

The thoughts of the past began to subside as Demi progressed along her journey towards the estate agents, where she had arranged to collect her new house keys. The excitement was beginning to bubble, the butterflies in swarms flapped endlessly within her stomach as she contemplated the new start her house move signified. Everything had been perfectly planned; she had the whole of the weekend to be able to put her new house in order, and then on Monday morning, she would also begin her new job.

Inevitably, her excitement was also infused with apprehension about whether she would like the neighbours and if her new colleagues would look favourably upon her. Her nervous energy began to intensify as the facade of the building she was visiting came into view. Demi felt like she was going to be sick as she found a parking space just beyond the little shop and began making her way towards it.

Her mouth was incredibly dry as her hand reached out to depress the handle, the little bell tinkling the moment she opened the door, which sprang back into place as soon as she released the handle. Alerted to her arrival, Kirsty, who was sat at a desk to the left of the shop whilst a lady Demi had never met before sat to the right, glanced upwards towards her.

Kirsty pushed herself up from her seat and greeted Demi in a warm embrace. 'How are you feeling?' she asked, beaming at her.

'It is such a major step for me that I am beyond excited. It's ridiculous how nervous I feel,' Demi admitted.

'It has been a long road that we have travelled to find you the right property, and I am sure The Crescent will be the perfect place for you to begin your new life. It is such a gem, and properties very rarely come up for sale or rent on there, so we did well to secure it at such a great price. Just take a seat whilst I get the correct paperwork out. I won't be a minute,' Kirsty said encouragingly.

Demi took a seat on the faux leather 2-seater settee that sat to the right of the door. In front of it stood a small wooden coffee table with a grey binder containing details of listed properties. Demi sat back, crossed her legs and anxiously swayed her foot back and forth like a pendulum on speed, her chest noticeably rising and falling more rapidly than normal.

'Are you ready to sign your life away?' Kirsty said jokingly, hoping to snap Demi out of her trance-like grip of fear.

'Oh, don't say that, Kirsty. I already feel like I am going to pass out,' Demi said truthfully.

'Come on, you will be fine. One signature and it is all yours, just one more before you can step forward into your new life,' Kirsty assured her.

Kirsty produced the paperwork and set it down on the desk in front of her. She re-angled her computer screen, pulled out a chair for Demi to sit on and retook her seat inviting Demi to join her. She clicked through the pages of her computer, explaining the parts relevant to Demi, then printed out the parts that she needed before also placing them on the desk.

Kirsty had already checked the status of the other properties in the chain and that it was viable to proceed with the completion of the sale, confirming that all the funds were in place. She made one last cursory look over the details of the paperwork, checking the bank details before laying out the different documents on the table, including a slip for the receipt of the keys. She smiled before pointing out to Demi where she needed to endorse her signature.

With a shaking hand, Demi reached out for the pen Kirsty was offering her, took a deep breath and signed on the dotted line. In that one solitary action of applying a bit of ink, onto the document, it had changed her whole life, instantly. Kirsty gave her time to drink in the moment, knowing full well what a momentous and overwhelming occasion it could be for her clients, and probably more for Demi being so young. Kirsty then dangled a pair of keys between her thumb and index finger up into the air in front of Demi just to get her attention.

'I think these may be yours,' she said supportively.

There was a keyring attached to her offering with an advertisement of the little estate agent shop, but all Demi could do was stare. Her arms no longer seemed willing to move as she just focused her gaze on the keys to her new home. For months, she had dreamt of this moment, having searched property after property, and negotiated deals only to get gazumped, for them to fall through or unexplainably removed from the market at the last minute. Yet, here she was, right now, having walked through the legalities, packed up all her stuff she was now staring at the keys to her new home, unable to believe the journey was finally over and yet just beginning too. Demi felt like she hadn't slept or breathed throughout the whole process, wondering if her dream was ever going to become a reality. Now, here she was, with the keys hanging in front of her for the taking, ready for her to finally embark upon the next chapter of her life. Tears began to well up in her eyes, the blood vessels in her nose tingling with the rush of emotion, as her outstretched arm willingly retrieved her prized possession. Not realising she had been holding her breath, she gasped as her hands encountered the metal, managing to suppress any leakage from her eyes.

'Just one more signature to say you have received the keys and our contracts are complete,' Kirsty said with a smile.

Demi's hand automatically responded, obeying the directions being given, as though driven by a remote control, a defining, almost tangible moment in time.

'How are you feeling?' asked Kirsty.

'I just feel elated, like I have crossed a portal into a new dimension. I know it might sound bizarre, but after all the studying I've done for my exams and living in student accommodation for years, I actually feel like I have finally made it.' She looked down at her hand. 'These keys signify me stepping into the professional world. The hard work has paid off, and I can leave it all behind me, including the failed relationship. Now it is time for me to join the adult realm in my very own home,' Demi said, melancholy.

'Congratulations, Demi! I am so pleased for you, and you should be exceptionally proud of your achievements,' Kirsty told her.

'I have got my own house! I am on the property ladder; I can't believe it,' Demi said.

'Well, make sure you keep in touch, won't you? I expect to get an invite to the housewarming party,' Kirsty said jovially, as she did to all her clients, never really expecting an invitation.

'Oh, definitely,' Demi said, thanking Kirsty again before picking up her bag, placing the keys to her new home inside, securing the zip and then slipping the bag over her shoulder before giving the woman a big hug.

Kirsty retook her seat as Demi left, the tinkle of the bell signalling another happy customer, or as Kirsty liked to say, 'Every time the bell tinkles, property joy has had a sprinkle.'

As Demi arrived back at her car, she could feel her legs shaking. She was unsure whether it was the excitement or the fact she hadn't even had the time to have a drink, never mind eat. She unlocked the car and sat a moment, a little overwhelmed. She felt as excited as when she'd received her new laptop to finish her dissertation; the old had been sluggish, unwilling to reboot at any workable speed. The processor was slow, the internet ridiculously unresponsive and the software old and outdated.

The new version was on point, although she felt trepidation at her inexpertise to navigate its software. It gave her hope that she would achieve success at a greater rate, along with stretching her abilities to produce a higher class of work too. Today, sitting in the car with her keys safely tucked away in the zipped pocket of her bag, she held the same trepidation, the same hope yet uncertainty for the future, and an excitement that bubbled under the surface at the milestone of her life being propelled into professional status.

As she sat there, thinking about everything that she was thankful for in her life, she offered up a prayer to God, grateful for His goodness, His mercy and His everlasting love that transcended all understanding. She knew that without Him, she was nothing, but with Him, anything was possible. As the word stated, if He was on her side, she could conquer anything and nothing would stand in her way because, whilst He stood for her, nothing could stand against her (Romans 8:31). She had been amazed throughout her life when doors had miraculously opened for her, and she had stepped through with a resounding faith, knowing that the plans He had for her were for her benefit. And now, here she was, on the precipice of a bright new future.

'God,' she said out loud, 'I am ready, ready to ride the crest of Your wave, so I ask You now to accelerate me into something so purposeful and wonderfully unique to me, where I can serve a greater purpose in my life. Amen,' she said.

Demi wouldn't have been able to recall anything about the journey from the estate agents to the new house, as she was on her autopilot setting, seeing yet not absorbing, hearing yet not really listening to the radio station as it played. She was experiencing waves of excitement mixed with conflicting emotions of a longing that Stephen should have been sitting in the passenger seat, revelling in the experience with her. She felt sad, not at his decision to take a gap year and travel, but because he had gone without telling her. She would have jumped at the prospect of being able to travel with him to foreign countries to create amazing memories together, but he had never even told her, let alone invited her.

'Oh well,' she consoled herself realistically, there was no way she could have afforded such a luxury, as her parents weren't rolling in money like Stephen's, and besides, she had a new job to begin. The other positive about not being included was she wouldn't have been the owner of a lovely little semi.

As Demi took the short road towards the entrance of The Crescent, her heart quickened as she realised this would be her route home now. She was here; this was her home—or it soon would be once she had everything in place.

Chapter 25
The Crescent

Demi Lee pulled onto the uneven dirt track and slowly ambled along until she was right outside the third house, her heart in her mouth, her palms sweaty and her mouth as dry as an arroyo in the middle of summer. The Crescent only housed 5 pairs of semi-detached houses, which all sat on the right-hand side of a horseshoe, culminating in a private walled footpath that led down to an old, cobbled road. It was a quaint beaten-track, a hidden gem that rarely had any passers-by, so it easily maintained its sense of seclusion.

There was no tarmac on the road; it was just made up of compressed dirt from where the inhabitants had driven in and out on a daily basis. There was the odd brick protruding, possibly from as far back as when the houses were first built, when the rubble was filled in, but no surface was ever laid. As soon as Demi had laid eyes upon it, she knew this was the house where she would be able to settle and call her home. It had a great motorway network close by and a small town within walking distance that had everything she could possibly need.

She pulled up in front of the house and looked at it, marvelling that this was now her house, no one else's, all hers—the long journey of purchase behind her. She sat, staring at the small buffer garden, the tired windows, which needed a coat of paint, and the cute window box hanging beneath the lounge window, and she was overcome with gratitude. She knew she might have to do an extra part-time job just to pay for the renovations, but it didn't matter; she was young, and once it was completed, she could ease off. She looked at the red brick with the little square PVC double-glazed windows; at least that was one major expense she didn't need to fork out on.

The front garden was compact, but whoever had lived here before had lovingly nurtured it having created a centre piece with a small Salix tree, a member of the Willow family. Around the edges were numerous plants, Hebe's and bushes framed by a small log border, with a gravel path and then grass, which wrapped around the Salix tree, standing proudly, exhibited in its own circular mound. Demi's thoughts returned to the previous owners as she tried to visualise who they may have been and why they would have wanted to leave such a beautiful home after investing so much of their time into it. Today, it wasn't as pristine as when she had visited for her initial first viewing, nor her second or third, but then maybe the owners had become sick, were elderly or had moved away with work. Regardless of the overgrowth, it would not spoil this moment for Demi as she was looking forward to getting stuck in and making it her very own.

Demi couldn't wait any longer; the anticipation of unlocking the door and going inside was beckoning to her. So, she pulled forward at an angle to reverse her red Fiat 500 onto the drive. The good thing about having such a small car was that you could generally negotiate any small space, so she carefully eased back, mindful not to knock the gateposts. She loved her car, which she had fondly named Little Bug due to its shape and size. Upon the centre of the dashboard, below the mirror, proudly sat a solar-powered ladybird that moved back and forth in its groove as she trundled along. She loved her car, and she loved her new home, where it would now sit proudly outside.

She jumped out, despite the car sitting a bit skewwhiff, took the two little steps onto the gravel path, turned right to take the two to the front door, and, with a shaking hand, placed the key into the old, green door. With bated breath, she tried to turn the key, but it wouldn't budge. Confused, she tried again, wondering if the lock was rusty or a little temperamental, but it still wouldn't move. Confused she wondered if Kirsty had mistakenly given her the wrong keys and was about to take out her phone when she remembered there was a door to the side of the property. As she slid the key into that lock, ready to give the door a push, she found that there was such little resistance that she almost fell into the kitchen, as though the house was finally glad to have a visitor.

Behind the door, she found a stack of mail for the previous owner, a number of flyers advertising gardening services, and what Demi called charity begging bags that people had shoved through the letterbox since her last viewing. She stooped down and collected them off the floor before placing them in the corner of the kitchen unit. It felt smaller and darker than she remembered, and there seemed to be a faint tinge of damp hanging in the air, but she guessed it had been shut up for months. She lifted the white slatted blinds, opened the windows and momentarily looked out onto the garden, noting the overgrowth and work that was required to bring it back to its former beauty. Leaving the door open, ready for the removal men, she was ready to explore the rest of the property, her property.

She immediately noticed how worn the carpet appeared now the previous owners' furniture had been removed, as there was a remarkable difference without the settee. Underneath where it had stood, the carpet was fluffy, bright and soft but a thoroughfare of footfall in front of it had reduced the area to a tatty, flatter, much dirtier, well-weathered and worn comparison. She crossed the room to pull back the curtains and open the windows to let the sunlight flood in, and turned to find shadow marks across the walls, evidence left behind of where pictures had once hung. In the rays of the sun, particles of dust danced their annoyance at having been aroused by the movement of the curtains.

None of it mattered to Demi; it was all inconsequential, as these things could so easily be rectified. She found a pair of keys hanging on a tiny hook in the cupboard of the hall with a tag clearly marked 'front door', so she unlocked it and swung it wide open to let the air freely flow and to give the house room to breathe. Demi retrieved the only thing she had stowed away in her boot—her tool caddy full of essential cleaning products—and immediately set to work. She selected a black bin liner and began by filling it with all the excess leaflets and charity bags, though elected to stash the mail inside one of the kitchen drawers, just in case there was anything important for the previous owner.

She then walked from room to room, picking up any debris left behind or things that were of no use to her before filling her bowl with soapy water and setting to work on washing down the kitchen units. As she reached the end of thoroughly washing and disinfecting every inch of the kitchen inside and out, she stood back to survey her efforts, glancing at every inch to ensure there wasn't anything left untouched. Then, realising the window also needed washing, she replenished her water and cleaned it along with its frame and sill. She made notes to buy a replacement blind, along with some paint for the ceiling.

Satisfied with her work, she took herself off into the lounge to take note of the work that she needed to attend to in there. Inevitably, the carpet had to be replaced, not only due to the wear and tear, but she preferred a plain, neutral colour, not a flowered affair, although she knew it would have to do for now. The paintwork could do with a refresh, as there were areas where the gloss had significant yellowing patches, and as far as the wallpaper was concerned, she felt confident she could remove it with a steamer, sand it over, wash it down and just give it a lick of paint to brighten it up. Demi was pleasantly surprised with the quality of the light fittings and curtains, so gladly did not add them to her 'to-do' list.

Demi wandered from room to room, making lists until she hit upon the master bedroom, where she opened the window and leaned out to look at her rear garden. Overwhelmed, not by the quantity of work, but by the sheer love she already had for the place, she again felt a wave of sadness that Stephen wasn't here to enjoy the moment.

'No,' she told herself, 'You are not going to feel sad for a decision that he made, and you had no choice over. This is your moment, and you do not need the approval of anyone else.'

With a renewed outlook, she walked again through the house several times over, telling herself this was her home and how lucky she was to have the opportunity, whether she was alone or not. What a big difference it was going to be from her not-so-long-ago college days, sharing a house with five other girls. Of course, she knew it was something that would take a while to get used to, but what a trade-off to be catapulted into the adult, professional world and into her own home. Demi satisfied herself that she had done well and felt humbled by the fact, so set to work washing down the walls, floors, skirting boards and windowsills, mentally taking ownership as she busied herself.

However, there was one item in the house that Demi was not so thrilled about, and that was the state of the bath—it was appalling. The taps looked like they were circa 1960, bulbous at the bottom, flowing straight down, with no protruding arms for this elderly design. The tub itself was larger and deeper than she had come across before and would certainly take a lot of water to fill it, but it was the state of the bottom of it.

She reluctantly slid her hand across the stained, rough surface to confirm what she already knew: it was scratchy and the enamel had long since worn away. This was the only part that let the whole house down for her, but with the cost of plumbers, the bath and fitments, there was no way she would be able to replace this at the expense of all the other jobs. It was beginning to irk her, as she knew full well that every time she used the toilet, she would smart over the state of the bath. But maybe it would just encourage her to work harder to get it replaced.

At that moment, an alarm system of a heavy vehicle reversing could be heard entering The Crescent. Demi didn't think it was possible for Eric, the removal man, to look any more dishevelled than he had earlier, but he was really rocking the old vagrant look now, bless him.

'Would you mind moving your car, Miss, so we can get the heavy stuff down the drive?' Eric enquired as he approached the door.

'I'm so sorry, I never even thought about it. I was that excited to get in here and have a feel of the place. Yes, I will do it now,' she said, taking her keys out of her pocket.

Demi jumped into her Little Bug and then moved the car down onto the road at the bottom, so she didn't block the vans exit once they had finished unloading. She hadn't thought about it before, but maybe she should have taken the time to inform her new neighbours of her moving-in day, just in case they needed access too. She sighed at her inconsideration and hoped it would not cause them to be irritated by her negligence so, as a precaution, she decided to engage in some last-minute door knocks to apologise for any inconvenience.

On her way back to the house, she decided to take a photograph of the removal van outside the house, just so that she could send it to Stephen. Part of her wanted to share it with him; part of it was to rub his nose in the fact she was moving on and moving up in the world, without the help of any parental finances. She knew he probably wouldn't care, but all the same, she decided she would document everything throughout and then send him updates along the way. She didn't care if he ignored her; she didn't even care if he didn't bother to look at the photographs. It gave her a sense of sharing it with him and, then hopefully, she would be able to finally wean herself off him.

Besides, whilst he was sunning himself, enjoying new experiences, probably seeing different women and generally having the time of his life, she was going to send them whether he wanted to see it or not, a result of his dismissive action. She mused over whether she still loved Stephen or was it the fact that his absence had just created a void. She didn't know, but realistically, the truth was he hadn't shown her the kind of love that she really wanted. So, perhaps this was the best end to their story.

For the rest of the day, she pointed Eric and his team in the right direction, of which was bedrooms one and two, to ensure the right boxes were being housed in the correct rooms, the positioning of her settee, bed and other heavy furniture. Eric was so dedicated that he even plugged in and positioned her fridge freezer and installed her washing machine to ensure she had a fully working kitchen. By the end of the day, her belongings were just waiting for her to unpack and find their new position within their new abode.

As Larry began to close the huge metal doors at the back of the removal truck, Eric and Joel brought in the last of her items. At realising that all of her possessions had been transferred, Demi suddenly became overwhelmed with emotion.

'Eh, come on,' said Eric. 'This is supposed to be a joyous day for you, a new beginning. It should be exciting, not upsetting.'

'I know, Eric, but like I told you about Stephen, it just feels a bit sad that I am on my own. No matter how much I want to rub his nose in it, I do miss him,' she said tearfully.

'Where's that camera of yours?' Eric asked.

'Here,' she said, taking her phone out of her pocket.

'Joel, come here lad,' he began. 'Our Demi here has been recording her journey, so step in beside her whilst I take a photo. At least then she will remember we were the ones who helped her.'

Joel dutifully stood beside Demi and, noticing she was upset, he put his arm around her and reassuringly looked into her eyes and said, 'Everything will be fine, Miss. You just wait and see.'

'Will it Joel?' she asked, then gave herself a shake. 'You're right, it will be. Thank you, I am so grateful for all that you've done for me today!'

A tear slid down her cheek as she turned to look at the camera. It was mixed with gratitude for all their hard work, Joel's kind words, the intensity of the move and exhaustion, all rolled into one. After thanking them profusely for their efforts, she slipped a £20 note into Eric's hand to buy them all a pint on her. He chuckled to himself as he climbed up into the cab to start the engine. Demi remained at the doorway, heartily waving them goodbye like an overprotective parent whose child was going on their first school trip, watching them until they had trundled out of The Crescent onto the road below.

As she shut the door and flopped down onto the settee, the silence was suddenly deafening after all the hustle and bustle of the day. She had thought that with all the kitchen equipment, the bed, wardrobe, white goods, and multitude of boxes, Eric, Larry and Joel would have been there for the whole day, but it had only taken them until mid-afternoon to complete the move. Whilst she sat contemplating the day's move, she took out her phone to scan through the photographs. It was only when she came to the last one that she realised why Eric had wanted to record their presence. The photograph of her and Joel was of them looking into each other's eyes, his arm around her, so close and content in each other's company that anyone, including Stephen, would easily mistake them for being a happy couple.

Bless him, she thought, with renewed warmth for the kind gentleman she had harshly judged as being unkempt. 'Please God, bless this man, his business, his family and his heart, and give me the grace to not judge based on appearances. Amen.'

Chapter 26
The Housewarming

Demi Lee did one more final walkthrough of the home she had now inhabited for six months, and what a transformation there had been. The food was prepared and neatly set out upon the dining room table, with each plate and dish covered over with cellophane. She'd worked all day cleaning, scrubbing, washing to make sure everything was just perfect. The curtains hung flawlessly at the windows, having been peeled from their wrappers, washed and ironed. The windows were streak-free after she had polished them with a micro fibre cloth, now reflecting the glean of the brightly shining sun. In fact, she could safely say that every single nook and cranny of her home had been delved into. And now, as she stood back and surveyed the efforts of her labour, she declared it had all been worth it.

The kitchen surfaces had an array of glasses neatly lined up with an assortment of drinks next to them, ready for her guests' arrival. The punch bowl, containing a mixture of alcohol and juice, had chopped-up fruit floating haphazardly within it, was in the fridge cooling.

She opened both the side and front doors to let the airflow. She observed the cushions on her new settee and the one in the solitary armchair to its right, compelled to rearrange it for the millionth time. She had no idea why she felt so nervous; her friends from the office were young, vibrant and sociable, having made her welcome the moment she had accepted the post of a junior journalist. Speaking of 'welcome,' she checked the banner above the fireplace along with the matching doormat. Both were flawlessly placed, straight and central.

She smiled to herself in anticipation of her first early evening soiree. She had carefully prepared a list of suitable foods that she had downloaded from the internet for such an occasion, rather than just any housewarming party. She looked around, not believing this was her very own house, and considered just how far she had come. It was safe to say that her focus on creating such a comfortable space resulted in her having no room for thoughts of Stephen. In fact, she couldn't remember the last time she had even considered him at all, which made her love the house even more. She chastised herself for still calling it the house and decided, from this moment on, she would only refer to it as her home. She absolutely adored it, with its envious comforts, the green and grey colour scheme with splashes of cream, and the odd personal touches. This was her space, her creation, her design, her choice, and she loved it.

Unable to relax, she decided to walk around upstairs, opening a couple of windows. She scanned her bedroom with its neatly, smoothed-out dark/light grey checked duvet on a cream background with a cerise undertone. The matching pillows stood to attention against the headboard, with a dusky pink fluffy fleece tucked in tight across the bottom half of the duvet. The complementary dusky pink curtains hung just below the window ledge, yet an inch above an old monk's bench that she had lovingly restored. She had actually bought a matching single duvet and a length of upholstery sponge, which she had cut, sewn, filled and placed upon the bench to create a sumptuous, padded seat.

As a backrest, she had created two smaller cushions in the same fabric, all matching and unique to her. She had been very careful to keep everything simple with clean, crisp lines, so as not to overcrowd the room. The whole house had a sense of space, with minimal unnecessary clutter that made it homely, inviting, yet chic all at the same time. She had taken advantage of the huge window by using tiebacks for the curtains & installing blinds to areas like the bathroom, kitchen, hall and landing. By ensuring she kept all the internal doors open, there was a sense of positive energy flowing throughout.

The only thing she wasn't ultimately pleased with was the bathroom. It's not that it needed a full suite replacement or a complete revamp immediately, as she could change the tiles later, but the bath was awful. Not only wasn't she keen on getting in a bath where somebody else's naked body had lain, but the bath surface was scratchy on her bottom. This was the only part of the house that she still had to invest her finances in, although she certainly wasn't looking forward to the considerable cost she'd been quoted.

Demi shrugged the negative thoughts away and replaced them with the recognition that she had only been in the property for six months, yet she had already completed so much. Demi had even begun designing her little garden, buying plants each week from the market to build up the borders and make them her own. The fresh, bright colours of tulips, lavender, freesia and peonies were framed by a trellis of sweet peas. Their vibrance gave Demi an inner pleasure each morning as she threw back her curtains. The combination of scents that permeated as you walked past was delightful. Demi planned to install a small decking area to the top right of the garden with a shed to the top left corner. Along the left-hand side, running down to the house, she wanted to build a raised walkway where some Hebe plants would be intermittently planted, and perhaps some footprint stepping stones. She had already purchased a small chimenea that doubled up as a barbecue, and an old chimney pot that she'd been using as a planter. She hadn't been able to believe her eyes when she saw them in the sale part of the garden centre, a bargain at £125 for both.

The other feature she had set her heart upon was a water fountain, which she intended to install to the right of her garden, between the back gate and her flower bed. Not only had she found an outside plug here, but the fountain would be the first item you would see on the entrance. She hadn't tested whether the plug worked yet, but if not, that could easily be remedied. The fountain she had mentally chosen displayed a huge barrel with an old-fashioned styled water pump handle at the top, the type she had seen on the reruns of 'Little House on the Prairie,' a programme she had watched with her mother as a child. Although she was hoping that by the next time, she went back to the garden centre, that this too may have been reduced.

Demi took a deep breath, closed her eyes and pictured herself again sitting on a sun lounger, surrounded by her completed garden. She could hear the trickle of water from the fountain, feel the heat of the sun on her face and smell the fragrance of the multitude of plants. Satisfied by the utter bliss of her thoughts, she continued with her walkthrough.

As she glanced into her bathroom, utter dismay filled her heart at the state of the old bath with its massive downward pointing bulbous taps. She suddenly felt embarrassed that her new colleagues and friends would see where she had to perform her personal care. Demi cringed at the thought of hearing the high-pitched whistle of the taps every time someone came upstairs to use the bathroom. It was quite unmistakable, but would they judge her, laugh, be sympathetic or understand these things took time and money? Demi promised herself that replacing the bath would take priority upon her list of things to get the house to completion as soon as possible.

As she stood there visualising the type of bath that she would go for, imaging a line-up of different contemporary taps, she heard a car pull up outside. Demi glanced through the front bedroom window, not daring to assume they were attending her house. Before Demi Lee had got halfway down the stairs, her first guests were arriving at the front door. Demi Lee ran down the rest of the steps to greet Taylor and Jonah, her partner.

'Oh, it is so good to see you,' Demi began, giving them a hug. 'Come in!'

'Well, this is really swish!' Jonah commented, genuinely impressed.

'What a lovely crescent to be on; it feels so private, tucked out of the way,' Taylor said.

'Yeah, we drove past twice,' Jonah emphasised. 'I told you; you should have let me drive,' he teased.

'I don't think it would have made any difference. I must admit, when I came to look for it for the first time, I couldn't find it either,' Demi told Taylor supportively. 'But you're right, it is a lovely little crescent, isn't it? And so private.'

'So, do we get the grand tour?' asked Taylor.

'Yeah, sure,' Demi said, absolutely thrilled. 'Shall we start upstairs?'

Demi Lee retraced her steps back upstairs and went into the spare bedroom at the front first with its neat little single bed, bedside drawers and little TV fixed to the wall.

'This is the spare room, but I haven't had a chance to put any curtains up in here yet. Some areas are still a work in progress,' Demi apologised.

'I wouldn't worry too much about it,' Taylor said. 'It is not like you need them unless someone's staying here.'

Pleased with Taylor's kind and supportive words, Demi led them into the master bedroom next, where Taylor immediately gushed.

'Ah, I love your bedding and colour scheme. It's beautiful, Demi, and look at the matching cushions, Jonah,' Taylor said, pointing.

Jonah walked over towards the window and peered out onto the back garden.

'Taylor, come and have a look at this,' he said.

Taylor and Demi joined him at the window, also gazing out over the garden, whilst Taylor pointed out and named all the flowers. Demi then described the things that she wanted to add, like the water fountain, seating area, decking and where she wanted to put everything. Feeling much more confident in her little abode and driven by their positive reaction, she was ready to face the dreaded bathroom.

'This is the only place in the house that I still have to do, so please, excuse the bath, because as soon as I have enough money that thing is coming out!' Demi stressed.

'Are you sure you wouldn't want to keep it? You could have that in your garden as the new water feature, help save you a bit of money,' Taylor joked.

'Honestly, I hate it but the quotes I have had so far are way out of my ballpark, so it will have to stay a little longer. I cannot believe how expensive plumbers are,' Demi said.

Jonah stepped forward and rubbed his hand along the bottom of the tub. 'Oh my goodness, the enamel has basically worn off the bottom of here,' Jonah detected.

'Don't you think I know?' Demi said, playfully tapping her behind.

'Now, that's where I might be able to help you,' said Jonah.

'Sorry?' Demi asked, puzzled, looking from Jonah to Taylor & back again.

'Jonah is a plumber,' Taylor told her.

'Could you really help me?' Demi Lee asked, barely able to contain her excitement as she waited for Jonah to continue to speak.

Jonah smiled at the two women. 'It would be my pleasure, Demi, especially if this is the only thing you have left to do to complete your home,' Jonah told her. 'What exactly are you wanting to achieve?'

'At the moment, the only thing I can really afford is the new bath,' Demi admitted.

'So, you want to keep those magnificent taps?' Taylor joked.

'Obviously, you will need to replace those at the same time. They must circa in 1960s, at least,' Jonah said, laughing.

'Don't make fun,' Taylor chastised.

'It's okay, Taylor, I don't blame him. They are horrible but as they weren't my choice, I'm not offended,' Demi told her friend. 'But yes, Jonah, I would love to get the bath, and the taps changed as soon as I can, to be honest.'

'What about an over the bath shower?' Taylor asked.

'I would love to put a shower in and change the tiles as well, but I simply can't afford it all right now. So, the bath must go, but the rest will have to wait for now,' Demi explained.

'How about next weekend?' Jonah interjected. 'I have a brochure in my car, if you want to look through it this week, you can pick out what you want. Then I will take you to the plumber's merchant I use, and I am sure with my discount you'll be able to get it done sooner than you think.'

'Really?' Demi said, overwhelmed by his kindness.

'Yes, and I will throw in labour for free!' Jonah declared.

'You can't do that,' Demi began, astonished at his generosity. 'I would hate for you to be out of pocket.'

'I can and I will. So, I'll get you a brochure out of my car, have a look at what you want and we'll go next Saturday. I'm working till around 11:00 hours but we can be here for around 12:30, can't we, Taylor?' She nodded vigorously, so he continued. 'Then the three of us will go to the wholesalers together,' Jonah told her.

'Ah, that's fabulous, thank you, so, so much!' Demi stuttered. 'I don't know about you, but I think I could do with a drink.' Demi finished, skipping off down the stairs, excited not only because her home would be complete much sooner than she'd anticipated but she would be rid of that bath.

Once in the kitchen, Demi removed the punch bowl from the fridge and carefully placed it on the counter. She selected three little glasses before using the ladle to scoop a measure into each, handed Taylor and Jonah theirs before they all raised their glasses and heartily chorused a 'cheers.'

'Hello. Is anybody here?' A voice called out from the front door.

The trio looked at each other and immediately said, 'Sandra' in unison. They put their glasses down and shouted, 'We are in here,' before moving into the lounge to meet her.

'Wow, I love this, just look at that inglenook fireplace and log burner,' she marvelled, giving her colleagues and Jonah a hug. 'These are for you, Demi,' she said, handing her some beautiful sunflowers and then catching sight of the TV. 'Goodness me, Demi, I don't think you could have got one any bigger.'

'Thank you so much, Sandra. They are lovely,' Demi gushed, taking a little package stapled to the cellophane off to examine it. 'Look, everyone, they come with a packet of sunflower seeds. Just what I need for my garden.'

Demi led the group back into the kitchen to retrieve their drinks and find a vase for her flowers. 'I don't know about working in publishing; I think you should be an interior designer. Your home is absolutely beautiful,' Sandra told her

Demi Lee threw her arms around her boss. 'Thank you, Sandra. These flowers are beautiful. It's good to see you, and I am glad you could make it. How are you?' Demi enquired.

'Did you find it alright?' Jonah asked, having a little dig at Taylor.

'Yeah. Yeah, it was a breeze. Satnav brought me straight here,' Sandra told him.

Jonah shot Taylor an 'I told you so' look. 'See, it wasn't that hard to find. Maybe I should have got a lift here with you, Sandra.'

'To be honest,' Sandra said, 'I knew the whereabouts of the Cresent once I had reached the bottom road, because a friend of mine used to live here, years ago.'

It was now Taylor's turn to give Jonah a knowing look as they all started laughing.

The party was a great success with everyone chatting easily, sharing stories on topics from first-time dates, holidays, the different countries they had been to, cars they had bought, family feuds, decorating disasters and even running around the park after a lost pet. At the end of the night, when Demi had said goodnight, she sat back on her new settee, put her feet up on the pouffe, then kicked off her slippers, laid back and relaxed. Demi was satisfied that she had cemented her friend base after hosting such an enjoyable evening. Also, now that she had officially held her housewarming party, she really did feel that this had become her home more than ever before.

A deep sense of peace fell upon her, radiating a new contentment and happiness through her. She realised a new chapter had finally opened for her, one that she was ready to embrace and enjoy to the fullest. So, what if she was single? She had a new job, new friends and a new home. This created a different type of love for her life: one of hope, gratitude for all she had and a genuine excitement at the possibilities for growth. As she sat enveloped by the warmth of her future prospects, she was certain she was going to be really happy here.

What Demi Lee could not have foreseen was that, through the discovery of a hidden package, she would soon be faced with many important decisions. Things were about to change, and this new chapter would absorb her every waking hour, unleashing an exciting career opportunity, that would also be the key to unlocking an entire investigation.

Chapter 27
Friendship

The following Saturday morning, Demi Lee was like a coiled spring. Not only was she immensely excited to be able to select the bath that she wanted but she was glad to be able to spend some of her weekend with Taylor and Jonah. Demi had got so used to spending her weekends alone decorating the house, shopping for products or surfing the net. During the week, they had arranged that, when they had finished at the wholesalers, they would go out for lunch to a little pub that sat between Wakefield and Normanton. Apparently, it was a favourite of Taylor and Jonah's and was nestled between fields in a beautiful country setting. Demi Lee had never been before, so she was looking forward to this new experience, especially as it was with her two good friends.

She giggled to herself as she got ready not believing how excited she could become at the prospect of choosing taps. The last half hour of waiting for Jonah and Taylor to arrive seemed to take forever as she persistently checked The Crescent to see if their car was in view. When she finally heard the car trundling up the uneven track, she immediately grabbed her bag, threw it over her head across her chest and was out of the door, leaving it to spring back on its latch. Demi reached the car just as it came to a standstill, before they had even had a chance to remove their seatbelts, never mind open the door.

'Someone's in a hurry,' Jonah said, startled by Demi eagerly opening the back door and climbing in.

'Sorry, I am just so excited,' Demi gushed.

'What, to look for a bath?' Taylor asked, gobsmacked.

'Seriously, you have no idea just how much I hate those taps and that horrible scratchy bath! So yeah, I am eager to get this show on the road, even if it is only the first step at choosing the replacements,' Demi said, her excitement evident by the pace of her speech and animated gestures. 'It will be good to get rid of it and take a nice hot bath lying on the smoothness of a new bath.'

'Yep, no more scratchy bum for you,' Taylor joked.

Demi then proceeded to tell them about all the taps she had looked through, describing each one by name, the three she had narrowed it down to, and of her full design plans, including the shower, screen and tiles she eventually wanted to incorporate. Jonah nodded along, knowing exactly what she was talking about, whereas Taylor interrupted every now and again to ask, 'What does it look like?' Of course, Demi was more than happy to fully describe everything in the minutest of detail.

When they approached the wholesalers, Jonah was able to pull into a space right outside the front door, much to Demi's delight, as she was out and off like a racehorse at the starter gate the moment the car stopped.

'Wait for us!' Taylor shouted light-heartedly, getting out of the car, whilst Jonah got his tape measure and a little notebook out before sliding a yellow HB pencil behind his ear.

'Now you do look the part of an expert tradesman,' Taylor smirked.

Demi stood at the entrance, patiently trying to suppress her excitement, propping the door open for her friends.

'Come on giddy knickers,' Jonah mused, leading the girls to the appropriate area where the baths, taps and plugs were displayed.

As Demi intently spoke about each item, Jonah took notes, measurements, answered questions and gave his professional advice. Once she had made her final choices, Jonah led her to the next aisle where there was an array of showers, cubicles and screens on show.

'We might as well have a look at these whilst we are here, Demi. If you decide what you want now, I can make a note and then order it when you are ready, so it will save us time later,' Jonah encouraged her.

'I don't dare to think about it, Jonah, as it will be ages before I can afford to invest in a shower too. I will have to wait for that luxury for some time, I am afraid,' Demi said, a little disappointed.

'It doesn't hurt to look,' Jonah pushed, examining a shower head just to entice Demi to step forward and engage herself.

'Oh, my goodness, look at these tiles!' Demi exclaimed. 'They are absolutely amazing!'

Demi was soon in her element, describing exactly what she wanted and how she envisaged the finished product would look, whilst Jonah took notes of every single detail. Finally, Taylor approached them, having been wandering aimlessly up and down the aisles without any real interest in any products, just waiting for them to finish their task.

'Have you two finished yet? I am starving, and I can hear the chicken Caesar salad with a side order of fries calling my name from here,' Taylor moaned, 'not to mention their magical chocolate muffins with the extra thick double white chocolate sauce.'

'Yes, I think we are all done here, aren't we, Demi?' Jonah asked for confirmation.

'Yes, I have even decided on the shower, screen and tiles. When I can afford them, it's going to look amazing!' Demi beamed.

'If you're absolutely sure about your decisions, Demi, I will get it ordered through my account. That way, you will have an extra 28-days grace period before you have to pay the full amount,' Jonah told her.

'Are you sure that's okay? I mean, you seem to be doing an awful lot for me already?' Demi enquired questioningly.

'Honestly, it's fine. What is the point of having a friend with an account if you cannot make use of it? Also, don't worry about paying it off in one big lump sum either, you can pay in instalments or give me so much each week if it makes it easier,' Jonah told her.

Speechless, Demi looked at Taylor for verification.

'Don't look at me! If Jonah says he is happy to do it this way, that's up to him. It's his business, so that's his affair, not mine!' Taylor specified.

'Oh, Jonah, I cannot believe how kind you are being to me. You are such a good friend, thank you so much but only if you are sure,' Demi stammered, overwhelmed by his generosity.

Jonah didn't wait to hear Demi's last words, nor did he feel that an answer was necessary. As far as he was concerned, he had said what he meant, and he knew what his intentions were before they had even arrived. He strode towards the counter, whilst Demi was distracted excitedly showing Taylor the things she had chosen.

'Hiya, Jonah, we don't normally see you in here on a Saturday. How are you doing?' the salesperson greeted him.

'I am good, Mike, thanks. I want to organise an order for delivery next Friday, if you can make it the last drop. I'd appreciate it,' Jonah requested.

'Sure thing, if you want to start with the first product details, please,' Mike said, opening the order sheet on his computer.

Jonah proceeded to order the entire contents on Demi's wish list, including the shower screen, tiles, taps, shower, side panel, grouting, tools he needed for the job and, of course, the bath. He then gave his account details and the address for delivery the following Friday when he knew the girls were going away for the weekend together. All he needed now was to obtain a key for Demi's house, and then he would be able to surprise her with the finished product when she arrived back.

Over lunch, Jonah waited patiently for the chatter to turn to the girl's time away together the following weekend, and when it did, he pounced like a cat on a mouse.

'Oh, is that next weekend?' he said casually.

'I only told you this morning that I needed to get some bits, as it was next weekend when Demi and I were going away,' she said, confused.

'Oh, sorry, I can't have been listening properly. So, you say it is next weekend?' he asked.

'Yes, we have been looking forward to it for three months now. It is going to be great to have our first trip away together,' Taylor said.

'I am so looking forward to walking across the beach, feeling the sand between my toes, the wind in my hair and listening to the waves crashing across the rocks whilst the sun beats down on my face. Absolute Heaven!' Demi imagined.

'And we splashed out and paid for a sea view,' Taylor told Jonah.

'What's wrong, Jonah?' asked Demi.

I was just wondering what time you are setting off?' enquired Jonah.

'We both put in for a half-day holiday, so we're finishing at lunchtime and setting off around 2 pm, as we can check in from 3 pm,' explained Taylor.

'Yes, and I am driving,' Demi began, 'as it is so much easier to park my little car.'

'At least you will be more likely to get there,' said Jonah. 'You know what Taylors like at driving.'

'You are so rude!' Taylor sulked.

'Well, come on, if you didn't have a satellite navigation system installed in your car, you would end up in Sheffield if you were going to Leeds,' Jonah pointed out.

'He does have a fair point, Taylor,' said Demi, laughing. 'What have you got planned next weekend whilst Taylor and I are tripping the light fantastic?'

'To be honest, I haven't really thought about it,' he paused for effect. 'Oh no, I have just remembered,' he said, taking the delivery note out of his pocket. 'The bath is being delivered around 5 pm next Friday.'

'You will just have to change it, Jonah. We cannot waste our half day's holiday waiting for a bath to be delivered before setting off!' Taylor demanded.

'I would but it was the only slot he had for two weeks,' Jonah sympathised, looking at Demi.

'I know it's an awful lot to ask, especially as you are already doing so much for me, but would you be available to receive it if I left my keys with you, Jonah?' Demi asked hopefully.

'I have a really busy week, but I guess I could squeeze it in,' Jonah feigned.

'Oh, thank you, Jonah, you are a star. I will leave them at your house when I collect Taylor next week,' Demi said, relieved.

With the possession of the key safely secured for the following week, Jonah knew he would be able to proceed full steam ahead with his plans for the following weekend. Of course, he was aware it would be a back-breaking, full-on weekend for him, whilst the girls were having their chilled-out girlie time, but he also knew it would be worthwhile. What Jonah didn't know was that his decision to help Demi would have unrestricted, far-reaching consequences that would assist a number of people beyond the realm of his own comprehension.

Chapter 28
Bonding

It was 11:10 the following Friday morning when Demi Lee glanced across at Taylor, rolling her eyes at the clock, which had seemed to be on a particularly go-slow mode that morning. Just to ensure her friend had understood her meaning, she raised her right hand and tapped her outer wrist with the index finger of her left hand, demonstrating the time. Now it was Taylor's turn to roll her eyes. She had also been clock-watching for the past hour and a half, desperate to finish so they could get home, collect their things and set off for their girlie weekend away. Funny, how whenever you were waiting for something or in a rush, time always seemed to slow down and, at times, almost stand still.

'Can I have a minute, Demi?' Sandra said, interrupting their secret communication.

Demi jumped up and followed her boss into her office. 'Is something wrong, Sandra?' Demi asked nervously.

'On the contrary, I have just come out of an editorial meeting where your praises couldn't have been sung any higher. It seems not only have you been steadily making quite an impression over the last 6 months, but your style of writing in particular is a hit with our readers,' Sandra said encouragingly.

'Oh, wow, Sandra, I don't know what to say. Thank you, that's made my day,' she said, turning to leave the office, thinking the great feedback was sufficient praise.

'That's not all,' Sandra began. 'Our senior editor has put forward a proposal to offer you your very own column with the magazine.'

Stunned, Demi stopped in her tracks before pivoting around to reface her boss. 'Sorry?' she asked in disbelief.

'It is just for a trial period initially for 3 months with the possibility of extending it to 6 months, pending the reaction of our readers,' Sandra delivered.

'I don't know what to say,' Demi responded, astounded.

'Say you will give it a go and then find something interesting that our readers can engage with,' Sandra told her.

'Yes, yes, of course I will. Thank you, thank you so much,' Demi gushed, walking back to her desk with her feet barely touching the floor.

Taylor glanced up at her friend as she arrived back at her desk, frowning a 'what was that all that about?' kind of look at her.

'Tell you later,' Demi mouthed in complete shock.

Amazingly, the time seemed to speed up from that point on for Demi, as her brain went into overdrive contemplating what topic she could use for the new column. Then doubt started to eat away at her as to whether she was good enough. As soon as the clock hit 12:30, both she and Taylor simultaneously sprung up like a jack-in-the-box, finally being released from the confined space of its dusty box. Once they had logged off their computers and collected their belongings, the two friends made their way to the lift, arm in arm and out to the car park. Demi filled Taylor in about her chat with Sandra, excitedly deliberating on topics she had already considered and discarded, before she bid her farewell until she collected her at 2 pm.

On her way home, Demi's head was like a match at Wimbledon, batting ideas back and forth until, yet again, that seed of doubt started to germinate about whether she was good enough. What if Taylor was just being kind? Did she think she was good enough to write her own column? Oh no, Demi thought, what if Taylor felt she should have been given the opportunity first? After all, she had been working there a lot longer than Demi. She did hope that her friend wouldn't be disappointed, although Demi had to admit she had seemed to be positively receptive to her news. This was the problem with Demi: the enemy always attacked her mind with questions of whether she was good enough. The fact was, having read her work to date, the senior editor believed in her, so she had to believe in herself if she was going to do it justice. For now, she would have to put it to one side so that she and Taylor could enjoy their weekend, as she didn't want her to feel like she was rubbing her nose in it.

Demi arrived home, loaded her weekend bag, cosmetics and toiletries into the car, ensured she had her phone charger in, then got a quick shower. Even the surface of the bath under her feet had no sting today. In fact, it was the first time that she barely noticed its ugliness. She grabbed herself a quick sandwich before setting off for Taylor, who was standing on her front doorstep waiting as she arrived.

'You're eager,' Demi called out, laughing.

'I am so looking forward to spending this time together and enjoying a bit of pampering. It will be good for Jonah and me too, to have that bit of time apart,' she smiled.

'Oh, I nearly forgot, he will need my keys for the delivery of the bath,' she said, about to take off only the garage key, then she bethought herself. 'Oh, he may as well just take the bunch. I will pick them up when I drop you back off, but don't let me forget them.'

'No problem,' Taylor stated, taking the keys into the house and placing them onto the kitchen counter for Jonah. Then she secured the house and finished, 'Right, can we go now, please? I am itching to get started.'

The girls had the most amazing time bonding through facials, massages, swimming, eating, drinking and generally lazing away their weekend together, getting to know one another more deeply. They laughed, they shared and they grew closer like only true friends could, until their weekend had somehow come to an end.

'I cannot believe it's over. I have had the best time ever, Demi,' Taylor gushed.

'Yes, I am a bit sad I must admit, not because we must go back, but because I have enjoyed it so much. Maybe we could do it again?' Demi said hopefully.

'I think we should book to come back in 6 months. That way we have something to look forward to, and if your column goes well, we can celebrate its success,' Taylor suggested encouragingly.

'Oh, I had temporarily forgotten about that. What if it doesn't go so well?' Demi said with dread.

'Demi, it's a great opportunity and you will be fine. Besides, there is only you who doubts you. The rest of us know it will be a success. If it's not, we will still come back here to drown our sorrows, so it is a win-win situation,' Taylor said playfully.

'Come on, you,' Demi said light-heartedly. 'Let's get our stuff in the car. Bye room, thank you for a great experience.'

'Yes, see you again in 6 months,' Taylor said, releasing the door behind her and allowing it to slip into the lock itself.

When the girls were within half an hour of home, Demi remembered about her house keys. 'Oh, can you ask Jonah if he is home, as I will need to pick up my house keys when I drop you off?' Demi enquired.

'He will probably have left them back on the kitchen counter, but yes I will do it now,' she said, beginning to tap away at her phone.

'I wonder what he has been up to all weekend,' Demi said.

'He will probably have been sat on the sofa, playing games, drinking beer and watching football; either that or in the pub,' Taylor laughed.

'Thank you for spending the weekend with me, Taylor. I have really enjoyed it, and you have been such a good friend. Since I started at the publishers, I have felt so blessed by our friendship,' Demi spoke from the heart as a notification hit Taylor's phone.

'Jonah says he has just called into the supermarket round the corner from yours, so he will meet us at your house to save you dropping me off,' Taylor smiled.

'Perfect, could this weekend get any better?' she asked, not realising it was about to become so much better, even beyond her wildest dreams.

Chapter 29
The Secreted Package

As the girls approached the entrance to The Crescent, they noticed Jonah's van parked on the right-hand side of the road at the bottom, but he was nowhere in sight until they found him sitting on Demi's front doorstep. As Demi reversed the car into the drive, he stepped down and manoeuvred himself around the back of the car to the boot in order to assist Demi with her luggage.

'So how has your weekend been?' he asked.

'Absolutely fabulous,' the girls gushed.

'You look shattered, babes. I thought you would have taken the opportunity to have a night out with the boys or watch a bit of footie,' Taylor said, planting a kiss on his lips.

'I would have loved to, but an emergency job came up that I had to take care of,' Jonah said.

'Oh no, what a pity that it was this weekend of all weekends,' said Demi. 'Couldn't you have put it off and had some time to yourself?'

'Unfortunately not. It's been a bit of a rush job, and it had to be this weekend, but it's fine, it's done now. So, are you going to get the kettle on or what? I am dying to know all about your weekend,' Jonah asked.

'I am sure Demi will want to get in, unpack and put some washing on, love, as do I,' Taylor said, confused.

'It's OK, Taylor. Jonah has saved me an extra hour not having to go over to yours, so I have time for a quick cuppa,' she told her friend.

'Here are your keys, Demi. I will do the honour with the bags,' Jonah said, picking up the luggage.

Demi slipped the key into the lock, stepped in and kicked off her shoes. 'Just dump my stuff there,' she said, pointing to the hallway. 'Can you put the kettle on Taylor? I am desperate for the loo.'

As Demi ran up the stairs and Taylor made her way into the kitchen, Jonah stayed at the bottom of the steps and waited. The scream penetrated through the house bringing Taylor rushing back to the foot of the stairs, whilst Jonah grinned from ear to ear. The look of shock and disbelief on Demi's face as she emerged from the bathroom, coupled with the grin on Jonah's face, generated a two-steps-at-a-time sprint up the stairs from Taylor. Demi slid down the wall and wept tears of joy, disbelief and utter relief, all mixed into one, with Taylor standing beside her, opened-mouthed and astounded.

'You see,' said Jonah, 'from the bottom of the stairs, this weekend's job really couldn't wait; otherwise, it wouldn't have had the kind of impact I had anticipated.'

'But?' Taylor uttered. 'How? We have only been gone two nights.'

'I hope you don't mind, Demi, but I stayed all weekend so I could work into the night to get it done for you,' Jonah said.

'Mind?' Demi blubbered. 'I can't believe it, Jonah.' She said running down the stairs and almost flattening him against the hall wall.

Taylor followed her friend in utter amazement at what Jonah had done for Demi with renewed love and admiration for this amazing man. 'Thank you,' she managed to utter.

'No, thank you for taking her away so I could just get on with it,' Jonah joked.

'But, Jonah, I thought we had only ordered a bath and the taps,' Demi said. 'How did you manage to do all of it exactly how I wanted?'

'Don't you remember? As we walked around the plumber's merchant, you pointed everything out and described exactly what you wanted the finished piece to look like. I just figured it was easier to do the whole lot in one fair swoop. Now you can enjoy the interior of your house whilst you complete the garden,' he finished.

'But, Jonah, I don't have the money to pay you for it yet,' Demi suddenly realised.

'No problem. I have already put it through the business so we can set up a payment plan that you can afford. Simple,' he said, grinning at her.

'Come on, let me show you how to work your new shower,' he said, setting off up the stairs with the girls following close behind him.

Demi didn't hear a word of what he said about the flow, the system, the hot/cold mixer tap, absolutely nothing. All she could do was marvel at the beautiful, polished tiles, the gleaming silver taps, the deep sunken sink, the cabinet underneath, the mirror above, the taller-than-average obscured shower screen, and the gleaming white toilet and bath. It was exactly how she had envisioned it.

'So, this was why we had to meet you here and you wanted us to come in for a cuppa,' Taylor said, hugging her man with such pride.

'There was one thing, Demi. I noticed that the panel on the end of the bath was slightly loose and that it slipped out far too easily,' he paused. 'The thing is I found something secreted underneath the bath. At first, I thought someone had stuck it under the bath to level it out, as it's amazing what we find but when I pulled it out, I found that it was a brown paper package,' said Jonah.

'A brown paper package of what?' asked Demi, perplexed.

'Well, that is what I have been waiting all weekend to find out. It wasn't like I could message you to ask if it was OK if I opened it when you didn't know I was here as it would have ruined my surprise,' Jonah informed her.

'So where is it now?' asked Taylor, intrigued.

'I put it on the mantelpiece in your lounge,' Jonah said.

The girls looked at one another and then raced downstairs to find out what he was talking about. There on the edge of the mantelpiece, was a package wrapped in plain brown paper and tied with string. There were no obvious marks on it, no label or anything to suggest why it had to be hidden in such an obscure place.

'Are you going to open it?' asked Taylor.

'I'm not sure. It feels a bit invasive, as though I am prying into something private, although it is a funny place to hide it,' Demi reasoned.

'Not half! Whoever put it there didn't want just anyone to find it,' Taylor offered.

'I wonder who it belongs to?' Demi asked.

'Perhaps someone who lived here wrapped up the present for someone and forgot all about it. My mum used to do that all the time—wrap gifts and hide them for us to find, especially just before we were going to bed on our birthdays. By that time, we thought we had opened all our presents but there would be that one present that she had left until the end of the day. It was such good fun,' Taylor said fondly, as Jonah joined them.

'Haven't you opened it yet?' he asked.

'I am not sure I want to, Jonah. It is so dusty; it looks like it has been there for some time,' Demi pondered.

'Well, I am shattered, and I am sure you want to enjoy the delights of your new bath, so can we get back now, Taylor?' Jonah asked.

'Really, Jonah? I am desperate to see what is in the parcel, even if you aren't,' Taylor confessed.

'But if Demi is unsure about opening it, you will have to wait until she does. In the meantime, I am ready for a shower and a pint,' Jonah told Taylor and turned back towards the door.

'Sorry, Taylor, but I promise you will be the first to know what is inside as soon as I feel comfortable about opening it,' she said apologetically.

'Come on, Taylor,' Jonah called from outside the door.

Demi gave Taylor a big hug and thanked her again for the weekend before following her friend outside and walking with her down to Jonah's van at the bottom of The Crescent.

'I cannot thank you enough, Jonah. I could never repay your kindness; it is overwhelming, and I promise I will pay you back as soon as I can,' she said, holding on to him for dear life.

The trio embraced, having solidified their relationship, each like a leg of a stool—supportive, unique and equal to the other. Once Demi had waved them off down the street and returned to her home, she sat on her settee, staring at the package, contemplating what could be inside but was soon fast asleep.

Chapter 30
The Unveiling

The next morning, as Demi arrived for work, Taylor was just emerging from her car when she pulled into a parking space, almost as though she had been waiting for her.

'So, come on then, what is in the package?' asked Taylor.

'Good morning to you too, Taylor,' Demi giggled.

'Sorry, I have been thinking about it all night, wondering what it could be and the mystery surrounding why someone would have hidden it in such a bizarre place.' Taylor confessed.

'Yes, it must have been well hidden if it was secured beneath the bath. I wonder why someone would choose to secrete it there, unless they didn't want it to be found,' Demi pondered.

'Maybe this could be your topic for your new column, the mystery of who the person was and the story behind why it was left there and how it was found,' Taylor suggested.

'When you put it like that, Taylor, it sounds like a great idea, although in reality, it could just amount to nothing,' Demi said sadly.

'So, come on then, put me out of my misery, what was inside it?' Taylor implored her friend.

'I don't know,' Demi said blankly.

'What do you mean, you don't know?' asked Taylor, surprised.

'I didn't open it,' Demi confessed.

'How on earth have you been able to stop yourself? I would have ripped it straight open, my curiosity getting the better of me,' Taylor stipulated.

'I don't know, it just seemed wrong, like digging up a pet when you have laid it to rest. Whoever left it there probably didn't want anyone finding it, so it's making me feel as though I should put it back and leave it well alone,' Demi said solemnly.

'You will not put it back! What if it has been sitting there waiting to be found, desperate to be found? We cannot just ignore it, Demi,' Taylor told her friend earnestly.

'Doesn't it feel wrong to you, Taylor, like we are invading someone's privacy?' Demi enquired.

'No, quite the opposite. I think we have a duty to open it, see what it is and then we can make a decision what we do with it when we know what we are dealing with,' Taylor expressed.

'Is that you wanting to do the right thing or is it you just being nosey and wanting to satisfy your curiosity?' Demi asked directly.

'To be honest, it is a bit of both,' Taylor admitted. 'But we cannot possibly make a decision about it until we know what it is, Demi,' Taylor said sternly.

'Ok, I will open it tonight,' Demi said.

'No, *we* will open it tonight! You have heard of the phrase 'curiosity killed the cat.' I cannot wait until tomorrow to find out what is in it!' Taylor said, linking her friend and leading her into the office.

If the girls thought that Friday morning had gone slow, then they must have felt that Monday was on freeze-frame, as each minute throughout the day had felt like an hour, and both were shattered by the time they walked back to their cars.

'That has got to have been the longest day in history!' Taylor moaned.

'I honestly do not know how I didn't fall asleep in that last meeting. I was seriously giving up the will to live. Shall we grab a coffee from Chica's on the way home? I think I could do with a caffeine hit,' Demi suggested.

'Are you crazy? No! I cannot wait a second longer,' she said, opening her car door. 'We are opening that package without any more delays. See you at yours,' she said, slamming her door.

As Demi drove back to The Crescent, there were so many possibilities circulating in her brain as to the contents of the brown paper wrapping tied with string. Maybe it was the string element that was making her feel like it was something private, a metaphoric barrier that she shouldn't cross. She didn't know. What she did know was that there was something about the seemingly innocuous parcel that made her feel very uneasy. Demi had a hunch that, somehow, like a genie being released from its bottle, she wouldn't be able to stop it from potentially impacting her in some way.

As she reversed into the drive, she saw Taylor walking down the path towards her, and she knew that soon there was no going back, and the truth would soon be revealed. Would it be something she would live to regret? Would she feel relieved? Was it just a gift that someone had hidden, or was there a secret inside that they were going to uncover? Demi began to feel nauseous and now wished she had ignored Taylor and called at Chica's for that caffeine hit after all. As she clambered out of the car, her legs felt like jelly and her mouth was as dry as an old rotten tree.

'Come on,' said Taylor impatiently. 'I honestly can't hold in my excitement any longer.'

'Thank you, Taylor,' Demi laughed.

'What?' Taylor said innocently.

'You just have a way of releasing my tension, and I love you for it,' Demi began. 'Come on, let's do this—together.'

When the girls bustled in through the front door and then stepped into the lounge, Demi stopped abruptly, staring at the package still sitting on the end of the mantelpiece.

'Don't stop now,' Taylor said, shoving her friend inside. 'We are doing this.'

Demi took a deep breath and sat on the edge of the settee, leaving Taylor with the responsibility to retrieve the parcel, which she placed onto Demi's lap and then sat down beside her. For a few moments, Demi just stared at it—like it was an urn full of a loved one's ashes—not wanting to touch its contents, until she felt an elbow in her side.

'Come on then, it is not going to open itself,' Taylor urged.

Demi swallowed hard, the lump catching in her dry throat. Her palms were sweaty and with shaking hands, she reached out to pull the string free, but it had been knotted and was too tight to pull over the edges. Like a gazelle sensing a potential threat, Taylor sprung up and dived into the kitchen, returning in seconds with a pair of scissors. Nothing was going to prevent Taylor from gaining access to this package, and in one swoop, the string had been cut before Demi knew what had happened.

She gazed at the string's severed edges—the violation of its tightly kept form now free and sagging at either side of the loosely fitting brown paper. In suspended animation, unable to rewind or go forward, she felt like a film left on the screen on pause until Taylor again pressed play.

'Come on, Demi,' she urged. 'This bit has got to be your decision.'

'But what if it is something bad?' Demi asked.

'And what if it is something good?' Taylor counteracted. 'It could be something that is worth a fortune, and as the property is now yours, so is the treasure.'

Very carefully, Demi began to unwrap the brown paper, unfolding it neatly yet easily, as it wasn't even fixed down with Sellotape. The girls looked at each other in stunned silence when a brown, embossed leather-bound book with a leather strap tied to its right was unveiled.

'It's hardly a treasure,' Taylor finally said, feeling somewhat deflated.

'I wonder who it belonged to or why it was so precious that they had to hide it, it doesn't make any sense,' Demi said perturbed.

'I doubt you will ever find out. Maybe it's someone's memoires or secret formula on how to live a good life,' Taylor said, no longer captivated. 'I will see you tomorrow.'

'Oh, alright Taylor, I will see you tomorrow,' Demi said a bit disappointed that Taylor's interest had suddenly expunged, the excitement in her voice gone, now the package had only contained a book.

As Demi glanced back at the book, she heard the front door close behind her friend. That was it—no mystery, no wonder, no interest—just herself left with the book sitting in her lap. Demi retied the string around the book, replaced it on the corner of the mantelpiece, set on top of the brown paper that it had been wrapped in, the ends of the string haphazardly hanging down, equally as disappointed as Taylor. *Never mind,* she told herself. She had at least enjoyed the potential adventure, even if it had only lasted 24 hours it had definitely ignited their imaginations.

Chapter 31
Three Excerpts

Demi didn't give the book a second thought throughout her working week; she simply got her head down and focused on the tasks passed down to her. It stayed on the edge of the mantelpiece, overlooked like any other ornament that had been there long enough—ignored and blending into the background.

It was only on the Friday evening, as she treated herself to a luxurious soak in a mountain of bubbles in her new bath, that her thoughts drifted to the book that had been laid beneath her bath. Maybe it was a sketchbook of a famous artist or an unpublished manuscript waiting to be discovered.

As she lay there, basking in the warm, silky water, it dawned on her that all this speculation was pointless, when all she really needed to do was open the book to find out. Maybe, after the disappointment of finding it was just a book, she had not wanted the further blow of finding there was nothing inside, so had refrained from looking. Or perhaps it had been Taylor's dismissiveness and sudden lack of interest that had robbed her of her inquisitiveness.

As she stretched out her foot to flick on the waterfall hot water tap, she was relaxed and content, listening to the low, tranquil, sound of meditation music. She was neither motivated by her curiosity, the need to know what was in the book nor the earlier feelings of violating a stranger's privacy when she made the decision to look inside.

She had merely concluded that it would be silly to ignore its existence and take no responsibility. She believed that everything happened for a reason: she had bought this particular house, the bath was ripe for modernisation, and this was the time it had been found. Therefore, this was the right time to discover its contents, and so she thanked God for placing it into her care and giving her the responsibility to decide what happened to it.

After all, hadn't she asked God to 'accelerate her into something purposeful and wonderfully unique to her'? Maybe this was it, and He was propelling her on the crest of His wave so that she could serve a greater purpose in her life by entrusting her with the contents of this book.

Demi eased herself up into a sitting position, filled with a renewed excitement of hope at the endless possibilities with God. She scooted herself forward, grabbed the silver control dial and turned it to release the plug so that the water could drain away.

As she got to her feet, she wiped away the excess bubbles from her body, then reached for her towel before stepping out, after drying one foot at a time. Clothed in the towel, she padded into her bedroom, where she selected a thin sleeveless top and a pair of light pyjama bottoms.

She smiled at her reflection, having realised they were the ones Stephen had bought her the year before for Halloween that glowed in the dark. Then she made her way downstairs, flicked the kettle on and settled herself on the settee with the notebook on her lap.

Ever so gently, she tugged the leather strip binding it together and allowed it to release its hold upon the book before carefully opening the cover. On the first page was the following message:

Dear Diary,

I am not sure where to start, but I guess the acknowledgement that, although it may seem preposterous, I have decided to write this journal if only to get the thoughts of self-recrimination out of my head. Some things I know will be very hard to confess, but I am more than willing to lay myself bare to unburden and purge myself of the blackness that is killing me from within. It may work, and then hopefully I will feel better, but if not, at least I tried.

That was it. There was nothing else beneath it, so she turned the page, and then the next but again there was nothing.

Demi picked up the book with both hands. Holding on to its spine with her left hand, she bent it with her right hand and then firmly skimmed through the pages with her thumb. A third of the way through, she found a multitude of handwritten pages and, compelled to continue, she committed herself to read on.

Dear Diary,

Tonight I didn't want to go out to the pub, as it seems to be every night of the week he suggests going for a drink. This is not how I wish to spend my evenings, nor do I consider it being a good steward with my finances, so I declined. Seriously, you would have thought I had stabbed him in the back. He spent over an hour skulking around, banging and slamming cupboards in the kitchen before slumping on the settee, refusing to talk to me.

I knew he was trying to guilt-trip me into changing my mind, but this has happened too many times now where he doesn't respect my right to choose what I want to do. I suggested that if he wanted to go out, then he should, as I wasn't holding him prisoner—and if truth be known, I would have loved the opportunity to chill out without him. I was then subjected to persistent pressure to just go for one.

Why does he always ignore my right to choose to stay at home? In the end, he wore me down to such a degree and, despite it being almost 10 pm, I agreed, although I really just wanted to climb into bed. I honestly do not know why he has to control everything I do. Surely, if I want to stay home, he could just go on his own. This is beginning to feel extremely toxic.

All I want is some time without him, but he will not allow me that freedom. It's so exhausting.

In just those few words, Demi could feel the person's anxiety and was instantly captivated. She tried to picture who she might be, what she looked like or what had made her start to record events in her life—and, more importantly, who was the person she was talking about.

She read on:

Dear Diary,

Today has been yet another incident of Robert demanding immediate resolution. He does not seem to have any emotional integrity or the ability to put himself in my shoes to understand that I am not a machine able to overlook his coldness. There is something deep in my spirit telling me to get as far away as possible, but he will not allow this it is like he thinks he owns me.

He has said lots of times that he is mine but to remember that I am his. At first, this felt like a cute statement to be so connected, but now it feels possessive and, therefore, only his needs matter. I do wonder if he sees me as a person or just his possession, as the way he talks to me is that I am not his equal but subservient and below him.

The trouble is, when Robert is in the mindset of wanting an immediate resolution, he uses his size to intimidate me, uses his voice to drown me out, persistently talking over me. In this situation, all I can do is retreat into my shell to remove myself to make it stop because he has no capacity to listen.

I feel I have not only lost my voice but my right to function as a human being. But there is no point protesting, as I am just wasting my breath. In times like this, every rational, reasonable thought or action goes out of the window, and all that remains is his determination to stop me from disengaging or walking away.

I firmly believe the luxury of a little time to calm down will allow us to, not only process the events more clearly, but to find a mutually beneficial way forward rather than being railroaded to agree to anything for the torment to stop.

Demi sat back, as though the space the writer had suggested would allow her to take in the words she had just read. But in reality, she felt scared for the person and where the events were taking her. Demi read and reread the three entries. Deep in thought, she created a distance, hoping for the clarity the author had spoken about and re-boiled the kettle to finally make the drink she had begun earlier. She wondered if the woman had sensed she was in danger and that was why she had taken to recording her thoughts and experiences with this man, whom she felt intimidated by. Why did she stay in the relationship? Was it because she loved him or couldn't escape him? After only three excerpts of this person's real-life experience, Demi knew she had been drawn into something bigger than just a book under a bath. What if he had hurt her in some way? She must have felt that her safety had been compromised to make the decision to record events. And she must have been terrified he would stumble upon her writings, which is why she had hidden the book in such an obscure place. The poor woman. But where was she now? Intrigued, and with a yearning to help the woman, Demi knew she would have to continue reading to find the answers and to expel her fears. This book was in her safekeeping, and she alone would have to determine the appropriate action she would have to take. What she was not ready for was the avenue it was about to take.

Chapter 32
Full Speed Ahead

Demi arrived at work on the following Monday morning with bags under her eyes and a heart full of love for a woman she felt she knew but had never met. She had one determined thought, and that was to find Sandra in the hope she would help her find this woman in some way or another. With the magazine having such a wide audience, she felt it was possible that somewhere out there, one of their readers might know her identity and they could reach out to get her the help she required.

As Demi laid out her plan to use some of the excerpts for her new column, simply titled *Dear Diary,* Sandra listened intently.

'So, what do you think, Sandra?' Demi asked.

'Obviously, I haven't seen what you have read, but from what you are saying, I think the readers will be captivated by the curiousness and mystery of the hidden book, along with the concept of finding the person. However, it could be construed as plagiarism to put into print the writings of another person without their consent,' Sandra warned.

'That did concern me at first, but the only people who know about the content of the book are you, myself and the person who wrote it. I think if you read the book yourself, you would see she is crying out from the pages, and this may be the only way we can help her. Why else would she have hidden it unless she was hoping that one day someone would stumble across it?' Demi rationalised.

'We don't even know how old it is or how long it has been there, Demi,' Sandra said wisely. 'We may do all this, but the diary could be a hundred years old,' Sandra said flatly.

'But then it is just a story to captivate our readers, so it will stimulate their opinions and interactions. What a great first column on my road to journalism,' Demi said hopeful.

'It could also open a floodgate to sharing similar, personal experiences, so you need to ask yourself where you want to go with this and if you really want a deluge of agony aunt letters to respond to,' Sandra said wisely.

'Will you at least take a look, please, Sandra?' Demi said.

'I will, but only because it has got you so fired up and, inevitably, this is what we look for in investigative reporting,' she began. 'Bring me it in sometime this week, and I will take a look at the weekend, but no promises!'

Demi fumbled in her bag, and producing the book, she laid it down on Sandra's desk.

'I have it here,' Demi said, sliding it across to her.

'Oh, alright, but no promises,' she reiterated. 'Now go and get on with some work!'

Relieved that Sandra hadn't said a flat-out 'NO,' Demi was able to return to her workstation, where she put the book out of her mind to concentrate on her work. However, by Thursday afternoon of that week, it was a completely different story.

'Demi, my office now,' Sandra said on her arrival.

Worried her work was not up to scratch, she dutifully closed the office door behind her and waited for the words of disappointment to hit her like a hailstorm.

'I have just come out of a meeting with Justine,' Sandra informed her. 'The boss, boss,' she stipulated, raising her eyebrows for effect.

In stunned silence, Demi remained as still as a statue, worried she was about to get the boot, when Sandra continued, 'She agrees with me. We print the book!'

'Really? But how?' Demi stumbled.

'When you handed me it on Monday, I have to say I was sceptical, but curiosity got the better of me, and I thought I would read a couple of pages just to get the gist of it. Well, I couldn't put it down and ended up absorbing it through the entire night. You are right—it is a scoop and a half. Its origin is intriguing, the story captivating and the woman's experience breathtaking. It will have our readers engrossed. It is perfect!' she said triumphantly.

'I don't want to feel as though I am capitalising on this woman's suffering, though,' said Demi.

'Capitalising? Demi, her experience will send out a warning to other women on what to be aware of when getting into a new relationship and the signs to look out for if women are stuck and unable to break free. It could almost act as a self-help guide a warning not to stay in an abusive relationship and to get out before it is too late. You have struck gold with this. Justine has read it too, and she is in full agreement. We have a responsibility to not allow this woman's suffering to go unheard and to help free other people in a similar situation,' Sandra declared.

'Do you really think so, Sandra?' Demi asked tentatively.

'Think so, my girl? I know so!' she stated. 'And we are not running it in the monthly magazine, we want it in the weekly paper. So, clear your decks because we want 100% of your attention on your new column. So, get writing.'

Demi turned to leave the office when Sandra gave her a further instruction.

'Oh, there is one other thing, Demi. Justine has stipulated that you keep this to yourself. She wants it to remain under wraps to make it as impactful as possible. You deal directly with me—no one else. OK?'

'Yes, Sandra,' Demi stammered, a little overwhelmed.

Then as she walked away she worried about whether she had done the right thing and hoped she would do the writer justice. The last thing she wanted to do was exploit the woman further.

Chapter 33
Dear Diary

Over the next few weeks, Demi had no time to engage with anything else other than her *Dear Diary* column. In the first print, she introduced herself to the reader as though she was a character in a story to enable her to remain detached and anonymous. As far as the reader was concerned, her column was nothing more than an elaborate tale made up for entertainment purposes.

She began by detailing the uncovering of the book, using descriptive words to engage and pique the reader's interest. Then she would deliberately leave the passage on a cliffhanger, tantalising and intriguing them as to what would happen next. By indulging the reader's natural curiosity and desire for undisclosed answers upon the outcome, she began to slowly build a following.

After the first two excerpts were published, a flurry of emails were received from women stating how much they were enjoying the suspense of the story. Each week, the written accompaniment to the column that Demi had to contribute lessened, whilst the emails and personal letters began to flood in. A wave of excitement within the office was being whipped up as the general public jumped on board with who was the *Dear Diary* woman in the so-called story.

Demi was overwhelmed by the inundation of the public's response, resulting in Sandra having to appoint staff to assist with the responses. Demi then began to select letters that she felt required a reply, which were subsequently printed alongside the next excerpt of the book to generate more interaction.

After a couple of months, the tone of support changed to include letters of similar personal experiences and requests for advice and support. Carolyn, the resident counsellor, was tasked to join the team to offer her expertise and insight.

It was at this point that Demi was called back into the office with Sandra— only this time, when she walked in, Justine was sitting there waiting for her too.

'Hi, Demi. I just wanted to congratulate you on the column that you are currently running,' Sandra began.

'Yes, and we were just talking about giving you the go-ahead to take it to the next level,' Justine butted in.

'The next level?' Demi queried, not quite understanding.

'Yes, social media,' Sandra revealed.

'The feedback we are receiving is quite extraordinary. It seems that this little whodunnit, so to speak, has got our readers gripped. I think it is safe to say we all want to ensure that the lady has escaped this man's clutches and is living safe and well somewhere,' Justine delivered.

'So, we thought we would use the power of social media to discover her true identity and maybe see if we could track her down so we can conduct an exclusive interview,' Sandra said triumphantly.

'What do you think?' asked Justine.

The problem was Demi was not sure what she thought. If it became more of a phenomenon, would it expose the man and then put the lady in further danger? There was no doubt Demi had been intrigued from the start about the woman's identity, but she also felt an obligation to protect her too, and right at this minute, she felt like she was no longer in control of what would happen to her.

Demi suddenly felt very young and naive in an adult's world. She had not wanted to exploit the author, but now she felt like she had betrayed her confidentiality by being propelled along. Was it too late to pull the plug on the column? By the looks on both Sandra and Justine's faces, she guessed that it was.

Maybe the book had been under the bath for so many years the woman's grandchildren would be the only ones to come forward. Or perhaps the lady never even told anyone of her experiences because she was too ashamed and cut off to have voiced her thoughts. Hence, that was why she had recorded her thoughts in the little leather-bound notebook.

''So, what do you think?' Sandra pressed.

'I am not sure, to be honest. I understand the fascination about the story and indeed whether she is alright, but maybe to publicly name her could be to shame her,' Demi said carefully.

'I hardly think it will be a case of shaming her, Demi. We are looking to support her, not judge her. Besides, she has become a figure of public affection, not scrutiny, which has the potential to propel her to celebrity status. Who are we to quash the public's interest? We have a responsibility as journalists to report on stories without bias or judgement and deliver what is in the public interest,' Justine said.

'Justine is right, Demi. As a tabloid, we have a duty to not only investigate the story but also the means to find out the identity and location of this lady,' said Sandra.

'But we don't know how the woman may feel to be publicly exposed and have her secrets revealed upon how she was treated,' Demi protested.

'I think it's a bit too late to worry about that now, Demi. Your article has exposed the treatment she has sustained, which is another reason why we need to locate her,' Sandra soothed.

'I don't follow you,' said Demi naively.

'To ensure she doesn't take her own life,' Justine said bluntly.

Weighed down by the responsibility of having this lady's life in her hands, Demi returned to her desk sombre, no longer energised by the buzz of the office nor the joy of her column. She closed her eyes and quietly asked God to give her the strength to keep going, the skills to find the lady before anything happened to her and the grace to conduct herself with integrity.

Before the end of the day, posts were circulating on social media platforms gauging public opinion about *Dear Diary's* identity. Within 24 hours, they had been randomly shared multiple times, and after only a week, they were reaching a global scale.

At the bottom of each post was a link connecting the reader to all the excerpts from the book:

Dear Diary,

I know it may seem a little crazy, but I often wonder what advice I would give to myself if I could go back to that first moment when Robert and I met. I guess it would be a frenzied conversation to ensure I continued walking and didn't look back.

It makes me want to scream out to the world to prevent any other women from being taken advantage of by unscrupulous characters like this. Each time I have managed to loosen his grip and fend off the clutches of his emotional trappings, he has somehow managed to worm his way back in on the pretext of just being friends. Inevitably, having removed myself from the hamster wheel, I have tried to establish boundaries to maintain a healthy relationship for us both.

I suggested us having a few nights a week apart, of him working from his own house, and us both making time to see our friends too. After all, high dependency on just one person limits our social abilities and is counterproductive to our personal growth.

Expectantly, he readily agreed—as, like me, I believed we were moving into a more settled sphere of an established relationship. Time apart stimulates a healthy longing when you regroup as a couple. I could never have foreseen the shift that occurred.

To me, it was healthy, so I was glad to see we were on the same page. But to Robert, although he affirmed my suggestions, they were a compromise he was totally unwilling to succumb to, nor did he seem able to cope with. This has been the greatest sticking point that has spiralled me into experiencing the very worst Robert has to offer.

Do I feel stupid? Yes! Do I feel duped? Yes! However, I will no longer continue to allow him to impede me as a person, nor inhabit my home, as the beauty is I can walk away from him and live a full, happy and interesting life if I really want to. He, on the other hand, is just chasing his next victim to live on the surface of life that someone else can provide for him. They say that time is a healer. Well, 6 months ago, I couldn't have foreseen my progression, as I was broken beyond measure and absolutely smashed to smithereens. Today, I am determined to regain my strength, independence and confidence to become the woman that I have always been. Only now, I will become more powerful because of my experiences.

Dear Diary,

This afternoon, an old work colleague dropped by for a coffee and a catch-up, but I was not allowed the privacy for this to take place without him. He turned up unexpectedly a few minutes before Joanna arrived and bizarrely busied himself drying some pots up before producing his work folder and seating himself at the table. It was very uncomfortable, to say the least. It is like he cannot bear me to be with anyone else unless he is there. It is suffocating me. I have set up numerous friendship bases over the past 12 months, but he always finds a way to sabotage them. He finds fault, picks arguments or makes everyone feel uncomfortable and then he blames these people for why we are arguing. I have had to cut more people off than I care to remember, with the underlying reasons associated with being with him and not them.

Dear Diary,

I am so exhausted and feel mentally drained. Tonight, after my resistance at being harassed to go out late at night in the pouring rain for a drink, I was forced to give in to make him stop. Later, I heard him describing me with very negative and hurtful words, but when I tried to address this, he put a totally different spin on how or what was said. It was blatantly obvious he was lying, trying to make me believe it hadn't occurred, and he even questioned the validity of my perspective as though it was my interpretation of events that had caused a miscommunication.

The fact that I could give specific details or recite exact words was of no value to his new perspective, so what I was saying simply was not true, and as far as he was concerned, I was mistaken. I actually think he may believe what he is saying, but I don't know how he expects me to trust him when he does this—not to mention that it is also chipping away at my love.

Dear Diary,

This morning, I was sitting opposite Robert, listening to him on the phone trying to clinch a deal from an opposing company, and the lies that he told were outrageous. Afterwards, he batted it away as 'everyone does it,' but it made me think that, being a salesman by trade, he was a professional at making people believe what he wanted them to believe. I had just witnessed him saying whatever he needed, to make the client submit to what he wanted. Is that what he has been using on me when all else has failed—so he has reverted to tears, playing the defeated, hangdog, submissive card? Inevitably, it has worked before, so he knows full well that I would feel sorry for him. So, it has become the default mode of success in sealing the deal by emotionally blackmailing me into forgiving him.

There have been times when I have been unrelenting to these methods, so he has attempted to gain a footing by suddenly being overhelpful or dropping me some lunch off to show he is thinking about me. When I think about it now, I wonder if he felt his position was threatened and so he just wanted to highlight how indispensable he thought he was. This has been a persistent pattern. though I think perhaps it is his unwillingness to let go of the standard of life he could have with me, without adding any value himself.

When all these methods have tirelessly been exhausted, I have had the indignity of being stalked. I feel as though my eyes are opening wider and wider as I wise up to him, although I secretly manage to keep this to myself. I need time to decide how and when I am able to free myself of this parasite.

Dear Diary,

Tonight, I had to come home on my own because he was vile. We had been out for drinks with my friend Janet and were about to come home when Sammy, a girl who went to school with Janet's children, came in. She was with her mum, dad, brother and their friend, and they were celebrating her 18th birthday. Inevitably, Janet wanted to stay for a couple more, so I got another round in. I knew it was a fatal mistake when Robert glared at me over the top of his pint. I mouthed 'sorry' because I had failed to ask his permission.

Apparently, it wasn't OK. But then, he could have left if he had wanted to. However, he won't allow me to be out without him. I am not sure if he is scared of missing something or if he wants to keep his eye on me. Anyway, Janet was standing to my left at the bar and Robert to my right, with the birthday group sitting opposite us at a table. Unfortunately, as I turned to talk to them, Robert was kind of behind me. Another vital mistake.

Sammy was keeping us spellbound with talks about being a bit of a rebel at school and later divulged she had been adopted. As quick as a flash, Robert interjected, 'At least you weren't found behind the bins.' It completely cut me to the quick, like a knife being thrust straight through my heart. He knew it had hit the target and smirked in triumph. This was the phrase I had been tormented with when I was a child to show disdain for me that I wasn't worth anything and that my own mother didn't even care about me.

I had all on not to burst into tears. I quietly made my way through to the toilets and then exited out of the back door of the pub, completely destroyed. How cruel, just because I was having a good time and he wanted to leave. Later, Janet messaged asking if I was OK. I wasn't going to protect him, so I told her what he had said and asked her to make sure he didn't follow me but that he went to his own home. I really did not want to be around him right then, preferring he didn't revel any further in the hurt he had caused or to put the knife in even further. More and more, I seem to have to revert to self-protection mode where he is concerned, but then he will feign innocence.

Tonight, I just need to have a bit of space to help myself heal in private.

Dear Diary,

Well, last night did not go to plan. I had wanted him to go home, but as usual, he violated my boundaries because he wanted to explain. It didn't matter that I was hurt, upset and needed to be alone—what he wanted was more important to him. As usual, I had to listen to lies that it had been nothing more than a 'throwaway comment', that 'he would never hurt me,' and that 'I had got it all wrong and that was never his intention.'

He doesn't seem to get that it's hardly a throwaway comment. His excuse was then that he had 'no idea where he had heard the phrase.' How ridiculous! But this is what he so expertly seems to do—he turns things around to make out the way I have seen things is merely my interpretation, and as they were never his intentions, then I have got it completely wrong. At times, he has me questioning my own sanity.

I still wanted time on my own, but he wouldn't leave. In fact, he totally ignored me and just started cooking himself something to eat as though I was insignificant. So, I was forced to go upstairs, get dressed and leave instead, as I couldn't bear to be in his company. It sounds crazy now, but I knew if I walked out of the kitchen door, he would have prevented me from going anywhere, so I had to sneak out of the front door. Once out, I ran down the steps, across the lawn and over the wall but managed to split my trousers in the process. It was around midnight and there was no one on the streets, but all I could think of was I needed to get away from him.

I didn't know where I was going. I was just so upset at having to leave my own home in the early hours because he refused to ever put me first. Now I was out on the street—unsafe, alone, hurt and potentially at risk. I knew his daughter was nocturnal, so I ended up messaging her to see if she was still up. She was, so ironically, I ended up at his house. Her first words were, 'What has the man-child done now?' which spoke volumes of her own impression of him. It was the first time I opened up about how he made me feel. Whether rightly or wrongly, I was desperate to talk to someone.

She told me something so outrageous I felt numb all the way home. Apparently, when he met me three years ago, he was £235,000 in debt. He has never revealed this to me. I feel like I have been smacked in the face with a sledgehammer. There were clear conditions for my entering a relationship, and they were that I did not want to get involved with anyone in debt, a gambler, a smoker or someone who drank excessively. He has obviously intentionally lied

Dear Diary,

When I got back last night—or should I say, in the early hours of this morning—he was in my bed fast asleep. He hadn't messaged to ask where I was or to enquire if I was OK. He had simply eaten his food—or should I say, my food—then gotten himself tucked up into my bed, not a care in the world. Seeing him there, relaxed and comfortable, actually made me feel sick to the core that I was unable to even get into my own bed. I couldn't bear to be near him, so lying down next to him was totally out of the question.

For the first time, I didn't feel safe. Knowing I could be at risk of being woken inappropriately in the middle of the night, I decided to sleep in the spare room. Today, he has acted as though nothing has happened. It feels like I am in purgatory, having to tread on eggshells in my own home. I just want him to leave. I don't want him here anymore, but I do not seem to be able to get rid of him.

Dear Diary,

With only a few days to Christmas, I have tried to overlook the situation as I do not want to spoil the festive season for those around us. With so much to organise, we had planned to set yesterday and today aside to give the house a really good clean together. He has done nothing but walk from room to room, drink coffee or go out for a smoke. Now, he has made the excuse of going to his office Christmas party to not help at all, despite not being interested in it last week. So again, I am left doing everything along with buying and wrapping 165 Christmas presents for 34 members of both families and friends.

This one-sided effort grinds me down whilst he sits back and revels in all my hard work. He then rings me, pleading for me to meet him as he wants me to meet his colleagues. Like I have the time! After several calls and being sick of listening to him, I finally succumbed just to stop him from harassing me. I sometimes wonder if I will ever learn, as I never win in these situations—and this was no different.

First, I had a drunken yob verbally abusing me whilst Robert sat watching like a spectator at a football match. Then, he looked on whilst the same colleague sexually assaulted me, grabbing my boobs. It was Robert's boss who stepped up and intervened to protect me and ensure I was OK. Robert just looked on. He did absolutely nothing, then later excused himself by stating if he had got involved, he would have killed the guy.

The ugly truth is that he didn't care enough about me to even step in the gap or protect my honour—nothing. He just observed, letting the situation play out. This is so confusing when I have stood up for him on numerous occasions, immediately going into battle mode and putting myself in the mix without a second thought. I was humiliated, verbally and sexually assaulted, and he did nothing. I feel so hurt, so let down and inside I am crying with deep grief because this relationship means absolutely nothing to him. I mean absolutely nothing to him.

Dear Diary,

Today, it is Christmas Eve. I am excited for the festive period and cannot wait to go toast my late father with friends and family. It's the most important time for me. Before setting off, I was relaxed, happy and in a joyful mood. Robert had inadvertently spoilt the last two Christmases, where everything revolved around him, his family and how much I could put out for them at my own family's expense. On reflection, I can see he has purposely put a spanner in the works many times, causing ill feelings between people and spoiling important events.

He has this innate ability to never put any effort in himself but of ensuring he reaps all the benefits—or his habit of ruining your plans just so he can become the night in shining armour who has come to save the day. He would then be surprised at your response to his transparent actions and make you feel guilty for reacting to his bad behaviour. It is seriously difficult to win with his twisted view of what is normal interaction between people. So, I decided nothing was going to spoil today, and I would overlook anything he did by staying in my own lane and focusing on enjoying my afternoon.

On our arrival, he took a call outside and then came back in with the bombshell: all plans for Christmas had been scuppered due to his mum's selfishness. After a massive fight over the phone, he was in tears and began emotionally blackmailing me to respond to her, actively telling me what to say. At the time, I didn't even contemplate the manipulation. I just didn't want our afternoon overshadowed by him or his family again, so I willingly fired the bullets he loaded. It ended up clouding not only the whole of the afternoon but Christmas Day and Boxing Day too because I was left with a sulky adult who hadn't got his own way. And here he is—he has ruined our Christmas again for the third year running. Why do I allow him to draw me in?

Dear Diary,

Today he really scared me! Thankfully, we were out with another couple who witnessed his horrific behaviour. He has told me many times that as a younger man, he was prone to fits of rage—actually seeing red and not being able to stop himself from beating the shit out of someone. I had thought it was just bravado, you know, him trying to look big because he seemed so gentle and self-controlled. Anyway, we were sat having our first drink, so he didn't even have the excuse of being drunk—not that it would have excused what he did. So, I could see Robert was becoming agitated, although there was nothing evidential to suggest why. I thought perhaps a distraction would help, and as the couple had their 14-year-old grandson with them, I asked if Robert would like a game of pool. To my relief, he did.

But then I made a fatal mistake when I asked the young boy if he wanted to give him a game. He was thrilled and jumped at the chance. My error was not detecting the anger that had instantly risen to boiling point. How was I supposed to know that Robert would view this as a punishment and my disdain for him? The couple glanced at each other as Robert and their grandson made their way across the pub. It instantly put me on edge when they didn't offer an explanation and dismissed my questioning look. As we sat and chatted, I soon became aware of raised voices near the pool table. Since the boy was so young and his grandad had gone to the toilet, I went over to see what the problem was.

It was hard to understand at first, but apparently, there had been a glass smashed on the floor. A young woman, having alerted the bar staff, was waiting for them to remove it when Robert had trodden on it. I have to say she was very drunk, loud and out of order, but what Robert said chilled me to the bone: 'It's a good job you came over because I was about to stick this cue straight into her throat.' And then he calmly continued with his shot.

When I went to chat with the young woman, it turned out she had just had a miscarriage and was beside herself with grief. Bless her. Back at our table, Robert was unrelenting about his behaviour and was stalking the woman with his eyes like he was about to spring up and take her out. His unpredictability terrified me, and thoroughly embarrassed in front of my friends, we left. But it didn't stop there. On our way home, we decided to call at our local, where he took great delight in some random woman kicking off at me because I had misunderstood what she had wanted from me. He literally stood there smirking

271

as she was shouting and carrying on, whilst shell-shocked, I just stared at her. For the second time today, I felt at his mercy, and it wasn't a pleasant experience.

Dear Diary,

I literally feel like I cannot breathe. The stress that he induces is so overwhelming it is like nothing I have ever experienced before. He is like an emotional vampire, draining my energy and I cannot get away. I feel trapped, suffocated to the point I have been experiencing great anxiety and tonight, my first ever panic attack. Tonight was a whole new level. When his pleading eyes routine failed to work, he started using his physiology to bar my way. It was so emotionally and psychologically damaging, trying to assert boundaries against his need to control me.

Again, he had pressured me to go to the pub despite my just wanting a bath and an early night. I had to endure barbed comments when anyone came to speak to me. He wasn't the centre of my universe, so he demonstrated embarrassing character portrayals with silly facial expressions, mocking me. I decided the best course of action was to leave the situation. After all, it was he who wanted to be there, I didn't need to stay. I tried to secretly exit out of the back door, as I couldn't deal with another unnecessary confrontation. I just wanted the safety, comfort and peace of my home.

However, he followed me out of the back door of the pub and wouldn't allow me to go. He went on and on at me, trying to break down my resolve to gain a footing so I would do as he wanted. I just wanted to leave the situation, but he was intent on making me stay by barring my route and preventing me from going home. At one point, he grabbed hold of my arm hard at the elbow, grimacing into my face, dictating that I would participate in yet another showdown.

This is so exhausting. I love him, but does he really love me?

Dear Diary,

I feel so helpless. It doesn't matter what I say or do; I cannot win. I try to live by example and treat him with the respect I require, but how is it respectful to prevent me from leaving a toxic situation—to actually grab me and only effectively communicate his needs without also listening to mine? I have no space to call my own, no hobbies anymore, no decisions or choices that don't benefit him, and I feel like I am going under. Of course, this morning he was really sorry for barring my way, for grabbing me and being argumentative. Apparently, it won't happen again, but despite trying to communicate how his unpredictability makes me feel, according to him, it didn't happen the way I suggested because, again, that was never his intention. I cannot win. He doesn't listen, and I am beginning to wonder if he even has the capacity to connect with anything other than his feelings, his thoughts, his needs or his goals. I feel so depleted. I just want my home back without him in it, but he won't leave.

Dear Diary,

I was so looking forward to going out tonight, as Robert had promised me that I could go out with Janet on my own. All week he has told me how much I need this, that it will do me the power of good, that he is staying in, so I don't have to rush back. He even offered to drop us off in Horbury to enhance the night. I was thrilled at his support, but now I just feel utterly stupid for believing his lies. Janet and I went into the first pub, got a drink and decided to sit at a corner table so we could chat. I had probably only had two mouthfuls when Janet said, 'Knobhead's here.' That's what she calls him. Inevitably, I thought she was joking, so I was not taken in at all.

'He has just walked past the window,' she urged. I didn't believe her at all and thought she was just making fun of the numerous times he had turned up uninvited. Then I saw him, and I was gobsmacked. Janet just said, 'I told you.' Dismayed that our evening had been hijacked yet again, I couldn't believe it. He waltzed over and plonked himself down next to me as though his presence was expected. When I questioned him about why he was there, he said on the drive home, he had changed his mind about staying in and had decided to ring a taxi to bring him straight back down.

This felt like a serious infringement of boundaries and yet again him controlling the situation. I don't understand why he cannot leave me to enjoy a night out. It's not like I am doing anything wrong—I was just catching up with a friend. This is why I feel so suffocated: because he doesn't let me breathe without him. It's as though he possesses no moral compass, just an arrow pointing towards 'what Roberts wants, Robert takes.'

I felt so disappointed and let down by his inappropriate arrival that, whilst he dominated the conversation, I just felt on edge all night. The worst part of it was that I had built myself up to share my concerns about Robert with Janet just to get another perspective. In the past, when I have had conundrums to puzzle, just hearing my own voice saying it out loud has revealed the relevant answers.

I find having Robert in the mix promotes continual confusion; therefore, I am rendered with no ability to move forward or around the situation. He either creates a stumbling block or an impenetrable brick wall that is impossible to get through or remove. I am so tired. My thoughts do not feel like my own anymore— it is as though I am his ventriloquist's dummy. I can no longer see where he ends, and I begin. He has fused us so tightly together I almost feel brainwashed because if I don't accept what is happening, I will have to tolerate the emotional and mental abuse.

I am so tired I just want it to stop, but he hasn't finished with me yet, and so I have no choice. I am an unwilling participant in his game without access to the rules. Please, God, help me. He is taking my very soul and replacing it with his nothingness.

Dear Diary,

I feel absolutely sickened! My head is in turmoil. I actually woke up at around 4 a.m. to find he was—what I can only describe as—sexually abusing me in my sleep. I subconsciously turned away from him, but this was no accident. Despite my drowsiness, an inner red flag must have woken me. But once I had shifted, I didn't dare move again.

As I lay there, his words as I went to sleep suddenly bolted to the forefront of my brain: 'Don't forget your sleeping tablets,' he'd urged me. He has said this a lot to me recently. What if he has been doing this whilst I have been under the influence of strong sleeping tablets? They are also oral dissolving tablets, so he could have added extra into the tea he has suddenly started to bring me before bed. Oh my goodness, it doesn't bear thinking about. Perhaps that is why I have felt so drowsy and unable to formulate my thoughts, and why I have been having to come to bed mid-afternoon. I laid there frozen, unable to move in case he thought it was open season. I could feel the bed moving ever so slightly, and I am sure he was jerking himself off. This is the action of someone who associates the closeness of sexual unity only for their own gratification and pleasure. What the heck am I to him? He cannot possibly understand the true element of two people bound together in love.

Dear Diary,

Last night's issue was not something I could ignore, but it was very difficult for me to approach the subject. I did not want it to come across as though I was being judgemental or that I was criticising him or making unfounded accusations, but I needed to feel safe in my own bed. I waited until we were away from the house, as I didn't want the negativity to be held there. My thoughts were if we went for a walk, then we could say what needed to be said and let the words evaporate in the wind. At first, he played the confused card, like he had no idea what I was going on about, but I wasn't about to let it go. He does this a lot—whenever he behaves in some inappropriate way towards me—pretending in order to deny responsibility.

He then tried to make out that he thought I was awake but denied completely that he had been masturbating. I don't know why he can't ever own up and admit where he is wrong. He then devalued me further by insulting my intelligence, trying to convince me that I had misread the situation. But the facts are I was awoken by him inappropriately touching me in a sexual way without my consent. However, according to him, because that was never his intention, my perception of the situation is completely wrong. Amazingly, I am left broken—having been sexually violated—compounded by my feelings also being invalidated. If only he would take some responsibility, then the consequences of his actions may not feel so detrimental, and I wouldn't feel so hopeless.

Dear Diary,

The hopes and dreams I had for this relationship in the beginning have all but gone. He is chip, chip, chipping away at my willingness to keep banging my head against the brick wall. The trouble is my faith and belief that things will change has diminished along with my trust in the promises Robert makes. I sometimes want to tell him to use some mouthwash because the stench of bullshit literally permeates from every word breathed. I truly loved this man so much and believed he felt the same, but the recklessness of his destructive behaviours is destroying me in every conceivable way. Yet he displays no care for my well-being—my emotional health nor mental health. It is simply exasperating and draining beyond measure. God, please help me before I go under.

Dear Diary,

I am so exhausted! Yesterday was such a long day—running from one chore to the next without any help from him whatsoever. He just sat there on the settee, sulking again because I didn't want to go out for tea. I was so tired; I just wanted a soak. But as usual, he wanted to consume alcohol, and he wouldn't let the subject drop. This time, he physically blocked me into a corner of the kitchen, putting his hands on the unit at either side of me, forcing me to receive what he wanted to say. Why does he devalue me—talking at me and never hearing what I try so hard to communicate? I just want to cry all the time because he is forcing me to do things against my will, and I have little pleasure in anything these days. My head feels like there is a cavity of where I used to reside, but now there is just air with a mass of his words floating around. My insides feel as infected as a rotting tooth—my light almost extinguished by the dumping ground of his blackness. He seems so comfortable with mistreating me, and dare I say, at times, I even think he enjoys it. Yet his mouth proclaims his innocence. Well, this game is wearing as thin as a cheap kitchen roll, and I have absorbed as much as I can. I need to get away.

Dear Diary,

Tonight, his behaviour has gone to a whole new level. It has actually felt like I have been forced between the jaws of a baling press. Again, it manifested out of my simply wanting a night to myself. There was no argument, no drama—just a request for some 'me-time.' Anyone would have thought I had stabbed him in the heart as he paced around the house in a distressed state, trying to browbeat me into allowing him to stay.

He still evidently sees it as a punishment. I tried to placate the situation, play it down, explain and appeal to his better judgement but he was literally blind to my needs and deaf to my words. This time, he tried emotionally blackmailing me with the fact he hated his house, he couldn't go there, wouldn't go there and that if I made him leave, then he would check into a hotel. This pendulum swung from playing the victim-trying to coerce me into doing what he wanted at my own expense—to trying to manipulate a different outcome.

After two hours, I was actually sitting outside, crying uncontrollably, resisting being forced into submission as I knew survival mode would be initiated again. I just wanted him to leave as I find his pleading, needy behaviour so destructive. He could see the distress he was causing me as I rocked back and forth, trying to comfort myself, yet still his onslaught continued. I ended up lying down on the wet grass, pleading with him—my mind actually beginning to fragment to protect itself from serious harm of the trauma I was enduring. And still, he kept pretending to leave and then returning to me moments later. I think I actually screamed in mental anguish.

He is crushing me in every conceivable way, and I am beginning to wonder if he has some undiagnosed mental impairment because this is not normal behaviour. It is torturous to be on the receiving end. His methods have already systematically isolated me from my friends, ripped me of the confidence I once had, depleted me of my self-worth and now I am questioning my own sanity. My only wrongdoing was feeling sorry for him, offering him solace in his time of need, then doing my very best to help him restore his life and being willing to share with him all that I had. Now he seems to think he actually owns me. I begged him to go home, to stop the onslaught, to just leave me be. But he viewed me as the problem—and that I had got myself worked up over nothing—so he couldn't possibly leave me now.

I was having a mental breakdown in front of him, and still, he wouldn't acknowledge he was the problem, which could have been solved if he had just left. This is mind-bending. I don't know if he has mental health issues or what, but it's not normal to inflict so much mental abuse and then blame the other person for their response to the treatment they are enduring.

The only way to escape was to again agree with him that it was over so I could at least get him away from me. At times, having been forced into submission, a survival mode is initiated, so I complied but then he persisted in begging me to let him stay, not recognising that the situation had been caused by the same behaviour trait. I feel like a shadow of my former self. He played me, for sure, which sickens me because it is now clear that whilst I loved him and stayed true only to him, he was only loyal to himself.

Dear Diary,

I feel so cut off from everything. Every so-called friend I have richly invested in over the years—my thoughts, feelings or any other connections with the outside world—have been severed. There have been numerous times I have come to lie down in the afternoon, specifically on a weekend, shattered and just wanting time alone. But within minutes, he is following me and then wanting to get in. He doesn't seem to get the concept of downtime or my need to be alone. It almost feels like he needs me there as his comfort blanket, and yet he is destroying me. He doesn't seem to appreciate that we can be in a relationship and yet have time apart. As I began to pull away, he has become more rigid—unbendable—holding on to me for dear life. All he says is, 'I just want to be with you,' like I should succumb to meeting his wants, but it is at the expense of my own needs. So, I am being forced to sacrifice any time I want to be alone, which is another prime reason for him to go home.

Dear Diary,

I have been going back through my journal more and more to look at incidents that may have happened to try to understand how I have reached my current situation. Maybe one of the earliest signs of his materialistic side was right at the beginning when he arranged for his ex to drop their son off at my address because he had wanted to show off the size of my house. He made out to me that she had left him in considerable debt, but I have since found out it was all him.

I am very confused about who Robert really is because he has so many fake personalities depending on who we are in front of. It's ironic how much I have always hated bullies, yet I couldn't see the techniques he has used to wear me down—to get his own way by bullying me to comply to meet his needs at the expense of my own. This was evident during disagreements when I had requested over and over again for him to leave my property, but he would become forceful, determined and intensive to make me change my mind. There have been so many times that even when I have left the room, he has continued to pursue me. I would ask him to post the keys on his way out to signify I was done with the situation, but he would then follow me upstairs, persisting like the repetitive jibes of a woodpecker's beak.

Relieved at his final retreat, I would begin to relax until I could hear him banging about downstairs—another demonstration of his annoyance—until his reappearance to attempt to force me to relinquish my position. I have stood firm with the broken record technique, communicating my resistance to his futile opposition, but the same repetitive pattern ensues: his fight to stay and my right to be alone.

It thoroughly baffles me how a grown man cannot see the error of his ways when his only emphasis is on securing only what he wants at the expense of my health and welfare. It reminds me of a child behaving badly in public in order to manipulate their parents through embarrassment to get their own way. It then poses the question of whether he has learnt this persistence in childhood or if it is a pattern that has been successful in his early relationships, and so he is simply continuing to use it. There have been so many very disturbing issues with him, but the lack of respect for me as his partner, my home, family, and treating me *with dignity raise just a few elements. I seriously do not know where I am with him.*

Dear Diary,

I feel so desperate for some other adult conversation rather than it being with him. I have not been able to go out with my friends at all without him either gatecrashing the event or making me feel so guilty I have had to cut my evening short. The girls at work were planning a week's retreat to an amazing, picturesque cottage in France, so I was thrilled when they asked me along. That was until I mentioned it to Robert. Stupidly, I thought he would be happy for me, but his response was, 'Well, I don't think I want to be in a relationship with someone who will leave me for weeks at a time.'

I don't know who was more shocked by my response when I told him, 'That it would be his decision to make, as it would be my choice to go if I so wished!' I am sick of the controlling element, so at this point, I think we are coming to the end of the relationship; therefore, I no longer care about upsetting the apple cart. However, as I have begun to pull away, his toxicity has intensified to the point that I am waking up more regularly to find him sexually abusing me in my sleep.

I have no idea how long this has been going on because, for around six months, he has repeatedly been reminding me to take my sleeping tablets. Up to this point, I had not been able to fully detach myself due to the tentacles of his emotional strangleholds, my love for him and the hope it was going to get better. I had thought that we could rekindle our early love story, only I was slowly realising that this had just been an act, and the mask has been well and truly slipping.

I now just want it to end to allow myself to thrive as an individual, so I can regain my self-worth, rebuild my confidence and begin to experience life again. Much to Robert's surprise, I went on the trip and came back energised, excited and confident in my abilities once more, but was greeted with the same disdain, unwillingness to compromise or to treat me respectfully. I have slowly but surely realised he is definitely not for me as he suffocates my spirit, diminishes my light, weakens my strengths and makes me feel less of a person. The only trouble is I know he will not let me go without a fight.

Dear Diary,

Tonight I saw a different side to Robert that actually scared the shit out of me! I do not know what was wrong with him or whether there was some residue he was harbouring from yesterday regarding the airport situation and my subsequently going out, but I got the silent treatment all day. I wouldn't mind if he had done it from the sanctuary of his own home, but he just sat in my house, making me feel uncomfortable, ignoring anything I asked him. Anyway, when he realised it was a bank holiday, of course, that was yet another excuse for him to spend it in the pub. To be honest, I would have preferred it if he had chosen to take himself off—then I could have chosen my own personal space.

Apparently, my wanting to do my own thing was an outrageous suggestion. It was a bank holiday, a time for us to be together, with the fact that he had been ignoring me all day suddenly forgotten. I am expected to turn my feelings on and off to match his mood changes, a bit like a closed/open sign on a shop door. Also, my resistance due to being at the pub yesterday didn't matter either; he wanted us to go again today with the stipulation it was also without Louise.

Despite only being home for 24 hours from a week's holiday, for the first time ever, I really didn't want to be on my own with him. There was something about his behaviour and the way he had treated me yesterday that gave me cause for concern, so I organised to meet up with a couple we know. Oh my goodness, I could never have predicted the outcome!! Literally within minutes of arriving and without warning, he went from 0–100 within seconds. For some reason, he blew a gasket because a guy had accidentally caught his arm as he turned away from the bar, which resulted in him threatening to rip the guy's head off. I had never seen him like that before, though I have been told he used to be very handy with his fists as a young man, so I was terrified for his safety. I was able to placate the situation and move him away, but his level of anger continued to smoulder with absolutely no remorse or concern at the level of fear it had induced. Inevitably, I had to get him out of there before the situation escalated further, but he wouldn't let the issue drop.

Dear Diary,

I don't think I got a wink of sleep last night. I am not sure if it was the fear of what could have happened to the guy if he had completely lost it, or the anxiety of what he may do if I closed my eyes. I didn't want him here; I felt nervous for my own safety, and now, of what he is potentially capable of, so I became conditioned not to challenge him. It worried me that if I had suggested he went home this time, he could have turned his rage onto me, and I wouldn't have been able to defend myself. I have been inwardly anxious all day knowing I would have to speak to Robert. Why does he make me feel so nervous and panicked? When I saw him pull onto my drive, I seriously wanted to run out of the back door or hide in the house and hope he'd go away, but he would just keep coming back. Again, I suggested going for a walk; at least then I would be in public, but why should I have to think this way?

He came in with a bunch of flowers and genuinely seemed pleased to see me. This has become a pattern;, to somehow cancel out a misdemeanour, he turns up the next day with a gift. Yet he knows I hate flowers in the house as it reminds me of when my father passed away. It's like a double-edged sword because he is more than aware of this fact, yet continues to bring what I hate to make himself feel better. It's like when I told him I hated knick-knacks, so that was all I got for my birthday.

Or when I stressed, I didn't want any perfume for Christmas, so he got me 4 different kinds. Again, I have no right to choose what's right for me; I am not supposed to be disappointed or say anything; I am just forced to accept whatever he dictates. It's so confusing, especially when he acts like we have never even had the conversation, and again it's all a misunderstanding. Apparently, I had blown yesterday's events out of proportion too, but he offered to apologise to the couple we were out with, even though he didn't think it was necessary. I truly am at a loss. Is it me? Have I completely lost the plot? He suggested that I may have bipolar.

Dear Diary,

I am beginning to notice an almost sadistic pleasure that Robert seems to get out of the way he treats me. Personally, I have always believed that if you have communicated with another individual about traits of their behaviour that affect, harm or give you cause for concern about your safety, etc., that if they continue, then this is bullying. I have told him over and over again that his neediness and pressure for instant reconciliation is detrimental to our relationship when he persists to the point, he is breaking my spirit. Yet it continues.

I had been subjected to the silent treatment, devaluing comments, blocking my exit, stalking and control measures, but now he is punishing me in a new measure that scares me. I had asthma as a young adult and was on 3 different inhalers a day at one point but seem to have outgrown it, to some degree. However, there are some instances that trigger issues with my breathing, and the main one is aerosols, particularly talc-based deodorants. I noticed this more when Robert and I were away on holiday and living in such a confined space, so I asked him to use it on the balcony. It helped tremendously, so he cannot say that he isn't aware of the situation.

As I am beginning to become immune to his pity party routine or the intensifying silent treatment, he has now taken to spraying talc-based deodorants in my room. It literally feels like my lungs, inner chest wall and the back of my throat are coated in a thick, irritating substance, and my airways seem to narrow. Once it has hit me, my chest does not feel like it can expand due to a tight elastic sleeve wrapped around me. The coughing is immediate, and if I take too many breaths in the vicinity, the wheezing begins.

It is a very worrying situation to be in, but when you feel this is a purposeful decision by a third party, it is hard to comprehend. Interestingly, he only makes this 'mistake' when he is annoyed with me over something he has not been able to manipulate me to do. It has started happening very frequently lately, and despite its effects, a wry smile seems to cross his face each time he is successful. I know it is not by accident, as I have addressed it with him several times just this month, and now, he is spraying it in other rooms too, then leaving the doors open. I am worried for my safety and wonder exactly what he could be capable of.

Dear Diary,

Oh my goodness, I found something else out last night that has literally floored me. He has intermittently said over the past few months how he is struggling financially, but to be honest, so am I. He keeps saying how much he hates his house, the one he will never go to is costing him £2k a month to run. I don't get involved because your financial affairs are private, but he kept saying, 'I would never ask to borrow anything from you though.' Indirectly, he was trying to coerce me to offer it to him as he was in dire straits, but it's not my debt. He has said it repeatedly, but I have not bitten.

I wonder how many other people he has done this to. He then let it slip he had remortgaged his house, and to help make ends meet, he had borrowed the money I was saving for my holiday. I was absolutely shell-shocked! Not only had he gone into my private drawer, without my consent, but he had removed money that wasn't his to take, and he had done so when we had been on a break, months earlier.

He completely failed to perceive why I felt violated, or that he had committed theft because he was going to give it back. His defence was that he needed it, as though that was reason enough to take it. I am sickened. I had no reason to contemplate that this money was under any threat. I am flabbergasted and outraged. It makes me wonder if anything that ever came out of the philanderer's mouth was ever true. I feel as though he is using me to have his needs met at every expense to me that he can use. I feel angry. I feel like a fool. Not only myself, but my home has also been disrespected.

Dear Diary,

I have never been so embarrassed in my entire life! Today, I had arranged for a get-together with my friends for my birthday at our local. I have done parties for everyone else, including Robert and his family, but knew unless I organised something for myself, I would be sitting home alone as he wouldn't have made any effort. So, I bought lots of trays of sandwiches, cakes, and salad stuff and got a delivery of 10 pizzas and chips. I was really enjoying myself socialising with everyone when a sleazy guy I don't like tried to include himself. Robert's mum and his auntie could see my discomfort but went out of their way to include this stranger. I chose to ignore them but could hear them making cutting comments behind my back.

Robert then told me he was annoyed with his mum because of some altercation and asked if I would assist him with something, as he didn't want her to interfere. I willingly obliged, but then she wanted to take over, to which Robert told her to 'sit down.' I didn't think anything of it as I was having a lovely, relaxed time until she suddenly kicked off in a massive way, verbally abusing me, towering over me, shouting and pointing her finger in my face. Meanwhile, Robert, who was sat right next to me, witnessing her tirade of abuse, said absolutely nothing. She even grabbed him, screaming and pointing in his face, making a right spectacle of herself, in front of my friends and family. At first, I tried to appease it, but her sister, who had drunk over a bottle of wine, also began with negative, rude comments, even stating I was worse than his previous girlfriend who had apparently abused his daughter.

I certainly didn't want to get involved with their psycho behaviour, so I simply put my hand up, signalling for her to stop as she was out of control. This seemed to ignite her further, so, having been subjected to her irrational behaviour for long enough, I asked her to leave and informed her she wasn't welcome at my home anymore. It was an outrageous, vile and unwarranted attack which Robert admitted that he had fuelled and that she had been spoiling for a fight with him. This was my birthday, with my friends and family who were important to me, yet it meant nothing to either of them, so here I was, the lamb to the slaughter.

Robert did nothing to calm the situation he had caused, did nothing to stand in the gap for me, nothing to protect me from her outburst and nothing to defuse it by removing her. He simply sat there, impassive, non-reactive, unsupportive, uncaring, allowing her to disrespect me and the occasion. I felt so let down, humiliated, angry, hurt and outraged on so many levels. On the positive side, everyone congratulated me on handling the situation with dignity and made me see the funny side of how erratic her behaviour had been. As I sit here now, it does make me wonder if this is why Robert has no respect for women, because his mother has persistently shown such little respect for herself.

Dear Diary,

I am beginning to question my ability to see what is in front of me as people are coming forward with concerns about Robert. I bumped into a friend the other day who asked me about Robert's gambling habit. It took all my strength to stop my jaw from hitting the pavement to compose myself enough to respond nonchalantly, 'Oh, I didn't realise he had shared his situation with you?' I pretended.

'Yes, I saw him on Saturday night. He was absolutely hammered and was telling me about his massive gambling problem, but he has got you, so I am sure you will sort him out,' he told me.

I felt sideswiped straight in the gut. Was he joking with me? It was the first time I had heard anything about a gambling habit. This filled me with dread. I don't do debt; I don't do smoking, and I don't like excessive drinking. Seems like he has just scored the hat trick! My friend Janet is also concerned at his demeanour, describing him as only being half there, like he has got his head in the clouds or something. Her observations mirror my own concerns that Robert does not have the capacity to actually be with me in this relationship on a connective level to align with me in a supportive emotional or mental role.

The fundamentals of an equally fulfilling and productive relationship seem impossible with a person who is only happy if we are doing what he wants, if not he sulks, gets moody, makes everyone feel uncomfortable or tries to get his own way. I feel so conflicted. For the first year, he bombarded me with love and couldn't do enough or was this to create an image to keep me in it of what it could be like if I kept trying. The truth is, he drains me with his persistent negative view of the world & his depressive, unpredictable mood. If we argue, he shifts the blame, making me question my own perception of a situation, invalidating my feelings thoughts, expectations and rights to have my needs met.

He has made me feel so alone, to the point of invisibility, like I do not matter, and his wants come before my needs. His efforts are only surface-deep, and I need more, but the pull to stay is so much stronger because I do love him with all my heart, I am just not sure he can love anyone but himself. I wish there was someone I could trust enough to air my thoughts to get an honest second opinion, but I do not think anyone is interested. I did try with Anne, but rather than listen and really hear my heart, she just reverted it to what more I could do to better the situation and suggested I look at it from Robert's perspective.

I can't reach out to anyone because he has got them all under his spell with the wave of his charming wand, but it really is rubbish. I wish someone loved me enough to see my inner desperation instead of happily assuming everything is perfect just because it suits their narrative. Please, will someone help me? I feel like I am going under

Dear Diary,

I am feeling so sluggish at the moment, with a mind filled with clouds, unable to grasp any thoughts, never mind process them. Straight after church, I had to go lay down. I was so tired I could have slept on a washing line. The warmth of the duvet wrapped around me gave me comfort as I began to drift off, but then I was alerted to the movement beside me before an arm stretched around my waist. He had not only let himself into my house but made his way up to my room and invited himself into my bed. I tried to move, but he hushed me to relax and go back to sleep. I was far too tired to fight, so I willingly surrendered to the call of sleep.

However, he was not there to support me; he was there to take advantage of me and soon began breathing heavily down my neck. I was comatose until I felt him slide my shorts to one side and felt the hardness of him pushing his hips towards me from behind. I know I resisted his advances. I know I told him 'No.' I know I told him to stop, but he continued anyway, telling me it was because he 'loved me so much' and that he just needed me. He did not listen; he did not care about me or how I was feeling. He just wanted sexual gratification, even though I was too incapacitated to protect myself. And then he got up and left.

Is it true that, because we are in a relationship, he has a right to my body whenever he decides, whether I agree or not? I have never felt so worthless, objectified or disrespected as a woman and disregarded as a human being. Why would he do that? Am I being too sensitive, as he says? I feel so messed up. I am sore and bleeding again. How can this be deemed as love? You absolute fool! Why didn't you just report him? Now he has raped you on numerous occasions, and yet you still make excuses for him. WAKE UP BEFORE IT IS TOO LATE!!

Dear Diary,

When I look back over the last 3 years, I can see that all the special dates that were important to me were the ones he ruined time and time again. He would provide wrong times, and dates, turn up late, cause stress beforehand, sulk, give me the silent treatment, incite pointless arguments or continually put me down so that I would leave and walk home. He would even get arsey if I spoke to friends, block my route, redirect me in a different direction and woe forbid any man who dared to speak to me or, worse still, put his hand around my waist or lean in close to speak to me. I have persistently walked on eggshells so I do not upset him, whereas he doesn't care a hoot about my feelings at all. My head is mashed. What is it about me that he hates so much to treat me so badly?

Dear Diary,

Today I wept for most of the day. I cannot begin to get my head around what he has done, and I cannot even tell you as it will make it real. Why does he make me feel so bad when all I do is love him?

Dear Diary,

I feel so sick. For the 3rd time this month, he has woken me for sex. What is wrong with him? I am sick of telling him that he may be aroused and primed for sex, but I am not. Tonight, he really hurt me, and I haven't stopped bleeding each time I have gone to the toilet. I have also had to change my pants three times today. I tried to use this fact to get it through to him that I do not appreciate being woken in the middle of the night, nor is it enjoyable. In fact, it just feels like I am being sexually abused. Rather than empathise or try to understand, he got really angry and told me never to repeat the words. He became defensive and, before I knew it, he was the victim again. He actually challenged me to consider how it felt for him to be accused of being a sexual abuser. I honestly cannot win. I do not feel loved, yet I love him and do everything I can to make myself loveable.

Dear Diary,

I am ashamed to say I feel such loathing for him. It makes me sick to the core that he is infecting me with his blackness, his sordid desires that he is acting out on me. I no longer feel like my body is my own because he possesses it whenever he chooses, whether I am a willing participant or not. No matter how many times I explain to him how his behaviour affects me, it doesn't change. Again, today I was met with the same response, and he was suddenly the victim again. I don't know how he manages to disown his actions in favour of it somehow making me feel bad for telling him to stop sexually assaulting me.

Today, whilst we were out walking, I told him that when he touches me, it hurts. He seemed alarmed at first, as though he really cared that he had caused me some discomfort. But when I spelt it out, he got angry and then dismissed me. Conversation over. I feel defeated. Am I being 'dramatic,' as he says, or is this normal behaviour when you are in a relationship with someone? I feel so out of my depth. I love him with all my heart, and it feels so wrong, but I have not had a relationship for almost a decade, so I simply don't know. But who can I turn to? Who is there that I can ask? He says it would be a gross breach of our intimate details and that this should remain confidential between us. I am so confused.

Dear Diary,

I feel as though I have lost my inner self, having had my insides sucked away with a dentist's vacuum tool. He has systematically drained me to the point I do not recognise myself, and still, it continues. I have taken to begging him to stop now, to please just leave, as I fear for my own sanity, but he is a parasite eating away at me from the inside out. I cannot make it stop; this is not normal behaviour, and I think he must have something seriously wrong with him. I also cannot believe that I am the first, as he is very well adept at the techniques he is using. They are savage and only seek to destroy.

Repeatedly, my mind has driven along the one-way street of how many other women's lives has he destroyed? If only I had their details, I could meet with them in secret and at least then I would have some answers to my questions. What has happened to him that has created this monster seeking to use, abuse and defile me? He is sick yet parades himself like Jekyll and Hide. No one would guess that beneath the surface is this evil lurking.

I used to love his piercing blue eyes. Now they bore into me as black as day, seeking to devour. I am at the point of no return because he is so embedded within me, like the talons of a vulture, the sickness seeping into me, running through my veins. I feel so poisoned by his spiritual blackness, disarmed and unable to save myself.

What was my crime to have deserved being tortured like a cat perpetually tormenting a vulnerable mouse? Is that what he first saw when he intently watched me from afar, researching who I was? Did he see a vulnerability in me that he knew he could so easily exploit? He must have, because this was not a coincidence. It was a premeditated, orchestrated attack, like a paedophile preying on a child, only we are adults.

Did he see my carefree, fun-loving approach to life and thought it would look good on him, so he decided to extract it to retain it for himself? That is exactly what it feels like. The essence of who I am has been literally extracted, and he now walks the earth in my place, after robbing me of me.

My only ability to survive at the moment is by blocking out any thoughts as I travel through each 24-hour period. Feelings? I cannot allow myself the luxury of stepping into those or allowing myself to engage, as the fragile shell holding me together will undoubtedly splinter and shatter like toughened glass. I find myself watching the drug addicts as I take solace on a park bench and envy their ability to at least escape their nightmares. I honestly do not know how much longer I can survive or the depths of depletion he will take before it is time for him to move on. I yearn for the moment he is gone from my life forever, and yet my fears for the next woman that I know he will simply sidestep into overwhelm me.

I do not know you, but your vulnerability will excite and energise him. He may already have his sights set upon you. Did the last victim feel the way I am feeling right now? Did she fear for me? If she did, I am thankful to her, although

I wish she could have stopped him, if only to have spared me. Is that selfish? He tells me I am selfish all the time, tells me I am fat, treats me like I am worthless, and ignores me to the point I feel invisible. Why is it that I have always promoted inclusion, always been hospitable, a good friend and a listening ear, yet I am so alone? No one has rung me for months, no one has just checked in on me, called for a cuppa, asked me out for a drink, nothing to reach out to demonstrate they care.

Maybe what he says is true: nobody ever really cared; they just used me for what they could get. I just wish someone would save me, but I fear if he finds my diary, he will end me for good.

Dear Diary,

I am so very tired. I just wish I had someone else to talk to, if only for my own sanity, but he has chased all my friends away. I feel stuck without a light at the end of the tunnel. I am alone, lost and forgotten by all who I once knew and loved. Why hasn't there been even one person available to reach out to me? Am I really so despised, as Robert continually tells me, that no one cares if I am dead or alive? If that is the case, then I may as well end my life now, as I cannot live this way. I won't!

Dear Diary,

I am now being subjected to the risk of sexual abuse whenever I want to sleep, have had a drink or want to take a rest. His behaviour utterly disgusts me! I cannot get into bed without him having to slip under the covers too, but it is not to cuddle or comfort me. he lies with his back to me and then inadvertently reaches back with his left hand to literally flick my clit.

It is a task-orientated action that is performed without care, love or pleasure. Ultimately, there is no engagement of foreplay—just a rough rubbing that is very uncomfortable. it makes me sore and is just a means to an end for his own sexual gratification. Multiple times I have said no. I have moved my hips away, but he is relentless, as though this area has a secret on/off switch that he has the power to operate. I have told him on numerous occasions I do not want him prodding and poking at me, as it is invasive, intimately abusive, and he does not have my consent to use my body for sex.

I do try so hard to say things in a way he will receive it, understand, reflect and stop. However, regardless of the eggshells I tentatively step upon, I cannot

289

win, as he becomes defensive at what he perceives is a rebuke, and then I am subjected to the moods again. The word 'conditioning' springs to mind, so for that reason, I will continue to exert my right to speak up. He seems to have this innate need to be in control that's as responsive as a knee-jerk reaction tested by a doctor. For instance, if on a rare occasion I was to touch him first, he would concentrate hard to make sure he didn't get an erection.

He must be in control, and it has got to be at his say-so. But this is happening every single time we settle down in bed, whether that is in the evening or my taking rest during the day. For this reason, I don't want him in my room when I want to rest. There is no way we could ever cuddle up, as it always must revert to sex. If we have been out and I want to go straight to sleep, he will pester me. I can turn over with my back to him and tell him no, but he will slip his dick out and start prodding at me.

I will reiterate I am not interested, stating that I need to sleep, but he will not be satisfied until he has forcibly taken me. Again, it is unsatisfying, uncomfortable and unloving for me, just the kind of act that he has described as having with his ex, to ejaculate. I wonder if she ever felt used like I do, or did she also become like a desensitised puppet? How I wish I could find out, as there is power in knowledge, and together we could stop him. It's just here on my own, I am powerless.

Dear Diary,

It's funny how things he has said in the past are like red flags suddenly flapping against the wind, whereas at the time I never gave them a second thought. Last night, he tried to wake me for sex, but I rolled over and ignored him. Again, I could feel the bed moving. It generated his confession of having masturbated every single day—sometimes twice a day—from the age of 12, whether he'd had sex or not. Maybe I should have taken note that this was simply a habit, an action to reach a result without any real feeling or connection with love. Alarmingly, he seemed so proud of his secret behaviour, as though it was somehow an achievement for the 'Guinness Book of Records.'

He revealed how sex with his ex-had been a non-pleasurable, mechanical event, so each morning he would enter his en-suite to relieve himself further. In the beginning, I tried to educate him on the difference between unfulfilling sex and the depth of a mutually loving relationship. However, when I look back now, the truth is it took over a year to become anywhere near compatible—and *shamefully, throughout that time, I reached an orgasm on only two occasions. Yes, that red flag is flapping wildly in the wind these days!*

Dear Diary,

I feel like Robert's sexual appetite now is insatiable. Perhaps he has felt me pulling away more and more over the past couple of months. He has commented on my inability to tell him I love him, but how can you love someone who treats you like an object for his sexual pleasure? His loveless sexual acts have intensified to the point that it is not just every single day, but it has been two and sometimes three times in one day. I feel devalued beyond belief, disregarded to the point that not only doesn't he hear me, but he doesn't care about me either.

I feel sick to write this, but his recent exploit is to assault me orally. Maybe he has got fed up with me moving away and telling him he is making me sore prodding and poking at me, so it is his way of lubricating the area to ensure he gets what he wants. It seems there is nothing that will deter him. No matter how much I complain, he minimises my feelings, and nothing will make him stop. I have physically pushed him away, moved myself away from him, explained how it makes me feel and tried to make him leave, but he is undeterred.

He is like a dog chasing a bitch on heat. He has one focus, and whether I want to participate or not, he is determined to finish. A couple of days ago, after subjecting me to oral abuse, he then pushed me over to take me from behind, which I didn't want him to do. It was awful and so very painful, just another to add to the many times that he has caused vaginal bleeding. I am so sickened that this person acts to everyone else as though he is such a nice guy, yet behind closed doors, he is anything but.

Whilst out walking this afternoon, I carefully broached the subject with him AGAIN about how unpleasurable and uncomfortable it was for me. I made it abundantly clear that I never wanted to be subjected to the indignity ever again. I actually likened his action to having a broom handle shoved up inside me. I also explained how it had caused me to bleed for the last two days. I felt relieved when he thanked me for letting him know and praised me for being able to speak openly with him. I am such a fool for believing in him or trusting that he would show me any consideration, as unknowingly I had just given him information to satisfy his sadistic side. This evening, he proceeded to do the exact same thing again. He cannot say he doesn't know what he is doing is wrong, as I have also told him that there is only one word for it, and that is RAPE.

Dear Diary,

In the past two weeks, the same vaginal bleeding has continued as he flicks, prods and pokes at me. Then, when that doesn't work, he orally abuses me, and then I am subjected to the same broom handle unpleasantness. Regardless of my protests, he is also still waking me up in the middle of the night wanting sex. Inevitably, like any normal person, I do not want my sleep pattern disturbed, but when I object, he belittles and undermines me.

Apparently, he would love me to wake him up for sex, and then proceeded to complain about how unfair it was that I could have sex whenever I wanted, but he couldn't. I am dumbfounded that he contemplates this as an acceptable approach in a loving relationship. It is quite an archaic, primitive, controlling and very frightening concept that he feels my body should be an open door for him whenever he decides. I am not making any excuses for him, as there aren't any viable excuses, but his belief explains his disgusting behaviour. I have made it quite categorically clear on numerous occasions that I never want to wake up in this manner.

As far as I am concerned, his thoughts/dreams may have caused an arousal, but he seems totally oblivious as to why I do not welcome the prospect of being expected to simply perform at his demand, especially in the middle of the night. Recently, I have been looking back over previous diaries and was stunned to find it had happened sporadically over the first couple of months. I guess it had never really registered with me before because they were far and few between, so I excused them as isolated incidents.

He had always excused himself stating, 'Sorry, I thought you were awake.' However, the regularity now with which he openly wakes me, along with the aggressive determination to take me against my will, is unmistakable. I feel so isolated, fearful and unable to reach out to anyone, as no one seems to even notice I exist anymore. I feel abandoned by every single person I ever loved, as there is no one willing to stand in the gap for me the way I so willingly dived into oceans for them.

I cannot bear the weight of the pain. I feel so let down and overcome by shame and loss. Not the loss of the people—because they were clearly never my people—but the loss of myself, buried somewhere beneath the rubble of who I was destined to become. I am such a loser. I cannot even make myself hate him because I am that depleted and void of all emotions. My saving grace is that God has not abandoned me, as without Him, I would surely die. I believe He will bring me through this and that my experiences will not be wasted, even if it is to help his next victim. Please, God, let me get out of this alive.

Dear Diary,

I simply do not know who I am dealing with or what will happen next with Robert. His character is interchangeable, along with his moods. I feel like I continually walk on a tightrope whenever I am around him. My life does not feel like it is mine to live. I have no rights, no say in anything. Even what I think and believe is apparently wrong too. I feel as though I am barely holding on to who I used to be. My mind is so distorted and polluted with the things he impregnates within it.

He once described his mum as being a negatively minded person who often put others in a bad light to elevate herself, but this is what he does. If it is just him and me, all appears to be fine, but should any of my friends join us for a meal or drinks, he is vile—goading people to stimulate a disagreement. He kicked off tonight at a waiter, blaming him for knocking his knife onto the floor, but I saw him intentionally do it himself. It reminded me of how he had described his mother as having an explosive temper—who would kick off unexpectedly with little provocation just because she couldn't get her own way.

He seems to do this all the time. When I try to ignore it, I am then subjected to a public dressing down about a perceived disrespect of him, but he demonstrates an inability to own the disrespect he shows others. He has acute tunnel vision, only observing matters from his own perspective. I don't like this controlling, unpredictable behaviour, and I do not know how he has hidden it from me for so long. Or maybe there is truth in the phrase that 'love is blind.' I feel sickened that I have so easily been duped by this vile, cold-hearted man, but I am now able to see with my eyes rather than with my heart.

I look back and can see how I have been second-guessing my own behaviours and reactions to ensure they didn't initiate another negative episode. It is evident that through my compromising, he has unwittingly been able to condition me to allow himself the pleasure to keep repeating the same patterns of abuse. I stupidly believed there was room for change because he would supposedly recognise the error of his conduct—often accompanied by tears of remorse—but they were nothing more than a ploy to maintain his control. I have misinterpreted his displays as a willingness to grow, but their cunning nature has simply given him licence to continue pulling the wool over my eyes.

How stupid I feel now, to have let the same damaging traits continue to fester beneath the surface until other issues arose—spawned out of his insecurities, neediness, jealousy or wantonness to control. Then the methods used would be to coerce, manipulate, gas light or emotional blackmail. It makes me feel ill that it inspired a desire in myself to want to try harder with the simplicity of his remark that, 'None of his friends would put up with my behaviour.'

This precipitates the message that it is my fault and that I should be grateful that he is with me, along with inducing the fear that he may leave me if I don't change! At this point, I just wish he would go. I am sick of trying to sidestep his moods, deflect his unwanted advances and navigate the dramatic changes to his character. I don't love him, and I don't want him here, but like a boomerang, he seems compelled to return.

Dear Diary,

I feel like I am going insane. By day, he is a needy, suffocating individual whose moods I must navigate, and by night, nothing less than a sexual predator. I have sent him home on numerous occasions, spoken up about not feeling safe in my own bed, and literally barred him from being here, but now I am being subjected to him stalking me.

Today, he has taken to persistently ringing or messaging me, making any excuse to get through the door. But I know if I open it, he will manipulate me to get back in. Wherever I go, he is lurking in the shadows and then randomly pops out right in front of me, just staring. Today, as I walked through the town, he circled around the bus station to bump into me accidentally on purpose. But I had already seen him, so I quickly doubled back. He then found where I had parked my car, so he hovered around it until I returned, actually walking up to my window pretending he hadn't seen me. It's such a ridiculous, juvenile act. Apart from it being very disturbing, he also displays no care about how this behaviour frightens me. His only focus is to obtain my attention, so I know it is just to apply pressure through emotional blackmail so I will feel sorry for him and agree to give it another go.

Last night, I went out into the garden to put the wheelie bins out and caught sight of him leaning against the lamppost, just outside my gate. Luckily, he was gazing down at his phone, so hadn't noticed me, and I was able to duck back inside without him observing me. Why is he doing this? I am beginning to feel like a prisoner in my own home now. When I have got to the point of not being able to take any more in the past and spoken to him, he only invalidates my feelings, thoughts and emotions with tears under the guise of 'they were never his intentions.'

However, the facts always remain that he has still created situations to ultimately cause anxiety and distress. His interpretation is always the same, and it results in him shifting the blame or minimising the situation, urging that 'we can get through anything, as nothing is irreparable.' I am beginning to wonder if it is me who is being judgemental and critical, because if not, I have to accept that he really does live in cloud cuckoo land. I am unsure how he can fail so miserably in not taking ownership of his actions—for himself—to not rectify his behaviour or to show any support for me emotionally or mentally.

They are unsettling behavioural traits which make me exceptionally uncomfortable, and I can see it is really beginning to get to Louise too. Is this going to be another friend who severs all connections with me because of him? Last night, Louise and I actually ran out of the back door of the pub. We went around the entire building just so he wouldn't see which direction we had gone in. Whether I am with him or not, he is like an emotional vampire, zapping my energy because he refuses to let me go.

He talks of us growing old together, promising to take care of me, suggesting he would happily push me around in a wheelchair. It is not a prospect I find appealing when he doesn't even look after me now. As far as pushing me around in a wheelchair, not only would I be scared for my life every time a bus drove past or he had me on the edge of a cliff, but I would probably have ended up in it by his hand. I cannot help wondering about his wife who passed away and whether he also sprayed deodorant aerosols in her presence too, to initiate her asthma attack. I used to feel so proud to be with him and that he would do anything to keep us together, but now it terrifies me that I will never get away from him. I really do believe I will either die by his hand or he will push me to suicide, as this will only be my means of escape. Help me, please, before it is too late.

Dear Diary,

Life with Robert has become so unbearable. I told him I wanted out, and all he can think of is the embarrassment it will cause him since we only got engaged a few months ago. He is holding on tighter to the point I cannot even use the toilet without him being in the bathroom. It is horrendous, not to mention an *invasion of my privacy. I am no longer able to express love towards him, and still, he won't go. He knows he has lost me; he knows I don't feel the same way about him anymore because I cannot hide the contempt that I hold for him, and yet still he keeps turning up.*

I may have been the kind, soft, pliable person who has been putty in his hands for the past 12 months, but he is finding that these days I am not so easily manipulated. I feel sick to the core when I think about how I have been subjected to his relentless advances for sex. Whenever he hugged me, he would stick his nether regions into me and make some derogatory motion or words for sex. His phrase, 'get up them stairs,' constantly rings out in my ears. Now I ignore him and walk away. I know people would judge and think why such an intelligent woman is allowing herself to be disgraced this way, unable to fathom why I don't just smack him in the face or kick him out. Like everyone else, I would probably have thought the same, along with a belligerent defiance that I would never let that happen to me.

How wrong could I be? After falling in love with the man whom I thought was my future, my one true love, that one person I had waited my entire life for, I was attached and then became trapped through his systematic abuse. In the beginning, he was everything I had dreamt of. But, after all the emotional abuse, manipulation, coercing tricks and guilt tripping I have sustained, it reduced me to an emptiness within and of actually feeling that I was lucky to have him. He has been telling me for so long that everything is my fault, that no other man would put up with me, and that women are constantly coming on to him. It conditions you to put up with almost anything to keep them. I have often asked myself if I am a weak person, but no, generally I am a strong, confident, independent woman. I just fell in love with a person who sought to exploit both myself and the things I had accomplished.

As a salesman, he has spent a lifetime assessing human nature to find a person's weak spots for the purpose of manipulating them for his own benefit. He has intentionally taken advantage of my good nature, demoralising me into compliance via tactics he has spent a lifetime perfecting, with only one goal in mind—to have his needs met.

Hence why I kick myself now at my blind trust in believing he was a man of integrity—honest, kind, thoughtful and generous like myself. To my absolute horror, I can see that this was just an assumption based upon the lies and images he intentionally portrayed, when, in fact, he is morally corrupt. I am sat here with tears pouring down my face at the confessions of my own stupidity.

Dear Diary,

Oh my goodness, what have I done? He pushed me too far, and I finally snapped. I am mentally exhausted. He makes me feel so nervous when he is around, and even when he isn't here, I am stressed because I know he will be coming back. The sleep deprivation is the worst because I am so scared to close my eyes in case, I wake up with him abusing me. I couldn't spend another night lying next to him—he is a monster. It was my intention to say anything just to get him to spend one night at home, which would give me enough time to pack his stuff. He instinctively knew there was something I wasn't telling him, but I just kept saying I didn't feel well. That just gave him the excuse to say he 'couldn't leave when I was ill.'

No matter what I said, he wasn't budging, but this time I was determined to stand my ground. I see it now—he has taken everything from me: my money, my friends, my independence, my life, my home, everything that was dear to me. And in return, I get him. It is not a fair exchange, and I want my life back. I will not live as a carbon copy of myself. I have one life, and I refuse to let him keep destroying it. So, I ran a bath and told him I needed to rest and would see him tomorrow. Without warning, he grabbed me by the throat, slamming me hard against the wall. When he brought his head close to the side of mine, a voice unlike, I had ever heard before came from his lips: 'You had better not be lying. You wouldn't like it if you made me angry.'

As he stepped away, his eyes were as black as the night sky, with the tinge of the reddest sunset. A demonic laugh escaped his mouth that sent chills throughout my being. I am utterly convinced the man is possessed with something that is not of this world. I opened my mouth to scream, but the panic rendered me mute, and no sound emerged. What have I done? He will kill me for sure if I dare to oppose him, but he is already killing me slowly from the inside. How did I get involved with this? He had showered me with praise in the beginning, made me feel like he was the answer to all my problems, that he was 'the one.'

I don't get it. How has he been able to keep this hidden without it manifesting before now? Or maybe all the times he has abused and raped me, it has been some demonic entity possessing him and taking me? No, it is too farfetched. This cannot be true, but there was no denying what I saw and heard. I need to get as far away from here as soon as I possibly can, if only to sleep so I can think more clearly. Am I going mad? Has he finally succeeded in pushing me beyond the bridge of no return? I have got to escape—I've got to get to somewhere safe until I can decide what to do. Maybe I should talk to the police because there is no doubt in my mind he has both the ability and will to kill me. First, I must find somewhere secure to hide you because if he reads what I have written, he will kill me for sure. But where? It has to be somewhere he will never find you, just in case he finds me.

Demi read that last sentence again, trusting that the writer was able to get away. But as it resonated with her, she realised that Sandra and Justine were right—they did need to get to the bottom of what had happened to her. Demi opened her desk drawer and took the brown paper the book had been wrapped in out. Why she had kept it, she didn't know. Perhaps it was just that they had belonged together, so therefore they should remain as one.

She began to open it out to lay it completely flat upon the surface of the book so that she could wrap the book back up like a jeweller presenting a gem on a black velvet cloth. Demi tied the leather strip back around the book and reached for the brown paper to slide underneath when something caught her eye. She tried to hold the paper up, but it was impossible to be absolutely sure. She laid the paper back down, took out her mobile phone, applied the torch and examined the paper's surface. Yes, she was sure there were further indentations of writing. Demi took a pencil and very carefully, lightly rubbed it across the surface of the hidden letters, back and forth, until the entire area was covered.

When she examined it with her torch again, her hand flew up to her mouth, and she instantaneously stood, the chair flying backwards to the floor.

'I know who the woman is,' she said out loud.

Closing In

The evidence is building, the case is secure,
I cannot wait 'til they break down your door.
The walls are moving, they're closing in,
Removing your arrogant smirky grin.
Do you feel it tightening the closer they get?
The wheels are turning; your fate is set.
But no, they're too clever, they have you in sight,
The darkest of shadows soon in the spotlight.
You thought I had gone, erasing my parts,
But I still exist in your 'Jar of Hearts.'
I will not rest 'til my work is done;'
The soul may depart, but my spirit lives on.

(Juli Flintoff)

Part 4
The Present

Chapter 34
Beneath the Veneer

When Robert Day Junior had reversed out of the drive of 357 St Michael's Mount, he was grinning inwardly—even more so when he took the time to nod his thanks in acknowledgement to the two policemen standing at the gate. He put the car into first gear and slowly pulled forward. Then, as soon as he had cleared them, he broke into the biggest smirk as he drove away. What fools the police could be, he mused.

With the carrier bag of garments secured underneath his seat, he drove steadily and carefully down to the bottom of the road so as not to induce any suspicion before accelerating off once he was around the bend. He blew out a sigh of relief as he recognised what a close call it had been.

Now what? he pondered to himself as he continued on his route towards the house that he had never truly felt was his home and absolutely hated. To Robert Day Jr, it was just a minor blip. At the end of the day, he knew he would soon find someone else to fill the vacancy—there were plenty of replacements just waiting to be told how special they were.

He chuckled at the thought of their stupidity and gullibility to think that someone like him could ever fall for them. These middle-aged women carrying their life's baggage with 'I'm a victim' so clearly splashed across it. If it wasn't so disappointing, the absolute desperation written on their faces would be humorous. He couldn't believe how easy picking their field had become: single parents, downtrodden divorcees, unhappy in their careers, hurt from a lifetime of disappointments—just waiting for someone to come along and rescue them. It was astounding how they stood out in a crowded room—a sitting duck with a target on their backs.

It was sheer stupidity how they submitted themselves so easily to him after being offered just a few select words that they wanted to hear. The digital era had made it so much easier to find them on Facebook when he would cast his line with a message to see if the bait was taken. Then, it was just a matter of doing a little bit of homework—looking through their news feed to find out their interests, the types of things that they posted, what family was important to them, and if there were any mutual friends. The friendship base was important, as this generally revealed specifically who they hung out with—photographs of where they socialised, usually accompanied by check-ins specifically showing when and how often they frequented these places.

They made it so easy that he could just sit in the shadows, watch and get to know them without them even realising it—until he was ready to put his operation into practice. This was usually as soon as he found the jewel to his crown: a post about their innermost thoughts about the type of man they were looking for. Never had he been disappointed, as every ounce of information he was searching for was already out there for his eyes to discover—they only had themselves to blame. At times, he couldn't believe just how easy they made it for him. So what if the last one had pushed him until he had snapped? She should have kept her trap shut—now look where she was. It didn't matter to him. He had the ability to just evade the issue by stepping into the next saps life that crossed his path, and he knew it was only a matter of time before he would find his next target. So, no harm done.

Robert Day Jr had only one purpose, and that was to basically get his needs met. He didn't care about them—in fact, he had absolutely no feelings, no connection, nor interest in them whatsoever. The words that came out of his mouth were just that: words, with no value, no emotion and absolutely nothing coming from the heart. He had perfected the disingenuous smile, the fake sympathy, the apparent listening ear to all their problems, with the occasional nod of the head or soothing word—when in reality, he was probably contemplating what he was going to have for tea.

What they had to say disinterested him. Who they were bored him. What they looked like was of no importance—they were nothing as far as he was concerned, other than a meal ticket. These silly women willingly offered themselves up to him like a sacrifice on the altar for his narcissistic pleasures, so it would be rude for him not to obligingly feast. Why should he feel guilty if they wanted to put a roof over his head, to lavish him with whatever gifts he desired—all for the minimal cost and effort of a token gesture here and there?

They should feel guilty at their stupidity for being so easily duped. Besides, they were lucky that he had chosen them, devoted so much time and brought life back into their mundane, desperate lives.

Did Robert Day Jr feel any remorse regarding Karen Blakely? Of course not. He was detached, unemotional and yet excitedly imagining what his next victim would be like, as though he was deciding his next serving at a buffet. He was so egotistical that he couldn't help but congratulate himself on having recognised the opportunity to exploit this bracket of women and the perfection of the plan that he had been able to execute time and time again. His favourite part was probably from the early stalking to the end of the first year, because this was fulfilling—manipulating as much out of them as he could obtain. Then, it began to be less of a sport and more tiresome.

At first, it was so easy. They would be fooled by his expressions of love, his desperation to want to be with them all the time, that he couldn't get enough of them and how he'd never met anybody like them. He would pour it on thick, get them to be fully compliant and reliant upon him—that they would do anything rather than lose his attentive claptrap. He would make them believe that he had wished he had met them sooner, and they would fall for it and actually yearn for the time they had missed out on and want to make up for those lost experiences.

They would automatically wish for that too, where he had actually witnessed them display regrets only to become besotted to the point of not wanting to let go in case they lost him. He was then able to experience life to the fullest whilst they paid for meals and holidays, gave him the use of their car to run around in and helped pay his bills. The best thing about it was the sex on tap—morning, noon and night—for a flash of his smile and the utterance of a few effective complimentary words that he had picked up along the way. What an exchange!

But this last one had proved to be a bit of hard work—always resisting, always arguing, always making him feel like he wasn't quite measuring up. But he wasn't one to throw in the towel or be beaten. He chuckled to himself as he thought, *Well, look who doesn't match up now, babes*—at least his lungs would continue to take another breath. As he pulled up outside his house, a wave of regret washed over him—not for what he'd done, but the fact that he was back here again. How he hated this place with its fake stone façade—yet, like him, there was nothing authentic nor respectable about it.

Even the building work he had attempted had been a disaster—having been built over the top of the decking rather than on solid ground. A bit like the lack of foundations to his own life, which was built on the surface of other people's achievements. The fake laminate in the dining room had been fitted to cover the manhole of a sewage pipe—not unlike the veneer of his character, thinly covering the faecal matter within his decaying heart. He walked down the side of the house, put his key in the lock and pushed hard with his shoulder against the door to free it from its swollen jamb.

It had been a while since he'd had to return to live here, so the smell that greeted him was pungent, like an open, old carton of milk had been left out. It had permeated the room, making him gag, so he stepped outside, took a gulp of air, then stepped back in before quickly opening all the windows and French door to let the breeze flow through. Luckily, the door to the room had been shut, so the smell hadn't carried itself through this area. He looked back at the kitchen, with its numerous pots and pans stuck exactly where they had been left, the food debris caked within them, the discoloured, heat-resistant silicon spoons still sticking out, their oval counterparts secreted in mouldy masses.

The tired kitchen was way past its sell-by date, with drawers tilted rather than secured in place, the cupboards ill-fitted and the handles spinning in their drilled holes. As he walked across the surface of the filthy kitchen floor, the soles of his feet sticking to it like the toilets of a backstreet pub, he couldn't ignore the brokenness of his surroundings—not unlike the women he had picked up along the way. The existence of life in this place was only evident in the multitude of spider's webs. He stepped forward to observe a movement and looked closely to watch as a spider began to devour a woodlouse in its finely woven silky threads, crushing it without mercy. Not unlike the way that he had smashed Karen Blakely's, face onto that island.

He closed his eyes to savour a replay of her startled eyes, the surprise on her face, the moment her head hit its target, the crunch and crack of her breaking bones, and her lifeless body dropping to the floor. He replayed it again, this time concentrating on the deep thud of her skull cracking and the pool of blood congealing as her brain juice seeped from its inner sanctum. He would keep the video safely locked in the vault of his own compartmental memory banks, where he would salivate over it at leisure, his finger always ready to hover over the start button. It would serve as a reminder to ensure the next one was fully compliant and under his complete control. never again would he make the mistake of allowing anyone the power to make him lose his self-control.

Karen Blakely had a lot to answer for, and he could feel hatred was beginning to manifest itself at the realisation that it was her fault he'd had to come back to this rundown hovel, that he absolutely detested. The putrid smell, the sight of his failed DIY efforts, the non-existent soul that bombarded him with an atmosphere of deathly stillness, and the lack of life within it. He wouldn't have admitted it, not even to himself, but it replicated not only his life but his heart and his soul too. He took himself upstairs in order to take a shower, wanting to be rid of the stench of her house, the hospital and the police station so he could leave the past behind him. The future was his only concern, but the drains were overwhelming.

As soon as he ignited the shower, the putrid smell intensified, assaulting the air like it was muck spreading day down on the farm. He glanced down to find the crawling of black mould around the edges of the shower base had multiplied significantly since his last visit. The glass screen was dull, covered by the rough, off-white chalky texture of limescale, with the same substance coating the majority of the tiles. How he hated this place that her selfishness had brought him back to. but she had paid for it, so it did give him some comfort, and with that, he decided not to give it another thought.

In an instant of the same breath, his thoughts brought him back to the interview with that beautiful young officer, Collins. He couldn't ignore the fact that she did have a nice, rounded, firm butt, small pert tits and the twinkle in her gaze as their eyes met. Yes, there was definitely something there. There was something deliciously coy and innocent about her   she was like a delicate little mouse, ripe for the picking. But was it a little too dangerous with her being a police officer, especially when they were going through the investigation?

'Down boy,' he told himself.

As he stepped into the shower, he couldn't get the thought of Officer Collins out of his head, mentally visualising what she would look like beneath her black cotton trousers and tight grey top. Before he knew it, the excitement had reached his nether regions, so the only course of action by then was to release the building pressure. Well, after all, he hadn't been able to satisfy himself the night before due to Karen Blakely's attitude—and look how that had ended, he soothed himself. For now, he would just have to make do with a one-on-one solo act of pleasuring himself. It didn't take long as it wasn't in the excitement of the moment or to do with feelings, it was the habitual action, which is why he was so carelessly able to screw around regardless of the mental anguish he caused.

After all, he had been relieving himself on a daily basis this way for the past 35 years, since he was 12 years of age, and his mother had walked in on him and leathered him. It was his psychological two-fingered salute to his dearly departed, darling mother, and it would have to get him by for now. He flicked the deposit of slime from his hand towards the plug hole of the shower base, leaving it to find its own way down the drain. He didn't bother to soap himself nor rinse away the deposits from his nether regions, but then this was a man who didn't see the value in washing his hands either after using the toilet.

He wiped his feet and stepped out onto the shower mat, grinning to himself about how he always ensured there were two imprints of his size 10s whenever he was at Karen's. He knew it annoyed her, which is why he continually did it— like banging her hoover against the units to damage them or putting his hot drink on every wooden surface he could and spilling his curry on the floor. Better still was the time he had intentionally spilt the curry on her brand-new settee. She had been as reactive as a cornered skunk, and her language had been just as foul. He smiled at the memory, pleased with himself even though it had cost him his supper. It had been worth it, especially the months of mileage he had seen it eat away at her. The silly cow.

He got himself a new pair of boxers along with a set of clean clothes before throwing the dirty ones he had taken off into the washing machine. Before turning it on, he went out to the car to collect the secreted evidence under the driver's seat, then took it into the house and shoved that in the washing machine too. He decided to put it on a hot wash, so turned the dial up to 60°, added the detergent and fabric conditioner, slammed the door and pressed the start button.

Hungry and with no food in the house, he decided to take a walk to find a little cafe where he could enjoy a hearty breakfast to help him formulate his next plan of action. He locked the door behind him and, as he made his way along the high street, he mused upon whom the next target would be and where he might meet her. He was in such a chirpy, happy mood as he contemplated if it might be at the library, in a shopping mall, would it be when he was buying groceries, or out walking in the park. The list was endless, and the possibilities excited him dramatically. He loved the hunt, but he was unable to leave it for longer than 2 weeks. History had taught him that if he became agitated, then his mental health would be affected.

If he did not have a woman standing beside him, adoring him, then his inner chastised little boy would submerge—feeling neglected, unwanted and unseen.

Robert Day Jr could not allow the feelings of the sullen, morngy brat to rear his ugly head, nor did he want to sink into the spiral of depression that had once threatened to drown him. No, he had to find his next target and quickly, as it energised and validated his whole existence—especially if they quickly became hooked and besotted with him. Robert Day Jr would never admit to any weaknesses, but the truth was that he couldn't function on his own. As much as he hated his mother and her unbearable interference in his life, he had been heavily reliant upon her.

It was his mother who had parented his child, she who had looked after her whilst he enjoyed holidays away with his *new* family, her who had cleaned and painted his home, and her that he had turned to when he couldn't cope. Never would he ever have admitted how she had guided, helped, supported and fought his battles for him throughout his life because he hated these inadequacies reflected on him every time he looked at her. It was the one part of himself that he despised the most, as it oozed weakness and demonstrated a neediness that ordinarily he personally found abhorrent in others. Oh, how he had managed to master that negative inner voice the moment his super sanctimonious mother had fallen on hard times and began coming to him to borrow money. This had given him great superiority over her and provided him with immeasurable satisfaction—to be able to control if and when he would sanction her rewards, or not.

He would also never admit that his feelings of desperation to be with a woman represented his early childhood yearning to be loved and valued by his mother. His treatment of women was borne from a direct parallel of both the type of relationship he perceived both he and his mother had and the feelings this induced. Therefore, he had to quench his addiction and secure himself another relationship quickly—to cease her laughing face from haunting his wakefulness and to silence her mocking voice in his head.

For this reason, Robert Day Jr could not function unless he had a woman doting on him, focusing all her time on him and believing in him—to ensure she didn't have the chance to question his motive or contemplate his true intentions. He wanted to have her totally reliant upon him, to be the focal point of her life and anything that got in the way of that—like friends or family—would be eradicated.

Most women loved the attention and the intensity of his seemingly open heart; it was refreshing as most men were reluctant to make a commitment.

Robert Day Jr had perfected the portrayal of the perfect partner, as it was the open doorway to ingratiate himself quickly and firmly into their lives without them even realising it. He would demonstrate being the personification of perfection long enough to ensure they were either hooked or he had stripped them of their entire assets and then he was gone. He marvelled at how, with such little effort, he had been able to wipe out the entirety of his lifetime of debt. How he travelled extensively on the promise of paying for his half but never coming up with the goods—or stealing the monies from one person to give to the next but never at a cost to himself.

Early on in his campaign to use and abuse women, he had recognised the golden nugget of being the victim of his previous relationship. This trick had never failed, as it immediately induced sympathy, created an immediate bond, stimulated a sense of openness to find out more about the woman and developed loyalty, as the new woman would not want to hurt him. They would think they were so safe in his hands, misled into believing he wouldn't hurt them, and even grateful to have him in their lives—if not lucky to have found him. Well, he had already been through enough, so with their mothering instinct ignited, he would be fully taken care of.

Robert Day Jr was the most conniving, manipulative specimen of immorally harmful behaviour that women could have been protected against if only they had quantified his claims. All they had to do was ask his previous partners, and then the truth would have instantly set them free. The biggest deceit was his knowledge that not one of them would ask questions because he'd done such a good job of isolating the previous partner and making them so unapproachable— if not hated—by the lies that he had told. The new woman would feel so sorry for what they had been deceived into thinking he had gone through, whilst the previous one was elated for finally managing to escape the monster's clutches.

Inevitably reluctant to want to deal with him again, despite grave concerns for his new victim, the injustice of the lies he was spreading about her or the need to tell her side of the story, she would fade into the background—a shadow of her former self. This solid protection provided a safe and secure method to perpetually create multiple virtual worlds at will. The truth regarding his success in convincing these women rested in the fact he had convinced himself all of what he was saying was the truth. He fully believed he was the victim—and so they did too.

Robert Day Jr's walk took him down to the end of his road, along Main Street towards the parade of shops, under the bridge and left into the park. In the distance, he could hear the sounds of children running and laughing, with the odd expressive squeal of excitement. There were numerous people wandering around beside the duck pond, throwing bread to the birds despite several signs asking them to refrain from the activity.

The sun had brought out an arrangement of colourful flowers all around, and the grassy areas were a mass of thick, lush green awaiting their next cut. Unsurprisingly, Robert Day Jr was not able to enjoy any of the beauty around him—as not only did he neither see it nor feel anything about it, but there was no personal gain in it for him. Devoid of any emotional connections, he passed by like an empty vessel out at sea with its coordinates set towards the nearest port, everything a completely unnoticed expanse as he passed by. There was a little gated cafe at one of the entrances to the park, so he entered, made his way to a chair, in front of a small window and took a seat.

It was not his intention to gaze out to enjoy the landscape but more to ensure his back was turned to everyone else in the cafe. Despite having made a career out of being an avid people watcher, he hated people staring at him as it generated uncertainty about what others were thinking about him, and he liked to remain incognito. A young lad of around fifteen years old with cropped hair—apart from a spiked-up fringe—approached him to take his order. He was about to say a vegetarian breakfast when he realised he didn't have to keep up that pretence anymore, so decided upon a full English breakfast with extra toast and a strong cup of tea.

He highlighted to the young man that he didn't want a lukewarm, wishy-washy, weak drink, nor one that was too milky, but that it should be a strong, 'envelope' brown in colour. He then set his eyes out of the window, though seeing nothing as his mind began formulating his next plan of action. He contemplated the strategies he would have to follow, but he first needed to secure himself a target; and decide on the approach—perhaps accidentally on purpose or nonchalantly. Then he had to anchor them down, and quickly; feed them a sob story and play the emotional card, thus embedding himself quickly. After that, he could coast along and play it by ear, but he had to move fast because there was no way he was spending any more time at his house than was absolutely necessary. Finding someone who could offer him a place to live was his number one motivation—then he could work his magic to absorb their life as if it were his own.

He smiled to himself at the stupidity of how these women voluntarily opened up their homes, their lives and their legs for him to so easily step into the shoes of their lives without him having to work hard for anything. No matter where they were in the social structure, he could obtain anything and everything he wanted with marginal effort. Such simplicity, yet the rewards were enormous for him, and the plan had never failed him yet.

'A full English breakfast with extra toast and a strong cup of tea,' the young boy said as he approached Robert Day Jr from his left side and placed the tray on the table. He positioned the plate neatly between the knife and fork, set the cup to Robert Day Jr's right side, and the side plate containing the extra toast to his left side.

'Can I get you anything else, sir?'

'Yes, brown sauce and ground black pepper,' Robert Day Jr stated without bothering to even look up, never mind say please.

By the time the young boy arrived back at the table, Robert Day Jr had taken to rearranging the contents of his plate. Two halves of bread were balanced up on the edges of the plate, one spread with beans the other tomatoes and on the top of each, was an egg. The bacon and the sausage had been moved to sit on opposite sides of the plate and wiped to ensure they were not contaminated by any other foods. The mushrooms had been completely isolated, and he was busy wiping the plate clean around the edges of them to create an island.

When the boy returned, he took one look at the man's strange etiquette procedure, slid the condiments onto the table and quickly scurried away.

Robert Day Jr may have been a needy, inadequate, dependent person who couldn't function well in his own company, but when it came to eating, he preferred to conduct himself in a solitary performance. Once he had arranged a rasher of bacon with a spoonful of beans on one of the extra pieces of toast, along with a sausage cut in half with a spoonful of tomatoes on the other extra piece, he took a moment to purvey his masterpiece.

He had a slurp of the 'envelope brown' tea—*not bad*, he thought—and then he was finally ready to eat.

Satisfied that by having his back to the other customers it would not induce any spectators, he did what he always did with food: he gorged himself, shovelling it into his mouth, barely having time to chew before swallowing and

312

shovelling the next portion in. The speed at which he could remove the contents of his plate to hit his stomach was inhumane and certainly not healthy.

He was unsure whether this had been generated from a lack of food as a child or the fact that he had been made to sit at the table and eat the full contents of a meal no matter how long it took him, but more from greed and an unhealthy relationship with food. Unfulfilled, he gained the young boy's attention to order a second full English breakfast, and after the same rearrangement of the contents upon his plate, he was able to satisfy his need to purge.

Robert Day Jr was usually a master at adapting so that he could blend into his surroundings, and today was no different. There was not a person in that cafe—or that he had passed on the way there—who would have guessed that his partner had died in a vicious attack only hours before. Any normal person would have been repulsed, if not outraged, to find out that the man sitting at the window seat, stuffing his face, had been the person who had administered the sickening blows himself. The only effect that had changed was his usual ability to smile appropriately, to maintain eye contact, and to remember to use manners appropriately. This was not something that had been ingrained in him as a child, nor was it something that came naturally to him. How could it be when he believed that everybody around him was to be used to serve him and meet his needs?

No one was of importance to him as he only viewed them in terms of what they could do for him, provide for him, make life easier for him or inflate and feed his superficial ego. It didn't matter to him what they looked like, their age or what they did for a living—it was all immaterial, just as long as they had their own house, plenty of money to exploit and could provide for his needs. He therefore did not consider himself to be a fussy man, although it was always a good sign if they had children because they would possess a motherly nature, which meant they would generally be caring and mother him too. Another plus side was that he could use the children as a weapon to manipulate her in every format—not to mention causing discord by playing them off against each other whilst he acted as mediator.

He believed that he was the perfect partner and stepfather figure despite the evidence of gross neglect and a lack of an ability to present any interest in parenting his own children. Robert Day Jr's issue was that he saw no wrong in anything he was doing and could not abide nor tolerate any personal criticism. His silver-tongued delivery to control, direct and engineer a specific outcome had been developed through the bedrock of his years as a salesperson. He was therefore more than capable of distorting facts to manoeuvre people into the positions he wanted them, like they were pawns in his personal game of chess.

Robert Day Jr decided that the place he would select his mark would be in the pub, as it was easy enough to identify who was the perfect target, and at least he would be able to enjoy a pint at the same time. In fact, there was no time like the present, so tonight he decided he would go out on the prowl, scouting for his next victim. Whilst Robert Day Jr was feeling positively hopeful, there was a lady somewhere who didn't know it yet, but she was about to have her life completely turned upside down. Like all the rest, she wouldn't be able to believe her luck. She would quickly fall head over heels for the lies and the image he portrayed. When it was too late and she realised who was behind the mask, she would discover he had as much depth as a life-size cardboard cut-out.

And by that time, it would be too late.

Chapter 35
Loss

June Brown knew instinctively that it was far too early for her to be waking up the second her eyes began to flicker open. She fumbled around on her bedside table, physically feeling for her phone to check just how early. 06:35!

'For goodness' sake,' she said out loud, having only fallen asleep at 04:10, after tossing and turning persistently for hours.

'This has got to stop,' she berated herself.

June slid back down beneath the warm, fluffy quilt—the one that she and Michael had purchased together from a mill near Halifax. It had been a particularly cold winter, alternating from severe flood warnings, heavy snow and temperatures below zero. June, in particular, had suffered from S.A.D (seasonal affective disorder). Her mood had uncharacteristically reflected the lows of the weather. From plummeting into deep depression, she had little interest in anything to feelings of despair that some days she couldn't even bring herself to leave her bedroom.

It was when she had swung from comfort eating to having no appetite and refusing to even get in the shower that Michael had suggested a day out. She didn't want to go out, she didn't want to be surrounded by other people, and she certainly did not want to be forced into making conversation with anyone. Michael was not taking no for an answer.

'The bath is ready for you,' he declared as he walked into the bedroom and made a beeline for the curtains. In one fair swoop, he had swished the first one back and was reaching out for the next.

'Michael, please stop,' June had implored him. 'I don't want to get up.'

'June, whether you want to or not is irrelevant. You need to get up instead of wallowing here in self-pity. There are some things in life that we can change, but the weather is not one of them,' he had told her and pulled back the other half of the curtains before making his way towards the door. 'Now come on, before the bath goes cold.'

June had lay there like a sulky little child for some minutes, debating whether to get up to redraw the curtains and then get back into bed. She pondered how long she had stayed horizontal but was ashamed to confess she had absolutely no idea.

Michael was right—she did need to get up, if only to give her body a wash.

June struggled to free herself from the quilt that she had wrapped so tightly around her body, kicking her legs in a futile attempt to get free. As she swung her legs over the edge of the bed and sat up, she immediately went dizzy and had to rest her hand upon the bed head to steady herself before rising to a standing position.

'Maybe Michael was right after all; she had been lying here for too long.'

Once June had got her balance and allowed her blood pressure to regulate itself, she staggered towards the door, holding on to the oak and light grey painted bedroom furniture. Michael was exiting the bathroom as she moved along the corridor and quickly came to her aide.

'Wow, you look very unsteady. Let me help you,' he said tenderly, feeling a tad guilty for making her get out of bed.

'I think you are right. I will feel much better once I have had a soak in the bath,' June managed, focusing hard on putting one foot in front of the other.

'You look like the grandpa off *Willy Wonka's Chocolate Factory*,' he said light-heartedly, 'the one who had been in bed for that long his muscles had wasted.'

When they entered the bathroom, an intoxicating infusion of vanilla, jasmine and grapefruit hit overload throughout her nasal passage. She suddenly felt such warmth for the man next to her and was immensely blessed for the care and love this man had shown her for the past 32 years.

She glanced up at him out of the corner of her eye and smiled lovingly, suddenly thankful that he had known what she needed even when she hadn't.

'What?' he said knowingly.

'Thank you,' she said.

'For what? Forcing your smelly self out of the bed I have to share with you just to make you get a wash so I can peel the sheets off and throw them in the washer? Seriously, the pleasure is all mine,' he joked.

'Yes, for that and for also just being you,' she told him.

'Do you need me to help you get in, or will you be OK?' he wondered.

'No, I will be fine. Besides, this is my pamper session, and I intend to enjoy every second,' she smiled.

Michael shut the door behind him to allow her the privacy she required, noting the click of the lock from the other side. He wasn't offended; he knew it was not a malicious action to keep him out but June's automatic safety mechanism, having been abused in the bath as a child by her uncle.

He stripped the bed, deciding to do the wash in two halves just to ensure that the drum was not overloaded, and the sheets were given a very deep, thorough clean. He poured lashings of powder into the tray dispenser—perhaps a little too much—but he could hardly scoop it back out, so he left it and added the fabric conditioner.

Michael then entered the kitchen to make his wife a good old-fashioned English breakfast.

Upstairs, June had slipped out of her two-piece pyjama set, which had a Monet painting emblazoned across the t-shirt—a gift from Michael when they had visited Rouen Cathedral, Normandy.

June smiled as she remembered him making some excuse to go back inside to purchase them for her from the little gift shop. Michael was like that—always thoughtful, attentive, giving and dedicated to loving her in every conceivable way. June teared up as she recognised just how lucky she had been to have had Michael in her life from such an early age. Some people can live a whole lifetime and never find their soul mate, yet she and Michael had been together since her late teens.

June stepped over the edge of the bath, wincing slightly at her aching body, the warmth of the water instantly easing her discomfort. She lowered herself down into the thick foam, allowing it to cover her skin in a blanket of luxurious foam bubbles. Her eyes involuntarily closed at the delight of the hot water mixed with the velvety moisturised bath foam, with the rich aromas delighting the entirety of her senses. At that very moment, she wasn't sure if she had ever loved Michael as much or if it was possible for her to love him any more than she did right then. June began to lose herself in thoughts of Michael.

She had met him the day she had taken her first administration position, fresh out of college, aged 19. She had felt out of her depth walking into the block of offices that first morning, unable to consider how she was going to transcend from student to fully fledged employee. That was until she saw Michael sitting at the desk alongside hers, flashing his award-winning smile her way. He finished his telephone call, stood and welcomed her with such a cheeriness that even the tone of his voice had her buckling at the knee. Everything else around him seemed to blur out of focus; the nervous edge within her was replaced with excited butterflies, and she instantly knew all would be well. Michael had always had the ability to calm her in times of stress, to bring clarity in confusion and joy in sad times. She knew she was lucky to have him, so, as she allowed the water to swirl around her neck, she relaxed further in the knowledge that this lovely man, who knew her better than she even knew herself, her rock, her tower of strength, had only her best interests at heart.

Her thoughts were interrupted by a light tap at the door. 'Breakfast is done. Do you want me to plate it up or give you a little longer?' Michael enquired.

'I am coming now, you beautiful man, just give me five minutes,' she informed him.

Once they had eaten a hearty breakfast of egg, tomatoes, bacon, mushrooms beans and sausage, June playfully said, 'I could do with a Nana nap now!'

'No way, Mrs! We are going out for a drive, and that's the end of it,' Michael had insisted.

That was the day they had simply got on the M62 motorway, travelling west with no particular destination in mind, and had ended up in Halifax, a place they rarely visited. The mill that they had quite unexpectedly fallen upon was in the little village of Sowerby Bridge. It was a 4-storey stone building with a huge integrated chimney set into one of its far corners. The ground-floor windows were arched, with a complementary arched wooden door set centrally. The next two levels had square Georgian-style windows, set with 8 smaller individual panes, and the top level was awash with light through several skylights set into the roof.

The mill was in the middle of nowhere, nestled in a valley that was surrounded by hills on all sides. If there hadn't been signs along the road, Michael and June would never have found it. A smoothly laid tarmac drive led to a well-marked parking area, with a bubbling beck and canal towpath running alongside. June followed the noise of the running water to find an enormous waterwheel powering itself with the aid of a massive wooden armed structure at the side.

As she approached, the methodical rhythm became quite deafening, like a hundred galloping horses, their hooves hitting the floor in perfect sequence. The rotating wooden hub of the wheel pivoted round on a central metal axle, through which the inner cogs helped to continually power it. June found the whooshing sound of the water exceptionally calming and the sight of the propelling wheel, mesmerising. In her head, she was picking up the wheel's tune as she watched the glistening light reflect upon the downward surface of each strut as it sent the water it had picked up cascading back into where it had come from. The more June concentrated, the more she felt connected—the way she always did in nature, alive, in the moment, at peace. She noticed the inner spoke beams of the wheel projecting shadows along the huge stone wall within which it was set. June closed her eyes, listening, enjoying the sudden spray of tiny droplets upon her face, feeling its tremble through her body, like the thud of heavy bass music.

'June, are you coming?' she thought she had heard Michael say.

When June opened her eyes, it was to the same despair she felt every day— the knowledge that Michael was no longer here, and she had been longing for him so much, he had visited her once again in her dreams. June reached for her phone again to check the time; it was 08:42. She gazed at the vacant space beside her, overwhelmed by the emptiness of where his body had once laid next to hers. She had to force herself to pull away, otherwise the full extremity of her loss— the one he had left in her heart, her entire life and deep within her soul—would have overpowered her, as it often did.

Even at Michaels's funeral, people were telling her that 'time was a great healer' and 'it would get easier.' She knew they had meant well, but she wasn't naive enough to believe it, as she knew nothing would ever be the same again. True, she may learn to live within the pain of her loss, and maybe the gaping wound would gently heal, but there would always be the psychological yearning and the invisible scar. June excused their insensitivity for not having the capacity to love to the degree that she loved Michael. Without experiencing the resolute devotion of two connected soul mates, she had to resign herself to the fact absolutely no one could ever understand her unimaginable loss. June glanced across to his favourite jumper, she had put on a coat hanger and hung at the back of her door, sad that the scent of him was now long gone. It had been 16 months since he had passed away, and although she didn't want to, she knew she needed to go through his things if she was ever going to come to terms with her new status as a widow.

Chapter 36
Stepping Out in Faith

June Brown had been on the phone with Katie, her friend of 13 years, for almost an hour.

'But, Katie, I am not ready to go out socialising, and a pub is the last place I would want to be!' June told her adamantly.

'I will be there,' Katie tried.

'Yes, you may be physically in the pub, but you are working behind the bar,' June stressed.

'It has been really quiet for the past couple of weeks due to the school holidays, so I will be able to talk to you whilst I am working,' Katie assured her.

'I will still be sat at the bar, on my own, like Billy-no-mates,' June said alarmed.

'Come on, June, you will be doing me a favour. I hate having no one to talk to,' Katie urged her.

'Ah, so a minute ago you were trying to get me to come out because I 'needed to get out of the house and stop moping about,' you said, and now it is so that I can keep you company—charming,' June challenged her friend.

'To be honest, it is a little bit of both. I have missed you,' Kate said honestly. 'And I have tried everything else to get you to meet with me, so this was my last resort.'

'I would feel so stupid not just being on my own in the pub but sitting at the bar, where everyone will see. Michael would never let me even go up to the bar to get the drinks, never mind sit at the bar. I will stand out like a sore thumb,' June said despondently.

'I get it, June, honestly, I do, but you have to start somewhere, and you are not going to meet people if you don't leave your house. I don't want to diminish your grieving process, but I am sure Michael would not want you to mope around at home on your own, day after day,' Katie attempted to appeal to June's better judgment.

'I think I am best qualified to know what Michael may or may not have wanted, don't you?' June hit back.

'I didn't mean anything by it, June, just that it has been 16 months. Michael may have gone, but you still have a life to live,' Katie urged her.

Katie's words landed harshly, and before June knew what she was doing, she had put the phone down on her friend. She sat for a moment in shocked silence, both at her friends' words but also her response to them. Maybe it was because what Katie had said was partially true.

As she continued to sit on the wicker 2-seater in her conservatory, she contemplated exactly what Michael would have said. It was true that he only wanted the best for her and always took care of her needs, so maybe she was doing him a great disservice now as she sat and *moped about the house*, as Katie had stated. She had to admit that she was beginning to feel as though life was passing her by and that she had accepted the rut of daytime TV, cooking, cleaning, and shopping. So maybe Katie was right—she did need to break the cycle. But to go to the pub? Did she really want to start there?

It was true that everything she was surrounded by reminded her of Michael: the things they had bought together, items from holidays they had enjoyed, photographs depicting all the milestones they had reached. Although each one had been incredibly special, it was now just her and her memories.

June did not want her mind wandering down the one-way street of the no-hope city again. She had travelled enough down that route to last her a lifetime, so maybe Katie was right—she needed to shake things up a bit. The self-help technique her grief therapist had encouraged her to utilise this week was to capture the thoughts in the rear-view mirror. Instead of looking back and allowing her mind to wander and thus dwell in a time that had past or that she could not change, she was to meditate on something in the present. The idea was to not allow negative thoughts to fester, but to train herself to look at the things around her that she could still be grateful for.

At the time, June couldn't imagine why her therapist would want her to ignore her feelings or want her to irradicate the memories she held so precious of her life with Michael. Apparently, it was OK to visit those moments, but not to set up camp and dwell there. So, taking the therapist's advice into consideration, June immediately decided to 'recalculate the route,' as the satnav in the car kept telling her. She smiled to herself at the number of times she had tried to follow a planned route before being told the system was 'recalculating the route.' It could be exceptionally frustrating, but maybe she needed to view her life that way—as if she was just 'recalculating the route.' At least it felt like there was still a plan, that she was still on track to a final destination, but that she was just taking a different route.

June smiled. It felt alien at first, as she hadn't felt what it was like to smile for such a long time—well, 16 months to be precise. Perhaps Michael did sit with her in those quiet moments, as she had often thought, and maybe he was here with her right now, helping her to take some baby footsteps forward. She smiled again to herself, took a deep breath and looked out onto her back garden, but this time wanting to see it, not just to stare at it. She gazed up at the hanging bird feeders and admonished herself for not being able to remember the last time she had filled them up. She was very surprised to see that there were daisies and dandelions all over the lawn—something Michael would never have allowed. There was a very fat pigeon sitting on the edge of the bird bath, taking a drink. June felt relieved that it had been raining recently; otherwise, that would have stayed dry and unreplenished too.

June considered how her current situation was like the garden: unloved, neglected, undernourished and uncared for. Katie was right—she had shut herself away for far too long. In life, Michael had only ever wanted the very best for her. He had cared enough to put her first, and when she had been depressed, he had made her get up, get washed and go out. As much as she had resisted and didn't want to comply, he wouldn't take no for an answer. Michael had always known what she needed, even when she hadn't, and he was usually right.

So, she decided she would step out in faith, turn up at the pub tonight to surprise Katie, and sod what anyone thought. Little did June know, but that decision would actually change every aspect of her life, in more ways than one!

Chapter 37
The Stranger

June Brown had been sitting at the end of the bar for almost 40 minutes when the tall, handsome stranger walked in. By the way he had strode purposefully towards the bar, June knew that he had been there many times before. He wore a lovely cerise polo with a pair of tight jeans, a little too tight, judging by the overhang of his waist, which had been drawn in unnecessarily with a thick black belt. He haphazardly glanced around the room, not as though he was searching for anyone in particular, just an automatic response. June averted her eyes quickly, wishing Katie would hurry up in the cellar, and then, right on cue, she reappeared. June was sure there was a knowing look between the two, but she didn't want to appear as though she was staring for too long, so picked up her glass and downed the last of the contents.

'Usual, Robert?' Katie asked.

'Yes, please. It's quiet in here tonight; where is everyone?' Robert asked.

'With the boss away, there is no karaoke, so everyone has gone down to The Swan instead,' Katie said casually, before adding, 'That's why I have got June here keeping me company.'

June wanted the floor to open up, as her face reddened when Robert glanced in her direction and smiled. It was hard to pin an age on him, but June surmised he could have been anywhere between 50 to 60, although he did seem to have a rugged kind of charm about him.

'Do you want a refill?' Robert asked, but June was deep in her own thoughts.

'June, Robert was asking if you want another drink?' Katie enquired.

'Oh no, I couldn't,' she stuttered.

'Of course, you can,' Katie told her, before addressing Robert again. 'It's half of Heineken.'

'Get one for yourself, Katie; it looks like it is going to be a long night for you,' he smiled.

As Katie continued to serve him, June found herself intently watching Robert as he greedily drank from his pint. With one hand on the bar and the other wrapped around his glass, she noticed that his hands were masculine, but he had very short-bitten fingernails. As he reached out to retrieve his change, June noticed a strange, nervous twitch that he had: an up-shrug to his forehead, where the bone seemed to strangely protrude above his eyebrows. He did have the most beautiful blue eyes, though. Within minutes, his mobile rang, so he excused himself, which June thought was very polite, seeing as they didn't know one another, and he went outside the back door to take the call.

'What do you think?' Katie asked almost immediately.

'Think about what?' June questioned.

'About Robert? I saw the way your eyes lit up when he came in,' Katie teased.

'They did not,' June lied, flushing for a second time.

'I saw you studying him; I was watching you through the mirror whilst I got the drinks,' Katie revealed.

Busted, June gave in. 'He seems OK; where is his wife?'

'He is actually single; he and his girlfriend have just split up, apparently,' Katie informed her.

'If it is a recent thing, he will need time to get over it, splitting up is pretty hard. How long were they together?' June enquired.

'About a year, I think, so not that long, and it was Robert's decision. By all accounts, she was moody, wanted more from him than he was prepared to give, and kept getting into debt. He only stayed with her because he had become attached to her sick mother, so he is as free as a bird!' Katie told her.

Four women arrived and approached the bar, so Katie left June to contemplate her words whilst she served the newcomers. June had to agree that Robert was a good-looking man, but he was nothing like Michael had been, and she wasn't sure whether she was even ready to embark upon anything new. What was she doing getting herself drawn into this way of thinking when she didn't even know the guy? Besides, she couldn't see someone like him being interested in her. Once the four women had claimed their drinks, they settled themselves on bar stools to the left of June at the corner of the bar. Again, June felt quite awkward, especially now, sitting all alone amidst the friendly banter of the women, when one of them seemed to notice her discomfort.

'Are you out on your own?' said a young woman who reminded June of the actress Nicola Walker.

'Yes, my friend,' June looked for Katie, but she must have gone into the kitchen behind the bar. 'She works here, and I wasn't doing anything tonight, so came in to keep her company,' June admitted.

'If you don't want to sit on your own, you can come join us if you like, but it's also not a problem if you'd rather not,' the Nicola lookalike said.

June readily got off her seat to join the ladies, glad of some girlie company, not really wanting to be still sitting alone in her seat when Robert returned. The girls were great fun and really welcoming that June found herself admitting how out of place she had been feeling and sat at the bar alone. When Nicola looked puzzled, June explained about the loss of her husband and how difficult she had found making new friends.

'I mean, as a middle-aged woman, how do you even go about meeting people, never mind the potential of a partner?' June concluded.

'We go out most weekends, don't we, girls? You are more than welcome to join us if you like,' Nicola said.

June liked this woman; she was warm, kind, caring and compassionate. Nicola (lookalike) excused herself to use the bathroom, and that is when Robert returned. June's heart did a little flutter, but surprisingly, he slammed his glass down hard upon the bar and walked out. June wondered if his phone call was bad news, but she was sure he seemed more angry than sad as he disappeared out through the front door of the pub. As Nicola returned to her seat at the bar, June was simultaneously delighted and surprised to see Robert reappear, walk back to the bar and purchase another drink.

For the third time that evening, June's face flushed as Robert stood just 10 feet away, avidly watching her interact with the 4 ladies. She found his intensity both unsettling and exhilarating at the same time. His eyes were literally boring into her, like they were desperately trying to communicate some secret language. The tension between them was electric, and June felt alive for the first time since losing Michael. The four women joked and laughed between themselves, but June found she was no longer hearing a word they were saying. The tall, dark handsome guy across the bar, the one she had just met and who was called

Robert, had locked eyes with her, and now all she could see was him. If only she had known the truth then, she would have run a thousand miles in the opposite direction to get as far away as possible.

Victory

The sins of the guilty will be unearthed,
A trial for justice will soon be served.
The truth doesn't lie, and lies don't win,
No more smirky, arrogant grin.
All the world will know your fate,
The case will bubble a lava of hate.
You reigned too long, devoured and stole,
But now you can rot in your pitiful hole.
Triumphant, the meek and mild will rise,
They unburden their hearts to claim their prize.
The sinner will fall into a deep, dark well,
To where you belong in the pit of hell.

(Juli Flintoff)

Part 5
The Present

Chapter 38
Eureka

With a single sharp sideways movement of the head, Shona Williams indicated to both Parker and Jacobi that she expected them both to join her as she followed Anita Collins out of the briefing room. In an instant, they had scrambled to their feet and were at her side. Collins strode towards the tiniest room in the station, what everyone else simply knew as the 'Tech cupboard.'

'So, this is where you have been keeping yourself,' Shona said as she entered the room. 'I thought you had gone off sick; it has been that long since I saw you.'

'Yes, sorry, I always find it a lot easier to shut myself in here when I am tasked with the media elements. It gives me the ability to shut off and concentrate properly,' Collins admitted.

Jacobi and Parker tried to step inside, but it was far too much of a squeeze, even when Collins had taken her seat. The room used to contain a single shower, that a Chief Inspector from years ago had used after jogging to work each morning. When he had moved on, it became a broom cupboard, but Damien Clarke had converted it to what later became the tech cupboard. Shona could never imagine being able to function appropriately confined in such a small place; however, Collins looked more than comfortable. The width of the room was only just sufficient to house a desk, which stood directly opposite the door. When Collins was seated, the chair gave just enough standing room for Shona to peer over Collins' left shoulder. Jacobi stood with his back pressed against the door to Collins' right so that Parker could stand in the doorway, attempting to see the page of the computer screen that Collins was now scrolling through.

'This is it,' Collins began. 'So, there is nothing really outstanding about Day's posts; he seems to persistently share random crap of things that are on in local bars. It could be to remind himself of the places he wants to use because there is evidence later of the places he has checked into. There is nothing of value and appears to be just a platform to tell everyone where he is going. Some things that I probably would have overlooked had I not done the interview with you, Dion, are an attempt to personify the 'Mr Nice Guy' act.'

'Like what?' Dion enquired.

'Just posts pushing people to be nice to each other or re-sharing random things that on the surface, may have you think, 'What a caring person he is',' Collins explained.

'So, what you are saying is he reproduces other people's thoughts and feelings, but there is nothing of value underneath the veneer that actually stems from himself?' Shona defined.

'Precisely! I spoke to my friend Carolyn, who is a counsellor at the Daily News,' Collins began before glancing over her left shoulder at Shona. 'Obviously, I didn't give her any details of the individual.'

'It's fine, Anita, what did she have to say?' Shona enquired.

'She confirmed what I had initially thought—that having the inability to muster up your own thoughts and feelings in favour of simply sharing random things is a massive red flag,' Collins revealed.

'Why?' asked Parker, perplexed, taking the risk his colleagues may think him unintelligent.

'It openly demonstrates a lack of a personal connection with the world around you, and when he does comment, it is nothing meaningful. They are just words like a standard automatic reply, similar to the ones programmed into a new phone when you cannot immediately physically send something personal,' Collins told them.

'That sounds more like a humanoid robot,' said Shona.

'That is exactly what it is, Shona. He has programmed himself to reproduce what he sees, though he is not able to engage and actually feel the same emotions as everyone else,' Collins explained.

'That is pretty deep for a counsellor. Does she have the credentials to correctly profile Day?' Shona enquired.

'No, but my dad is an international speaker on the subject of narcissistic psychopaths, so why not access my biggest asset?' Collins said meekly.

'You are a genius, Anita,' Shona stipulated.

'Why hasn't this information come up before now?' Jacobi enquired.

'We haven't come across anyone quite like Day before, well, I haven't. I am so glad I was part of the interview with him as some of his telltale behaviours, reactions and tics really did pique my interest. He literally intrigued me,' Collins admitted.

'Thank goodness for you being in the right place at the right time, Anita. So what is the bottom line with him?' Shona enquired.

'In other words, he is faking his interactions by mimicking what other people are doing as an ability to fit into society, but he is devoid of his own feelings,' Collins explained.

'But he certainly showed feelings when we interviewed him, Anita,' Jacobi stated, puzzled.

'He may have done, but these were in response to himself; at no point did he connect with the ferocious attack on his partner nor display the normal grief of losing a loved one. The most telling sign was the fact he showed no love towards Karen Blakely, the person he was about to ask to marry him, and he was flirting with me as though she was a disposable waste he had just got rid of,' Collins stated.

'Yes, I noticed his persona completely changed whenever he was around females. He seemed to soften, rising to the smallest amount of attention like it had energised him in some way,' Jacobi shared.

'Exactly! Whenever I complimented him or intentionally stroked his ego, he gushed as though it was a come-on,' Collins said.

'Ah, you realised that too,' Jacobi blurted out, surprised.

'Of course, Dion. What do you take me for? I could hardly miss his chest puffing out and those intense blue eyes boring into mine as though he was trying to penetrate my thoughts,' she said incredulously. 'Day is a classic narcissist— cold, detached from human connection, self-centred, manipulative and self-controlled unless you tap into what makes him tick.'

'And that is?' Parker asked.

'A pretty woman who he thinks he can control to get what he wants,' Anita delivered.

'And you got all that from our interview?' Dion asked. 'I mean, I was pretty much summing him up as I observed his reactions to you, especially if I interrupted his puppy dog routine.'

'That was what secured my thoughts about him. Every time I complimented him, he gushed, just like my cat purring and wrapping itself around my legs when I pick up his bowl after I get in from work. The cat is independent, it's a loner, it never gives me affection, ever, but give him what he wants, and he is your best friend, momentarily,' Collins defined.

'So, we are comparing our suspect to a cat now, OK?' Shona said, raising her eyebrows.

'Having been brought up and educated by my father on what partner not to get involved with, I have always been intrigued by the subject of a narcissistic psychopath. To be honest, Shona, I have waited my entire life to meet one, and I am convinced, as is my father, that Robert Day Jr is indeed a prime subject.'

'Wow, Anita, you sly dog. I didn't realise all these thoughts were being processed behind those excessively large glasses,' Shona laughed. 'I think I might have to watch out—you just might be a DCI in the making!'

It was now Collins' turn to gush. 'That is the other thing he loves, the attention of positive affirmations and sought validation continually, yet if you disrupted that connection with me, Dion, he displayed immediate and significant irritation,' Collins stated.

'Yes, I noticed that. He revelled in you as though I was not in the room, but when I interrupted his trance-like state, his jaw would clench, followed by the scowl and upward shift of his brow, then the sideways Paddington Bear stare,' Jacobi recalled.

'Exactly. I was meeting his need of admiration, so I received the superficial charm. You interrupted that, so it instantly switched to a more aggressive, hostile response,' Collins explained. 'These types of people have a high sense of self and are focused only on their entitlement, not the equal rights of everyone.'

'I am stunned, and I apologise for my arrogance,' said Jacobi. 'I was so caught up in watching him that I didn't even think that you had noticed, let alone observed so much information. I thought your sympathy was a demonstration of being Team Day,' Jacobi admitted.

'That is because there wasn't just one actor in the room,' Collins admitted with a grin.

'If we get caught up in our own emotions of what we think of a suspect, Dion, then we cannot fully open our eyes to see the full picture that is in front of us. Above anybody, you of all people should know that, Dion' Shona mildly reprimanded him.

'I will put it on the hard drive,' he said, tapping his temple, 'as a reminder to never get caught that way again. It is annoying because, as you say, boss, I do know better, but there was something so disingenuous about him, he made my skin crawl. Although there was one thing that did amuse me,' Jacobi began.

'Amuse you, Dion? We are running a murder enquiry, not a joke shop,' Shona interjected.

'It amused me that, in objection to only being provided with instant coffee, he distastefully left it untouched on the table, or the way he ensured he was sat on the comfier chairs. You're right, it gave off an air of entitlement, and when we interviewed him, Shona, there was an arrogant superiority about him where nothing was his fault,' Dion recounted.

'Don't knock it, Dion. It's usually a perpetrator's arrogant superiority that brings them to justice,' Shona said smugly.

'Oh, he is definitely arrogant,' said Jacobi.

'When I was discussing the case with my dad,' she paused to affirm, 'no names were used, Shona, we were considering the way Karen Blakely was killed. As my dad says, it shows uncontrolled impulsivity, and if he is the murderer, which we believe he is, then during his interview, we witnessed a complete lack of remorse too. Notice, Dion, how he jumped on your red herring and quickly produced a suspect for us, redirecting us to Marcus. It strikes me we have a pathological liar who has perfected his craft in saying absolutely anything to get himself out of hot water,' Collins suggested.

'So, what was it about the post you wanted to show us?' Shona enquired.

'Here it is,' Collins said, enlarging it for everyone to see. 'He has re-shared someone's rather lengthy random post about the need for people to look up from their phones to see—really see—what is going on in the world around them,' Collins described.

'OK?' Parker blurted out, confused.

'It was a response that a lady had written that caught my eye,' she said, flicking through the comments as the phone next to the computer began to vibrate. 'Here it is: *But if people looked up from their phones, we would all see who you truly are, Robert Day Jr, and then you wouldn't be able to sexually abuse your partners, would you?*'

As Collins finished reading the quote, her phone suddenly began playing Bizarre Inc's *I'm Going to Get You* starting with the lyrics, 'I'm going to get you, baby, I'm going to get you, yes I am.' Shona, Dion and Parker stared at the phone in surprise. This was not a song they would have pictured in Anita's playlist.

'Sorry, I need to check this. It could be really important,' Collins said excitedly, whilst Shona glanced at Parker and Dion, shrugging her shoulders in disbelief.

'Eureka!!!' Collins exclaimed. 'I think we have got him!'

Chapter 39
The Unveiling

Shona, Jacobi and Parker stood in the tight space of the 'tech cupboard' behind Collins as she furiously tapped away at her keyboard, with her phone logged tightly to her ear using her elevated right shoulder. They waited with bated breath, Jacobi leaning against the door and Shona grabbing the back of Collins' chair for support. The keyboard clicked on, but the time seemed to stand still until finally, 'I have found it, thanks Carolyn, I owe you, massively!' she said, turning round with a grin of triumph.

'Come on, Anita, the suspense is killing me,' Shona said, breathing out heavily.

'So, I put an alert out on each media platform to notify me whenever anything was posted with the name Robert Day Jr. My friend at the Daily News, Carolyn, remembered our conversation about the traits of the suspect I had discussed with her,' Collins explained.

'Come on, Anita, what has it yielded? I don't think I can take the build-up,' Jacobi demanded impatiently.

'She has just enquired whether my suspect's name is Robert Day Jr and advised me to check out their *Dear Diary* search, by a trainee journalist called Demi Lee. Apparently, they contain excerpts from a diary written by a woman who was in a relationship with him and who feared for her safety, so the purpose of the search was to identify her and make sure she was OK.'

'Do they have the woman's identity?' Shona pushed.

'Up until this morning, they didn't have anything, although the post has attracted numerous responses. One of those comments is from the same lady who I was originally alerting you to, who wrote the sexual abuse comment on his earlier post,' Collins said triumphantly.

'Do we have a name for her?' Jacobi asked.

'Yes, it's here, Josie Bellamy,' Collins pointed it out on her screen. As the trio lent in to look more closely at the screen, they saw that Robert Day Jr's name had been tagged on the *Dear Diary* posts. The person posting it as their comment was a woman called Josie Bellamy. Nothing else, just his name.

'That has just sent a shiver down my spine,' said Shona.

'Do you think this Josie Bellamy was too scared to put anything else but felt compelled to at least identify him?' asked Parker.

'Possibly, but there is one thing for sure: we need to know who she is and get her in pronto,' said Shona.

'Where did the excerpts come from?' Jacobi enquired.

'I don't know, I didn't ask because Carolyn said that Demi Lee was on her way over here with some evidence, she wanted us to look at. Perhaps that is what she is bringing,' Collins assumed.

'Did she say whether she had the name of the woman?' Parker asked hopeful.

'No, sorry, I lost my head a bit when she asked if the suspect in our case was called Robert Day Jr and then told me to take a look at their news feed of the *Dear Diary* posts,' Collins apologised.

'Not to worry, if she is on her way, we can ask her directly,' Shona said. 'Right, guys, let's get a welcoming committee together for Demi Lee.'

'I take it we will meet with her in your office, Shona?' Parker said, and on affirmation, he continued, 'Right, I will sort a tray of drinks for us, and I might throw in a few biscuits too.'

'An excellent job, Anita, simply excellent! And well done for utilising your contacts,' Shona said, turning to leave the now very hot, stuffy box room.

It was only when the door clicked shut behind them that Shona realised that Anita had remained at her workstation, so she retraced her steps and opened the door to find her attention back on the computer in front of her.

'Anita,' Shona began, 'are you not coming?'

'Sorry?' Anita asked, puzzled.

'To be part of the meeting with Demi Lee, after all, if it wasn't for your brilliance, we wouldn't have found these spectacular leads,' Shona stated.

'Oh, sorry, I didn't envisage you were including me as I am only a Constable,' Collins said humbly.

'Your present rank may be Constable, Anita, but I wasn't joking when I said I would have to watch out for you, you're a DCI in the making. So yes, you are very much included,' Shona stipulated.

'Thank you so much, I will just finish this search, and I will be with you before Jenson has got the tray of drinks sorted,' she said light-heartedly.

As Shona made her way down the corridor to take a bathroom break before her meeting with Demi Lee, she couldn't help marvelling over Anita's fastidious approach to her work. She contemplated her unmatched drive to ascertain the facts, her problem-solving techniques, her discernment of character, her ability to work under pressure, her self-propelled motivation, her copper's instinct and the fresh approach in her attention to detail. There was only one other person she had ever known to possess those qualities, and that was herself.

Anita Collins was her15 years ago, and one thing that Shona had always been in search of was that one prodigy whom she could mentor. Shona smiled at the prospect of finally finding the right person to invest her time and experience in, knowing full well it wouldn't go to waste. She glanced at herself in the mirror as she washed her hands and felt so content that even the dark circles under her eyes went unnoticed. As she turned to use the hand dryer, the door opened to reveal Anita.

'I have spoken with Josie Bellamy, and get this,' she began, 'she is happy to come in whenever it suits us. Her exact words were, 'About time'.'

'Are you on shift in the morning?' Shona enquired.

'Yes, I am in at 07:00 until 17:00,' she said. 'Why?'

'Ask her to come in for 11 am. I want you in on that interview,' Shona stated.

'Really?' Collins said, thrilled.

'Really,' said Shona wryly, 'I need to start training you up if I am going to have any chance of getting you through the ranks to DCI.'

Anita almost skipped up the corridor back to her little cupboard, feeling valued, her abilities affirmed and with renewed excitement at her future career prospects. It was twenty minutes later Shona received a call from the desk sergeant downstairs to let her know that Demi Lee had arrived, if she was free to see her. Anita readily volunteered to collect Demi Lee to escort her to Shona's office, not just because she was the lowest-ranking officer among the other three, but because she was intrigued to get to Demi Lee first.

It was around 10 minutes before the door opened again, with Anita showing Demi Lee into the office. It was clear to see the young woman's discomfort at being escorted through the core of such a large police station and ushered into a room with three detectives. Shona stood out of respect whilst Jacobi pulled his chair up to the desk, stood behind it and offered the young woman his seat. She nervously stepped forward, all the time her senses on high alert as her eyes kept flicking between the two men and the woman.

'Hello, Demi, I am Detective Chief Inspector Shona Williams, these are Detective Inspectors Jacobi and Parker,' she said, indicating who was who. 'And of course, you have met Police Constable Anita Williams.'

'Hi, I am Demi Lee,' she smiled thinly, looking very uncomfortable and out of her depth.

'Won't you take a seat?' Jacobi said helpfully. 'It's alright, we don't bite.' Shona raised her eyes at Jacobi as if to say, 'Give the lass a break,' before sitting back down.

It was only then that Shona took note of the book that the young woman was clutching. 'So, what can we do to help, Demi?'

'It's a bit of a long story, but I will try to condense it. So, roughly 12 months ago, I moved into a little house on The Crescent in Ossett, spending the first 6 months renovating it. One of my friends, who is a plumber, helped me to speed up the remaining renovation, by installing a new bathroom suite for me. I had been away with his girlfriend for the weekend, and he had done it as a surprise,' She stated.

'Wow, he's a keeper, wish I had friends like that,' Shona said to make the young woman relax.

'Yes, I couldn't believe it. Anyway, as he was leaving, he told me he had found a parcel secreted beneath the bath that he had left on the mantelpiece for me to check out when I got back. I didn't feel that I had the right to pry, but my friend kept badgering me about it, so in the end, a week later, I opened it. This is what was inside,' she said, placing the book she'd been clinging onto as though it was a protective mask to fend off the Covid virus, down on to the desk.

The three detectives looked at the inconspicuous book laid on some old crumpled brown paper, whilst Anita Collins, who had been stood back near the door, stepped forward to get a glimpse.

'So, what is the story about it and how did it end up being a feature on your news feed?' Shona enquired.

'Well, first of all I had been given the opportunity to write my own column, so when I read through the contents of the book, I felt it would be a great topical source to use extracts. It ended up being really successful to initiate conversational feedback, to raise awareness of abusive relationships, and for people to reach out with their own experiences. So far, we are in triple figures of the number of women we've either been able to sign post to agencies relevant to meet their needs or give them help to escape toxic situations. It all started with this book, but when my bosses wanted to use social media to find out the identity of this person, her story became real to me. I know you will think me naïve, but until then it was just a story. I hadn't allowed myself to contemplate the possibility of her being a real person,' Demi admitted defeatedly.

'So, how long have you had the book?' Jacobi asked.

'It has been almost 6 months,' she stated.

'I am not sure if I am missing something here, but if you have had it 6 months, why is it suddenly important to share the information with the police?' Shona asked.

'This morning, I found some indented letters on the inside of the brown paper, as though somebody had rested a separate sheet on top of it and had left an imprint on this piece of paper below' she said, reaching out and touching the outer wrapping.

'Ok, so you have my full attention. What did it say?' Shona asked, looking around at her colleagues.

'Bearing in mind the contents of the book are regarding the writer's experience of being in an abusive relationship, the passage reads as follows: *If you have read any of this, then you have found my diary, which means he got to me first. I beg you, no matter how farfetched this may seem, please take it to the nearest police station and urge them to check him out and also my whereabouts. Please, this is NOT a hoax, and my life could depend upon you acting upon this information. I am Amelia Jayne Peters, my date of birth is 27.10.73, his name is Robert Day Jr,*' Demi Lee stated.

'I am not at liberty to share any details with you, Ms Lee, but we are currently investigating a person with that name, and if it turns out to be the same man, let me say you may have just provided the key to unlock our way forward,' Shona said, getting up.

'Anita,' Shona began.

'It's OK, boss, I am already on it. You know where to find me,' she said, making her exit.

She looked towards Jacobi and Parker. 'Guys, it is essential we focus on past relationships, so pull Taylor and Davidson off their role into his earlier life and have them with you and Driver, Dion. Parker, will you escort Demi Lee out to the front desk and pick up Day's phone unless they have already sent it for downloading? Either way, I am personally going to drop in on Delia Paige to ensure we have that downloaded as a priority, along with Karen Blakely's. Whilst he is still out there, no woman is safe, so let's get on to it.'

Chapter 40
New Evidence

By the time Shona had arrived back to the open area of the communal workstation, there was a hive of activity. Taylor and Davis had found that Day had no known addictions, but more importantly, there were no registered underlying diagnoses of anything. This pleased Shona as it took away the element of hiding behind a health issue and having to disprove claims later that he had momentarily been unaware of what he was doing. It annoyed Shona when this little 'get out of jail card' was dipped into the water to test a jury's sympathy.

According to the report, there was no evidence he suffered from any form of mental health issues, whether that was bipolar, depression or a psychotic illness. There was also nothing registered regarding any addictions, and he was not on any medications. In fact, the last known prescription that had been dispensed was 18 months previously for an antibiotic.

As anticipated, Diana Blakely was only too keen to assist with their investigations and readily gave permission for the downloading of Karen Blakely's phone so Shona made arrangements for Delia Paige to receive it within the hour. As Shona stood gazing at the scene photos, it reminded her about the shoe footprint on the carpet in Karen Blakely's bedroom and the need to enquire about the Tupperware box. So, she put in yet another call to forensics.

'Hi Michael, it's Shona again. I know you are probably fed up with hearing from me, but do you have anything for me yet?' Shona enquired.

'Shona Williams, you are the most annoying person in this building,' Michael delivered.

'I know, sorry, but I really do want something to go on,' Shona apologised.

'I am referring to the fact that we have been running this at 100 mph. As you live and breathe the case, so do we in processing the details, but we cannot make them magically appear. They take time,' he said sternly.

'So, there is no point in me asking when you may have some results, then?' she queried, totally ignoring what she didn't want to hear.

'If you took the time to enter your office every now and again, you might have found the file on your desk,' Michael stated.

'Oh, sorry, thank you,' Shona said elated, and was about to disconnect the phone when Michael continued. 'And, before you ask anything else, yes, a footprint has been lifted from the carpet, and Jeremy, my top guy, is currently comparing the saliva of the Tupperware contents with the DNA collected from Day. Now please leave me alone, I have more than just this case,' he said, slamming down the phone.

Unfazed, Shona raced to her office, grabbed up the report from her desk and dropped down heavily onto her office chair. Having read these reports on numerous occasions, she skimmed down to what she called the 4f's: fingerprints, footprints, fibres and fluids. Firstly, the only clear fingerprints lifted were those of Day's and Karen Blakely's, which considering he had been controlling the people in her life for some time, Shona hadn't really expected any less. However, there was a very clean full left handprint removed from the edge of the island's granite top.

Shona stood up from her desk to measure out what she was reading so that she could visualise it accurately. When stood at the corner, the impact area was 1 foot into the right, and the handprint had been located approximately 1 foot from the corner to the left. This appeared to be evident in someone grabbing hold of the edge of the island to provide the stability to give a fuller memento of a downward drag with the right hand, essentially allowing as much force as was humanly possible again, with the intent of achieving the greatest damage possible.

There had been no credible footprints to speak of other than the one upon the upstairs master bedroom carpet, which she was still waiting to hear about.

Inevitably, the blood splatter was consistent with Karen's face being slammed onto the kitchen's island surface, and evaluating where this had then landed, it was deduced that the killer was standing to her left. Shona visualised the kitchen, surmising that if the perpetrator was right-handed, then this made sense, and it was the nearest area to the door. Although this fit with the handprint location, confusingly, there was absolutely no blood upon Day's clothing.

They had also recovered tiny fibres from a red garment upon the upper clothing Karen was wearing, but these also did not match the clothes Day submitted, nor did the black fibres upon her lower garments. Shona sat back in her chair, perplexed. What if she had got it completely wrong and Day was telling the truth that there had been an intruder after all?

Then she saw the information about the fibre that raised questions. It had come from a very recently laundered garment. The ingredients of the powder absorbed within the fibre were easily matched to a brand called Sun Blessed and was identified as their summer breeze fragrant option. Shona recalled the washing machine that had still been plugged in, and that Day had been at the house for hours whilst Karen was at work. So, it was possible he had laundered his clothing whilst he waited for Karen to return home. But what then? Had he changed them again to remove the evidence?

The only time he would have been able to do this would have been between the time of her death and the ambulance's arrival. But how on earth would she know that for certain? It was one thing thinking of possibilities and a whole different ballgame being able to prove it. There was nothing for it; she would have to return to the scene to check the brand of powder Karen used. It might not prove anything, but at least she could then contact the electric company to see if there had been a sudden surge in electricity consistent with the washing machine cycle running.

Whether there was any forensic evidence at this point directly connecting Day to Karen's murder or not, she wasn't prepared to let Day off the hook yet.

Shona needed air, so she decided to take the MR2 for a ride over to 357 St Michael's Mount to satisfy her curiosity about the washing powder and was rewarded with a match. It wasn't anything conclusive, but it was something. On leaving, Shona stopped at the door, trying to picture everything that had happened when Karen had arrived home before the paramedics had arrived. She knew Karen was annoyed that she had made a call to Marcus, and that she had been sitting in the car for a few minutes until he had disturbed her. What was she missing? There had to be something that she was not seeing, but what?

Shona took the steps that Day would have taken to approach Karen when she was sat in the car. As she stood, her eyes intently searching, thinking and analysing, she suddenly saw it. Marcus had said Karen Blakely had told her she had just got home to find him there, and that he knew she was still in the car because he could hear the engine running. Above the dashboard, secreted from view by the rear-view mirror, was a little dash cam.

The excitement began to build as Shona returned to the house and found a solitary car key hung on a nail behind the kitchen door at the side of the coat hooks. Barely able to breathe, Shona raced to her boot, selected an evidence bag, put on a fresh pair of gloves, collected the car key and unlocked the car. Shona knew she could have just removed the SD card, but she wasn't taking any chances, so she removed the full head of the camera and placed it in the bag, sealing it and labelling it with the appropriate evidential information. She had a quick scan of the car, but there was nothing else of interest.

On arrival back at the station, Shona tracked down Tony from the CCTV department to see if he could do anything with the dash cam rather than her having to pester Delia Paige for that downloading as well. Even though Tony was on his way out of the building, he immediately turned back around, sensing the urgency in Shona's voice. It was when Shona entered the communal work area that the noise seemed to be overwhelming.

'Where have you been?' asked Jacobi. 'We have been trying to reach you.'

'I needed a breather, Dion, sorry. What's up?' Shona asked.

'The list of past relationships that we have secured, I think you need to take a look,' Jacobi told her, walking over to Driver, Taylor and Davidson.

'OK, guys,' Shona sighed as she wheeled over a chair from an empty desk and slumped down onto it. 'What have you got for me?'

'I was looking at whether Day had previously been married, so inevitably I began by searching the obvious registrar database for documents. I found that he had been married to a lady called Heather Day in 1997, who had previously received quite a substantial payment due to a surgical error. This marriage ended in Feb 2006 when his wife died at the tender age of 35,' said Driver.

'Were there any suspicious circumstances relating to her death?' asked Shona, suddenly sitting on the edge of her seat.

'There doesn't appear to have been, although they did have a child together, Belle, and a substantial trust had been put in place for her should anything have happened to the mother. That trust was systematically syphoned away by Day himself, so when the child turned 18 and should have received the proceeds of the trust, it was gone,' Driver explained, dismayed.

'So, not only does our man Day steal from his employers, but he also steals from banks using credit cards and refusing to pay it back, he steals from tax credits, the tax man and now his own child?' Shona surmised, astounded.

'Yes,' said Jacobi. 'It is a case of how low can you go?'

'The next person we found,' Davidson began, 'was a lady called Daniela Conway. She was on the electoral roll at Day's property on Edge Lane, Walton from July 2006 to August 2017.'

'Hold on a minute. His wife has just passed away, and within a matter of four months, he has moved someone else in?' asked Shona incredulously.

'Yes, that's exactly what we all thought,' said Parker.

'OK, who was next?' Shona continued.

'It was a lady called Rosina Wray that Anita Collins found and brought her to our attention. Apparently, she had found a photograph of them both on Day's Facebook page, so she passed on her details to add to our list. It looks like he may only have been seeing her for a few months because we were then diverted by Marsh and Bennett to re-look at his financial records. They had remembered a standing order of £26 per week being transferred to a Josie Bellamy under the heading of utilities. When we took a look at it, those ran from July 2020 to May 2023,' Taylor informed her.

Josie Bellamy?' Shona asked quizzically towards Parker.

'Josie Bellamy is the lady who made the comments on his Facebook page and identified him on the Newspaper's *Dear Diary* Feed,' Parker reminded her.

'Ah, the lady who we are interviewing in the morning,' Shona recalled.

'Yes,' said Parker triumphantly.

'So where does our *Dear Diary's* Amelia Jayne Peters fit into all this?' Shona enquired.

'That is a good question, we are still working on that one,' Jacobi started. 'We have been able to find her through her date of birth but haven't got any further yet,' Jacobi stated.

'OK, that's brilliant. If you can stay on it, Driver, whilst you two,' Shona said, addressing Taylor and Davidson, 'can you focus on getting the contact details of Daniela Conway and Rosina Wray? The only way we are going to find out who Robert Day Jr really is will be from the women who really know him, so let's find them!'

Chapter 41
Two For the Price of One

The next morning, Shona Williams was trying her best to stop the incessant habit of clock-watching, but by 10:45, her stomach was beginning to mix and turn like the tickets being spun in a raffle drum. When 11:05 approached, her heart plummeted with the potential of Josie Bellamy being yet another no-show witness. Shona never understood why people came forward, seemingly willing to share information if they did not have the inclination to see it through to the end. She understood that some people may find a police station intimidating, but for her, it was just a place of work.

As she sat pondering the matter, the silence was suddenly broken by the shrill of her desk phone.

'Hello, Senior Investigation Unit, DCI Shona Williams speaking,' was her rehearsed reply.

'Good morning, Shona, it's Dan Clarke. We have two young ladies down in reception for you. Apparently, one of them has an appointment with you at 11?' he told her.

'Two? Oh, it's OK. Josie probably brought a friend for support. I will send Anita down to collect them,' she said.

As Collins entered reception from the secure doors to the right of the hatch, she found the two women sitting together behind a glass partition screen. She was immediately struck by how similar the women looked, not only facially but in appearance too. They both sported the same shoulder-length hair, though one was blonde and the other auburn. Unnecessarily, Dan pointed to the two women, who were the only people sitting in the waiting area. Collins raised her eyes at him, and he grinned in response nodding his head at their pretend secret code.

Collins strode straight over to the women and introduced herself, asking which one was Josie.

'I am,' said the auburn woman, stepping forward.

'Nice to meet you. Is this your sister?' Collins enquired.

'No, this is my friend, who I asked to come along with me for support,' Josie responded.

Dan looked up at Anita as she approached him, 'Dan, would you let Shona know that Josie has brought a friend for support, please?'

'She already knows. I told her when they arrived,' Dan informed her.

Collins turned back to face the women and invited them to follow her through the secure door, then along the corridors, up the steps and into the partially seated and open workspace. She offered them a drink, but they both declined. Perhaps their nerves were getting the better of them, Collins concluded. She therefore made an excuse to find her supervising officer, not only to alleviate the women's mounting stress but to update Shona prior to her entrance.

She found her at the drinks station, stirring milk into a fresh cup of coffee.

'Where is Josie Bellamy and her friend?' Shona asked, perplexed.

'They are sitting waiting at the seating area. I just thought you might want to take a moment to prepare yourself, Shona,' Anita said cryptically.

'Prepare myself,' Shona asked, unsure where Collins was going with the conversation.

'Josie hasn't brought her friend for support. She has asked her along as she thought we might want to interview her too,' Collins delivered.

'Why?' Shona asked confused.

'The other woman is Rosina Wray!' Anita revealed.

Shona suddenly had no control of her mouth as it gaped open. 'What?' she said, trying to recover her surprise.

'She has just told me on the way up here, and I have to say my mouth dropped open like that too. So, I don't know how you want to play this,' Anita asked.

Shona was contemplating the logistics of interviewing both women as, originally, she had planned to have Anita with her when she interviewed Josie, especially as she had already been in contact with her.

'I think you and I will have to conduct separate interviews, Anita. Are you comfortable with that? I don't think either of these women would be at ease in a small room with either Jenson or Dion,' Shona told Collins.

'That is exactly what I thought too, but is it alright if I still sit in with Josie?' Anita requested.

'I don't see why not. If you go back to Josie and Rosina, I will arrange for two video suites to be available. I am sure Tony and Charlotte will jump at the chance to get away for a couple of hours,' Shona said, taking her leave.

When Shona approached Josie and Rosina, she too thought about the similarities, but not just to each other—also to Karen Blakely as well. Day obviously had a specific type.

'Good morning, ladies. I am Detective Chief Inspector Shona Williams and, obviously, you have met Police Constable Anita Collins. Are you sure you wouldn't like a coffee, tea or anything before we get started?' Shona enquired.

Josie declined in a strong confident voice, whereas Rosina shook her head nervously.

'Ok then, if you would like to follow me,' Shona instructed and turned back out through the door, down the stairs and into the corridor they had just been led along. The women gave each other a puzzled look, and then Josie cottoned on. The interview was not just going to be recorded but videoed, in case the evidence that was given would be needed in court. She wondered what on earth Robert Day Jr had got himself into now.

'Rosina if you would like to come this way,' Shona said gently, holding a door wide open for her.

'And Josie, would you like to come this way?' Anita said, smiling opening the door next to it.

The rooms were set out exactly the same. To the right of the door were three kitchen cabinets with a sink, a kettle and beverage-making facilities. At the end was a small white fridge. There were no posters on the wall. Instead, were two commercially produced canvases of different landscape scenes and another of a bunch of flowers in a watering can set on a metal garden chair. The first two reminded Josie of her being in a sunnier climate, and the third of a cottage garden where someone had freshly cut the flowers ready to take inside.

There was a grey plain mat set in the middle of the room, laid upon a wooden laminate floor, with a small pine table and two soft, comfortable armchairs arranged opposite each other. Its intent was to give a welcoming, relaxing atmosphere, but due to the location, it did nothing to ease Rosina's anxiety. In fact, it reminded her of the hours she had spent with Isla, especially as she was here again, having to relive her experiences of being with him. It annoyed Rosina that, even now, after five years, that man was still having an effect on her life, and she was being forced into this predicament due to his selfish behaviour

Nervously, Rosina scanned the three shut doors—two on the wall opposite and one to her left.

'Are you OK, Rosina?' Shona asked, worried that she was about to flee through the door at any minute to make a break for freedom.

'Yes, sorry, I am just angry that my time is being controlled again by him. I naively thought that once I had got through the counselling, I would be able to move on once and for all.' Rosina sighed. 'But he just seems to keep popping up like that irritating 'Whack-A-Mole' arcade game.'

Shona couldn't help but smile at the analogy, visualising Josie and Rosina with a soft hammer apiece, fighting to bring it down hard on Day's head. Perhaps the game was a good description of how the past has a habit of raising its ugly head when we least expect it to bring you back down to earth again.

Once both Rosina and Josie were seated in their respective rooms, they were taken through the preliminaries of what to expect. They were given the spiel of what to do in case of a fire alarm and then shown the camera room behind the door to the right and the interview room behind the door to the left and indicated that the third contained the toilet. They were thanked for taking the time to attend and reminded that if they needed to take a short break at any time during the interview, then they just needed to say.

When all the information had been delivered, the paperwork completed, and the cameras and sound levels tested, then the women were invited to take a seat in the interview room. Tony sat recording Josie's interview with Parker listening in, and Charlotte was on the cameras for Rosina's, with Jacobi listening in.

As normal, the date, time, location of the interview and the people present were identified prior to the start of the interview, in case the video needed to be played in court. It gave the jury a timeline but also proved when the recording was extracted. Once everything was in place, both Shona and Collins invited their respective witnesses to give their testimony without interruption unless something needed further explanation.

At the end of the sessions, Collins liaised with Tony and Parker, whilst Shona liaised with Charlotte and Jacobi to find out if there were any questions that needed asking or further clarification. Once everything had been satisfied, the interview was concluded.

It was Josie who was led out of her room first and escorted back towards the reception area, where she was shown to a comfortable seating area just before the communal public foyer. She was again offered a drink, which this time she readily accepted, as she knew she could be in for a long wait.

'If there is anything else you need, Josie, don't hesitate to ring the bell at the side of the door, and Dan will come in and attend to your needs. I am sorry you may have a long wait on your hands whilst DCI Williams is extracting Rosina's statement,' Collins apologised.

'It is OK. I knew that would be the case when I invited her to come along, but I wanted to make sure that we saved you some time and that you could collect her statement at the same time. At the end of the day, Robert Day Jr has done enough damage, so if you are finally going to put a stop to it, I am happy to wait here for however long Rosina's statement takes,' Josie assured Collins.

'Yes, I can see why. Thank you for responding quickly to my messages yesterday and for being so proactive in attending the station today. It is very much appreciated. The information you have provided is not only parallel to what we have discovered already but will assist in building a picture of Robert Day Jr in our current investigation,' Collins assured her, stepping forward to shake her hand. 'Thank you again.'

'Oh, believe me, it was my pleasure,' Josie said heartily, shaking the police lady's offered hand and grinning widely.

Chapter 42
The Video

By the time Shona had emerged with Rosina Wray, Josie had been sat waiting for just over 1 ½ hours, so was relieved when the door finally opened, and their ordeal was over.

'How did it go?' Josie asked.

'She did great and came across really well,' said Shona.

'That is not how I would have described it,' said a tear-stained-faced Rosina Wray.

'It is over now,' Josie said soothingly.

'But is it though?' Rosina sniffed. 'He just keeps popping up like high blood pressure, going undetected for years until, like the silent killer it is, it finally claims your life.'

'Come on, Rosina, let's get out of here and promise me we leave what has been said here behind us. We do not give it another thought. That man has claimed far too much of our time already. Agreed?' Josie tried.

'Agreed!' Rosina stated.

When Shona had thanked them for their attendance, curiosity got the better of her. 'Can I just ask you how you two became friends?'

Rosina looked at Josie, who nodded her approval. 'There was a bar I used to go into with Robert, but when he was with me, he was always fawning over Josie. It wasn't just the odd glance; he was literally undressing her with his eyes. The more it went on, the more disrespected I felt, and no offence, Josie, but it gave me the impetus to get away from him,' Rosina explained.

'Yes, I wish she had warned me what he was like, and I would never have got involved with him. But we are where we are, and together, we can stand in the gap for any subsequent women that he may come into contact with,' Josie said, giving her friend's hand a little squeeze.

'Well, it has been a pleasure meeting you both and may I thank you for coming forward to help with our investigation? You have been a Godsend,' Shona stipulated.

She escorted the two women to the exit and thanked them again before intending to return to her office. As she walked through the door, there was a note on her desk asking her to make her way immediately to the tech cupboard. She presumed that Collins wanted to discuss the elements of Josie's interview and to compare their testimonies, so she readily obliged. When she arrived, there was Jacobi and Parker stood in the doorway, observing the screen where the interview of Josie Bellamy was playing.

'That was quick,' Shona said, referring to the speed Tony had obviously expedited the interview.

'This is not this morning's interview, boss; this was filmed 13 months ago when Josie first reported Day for sexual abuse and rape,' Parker stipulated. 'And it makes for a very uncomfortable interview.'

It was for the second time that day Shona's mouth dropped open, and she had to recover herself before speaking again. 'Sorry?' Shona asked.

'Josie had implicated Robert Day Jr on the *Dear Diary* News Feed because the excerpts of what Amelia Jayne Peters had written in her book is an exact replica of what happened to Josie Bellamy!' Anita Stated.

'And to Rosina Wray,' confirmed Shona sadly. 'Dion, can you find out if Driver, Taylor or Davidson have been able to locate Daniela Conway or Amelia Jayne Peters? I have a feeling we will find they are also victims.'

'Jenson, would you mind checking on the phone downloads to see if we have recovered anything, please?' Both Jacobi and Parker scooted off to attend to their individual tasks whilst Shona pulled the tech cupboard door shut so she and Anita could analyse the footage of Josie Bellamy's earlier interview.

'That is shocking to watch,' said Anita, sitting back and pausing the video. 'She only gave me a brief outline when we started filming, having assumed I had already seen this copy of her earlier interview. I was embarrassed to tell her that I had no idea it existed, as a different department had dealt with her 13 months ago and, as no charges had been made, it was left on file.'

'Shocking yes, but surprising no. What Karen Blakely had tried to communicate to those around her was that she had felt smothered and that her life was no longer her own. She had tried to get away from Day on several occasions during the year she was with him, but he wouldn't let go. By the sounds of it, like Karen, for the last 6 months of Josie and Day's relationship, she too had tried to get away from him. Unfortunately, she had resigned herself to the fact that unless he made that choice himself, she was going to be stuck with him for the rest of her life. It was during this time that she seems to have given up on the relationship, which he has assumed demonstrated her compliance and thus taken advantage of her sexually,' said Shona. 'And to be honest, there are clear replicas in Rosina Wray's statement too.'

''Clearly a replica of Josie Bellamy's experience too. Can you imagine not feeling safe in your own bed, of him turning up in the middle of the night when you are asleep to find him sexually abusing you?' Anita said dismayed.

'Yes, and then excusing yourself repeatedly with 'I thought you were awake' or 'I would never do that, that was not my intention,' as though that excused his abuse,' Shona said incredulously.

'How does it become the norm for the person being used in that way?' Collins asked.

'The initial love-bombing stage is to make the individual fall in love with them quickly, to form a bond and belief that they are 'the one' they have been waiting all their lives for. It is a means to form an emotional dependency through gross manipulation to gain the ultimate control. When there are sudden changes, the target will then be gaslighted to believe they are to blame, so they will try harder to win back the love that they initially had. It's all just a game to coerce them to do what the groomer wants,' Shona explained, disgusted at the lives this man had ruined.

'What did Rosina have to share?' Collins asked, although she was sure she probably knew the answer to her own question.

'With Rosina, it didn't get that far. She was able to pull away, although I think perhaps her knowledge and guardian angel saved her a worse fate,' Shona said cryptically.

'Sorry, I don't follow,' Anita said puzzled.

'Well, Rosina's best friend was Heather, Day's wife, who died. She was able to share quite an insight into his marriage and the fact she had always been suspicious that Day was responsible for her death,' Shona revealed.

'Ah,' Anita said, the penny dropping. 'So the guardian angel was Heather looking out for Rosina.'

'Yes, not only had Rosina witnessed things, but Heather had also opened up about Day's controlling behaviour. She did confirm her place on our relationship list, though, as being Dec 2018 to Aug 2019. It seems that we have a very good picture of who Robert Day Jr really is. We just need to interview Daniela Conway now,' Shona said.

'Oh, sorry I forgot to tell you,' Collins began. 'Taylor tracked her down and invited her to come in for a chat, but because she has a child with Day, she has refused to give any information. However, she did offer Josie Bellamy and Rosina Wray as alternative options and then stated, 'Whatever they tell you, just know my experience was far worse and it lasted for 11 years'.'

'These poor women are scarred for the rest of their lives, whilst he steps aside and literally moves on to the next, as though he is throwing out yesterday's garbage,' Shona said.

'I remember my dad saying that the reason they do this is because they have an inability to face the consequences of their actions. So, like the excuse of 'it wasn't my intention therefore I am not to blame,' they cut off one and delve straight into the next as this creates the belief system that they were never the problem,' Anita shared.

'It does not make them any less culpable, though, Anita,' Shona stressed.

'No, it doesn't. It makes them weak and unwilling to take responsibility, and finding another target quickly convinces them they are not to blame. So, where do we go from here?' asked Collins.

'Did you find anything else on Day's Facebook account or Karen Blakely's?' Shona asked.

'They were remarkably different. Karen had photos of holidays they had enjoyed together, meals out, adrenaline-filled experiences—you know, the stuff depicting a life they had shared. Whereas Day had no photos whatsoever of his wife, Daniella Conway, Rosina Wray, Amelia Jayne Peters or Josie Bellamy. I am wondering if, when he cuts them off, he completely cuts them out as though they never existed,' Collins mapped out.

'Sounds like a man who cannot deal with the guilt of his actions,' Shona surmised.

'Or a man that doesn't want to be reminded and therefore erases their existence,' Anita pointed out.

'Cold and callous, especially when you consider how he actually treats them,' said Shona.

There was a tap at the door, so Shona depressed the handle to see Driver standing there.

'I am sorry to disturb you, boss, but I have something to show you in your office, and it isn't good,' Driver said, walking away.

'Oh, my goodness, what now?' Shona asked Anita. 'Come on, we had better brace ourselves.'

Shona turned and walked swiftly after Driver, whilst Anita pushed back her chair before hurriedly pursuing them both. What could be any worse than the information they had just received from Josie Bellamy and Rosina Wray about Day?

Chapter 43
A Startling Revelation

As Driver arrived at Shona's office, he suddenly remembered his manners and stepped aside to allow his superior to walk in before him. When Shona opened the door, she was confused to see Jacobi pouring over several haphazardly stuck-together papers. Shona looked from one to the other in confusion.

'Would someone like to explain what is going on?' Shona asked.

Driver was still standing at the side of the office door, allowing Anita to enter before his intention to join the group inside.

'Come on, lad, this is your baby. Move yourself forward and present your findings to the boss,' Jacobi stated.

Whilst Driver stumbled his way over to Shona's desk, she couldn't help but notice the grave look on Anita's face as, together, they were both apparently hoping that there wasn't indeed any more bad news. Driver carefully picked up one side of the papers whilst Jacobi took the other side, and then they stuck it up on the wall with pre-applied Blu-tac. Shona stared at it, not sure what on earth she was looking at, and waited.

'So, when I was tasked to look into the author of the *Dear Diary* excerpts, I was coming up with blanks no matter what angle I tried to tackle it from, so I decided to conduct a kind of Family Tree. I reasoned that if we had Amelia Jayne Peters' birthdate, then I could perhaps find her by looking into the registration of her birth. This way I would at least be able to locate her parents or some close family member in order to get information about Amelia Jayne Peters herself. Anyway, without going through a rigorous or detailed account of all the people I found I just want to draw your attention to...' Driver was saying, as there was a light tap on the door.

Shona was about to say, 'Go away,' the tension rising within her, when the door opened to reveal Parker. Believing he had also been summoned to the party,

Shona turned back round to face Driver and Jacobi, waiting for the door to close so Driver could continue.

'So? Have you found a close relative that we can talk to, or have you found Amelia Jayne Peters?' Shona pressed for an answer.

Behind her, Parker cleared his voice at the same time as Shona's eyes fell upon the name next to Amelia Jayne Peters. When she turned around, Sallyanne Peters, the coroner, was doing her best to not allow the sobs to be fully expressed.

'The thing is, boss, Sallyanne has confirmed that her sister was seeing Robert Day Jr around September 2017 to Nov 2018. They had just got engaged when Amelia Jayne disappeared on her own to Spain, but she did not come back alive,' Parker said.

Shona held out a chair for Sallyanne, who gladly put her hand upon its back for stability before slumping down into it. At that moment, Shona realised that Sallyanne was clutching an evidence bag containing a small bound leather book—the one that had been loosely tied with a thin shoelace sliver of leather—whilst Parker had its brown paper wrapping in a second evidence bag. Shona looked at her dear friend with a compassionate heart filled with an overwhelming love of protection as the tears of grief poured down her face.

'Sallyanne has just identified both the writing in the diary as that of her sister's and Day's line-up picture as the man Amelia Jayne had been engaged to prior to her untimely death. Before revealing what we knew, I casually asked Sallyanne if she had a sister called Amelia Jayne, born on 27.10.73, and she kindly filled in all the blanks. Would you like to tell the story, Sallyanne, or would you prefer that I continue on your behalf?' Parker gently enquired.

'No, I will,' she gulped, trying to swallow down the emotion. 'Around September of 2018, Amelia—or Meli, as we called her—seemed to be having doubts about her new fiancé. They hadn't been going out very long when he proposed, but Meli immediately said 'yes' because, during the first 6 months, he was everything she had ever wanted. I remember warning her at the time to be careful and advised her not to jump straight into marriage with someone she barely knew. He seemed far too good to be true to me, and not only that, but my dad had just passed away and Mum had not long since been diagnosed with dementia. Therefore, I felt she was quite vulnerable, but I couldn't tell her I thought he was taking advantage of her,' Sallyanne recalled.

'What was your opinion of him, Sallyanne?' Jacobi asked softly.

'You know, only too well, that I love nothing more than talking about my work, but not everyone is a willing recipient to want to listen. Anyway, at their engagement party, I was talking to Day, but for the first time ever, he creeped me out rather than the other way around. He seemed to be a little too interested in the procedures of how I might conduct a postmortem, asking some very probing questions about the removal of the internal organs and even down to the weighing of them,' Sallyanne shuddered.

'So, what happened to Meli in Spain, Sallyanne, if she did not come back alive?' enquired Shona.

'They said that she had been found in the complex communal pool with a serious head injury, so the Spanish government put it down to misadventure. They believed she had potentially dived into the shallow end by mistake, causing the head injury, and therefore her death had been caused by accidental means. Inevitably, I was unable to perform a secondary postmortem due to the conflict of interest, but I'd always felt there was far more to it. Meli was an Olympic swimmer, and we had visited the same village in the Baztan region of northern Spain since we were kids. So, it was impossible for her to make such a simple mistake. I tried contacting the local authorities; I even went over there, making my own enquiries, but I just came up with blanks every time. And of course, Mum's dementia plummeted through the trauma of losing Meli, so I had to concentrate on her care at the time. It has always had a great big question mark over it for me though,' Sallyanne's voice trailed off as though it was far too painful to delve into the memory any further.

'For our records, would you mind telling us what her date of death was?' Shona asked.

'Yes, it was the 31.12.2018,' Sallyanne stated.

'Was that the actual recorded date of death, the date she was found in Spain or the one that was given on her arrival back in the UK? Sorry to be so precise, but I know paperwork has been lost in transit before now, and a subsidiary date is given instead,' Shona enquired.

'I can definitively state it was the actual date of death. As a newly single person, Meli did not want to bring the New Year in with the rest of the family, and so she chose to be on her own instead. She was then sideswiped to find that her ex-fiancé had got a new partner, so, finding this unbearable, she had chosen to go to the one place she felt safe—the small apartments Mum and Dad had rented each summer when we were children. I tried to talk her out of it, but she was adamant she could not bear to be in the same country as him whilst he brought the New Year in with someone else, no doubt promising them the world whilst he had ruined hers. She was in a bit of a mess and spoke of her life being in tatters, so she needed to get away to clear her head. I rang her earlier in the day on the 31st to wish her a Happy New Year and to ask how she was, although she wouldn't say what had happened, she did promise to tell me everything on her return. She was found later that same evening by a young couple who had gone for a midnight dip as the fireworks lit up the night sky,' Sallyanne concluded.

'Did she say anything else, anything about Robert Day Jr or their relationship?' Shona probed.

'No, she just wanted the space to decide what her next steps were going to be, and then, when she had made a decision, she said I would be the first to know, so I didn't pry any further,' Sallyanne said, then burst into tears before continuing, 'Maybe if I had pushed for answers, we could have prevented what happened to her.'

'Sallyanne, there is no way anyone could have foreseen what happened to Meli,' Shona said, comforting her friend. 'I am going to have a car take you home. I do not want you behind the wheel tonight,' Shona said kindly.

'It's alright, Shona, I can find my own way home,' Sallyanne said determinedly.

'It was not a request. Parker, can you make sure Sallyanne is driven straight home, please?' Shona asked him.

Parker nodded, then eased Sallyanne out of her seat, and before she could go any further, Shona took the woman in her arms and whispered, 'I will find out what happened, that I can promise you.'

Chapter 44
Daniela Conway

'Right, Anita, what exactly did Taylor say about why Daniela Conway would not speak to us?' Shona asked as soon as Parker had shut the door behind Sallyanne.

'Just that, due to her experiences with him and the fact she had a child with him, she would prefer to keep a low profile rather than inciting any further trouble involving Day,' Anita explained.

'Well, whether she wants to keep a low profile or not, there are now two women who have lost their lives, so I am not prepared to allow her to withhold information that might be imperative to this case. So, get me her details. Jacobi, I will be out of the office for the foreseeable. Get your team researching all possible routes from England to the Baztan region of Spain. I want to know if Day made that trip when Amelia Jayne Peters was there. Please get me some concrete evidence that links Day. We need to do this, not just for her but for Sallyanne too,' Shona demanded.

'On it, boss,' Jacobi assured her.

'Anita, why don't you come with me? Let's see Daniela Conway together,' Shona said, as soon as Collins returned to her office with Daniela's contact details. Then, not waiting for an answer, she strode out of the office.

Shona didn't seem in the mood to offer any conversation on the route to Daniela Conway's house, so Anita Collins remained silent, knowing that a lot of Shona's rationalisations were conducted in her head whilst she drove. As they pulled up outside the red-bricked council house, Anita was immediately struck by the well-tended garden, with its pristinely cut grass, weedless borders and power-washed cobbled drive. The lounge windows were both open, and the left curtain was slightly protruding, flapping in the light breeze. The lace curtain was abruptly hitched back to reveal a face at the window. It was a young boy, who was then seen to turn, apparently saying something to whoever was in the room with him. A few seconds later, a pretty, young woman emerged at the side of him, and by the time Shona and Anita had got out of the car, she was opening the door.

'Excuse me, I don't mean to be rude, but will you be leaving your car there long? Only my husband will be here any moment, and that is where he usually parks?' she asked politely.

'Is this number 273?' asked Shona, biding herself some time to manoeuvre herself around the back of the car in order to get closer to the gate.

'Yes, it is,' said the woman, helpful.

'So, you must be Daniela Conway?' Shona asked, passing through the gate to approach the door.

'Yes, I am, but who are you?' she asked, really confused, evidently not expecting anyone. And then, as she looked from Shona to Collins and back again, the penny must have dropped. 'Oh no, you can't be here. I told them when they rang, I don't want to get involved. I cannot be associated with any investigation regarding him,' she panicked.

'Mrs Conway, I appreciate your anxiety and probably your reasons with regards to your decision, but that will not stop us from asking you questions. We have an investigation to conduct, so you can either do it here or at the station. The choice is yours,' Shona stated, unwilling to take no for an answer.

'Just wait a minute, Paulie. Get your swimming things and go next door to Mandy's,' she instructed.

'But it is way too early yet, Mum, and I haven't even had my sandwich yet,' the boy moaned.

'Paulie, get your things and do as I have asked you, now!' she ordered him.

Reluctantly, the boy pushed his way past his mother and left, giving the newcomers his best sullen look, just to let them know it was under duress. Daniela Conway then reluctantly stepped aside to allow Collins and Shona access to her home. The hallway had a hardwood parquet flooring that led through to what looked like a newly installed shaker-style kitchen. As they entered the lounge, they were met with a luxury pile fitted carpet, and the aroma filling the room from the set of three candles on the hearth was fresh and pleasant.

'Would you like us to remove our shoes?' Shona asked respectfully.

'No,' was Daniela's curt reply; she evidently didn't feel they would be staying long enough.

The rest of the room was immaculately presented, and by the tread marks on the carpet and lines on the soft, plush velour three-piece suite, both had been recently hoovered. Daniela Conway made her way to the chair furthest from the door at the side of the fireplace, and took her seat, leaving the two women awkwardly hovering by the door.

'Do you mind if we take a seat?' Shona asked.

'Would it matter to you if I did? I mean, I made it clear I did not want to be involved with your investigation, yet here you are. I don't mean to sound rude, but you have absolutely no idea what that man has put me through, and yet I must see him every week when he comes to take my little boy out. Do you know how that makes me feel, to be forced into allowing my child into his company and to know that those hands that inflicted such harm upon me are resting on him? I have to watch as he embraces him, holds his hand and ruffles his hair with those infected, violating hands, all the time seeing my son flinch at the sensation of his touch,' Daniela Conway spat out.

'I am sorry,' said Shona. 'But we need your help so we can stop this man from ever hurting anyone again. It will be the one way you can rid him of both your lives, forever.'

'Is that really possible, though, or are you just saying that to get me to help you? He was good at that—making me believe one thing and then changing it, just so I would question my own recollection,' Daniela said, tearing up at the memory.

'Do you mind if we sit down, please?' Anita asked gently.

Daniela Conway didn't reply but held out her right hand, palm up, and gestured towards the settee, so they thankfully took a seat next to each other. Shona seated herself nearest to the door to allow Collins to take the one closest to Daniela and nodded to her to take the lead. After all, the woman had responded more favourably towards Anita than herself; maybe it was her gentler approach rather than her own more authoritarian one.

'Mrs Conway, we are not here to stir anything up or to make life any harder than it needs to be, but we are investigating some very serious crimes that we believe Day is guilty of and which he may also have committed against you,' Anita informed her.

'And then you will leave me alone?' she asked.

'If you allow me to record your story, then I promise we will leave you alone,' Shona indicated.

Daniella Conway nodded. Shona handed Anita her phone, who placed it on record before setting it on the arm of the chair where Daniela was sitting. As the number of seconds displayed on the screen raced by, Shona and Anita waited patiently in complete silence. At the 1 min 27 second mark, she took a deep breath as if to prepare herself before the gates of what can only be described as a damn containing over 10 years of abuse came flooding out.

Yet again, the same story of gross manipulation, intimidation, self-centredness, control, severing of her support network, desperation, lies, abuse and rape unfolded. It was as though Day had a 'one size fits all' mentality towards relationships; he had a system that was working for him and so he continued regardless of the devastation he was leaving behind. This reminded her of something that Josie had said about challenging him on his behaviour, where he would seemingly understand but then behave in exactly the same way, yet expect a different outcome and be shocked when the same thing happened again. It was as though he had one set programme, and this was stuck on repeat.

In reality, all he was trying to do was brainwash them. He had an expectation without acknowledging that they were people with thoughts, desires and choices of their own. The only change to his rigid script was that he imitated each person's mannerisms, and feigned interest in their likes, hobbies and places. Yet when that relationship ended, he dismissed all these things and, like a chameleon, it was all changed to blend in and become a carbon copy of the next person he was seeing. It was only when Anita cleared her voice that Shona realised, she was being handed her phone back and Daniela had expunged herself. The woman was sat with her head hung low, her hands in her lap, having no more to give, facing the reality of the monster she had spent years with and bubbling with a newfound, deeper hatred for him.

'I am so sorry for what you have had to endure and that you have been forced to relive those experiences today. Please forgive us for our unannounced intrusion,' Anita requested, as Daniela simply nodded.

'Here is my card,' Shona began. 'If you have any questions, or decide at a later date that you would like to bring a formal complaint at any time, please contact me. I will have your statement included as part of our investigation, but if you prefer, I will keep your name confidential. And if you would like any updates, feel free to contact either myself or Anita. We will happily keep you informed, but only at your request,' Shona informed her.

'Before we leave, do you have any further questions, Daniela?' Anita enquired again, just in case.

'Were there any others or was it just me that he hated?' Daniela asked, looking pitifully into Anita's eyes.

'There have been several others, Daniela; it wasn't that he hated you or that you did anything wrong to deserve what happened to you. Robert Day Jr is a psychopathic narcissist who has no ability to empathise with another human being because, as someone else described him, he is dead on the inside. Please be assured, you did what you had to do to survive, and for that, you should be proud. At least you are here to tell your story.' Anita stood up before she said too much, swamped by empathy for the broken soul in front of her.

'Thank you for your time, Mrs Conway, and remember, we are only a phone call away if you need anything,' Shona said before making her way back into the hallway and out through the front door to her car. Neither Anita nor Shona spoke until they had secured the car door, put on their seatbelts and were driving out of the end of the Daniela Conway's, street. However, their thought patterns weren't so quiet, as each independently turned over the information they had just heard. A pin could have been heard dropping onto the car's carpeted floor; the tension was so palpable, both desperate to surrender and break the silence. Almost as a mark of respect for the lady who had just spilt her guts, they waited until Shona had joined the traffic on the main road, and then it was Collins who succumbed first.

'So, what do you make of that?' she asked.

'Programmed,' was the word that came out of Shona's mouth. 'Programmed,' she repeated.

'Yes, I felt quite sickened when she used that word too,' Collins stated. 'How does someone become programmed to give him sex every night and morning?'

'Well, the word 'give' is not technically true, is it? She described herself as just lying there, waiting for it to be over,' Shona said.

'But when I asked her why she would allow him to do just as he pleased to her, I was genuinely astounded when she explained that his treatment of her would have intensified if she objected,' Collins said sadly.

'Yes, but don't forget that she would have been made to endure it for much longer periods of time if she refused to comply with the initial request, just as she had done before,' Shona explained.

'So, what you are saying is, it was far better to let him rape her every morning and every night because her ordeal would have been so much worse had she not. I honestly do not know what could possibly be any worse than that,' Collins shared.

'That is the art of manipulation and conditioning to gain compliance through the knowledge that, regardless of how bad a situation may be, hanging over your head is the threat that things could be so much worse. Therefore, she put up with one thing as it was a lesser option than the fear of what might happen. That was enough to control her, the subject, to comply with his demands,' Shona explained.

'I couldn't believe how she just shrugged off what he was doing to her and that she felt powerless to complain because it was his house. But, there again, I suppose if he has driven it into her that no one else would want her and his attitude is, 'If she doesn't like it, she can f**k off,' then she has stayed because she has nowhere else to go,' Collins said in anger.

'Did you notice how Daniela made a point of stressing to us that Day knew full well she was not consenting to sex, as not only had she told him verbally every single time but that she would not participate in any way?' Shona reminded her.

'Yes, and the specific words she used to describe it as being nothing more than an action to use her body as a means of relieving himself—that is sickening!' Collins stated. 'It is no wonder Daniela had never felt that she was ever good enough for him.'

'Can you imagine how degraded, humiliated and unloved she must have felt? And then to know that after every time he had forced himself on her, he would say nothing, just get up, go into the bathroom and then openly masturbate?' Shona said disgustedly.

'You can see why she felt used, abused, devalued and sickened by him, not only resenting him but later developing complete hatred.' Collins swallowed down the emotions that were stirring within her; although she was a very compassionate person, she did not want her boss to think she was weak or unprofessional.

'It is so hard to imagine his arrogance to keep doing this to her both night and day, especially as her description of the act was him being robotic, with an almost mechanical element of just pressing on full steam ahead,' Shona concluded.

'It does fit in with something that Josie Bellamy said in her previous video statement about when she and Day had first got together. She described him as being pretty useless in bed and that in their first 9 months together, she had climaxed maybe 2 or 3 times, unlike him, which was every time. She called it robotic and referred to it as the old Dean Martin song, 'Wham! Bam! Thank you, Ma'am.' I thought the reference was quite clever at first, but now I know the background, I feel quite upset. Josie said she'd had to teach him the art of lovemaking because he had absolutely no idea how to please a woman sexually, only himself,' Collins revealed.

'All I see is a heartless detachment that he has had not only for Daniela but for every woman that we know about to press. Seriously, I do not think he could have demonstrated a lower disregard for human life,' Shona hardened.

'You're right. Daniela said that it was the lack of love, respect and human integrity that had hurt her the most, but she would have done anything to keep a roof over her children's heads, and he knew it. She was only finally able to escape when she met that guy through a dating website. It must have given her not only a wake-up call but a warm feeling, igniting the sensation of love again, along with a bond through his protection and support to get her out of there,' Collins said, feeling such pride for Daniela at finding the strength to finally break free.

'It must have killed her inside, though, all those years of soul-destroying abuse, and then when she does finally escape, she has the further indignity of him immediately hooking up with Rosina Wray. After the degrading way in which he had treated her, she must have felt like she'd been disposed of like garbage when he started flaunting her instant replacement in her face,' Shona said, disgusted.

'Don't you think it's weird that all these women knew of each other, yet they didn't warn the next one to save them the same indignation? I can see that afterwards, a strong bond has been created between Josie and Rosina, probably to support one another through their shared experiences. But do you think they were too scared to get involved at the time in case there was further backlash upon them?' Collins enquired.

'Quite possibly. But we are then left with the question that if someone had spoken up sooner, would Karen Blakely still have met her untimely death?' Shona pondered. 'And besides, Josie Bellamy did try to come forward, but obviously there was not sufficient evidence for whoever investigated this to dig deeper. Either that or they didn't try hard enough.'

'More than likely, they wouldn't have been aware of his psychopathic tendencies, so perhaps he was able to charm them, and it was a case of your word against mine, because let's face it, he wouldn't have given anything away,' Collins pointed out.

'One thing that hasn't escaped my observation is the fact that our Mr Day certainly has a type. Each of these women looks very similar, and from the ones I have seen or spoken to, they are all intelligent individuals,' Shona stated, amazed at how he had been able to charm them so easily and why they had tolerated his intensive, stalking traits to keep them tied to him.

'My concern for all of them, but especially Daniela, is the extent of the emotional damage and psychological harm that he has inflicted, as she has kept it locked up inside and hasn't had help from a counsellor. And now we have taken the plaster off, it is possible that she could completely unravel, and with so much to unpick, it could be detrimental for her to do it alone. We may need to check with her in a couple of days just to be sure she is alright,' Collins said thoughtfully.

Whilst Shona waited for the traffic light to change to green, she contemplated the case as a whole. All had been abused, all had been raped, so maybe this was what had resulted in their demoralisation and inability to break away, coupled with his unpredictability every time they had tried. It must have been both very confusing and disconcerting to find him turning up at locations he knew they would frequent, as though nothing had happened, or just hovering in their peripheral vision, waiting for an opportunity to talk. She was actually starting to believe that Day possibly could have some undiagnosed mental health condition because he was neither embarrassed by his actions nor could he see any wrong with what he was doing. It was particularly strange that he was apparently quick to excuse his behaviour, but then Shona guessed that although it may not be deemed socially acceptable, to him, it was probably his normal everyday practice to sustain his dependence on them. Somewhere in the crevices of Day's mind, she was sure that he believed that they were the ones who actually needed him.

Shona tried to picture him senselessly sitting on a random bench in the busy market town, changing seats throughout the day depending on Josie Bellamy's schedule, just hoping she might walk past to beg her with his eyes to talk to him. It was beyond weird; so too was the fact that he couldn't see why any of these women might find it disturbing. She wondered if he thought he was being cool, as though he was somehow blending in, unseen in the background like he had remained when he was stalking them at the start. Surely to goodness, he must have known he had stood out like a sore thumb. Of course, he did, because their accounts were also of him turning up at restaurants, sitting a couple of feet away from them at the bar, standing in Rosina's garden looking in through her window or accidentally, on purpose, walking inches from Josie's car as soon as she pulled into a space.

Taking Shona's lead, Anita too took a moment to assess, and a shiver ran down her spine as she contemplated the women's utter helplessness of not being able to shake him off, like that one infuriating car tailgating you down the motorway. No wonder they expressed feelings of being emotionally drained; the desperation, anxiety and stress of their situations must have seemed utterly hopeless, like being buried alive, bound and trapped in a steel cage. The more Anita was hearing, the more outraged she was becoming at the disbelief of how he had got away with it for so long. She couldn't understand why no one had reported him before now. Was he really so able to control them by charming them, promising the earth, using their good nature against them, before manipulating, conditioning and then coercing them into complete compliance?

Shona reflected on the opening statement that Josie Bellamy had made in her first video interview: 'Not everyone will tell the truth, but I have nothing to gain from lying, yet me telling you the truth has the potential to set me free.' All Josie wanted was some semblance of regaining a normal life. In contrast, she stated that, 'Day had everything to lose by telling the truth and everything to gain by lying.'

It was a simple, flatly delivered statement taken the previous year in the belief that her only escape from him was to inform the police to get their protection. She had felt that she had nothing else to lose, as her only choices had become either telling the truth or taking her own life. She had insisted that it was either one or the other; there were no further options. From the video, you could plainly see that Josie was still in turmoil about the action she was taking, but her statement had clearly and succinctly summed it up for Shona. He had everything to lose by telling the truth.

If Shona was honest with herself, she really admired Josie's strength of character and her sheer determination that, through her despair, she displayed a resounding power to do the right thing. Her only goal had been to ensure that

Day was brought to the police's attention to prevent him from being able to do what he had done to her to any other woman. All she had wanted to do was to selflessly stand in the gap for any other women he might come into contact with and to stop him from committing any future abuse. It was true these subsequent women would never know what she had done to protect them, but that didn't matter; Josie knew, and that was enough for her.

She had described him as being callous, cunning and deceptive in all capacities, and of being a sexual pervert who persistently tried to sodomise her as though it was a coincidental accident every single time, they got naked together.

Shona wondered how intelligent Day really was, or perhaps it was a case of how unintelligent he perceived Josie to be. He was a mature man with years of experience, and yet she was supposed to fall for his explanation of he didn't realise which orifice was where. Farcical—that's how Shona would describe it— and yet another attempt to condition his subject into compliance by his persistent behavioural trait to keep on trying.

Shona had to concede that it was the same disturbing and unrelenting pattern used when waking her in the middle of the night to sexually abuse her. Maybe, again, he thought the more times that he did it, the less she would react and perhaps leave him to it. After all, isn't that what Daniela Conway had done? She had laid there and become complicit, 'waiting for it to be over.'

Maybe it was a case of this practice that had already worked, so why not see if it works again? She didn't know. What she was more than aware of was the aftermath and the self-torture these women were now experiencing with having to face what they had been subjected to once the healing process had begun.

Josie had declared how she hadn't been able to sleep in her bed for months after giving her video statement. She would wake in the middle of the night, plagued with terrifying flashbacks, frozen to the spot, lying alone in the dark rigid with fear in case he still had a key and could return at any time. The poor woman had changed her locks and had cameras installed to at least give her a measure of safety, but there was no quick solution for how she would be able to restore her inner peace.

Anita was also thinking about Josie's video and how depleted her energies were, at not only the despair of what she had gone through, but also at having to say the things that he had done to her in front of a complete stranger.

'I was just thinking about Josie,' Anita said, interrupting Shona's thoughts. 'I asked her how she felt after giving the video statement, hoping it might have empowered her in some way to take the control back.'

'Had it?' Shona asked.

'She told me she had arrived at the station by 06:30 on a cold, wet morning not allowing herself to forethink anything about what she was about to do. She said had she allowed her mind to wander or to consider the consequences, she knew she could quite easily have changed her mind and not turned up,' Anita recounted, before stipulating this is what Josie explained:

I messaged the officer to say I was outside because it was dark, and I was too scared to get out of the car in the middle of nowhere, just in case he had followed me. This was crazy, as I knew he wasn't even in the country, which is why I knew I had to do it then, otherwise I may never get another opportunity. It was either that or my other choice was suicide. My heart was in turmoil, I felt sick, and I was suffering from fatigue and acid reflux, but I had to draw the strength from somewhere to go through with it. It was my only option.

I thought I loved him, but I knew he couldn't love me to be sexually assaulting me both in my sleep and wakefulness. Besides, I had been abused as a child, so I was not going to be disrespected again. I had to put a stop to it, and that was the day. The officer was young, which had made it a little harder for me, but she was kind enough to give me the freedom to talk, and once I opened my mouth, everything just spilled out.

At one point, I had to take a break because, as I spoke the words out loud, it suddenly became very real for me. I could no longer ignore it; I couldn't pretend it wasn't happening. I was suddenly connected and no longer detached. It actually helped me to finally face who this man really was, so it felt like I was only just truly seeing him for the first time and not the person he had portrayed himself to be. By speaking out, the image of the earlier days was suddenly erased, and I was able to say everything that I needed to say because I felt safe with him not being in the country and protected by the environment of the police station.

However, knowing he would be back soon, I panicked and went abroad myself three days later, so he couldn't manipulate me to make me retract the statement. I had hoped I would be able to rest, relax and recuperate, but it didn't work out like that for me. I sobbed throughout each and every day. In fact, whilst I was there, I'd had to reach out to people at church to pray for me, and I know it is going to seem strange, but to also pray for him. I suppose I was still emotionally attached because the level of distress and anxiety that I was going through made me feel like my heart was going to burst. I can honestly say I was literally broken and a shadow of my former self, but I was determined to not weaken further, as I knew that could be a very slippery slope to depression.

'I found it incredulous that she had the strength of character and compassion to ask for people to pray for him, yet I had nothing else to offer her, so I just told her how sorry I was that she'd had to endure what she had,' Anita explained.

'Did she explain whether making the statement had helped, you know, for her to finally get it off her chest?' Shona enquired.

'She said that she thought by speaking out it would act as a sign of her taking the control back, but in truth, both her wakeful hours and sleep were haunted by the memories of what he had done to her. She stated that the aftermath had caused her considerable anguish, so she had definitely not found it empowering or cathartic. I think the word she used was that she had found it 'horrendous.' Apparently, her emotions were all over the place, rocked further when the police rang her a few days later to say they had arrested him,' Anita explained.

'Surely it must have made her feel relieved?' Shona enquired.

'Apparently not; she described it as feeling like a vacuum had sucked her insides out to the point, she thought she was going to faint from the hollowness because it had made her feel so fragile, like glass shattering throughout her insides. She said she couldn't remember what she had asked the police officer, but that his response had been to assure her they would look after him. It was at this point she became really tearful because she realised just how engrained he must have been in her head if she was raising concerns about his welfare,' Anita said sadly.

'Sounds like a classic case of Stockholm syndrome, doesn't it?' Shona said perplexed.

'It is funny you say that, because when I looked at Day, I did wonder if he'd had an early childhood experience where he had formulated a similar relationship with perhaps a parent. Maybe they had used the same techniques on him. His repressive memories in his subconscious sphere could be directing and driving how he behaves, which is why he is unable to acknowledge responsibility for his actions,' Anita theorised.

'Stop right there,' Shona commanded. 'You will be hypothesising that he doesn't know the difference between right and wrong! I will not give him a 'get out of jail card.' He knows exactly what he is doing. As Jacobi said, it is all an act. None of this rubbish about his mum didn't love him so it gives him free rein to rape, pillage and murder—this man is a sadistic, self-adulating, manipulative, control freak, full stop!'

'Do you feel better, boss?' Anita said, not knowing whether to laugh, feel reprimanded or scared. A bit taken aback by the young officer's reaction, Shona suddenly felt small until Anita continued describing her conversation with Josie.

'Deep down, Josie said she knew that Day had a basic need to overpower and control due to the knowledge of his inability to fit in. She said he was more than aware that he was different to everyone else around him and that he was unable to express normal feelings. Therefore, it terrified him to be alone in case it exposed him for what he really was. She believed that he only felt safe when he was in a relationship because he could successfully hide in plain sight. Josie declared she thought this explained the reason he'd hop from one woman to another, to hide beneath the cloak of normality. To be honest, I thought she had developed great insight,' Anita stated.

'She sounds like she has almost forgiven him?' Shona said jokingly.

'I know it will sound crazy, and it did to me to begin with, but would it be ludicrous for her to find it in her heart to forgive him?' Anita divulged.

'That is incredulous! How on earth can you let a man like that get off Scot free after what he has done to her?' Shona almost screeched, outraged.

'When she talked, she was very careful to explain about her need to love herself enough to grab whatever opportunity she could to heal, thus being able to create a future without remnants of his control raising its ugly head. She said although she wasn't ready just yet, she did hope to have another relationship. But first, she wanted to give the future Josie a chance to rid herself of the baggage he'd dumped on her. To be honest, I kind of get it. Perhaps if everyone took the time to self-heal and decompress prior to jumping into another relationship, instead of infecting the next person, it would save a lot of heartache and psychological harm. Josie is just taking responsibility for herself in choosing to forgive and following her beliefs as a Christian, and I have to say I really admired that about her,' Anita confessed.

'Sounds like she has chosen the path that is right for her own mental health,' Shona agreed.

'Inevitably, I was quite interested to know what had happened last October when Day was interviewed,' Anita told Shona. 'But when I asked her, Josie firstly wanted to know if I had met him. When I explained that Jacobi and I'd had the pleasure of interviewing him, she flatly said, 'Then you will know he is a compulsive liar who portrays one thing to suit his narrative, but it will never reflect the truth.' When I asked her to embellish more,' Anita continued, 'she told me that Day 'is unable to see himself as he really is and does not possess the moral compass to tell the truth because, quite frankly, he is a coward.' As awful as it had been for her at the time, apparently developing that knowledge assisted her to regain her strength. Even though again, only two weeks after being interviewed for rape and sexual abuse, he had already found his next victim,' Anita stated, disheartened.

'I wonder how she managed to find out. I mean, I didn't even know my ex was having an affair, and that was right under my nose,' Shona said.

'Apparently, he couldn't wait to splash photos of them together all over Facebook, and as he had befriended all of Josie's friends, having none of his own, she was inevitably very quickly informed,' Anita answered her.

'Just as he knew she would be. A case of 'Look at me, I have moved on and found someone new; see, the problem was not with me, it was you all along',' Shona said, disgusted.

'Exactly. More premeditated mind games to appear to the world as one thing, when really the truth is completely different. As you say, 'Look at me',' Anita said. 'But then, isn't that the fallacy of Facebook? The pretence that you are living your best life? Reality is the ones who are really being successful just get on with it and haven't got time to build a story.'

'It seems that a story' has been the underlying crux of Robert Day Jr's life, or at least for the last 25 years. Desperate to fit in and seek the approval of those around him by any deceptive measure possible. Seriously, it must be exhausting He probably doesn't even know who he is himself,' Shona stated.

'The chances are this will be why he imitates the woman he couples up with and steals their ideas, phrases, beliefs, holiday destinations, hobbies, goals, and dreams, because he does not have any genuine ones of his own. I know Josie said it really irritated her because she would come up with a good idea or a plan, and he would instantly repeat it back to her as though her words had been his inner voice. Once attention had been drawn to this, Josie began to recognise it all the more, until she felt he was actually morphing into her, which she described as being very uncomfortable,' Anita explained.

'And that will be why there is no depth to him, because at the end of the day, he is just a diluted, cheap copy of the person he imitates. And he believed they needed him. The man is deluded,' Shona said angrily.

'Josie told me that she had seen a photograph of this new woman and couldn't help but recognise how uncomfortable they both looked, which made her giggle. That was until she realised that the woman was actually her double. So, the sting didn't last long, although he had always said he couldn't be with any other woman as he had never loved anyone as much as Josie, not even his wife,' Anita shared.

'Really looked like it, eh?' Shona said, shaking her head. 'Obviously, the 'sting,' as you say, has got to hurt, but then it is just his way to continue to put the knife in.'

'Josie isn't stupid; she knew it was all an act, and before long, he would be living the good life at this woman's expense, plastering it all over social media just to rub her nose in it. But the reality was, she no longer cared. She had seen him for who he really was, and despite what charade he chose to portray, the truth was she no longer loved him and had let go. Josie knew she wanted to heal quickly, so she initially took each day as a blessing and worked on getting through that one without thinking too far ahead. Soon, she had got through a week, then two and a month. Now, it has been over a year, and she is not the same person. It's plain to see from her video the distance she has travelled, although she was keen to say, that she has 'restored herself,' not to how she was but into something far more superior,' Anita smirked.

'And that, Collins, is exactly how you beat the abuser—leave them to think they are winning on their multiple holidays, bragging about money and displaying scenarios for the world to be deceived, whilst you silently become more superior,' Shona stated.

'I must admit, I have solid admiration for her. You do not become so strong or experienced in how to achieve this power without first having had the bad experiences in life to develop such inner core strength. So, I asked her for some insight into how she was able to stay so strong,' Anita admiringly relayed her conversation with Josie to Shona.

'Without my newfound faith, I wouldn't have been able to get through this, but my God is good, and I believe the truth will set me free,' Josie delivered.

'But how can you believe in a merciful God when he has let this happen to you?' Anita said, disbelievingly.

'That is the world's misconception of who God is, especially when nonbelievers want to blame Him for every bad thing that happens in this world. But do they open their eyes and thank Him for every good thing in life, or give Him credit for everyday miracles? No! Don't you think it is interesting that no one ever thinks to flip the coin or recognise that it is the enemy at work who brings the devastation and creates evil? For you cannot have one without the other. You see, God gave man free will, so it was not God's decision to inflict this on me. Yet through His grace and mercy, He has stepped in to give me the strength to get through it. To blame God is to absolve Robert of his actions, and that is preposterous. How is God accountable for Robert's behaviour? He isn't, but Robert will be accountable to God for what he has chosen to do. So, I must trust that by coming forward, I am honouring God, and that Robert will be brought to justice,' Josie explained.

'I have to say, Josie, there is so much power and strength that oozes out of you, it is quite incredible considering what you have been through, and the transformation from how you were in your video to now—it is phenomenal,' Anita had told her, unable to contain her admiration for such an inspirational lady.

'That is my God at work in me that you can see, for in my own strength, I am weak and fragile. I am afraid and lack confidence, but I know that all things are possible with God, for He has removed those mountains that held me down,' Josie powered on. 'With Robert, I have come to understand he will do anything to preserve himself, so therefore his deceit has to be exposed by seeking the evidence to prove the truth. And even then, he will not believe it. Robert won't ever be able to admit what he has done wrong because he is too weak to face the consequences. As I said, he is a coward who will never take responsibility—not even if you back him into a corner. He only has the mental capacity to observe things from his own perspective. That is why he remains detached,' Josie had explained.

'It almost sounds like you feel sympathy towards him,' Anita said, confused.

'It may surprise you to know that I do. I feel sad for him, because there is nothing on the inside; he is dead, and whilst I can walk away, he is stuck with that for an entire lifetime. Whatever he is or has become as a result of his past, including what he has done to me, I have found it within my heart to forgive him,' Josie said softly.

'How, is it possible to forgive the degradation, humiliation, pain, hurt, distress and aftermath that he has inflicted upon you? Sorry, Josie, and at the risk of sounding unprofessional, I don't get it,' Anita said, outraged. 'Is that not absolving him of any wrongdoing?'

'Only God can absolve him of his sins, but I choose to forgive him to set myself free and therefore I am able to seek God's forgiveness for my wrongful part in this relationship. After all, I was deceived and chose to stay. I have made peace with myself now, but it has taken a lot of self-help, love, nurturing and inner forgiveness to put myself in that position. The most important thing for me and why I came forward was because I wanted to stop him from doing this to anyone else. I know it probably sounds dramatic, but Robert's unpredictability was reaching new heights, and he was beginning to really scare me of what he might be capable of. There is one part of my video where I share about him losing his temper and wanting to stab a girl through the throat with a pool cue, so if I can do anything to stop anyone getting harmed or worse, I am in,' Josie divulged.

Anita was quiet for a little too long, creating a slight tension that didn't go unnoticed to Josie, nor did Anita's break in eye contact, the shift in her seat and the dry swallow.

'Oh no, he has, hasn't he?' Josie instantly burst into tears. 'It is bad, isn't it?' But Anita remained silent. 'Please tell me she's OK or at least they survived.' When Anita solemnly shook her head, Josie was beside herself with anguish that her need to stand up and save others had come too late.

Anita sat for a moment before sliding a box of tissues across the small coffee table towards Josie. Then she got up to make them both a drink. Anita now wished she hadn't requested taking Josie's interview, but there again, she didn't know how Rosina's was going either. She placed the full cups onto the table and reseated herself, but the next sentence out of Josie's mouth horrified her.

'You do know he has selected a new victim, don't you?' Josie delivered.

'What do you mean, Josie, when, who?' Anita asked.

'I was out with a couple of friends a few weeks ago when I noticed this lady who was sat at the bar on her own. Bless her, she looked so uncomfortable that I asked her to join us. She seemed lovely but incredibly vulnerable as her husband had only just passed away, and she was like a fish out of water, having been thrust back into the world of singledom. Anyway, she talked of following her dreams, having just bought a new business, but was very lonely and desperate to get her life back together.'

'A few moments later, Robert walked in and stood directly opposite me, trying to get my attention as he always used to, but he had no hold on me. I saw him keep looking from me to her, and when I glanced at her through the bar mirror, I realised what he was seeing: she looked very similar to me. I think she saw him staring too, because her attention on our conversation suddenly diminished, and all she could see was him. I chose to leave but have since heard she has become besotted by him,' Josie revealed.

'How can she be besotted so quickly?' Anita asked.

'He has this ability to make people feel sorry for him, so after each relationship, he always depicts himself as the victim, so you develop a need to protect him somehow from further hurt because you believe he has been through enough. He is then the sweetest man that you fail to understand why anyone would mistreat him, especially as he bends over backwards to do what he can for you, to pay you compliments and give you, his attention. You really do think you have hit the jackpot and cannot believe why anyone would want to let him slip through their fingers.'

'Therefore, you believe that the woman is the problem. He even goes to the extent of being friendly towards them whenever you are around to give the impression of cordiality, which inevitably causes them great discomfort. Therefore, this reinstates what a good guy he is and what a forgiving heart he must have, whilst also demonstrating their angst towards him, generating an instant dislike for them in a 'protect your man' kind of way,' Josie explained.

'He is very clever, of that there is no doubt,' Shona butted in. 'But hopefully, with Josie and Rosina's statements, along with our other lines of enquiry, Day's reign will be over soon.'

'I forgot to mention that when I was looking through the video before you had finished interviewing Rosina, Josie mentioned that the police had confiscated Day's phone when they had spoken to him last year,' Anita recalled.

'So, what happened to those records?' Shona enquired.

'That is the weird thing about it. According to Josie, it is still pending download. The officer dealing with her case just keeps telling her they are still waiting for it to be downloaded and that there has been a backlog,' Anita smirked, knowing full well what Shona's response would be.

'For over a year? Are you kidding me? So, this woman reports the crimes that have been happening to her, against all odds she goes to the police station and makes a video interview, but they cannot find the time to even process the download of the phone. Key information could have been extracted, and he could have been investigated and saved Karen Blakely before he had a chance to murder her. I do not care what anyone says, it doesn't take that long to download a phone, backlog or no backlog. Where is the ongoing care for Josie whilst they mess about taking their time?' Shona said furiously.

'You know as well as I do, that she will have just been passed on to domestic abuse and signposted to talking therapies. It will be a case of 'We have a statement, we will process it in due course.' She must have been in turmoil over the past 12 months, tearing her hair out, wondering what was happening,' Anita surmised.

'You can imagine her ringing in for an update, expressing her distress and the officer calmly saying, 'I understand your anxiety, but I have several other cases to deal with too',' said Shona.

'Josie did mention trying to express her despair by detailing the panic attacks she was suffering, the anxiety when she went out, of no longer feeling safe in her own home and of only daring to walk her dogs around the block as opposed to the lovely field walks, they'd once enjoyed. Apparently, she even told them of the night terrors and of actually waking twice in the last month, having wet the bed due to the nightmares she was experiencing,' Anita said, repeating Josies experience.

'Surely they pulled their finger out then?' Shona said, almost feeling embarrassed for the people in her profession.

'No, the female officer said, quote, 'Whether you are calm and collected, able to get on with your everyday life or having the experiences you expressed, I would still conduct my job in the same way',' Anita said.

'I think we need to find out who this officer is, because I, for one, would like to explain to her the implications of what has occurred through her negligence of not conducting a timely investigation,' Shona said, pulling into a space at the back of the station.

As Shona made her way towards her office, Anita elected the privacy of her tech cupboard to finish listening to Josie Bellamy's interview, both taking a detour via the Karen Blakely's board of evidence. After pondering the information for some time and contemplating again the similarities of Amelia,

Josie, Rosina, Karen and now Daniela's experiences, Shona was assured now, she had to secure the evidence to put this man away.

As Shona slumped onto her office couch, she thought about Josie, who had used her faith to empower herself, whilst Rosina, on the other hand, still did not know how she felt. Perhaps this was because she had also suffered the internal guilt of betraying her friend's memory. Maybe she felt like she had let Heather down. Well, that was how she had perceived it. Rosina had believed that she loved him, but like Josie, she now realised it was just the ideological image he had purposefully generated that she had held on to. She also found that images of herself in distress in her own bed were being displayed on a video loop, constantly playing in her head, so she hadn't been able to sleep and had ended up purchasing a new bed. Daniela had also described flashback memories as being 'like a projector assaulting her mind.' Every sound had intensified for her, like an echo, as she lay in the darkness of the night, fearfully staring at the door, watching in case there was a shadow beneath it, or the handle was depressed. Rosina battled with depression and travelled through an army of emotions. The worst was the grief, as this was coupled with the loss of Heather, mixed with the loss of her hopes and dreams.

Rosina had explained how alone she had felt, trying to reach out to friends who didn't seem to want to listen to her pain. Maybe they had enough of their own problems to deal with. She had just felt that, on hearing what she had to say, they were not interested in actually supporting her through it, and some didn't even give her an ear to listen. She described them as having a disinterested, blank look on their faces, but she needed to keep talking to get it out in order to make sense of it all. That was why she had ended up going to a talking therapist, because she couldn't quite fathom out how she felt, and until she could answer that question, there was no possibility for her ever being able to move on.

Luckily, it had demonstrated to Rosina that within the majority of her relationships, she had tended to overcompensate for the lack of effort the other party imparted and forced her to question which people stayed and which needed to be removed. She wasn't quite at the stage as Josie in regaining her power, but she had made some very important decisions to protect herself, and if nobody cared enough to check in with her, then she didn't need to waste any of her time on them. Rosina was now at the point of restoring who she was, her worth, along with investing in herself rather than at her own expense, which she had been doing. She was more than aware she still needed to work on her self-esteem and confidence.

What surprised Shona was that Anita had divulged Josie had been to the same counsellor as Rosina and found her amazing, especially as she had turned out to be a Christian too. So, maybe Josie was right: God was putting everything in place to help her, especially if this lady shared her faith. Perhaps that knowledge had underpinned her yearning of not wanting to be judged and released her to be completely open and transparent, revealing her innermost feelings and thoughts. Shona was desperately trying to recall the term Josie had used about being allocated Ilsa as a therapist. What was it? A divine appointment given by God; she liked that concept. Hopefully, God would give Day a divine appointment with the right judge.

Rosina had described her need of wanting to get what felt like the heavy burden of his blackness dug out of her, with a desperation to get rid of it so she could let some light back in. Rosina had not found the same ability as Josie to power her way through the therapy. In contrast, she had found talking about her experiences with Day exceptionally hard and had needed to be alone. Shona had reminded her to evaluate how far she had come because the person she was in the room with had flourished and was articulate and impactful. This demonstrated, at least to Shona, the progress Rosina had made from then to now.

Rosina had admitted that she did feel more like a survivor these days rather than a victim, as she had previously felt. So yes, she agreed that she did feel like an updated version of herself. It was similar to when her internet was lagging, she would slide the offending page on her phone down, then, like magic, it would suddenly refresh, and open accordingly.

When asked if she was strong enough to testify in court should she be required to do so, Rosina had thought about it for a long time before affirming, 'Back then, I felt black on the inside, but all that rotten mass has been extracted, and I not only feel like I have been knitted perfectly back together, but that I am refreshed, renewed and ready to stand up and be counted with Josie and with anyone else. I know we will get through it together!'

Shona had congratulated her for becoming an even stronger person in spite of her experience and was thrilled when Rosina corrected her and told her she had 'become a stronger person because of her experience, in spite of him.'

Shona's office door suddenly swung open abruptly, returning her to the present moment.

'What the heck is going on?' she yelled as Jacobi took it upon himself to burst in without knocking.

'Haven't you heard the commotion?' Jacobi challenged her.

'Commotion?' Shona asked, jumping to her feet.

'There are murmurings circulating of new vital information that has been found regarding the Day case. Where have you been?' Jacobi enquired.

'What information?' Shona asked, puzzled.

'That is what we are all waiting to know. Have you not even looked at your messages?' Jacobi asked, aghast.

'Sorry, I hadn't got that far. I was still processing my chat with Daniela Conway,' Shona began before picking up the printouts left on her desk. She scanned through the first one, her mouth falling open and then she reread it more carefully, giving it her undivided and full attention.

She grabbed the phone and speed dialled the Chief, 'Damien, it's Shona. It looks like we have got him.'

Chapter 45
Warrants Galore

There was an immediate silence as Damien Clarke, the Chief Inspector of Basic Command, entered the room, followed by Shona and Jacobi. Damien Clarke got straight to it.

"For all of you who do not know her, this is DCI Shona Williams from the Senior Criminal Investigation Unit, so simmer down and show some respect. We have two deaths that we are investigating, along with multiple allegations of rape against our suspect. I want everyone to focus their attention, please!' Damien commanded. He nodded at Shona to give her the go-ahead.

'As you all know, Karen Blakely's death was the start of our investigation, and throughout, we have had our eyes on just the one suspect, her partner Robert Day Jr. We have found out that Day has a history of using and abusing women; this was initially evident through our interviews with Karen Blakely's colleagues and friends. We then looked deeper into Day and found that, in at least five of his previous relationships dating back to 1997, he has displayed the same systematic patterns of abuse. These have ranged from emotional, psychological and mental abuse to conditioning, coercive manipulation, sexual abuse and lastly, raping his victims on the pretext of being in a loving relationship.'

'It is a very complex case, but the resounding positive in our favour is that at least two of our victims, Josie Bellamy and Rosina Wray, are prepared to give evidence, and I have managed to secure the evidence of a third victim whom I am not at liberty to identify at present. Nevertheless, we have sworn testimonies. This morning, Marcus St John sent transcripts of his conversations with Karen that clearly identify she was experiencing the exact same abuse that Josie, Rosina and my third victim have detailed. More importantly, there was a recorded voicemail that St John was unaware of. On the night that Karen Blakely was murdered, she arrived home to find out that Day had not only turned up at her home, but that he had let himself in and was awaiting her arrival, despite her expressed wishes that he gave her space.'

'Now, we know that when she arrived home, she placed a call to St John to let off steam, but that this call was abruptly ended when Day appeared at her car. St John disclosed that, once the call had ended, he proceeded to take a shower as he did after every shift, but what he was not aware of was that Karen Blakely had either recalled his mobile or it had redialled the last number when she dropped it back into her bag. I will now play you the voicemail that St John has released to us and that it has been verified as being made from Karen Blakely's mobile to his, and that it is her voice,' she nodded to Tony to play the recording.

There was utter silence as the full conversation of what had transpired in Karen Blakely's kitchen on 5 July 2024 was played to the room. There were some parts that were difficult to decipher due to them being more muffled, as though the parties had moved further away from the microphone, but it did not detract from the overall gist of the conversation. She instructed Tony to pause the tape before congratulating him on doing an excellent job of eliminating the inconsequential noise whilst highlighting the background conversation and sharpening the words and tone of the voices. It was clear for all to hear that Day's account was nothing more than a fabrication. The room was silent whilst they absorbed what they had just heard and waited for Shona to continue.

'As you continue to listen, you will hear Day fumbling about, searching for something in the cupboards, before there is the faint crinkling of what appears to be a carrier bag. I would suggest that it is highly likely that he was removing his blood-stained clothes and depositing them into this bag. An inner door is then opened and left to close on its own before we are left with the gurgling sounds of Karen Blakely choking upon her own blood.'

'Whether Day lashed out on the spur of the moment or not is irrelevant, as it is evident that he purposely did nothing to help Karen Blakely; instead, his only concern was with saving himself. I believe that he went upstairs to set the scene he had prepared for our arrival before putting on a clean set of clothes. I had a shoeprint analysed from the carpet taken from Karen Blakely's master bedroom that had been left below a fitted wardrobe at the side of the door. This contained only Day's clothes, and there was an open, empty shoe box inside.'

'In an interview, Day stated that they never wore shoes on the inside of the house due to the new carpets Karen had just fitted. After being interrogated, Jacobi collected the clothes and shoes that Day had been wearing on the night of the murder; those shoes were a match for our sample. So, after leaving Karen to choke on her own blood, he then went upstairs to set up a fake romantic scene to support his lies about a loving relationship before a quick change of clothes. He will then be heard re-entering the kitchen before the outside door handle is depressed heavily, and then it is slammed back into place quite harshly, like someone is in a hurry. Perhaps this is what gave Day the idea of blaming an intruder.'

'He stated that Karen had new doors fitted three months prior to the night she died and that due to the 5-point multi-locking system, it was difficult for it to just slip into the frame unless the handle was depressed. He said it would, but the only way for it to happen is for the door to be slammed to achieve this. To give credence to his statement that he had heard an intruder, he gave a convoluted example about it having occurred the week before when Karen was in the back courtyard hanging out washing. He described the wind as having apparently caused the door to slam shut, and Day was adamant that this was the same sound that he had heard as he raced down the stairs to apparently run to Karen's aide.'

'As you have heard, the only other person in the room when Karen Blakely was attacked is Day. He was not upstairs as he professed, but more importantly, the recording demonstrates that he did nothing to assist Karen in any way as she lay dying on the kitchen floor. This was supposed to be the woman he loved, the person he had just bought a ring for so he could ask her to marry him. It was only after setting the scene and changing his clothes that he returned to the kitchen and rang 999. The voicemail recording cuts off at this point, but Tony has the official 999 call for you to listen to. Tony, can you play everyone the part I have just explained along with the 999 call? Thank you,' Shona said.

There was a strained silence as every member of staff concentrated on identifying each sound that Shona had highlighted.

'After I had listened to the call, I rechecked the time that the ambulance log had registered its arrival at 357 St Michael's Mount and found a huge discrepancy. Day stated to the operator that 'the ambulance has arrived,' giving the impression that it was there when he hung up. However, there is a delay between when Day ends his 999-call stipulating that the ambulance had arrived to when it actually arrives, which is 8 minutes later. This time-lapse has also been verified via the 999 logs in conjunction with the exact time of arrival of the ambulance. The paramedic Susie Bradshaw and the driver Ian Blackwell have independently testified that Day was on the phone as they arrived, and both believed he was disconnecting the 999 call as they got out of their vehicle.'

'It is quite possible that during those minutes, Day gave the scene a quick check before stashing his bloodied clothes in his car, which is another reason he was eager to collect it from the crime scene. He was then able to remain at the door awaiting the ambulance, where he fabricated still being on the line to the 999 operator.'

'Tony has also had the opportunity to download the contents of Karen Blakely's dash cam footage. He found a clear video clip of Day approaching Karen's car, wearing a red polo shirt, black cargo pants, and a pair of black-and-white Adidas trainers. On top of that, he checked the settings on the dash cam and found that the in-cabin camera recording setting was activated, so we have a clear recording of her conversation with Marcus St John prior to Day approaching the car. Tony, if you would like to play that, please,' Shona instructed.

Once the recording had ended, Shona stated, 'As you can hear, this clarifies Karen's feelings towards Day, that she definitely was not expecting him to be at her home when she returned from work and nor was, she impressed. What Marcus St John told us both about Karen and Day's relationship and the conversation that they had shared that night is true. Jacobi, over to you,' Shona said and sat down.

Jacobi stepped forward and took centre stage. 'My team have been working tirelessly to discover the different routes to the Baztan area of Spain from the UK. We have looked at land, sea, plane and tour operators that also offered coach trips. We have found several routes, but after digging a little deeper, Driver found that, back in 2018, the most undetected route would have been to drive down to Plymouth and hop on the ferry to Santander, and then it would have only been a 3-hour drive to Baztan. Inevitably, the chance of any passenger logs still being in existence from 6 years ago is slim, but luckily for us, DVLA confirmed that Day has been the registered keeper of his Honda Civic since March 2017. That specific make and model does have an inbuilt satellite navigation system as standard; therefore, we will be impounding the car to assess its data to definitively prove that he took that trip,' Jacobi informed them.

As Jacobi retook his seat and Damien stood, Parker entered the room holding up a wad of papers in his hand. 'It looks like your signed warrants have arrived, Shona,' Damien stated.

'The judge has a warrant for Day's arrest on the suspicion of the murders of both Karen Blakely and Amelia Jayne Peters, along with the rape of Rosina Wray and Josie Bellamy. I have also obtained a separate warrant sanctioning the search of Day's house, car and outbuildings,' Parker delivered triumphantly passing them to Shona.

She quickly scrutinised through them, checking that the address was correct and that the registration number corresponded with the plate the DVLA had provided. The last thing that Shona wanted was for Day to be able to get off or delay the process due to a technicality. She was determined to hit Day hard and fast before he had a chance to comprehend what was happening, and more importantly, before he could convince his new 'victim,' as Josie Bellamy had described her, that he was the answer to all her prayers.

'Tomorrow morning, we will be executing a dawn raid at 06:00 hours,' Damien Clarke delivered earnestly. 'The noticeboard has a list of all those who will be operational and the teams that you will be working in. So, absorb the details, iron out any concerns with Shona now, then get home, have a good night's rest and be back here at 05:00 hours for the briefing. We need to find those blood-stained clothes and his passport displaying the stamp to prove he left the country and that he returned around the time that Amelia Jayne Peters was killed on 31 December 2018. Apart from that, seize anything that you think may be of relevance to this case. the last thing we want is for Day to have any opportunity to destroy evidence. Is that clear?' Damien Clarke bellowed.

'Yes, Chief!' Everyone chorused.

Chapter 46
Crème de la Crème

Three teams of four left the station early the next morning. Two vans made their way towards 357 St Michael's Mount, whilst the third, holding Jacobi, Collins and two others, quietly cruised towards 71 Park Grove on the other side of town. Word had reached Shona that Day was shacked up with this new 'victim,' as Josie Bellamy had called her, who they now knew was called June Brown. Jacobi was tasked with lifting Day at the same time as Shona and her teams would be searching his house. It was her intention to let him stew in a cell for a few hours until she was good and ready to throw the proverbial book at him.

At precisely 06:00 hours, the inhabitants of 71 Park Grove were abruptly awoken by the hard arm of the law braying on their door. 'Open up, this is the police!' Jacobi bellowed through the letterbox.

'Oh my goodness! Did you hear that?' June Brown was startled into consciousness. 'Robert, there is someone banging on the door,' she said, alarmed, but Day only stirred and murmured something inaudibly.

'Robert,' she tried again, almost pleadingly. 'Robert,' she said, shaking him gently.

'What?' he said, trying hard to open his eyes to make out what was happening.

'It sounds like the…' she stopped as the banging continued, and again came the bellow announcing their presence, delivered through the letterbox. 'Police are at the door,' she finished.

Robert immediately sat upright, no longer struggling to join the living world. 'What am I supposed to do about it?' he asked without any interest in her answer.

'Go and see what they want,' June stated, pulling her duvet up towards her chest.

Day reluctantly slid out of his side of the bed. He flicked on both the bedroom and landing lights to signify that they were well and truly awake and that someone was responding to their demands. He made his way down the open slatted stairs, grasping hold of the banister as he carefully moved down onto each wooden step, mindful not to miss his footing. Through the obscured glass-panelled doors, he could see the outline of at least three figures, which, at that moment, he thought was overkill. He then considered whether they were actually the police or someone incognito here to threaten harm. So, he hesitated.

'Mr Day, I can see you. Please open the door, otherwise, we will have to use force,' Jacobi declared.

'How do I know you really are the police? You might be here to harm us,' Day stalled.

'My name is DI Dion Jacobi, and I saw you 357 St Michael's Mount on the 5 July. I collected you from the hospital afterwards, and Officer Collins and I interviewed you in the early hours of the 6th. Is that enough proof to satisfy your concerns?' Jacobi asked.

'What do you want? I cannot understand why you are here. Has June done something wrong?' Day asked, perplexed.

'Mr Day, if you open the door, we will be able to clear everything up for you, but I am not prepared to talk through a door. Now, for the last time, are you going to open up, or do I have to give the order for it to be forcibly opened?' Jacobi said clearly.

'You cannot do that. We have rights as law-abiding citizens,' Day began.

'I have a warrant here, signed by a judge, that tells me I can do that. Plus, I have a great big red key that will open any door. Now, open the door,' Jacobi demanded.

'Oh, just open it, Robert. What is the point of delaying the inevitable? Besides, the sooner this is cleared up, the sooner the shouting stops. The last thing I want is to be a spectacle of the nosy neighbourhood watch brigade,' June stated.

As soon as Day had turned the key and the lock was heard to click, signifying its release, the door was abruptly shoved inward, knocking him off guard. Two burly coppers were on him and had him in cuffs before he had a chance to release another word. Poor June Brown was mortified, unable to control her despair she screeched for them to not hurt him and to be careful, stating he wasn't resisting.

Collins stepped in, taking her by the elbow, and led her away from the scene and through the nearest door, which led into a rather grandly designed lounge.

'Would you like to make yourself a cup of tea, June?' Collins asked.

The use of her name stopped her in her tracks. 'How do you know my name?' she asked.

'We know many things, June, but the only thing I can share with you about why we are here is because Robert Day Jr is under arrest for some very serious charges,' Anita stated succinctly.

'Serious charges?' she queried. 'What serious charges?'

'I am sorry, June, but I am not permitted to discuss that with you at this moment. All I will say is you have at least two amazing angels who have stepped in the gap to save you,' Collins delivered cryptically.

'Angels?' she asked, perplexed. 'I don't understand.'

'You may not understand right at this moment, but believe me, you have just been saved from a fate worse than death,' Collins delivered.

Jacobi's head appeared around the door jamb. 'He has been read his rights, we are done,' he said, before returning to his two uniforms and asking them to transport the prisoner to the station.

'This is my card, June. I know you will probably have 101 questions, but I just have one for you. Does Mr Day have any of his belongings stored on your premises?' Collins asked.

'No, not really. He just has a few clothes in a drawer in the utility, you know, to change into when he spends the night. But there is nothing else of his here, why?' June enquired.

'Mr Day is part of a wider investigation, and so therefore we need to ensure we do not miss anything,' Collins explained.

'Do you know where his car is parked? I noticed it wasn't anywhere on the street,' Jacobi rejoined the conversation.

'Yes, he left it at the Cock and Crown. We met there last night for a meal, and it seemed silly us both driving, so I suggested he leave his so he could have a couple of drinks with his meal,' June explained.

'Thank you,' Jacobi said, whilst redialling Shona to inform her where to send the impound truck to seize the vehicle.

'Can you show me this drawer that you were describing, June? The one that contains Day's clothes, please?' Collins asked her, hoping she would automatically comply with the request without resistance. She did. Collins searched through the items, but there was nothing associated with the investigation, so she thanked the woman and explained that the station would not be able to update her on anything until they had officially interviewed Day or released him. Collins knew that the latter was a highly unlikely possibility, but she was not prepared to get into any unnecessary discussions with the woman. Both she and Jacobi then made their way towards the Cock and Crown in order to secure the car ready for its seizure.

Despite being aware that Day was not on the premises of 357 St Michael's Mount, Shona followed procedures by having one team approach from the back of the house and a second to the front. Once in place, she gave Parker the go-ahead to bang on the door to alert the house to the presence of the police, stipulating the door would be forced if the occupants failed to open it. As far as Shona was concerned, the greater the kerfuffle, the better, as she was sure Day was not going to just accept his fate gracefully, so she was doing everything by the book.

So, what if the twitchy neighbour crew were hovering behind their curtains wondering what on earth was going on? She wasn't in the business of shying away from things to protect the reputation of someone such as Day. She gave the go-ahead for the battering ram to forcibly knock the door from its frame which it did in three fluent strokes.

The first thing that hit them was a putrid stench of dampness mixed with the acute ammonia of urine, cats to be precise, as a grey tabby made a run for freedom. They allowed the clean air to flow in whilst they were besieged with this unfair exchange in return. Shona couldn't imagine being sealed inside and wholeheartedly understood why Day wouldn't have wanted to return to this place, as Josie had relayed. After gulping in a few deep breaths, the team advanced forward in a synchronised formation, determining that each room in turn was 'clear.' With latex gloves and a multitude of searching equipment at the ready, the teams systematically went to work, one taking the upstairs and the second the downstairs.

'I've got something in here!' shouted Driver, after about 10 minutes of rummaging.

Shona took the steps two at a time to the back bedroom from where Driver's voice had emanated. 'What have you got?' She asked.

'Sorry, false alarm,' he stated, wafting a passport in his hand. 'The issue date states 3 February 2020. We need his previous one,' he said, gutted,

'Never mind, keep looking,' Shona said, heart-sluffened.

'Wait!' Driver said sharply, opening the pages of another passport that had characteristically had its outer cover cut across one corner. 'This is it,' he said triumphantly.

'Yes,' said Shona, thumping the air and stepping over discarded garments on the floor, she made her way round the bed to Driver.

He smiled as he held out the specific page, he knew she wanted to view. 'Bingo.'

'Fantastic work, Driver. Here, put it in this evidence bag and scribe the details of where it was located, along with the date, time, your rank and name. I will set up a clean area downstairs where we can compile our finds,' Shona told him.

'Ma'am,' someone shouted, much to Shona's irritation, as she not only hated the word, but it gave her the impression of an elderly woman. However, today she was in no mood to reprimand anyone.

Shona followed the voice to an officer she was unfamiliar with, as he'd been drafted in from a different department specifically for the search. 'What have you got?' she asked.

'It's hard to tell off the bat, but I think these could be his tax returns for 2018 to 2019. It is quite possible that if he did make the trip in December of 2018, he would have tried to claim some of the money back. I might be wrong, but he could have used the trip as a means to offset some of the expenditure via the taxman, you know, by making out it was a work-orientated trip or something,' he suggested.

'Excellent thinking, I like your style. Let's bag it,' Shona said, impressed, feeling that this was exactly the kind of thing that Day was likely to have done.

Each room throughout the house was thoroughly searched, so it didn't take half as long as Shona had imagined, with two of the bedrooms being completely empty and barely any furniture or personal belongings anywhere else inside the place. It made Shona wonder if this was because Day had been forced to travel light whilst he hopped from one woman to the next, never really having the opportunity to amass either anything of value or personal effects.

Or if it was because he was dead on the inside, as he had aptly been described, and therefore, he had no connection, value or character for such trivialities. Either way, the spoils of the search were a little sparse for Shona's liking, and the sucker punch had been that the clothes he had been wearing on the night of the murder were nowhere to be found. Deflated, they moved to the garage area, which was full of debris. Whatever he had in there was going to take some time to sift through.

'Sorry, guys, but we need to remain focused. Let's stay in the mindset of finding the evidence exclusive to securing a conviction so we can put this creep away,' she urged before putting them into teams of 2 so they could section off a quarter of the garage area each. She then took the remaining two outside so they could do a sweep of the garden. Her mobile rang.

'How's it going, boss?' Jacobi asked.

'Slowly but surely. We have cleared the house and just started on the garage. You ought to see it, there are bin bags all over the place. It looks like the bin van has dropped its load off,' Shona said light-heartedly.

'Then, on behalf of Collins and myself, can I personally thank you for detailing us to lift Day and supervise the seizing of the car? It is very much appreciated,' Jacobi mused, as Collins cocked her head, looking confused at him.

'How did it go?' Shona asked.

'Pretty much as you would expect. He was slow to respond, disbelieved we were there for him, and actually asked what it was that June Brown had done wrong. He won't be going down telling the truth, I am sure of that. The man is deluded. I really do not think he feels he has done anything wrong. He protested all the way to the van, but Mick and Pete from custody threw him into the back of the bus without breaking a stride. I was just ringing to let you know that the car is being secured now, so unless you need us there, Collins and I are going back to the station,' Jacobi told her.

'If I told you we needed your expertise here on site, would you come?' Shona teased.

'Definitely not, now I know you only have the garbage to sift through,' Jacobi laughed.

'Actually, Jacobi, that is a point,' Shona said abruptly, disconnecting the call.

Jacobi removed the handset from his ear and glanced at it, puzzled, as though it was about to answer the question that had formulated in his head. 'What's wrong?' asked Collins.

'I have absolutely no idea, but we are all in the clear to return to the station. Fancy a breakfast run on the way?' Jacobi asked.

'Need I even answer that?' Collins mocked, as they made their way to the car.

Shona walked around the side of the house and found exactly what she had been looking for: three wheelie bins boxed into a concealed, hidden partition that was cleverly indented into the end of a little passage. At first glance, you would not have known they were there, and let's face it, they were quite unsightly, so most people tried to dress them up with colourful stickers or created purpose-built alcoves for them. Days had inevitably taken a little more effort, with its stone-built barrier wall that blended into its surroundings and created a mirage effect from a distance against the house. It was only because Shona had been able to follow the freshly made tracks of the bin wheels that she discovered their hiding place. She opened the first lid, which was the garden bin, but thankfully, it was empty.

There were no grass clippings, no unrecovered twigs branches, leaves or weeds, and the bin was shiny clean as if it had never been used. The second lid she flicked open was the recycle one, so rather than tipping it over and spewing its contents all over the path to contaminate any possible evidence, she carefully removed each individual item and placed it into the clean garden bin. There was absolutely nothing of value for her case, so she decided to get to work on the household rubbish bin. As soon as she opened the lid, it provided her with the second invitation of the morning to fill her lungs with a rancid stench, this time of rotting food mixed with what smelt like faeces.

Shona instantly released the lid she was holding, and it banged back into place. There was no way she was going to expect someone else to do something she wasn't prepared to do herself, but equally, it also wasn't going to be performed in the careful extraction of each item either. Shona pulled the bin free, dragged it out into the open of the driveway, and then kicked it over so the contents spilt out in the opposite direction from where she was standing. The putrid plume of decomposition willingly escaped its imprisoned coffin, along with a stream of rotten, slimy food juice. Shona was taking no chances of being infected by whatever was now growing amongst the contents of the waste, but neither was she prepared to ignore the mantra of Euripides that she lived and worked by: 'Leave no stone unturned.'

'Can one of you give me a hand here, please?' she called to the two officers working the garden.

The male of the 2-person team lifted his head from being bent down, dragging the small pond, and acknowledged her plight. He stood and made his way towards her, but soon wished he had kept his mouth shut.

'What the heck died in there?' he asked, screwing his face up.

'I am not sure, but I intend to find out,' Shona informed him.

'Really?' he questioned.

'Grab this end, will you?' Shona said, ignoring him. 'And I will hold this end. If we shake it up and down, the contents should easily slide out, and then we can see what we are dealing with.'

He grabbed at the wheels where she had indicated, and together, they shimmied the contents out onto the floor. There wasn't nearly as much in quantity that Shona had contemplated, but she was correct when she estimated a few shakes of the bin would enable it to easily slide out. Most of it was covered in mould, and it had obviously been sat in the bin for a very long time—perhaps since the beginning of his relationship with Karen Blakely, over a year ago.

Shona pulled a small cane out of the ground that had possibly been placed into the earth to support a plant at some point but now stood randomly serving no purpose. She prodded and poked at the pile of goo, dismayed that it had borne no fruit when the cane snagged upon something. She tried to pull it free but instead was treated to a splatter of the slimy juice contents flicking across her face.

Disgusted, she cursed loudly before succumbing to the automatic reaction of spitting a globule of saliva at the ground, despite the offending matter not reaching her mouth. She slid her sleeve across her face as though the deposits were particles of lava burning through her skin. Undeterred, she prepared to joust the pile of trash again as though it was a rival opponent in combat, but this time, the male officer quickly retreated out of arm's length. She stabbed and jibed until she was finally able to lift the item suspended in front of her, mid-air, like a child at the Hook-A-Duck stand.

'Get me a clear sheet of plastic to place this on,' she called out to the male officer, and once in place, she carefully laid it down away from the rest of the garbage. The officers in the garage filed out to see what the commotion was all about.

'Anyone got a peg?' Shona asked sarcastically before lightly gripping it.

'No, but I have got a mask, for what good it will do,' Driver said, handing it to her. Shona gladly received the offering before approaching her prize upon the plastic sheet.

She bent down, swallowing hard trying to hold her breath for as long as possible as the nauseating smell was beginning to overcome her senses. She

carefully unknotted what she could now see was a used carrier bag that had been submerged beneath the waste, endeavouring to not allow the outer part to impregnate the inner sanctuary. As soon as she caught sight of the red fabric with the white-edged short-sleeved cuffs, she recognised that she had the crème de la crème.

The last time she had spoken to Chief Inspector Damien Clarke, she had said, 'It looks like we have got him.'

Now she knew for certain that she had.

Chapter 47
All Rise

As expected, Day not only denied all charges but appeared bewildered at the very thought that anyone would describe him with such derogatory words. In his opinion, he had treated the women in his life with nothing but love, respect, kindness and dignity. As the charges were laid out to him one by one; he simply shook his head in disbelief. From that moment on, he refused to answer anything other than remaining in consultation with his solicitor, two of whom he sacked in the lead-up to the case being presented in court. The only verbal response he would give throughout his incarceration was 'no comment' and, predictably, pleaded 'not guilty' when the judge asked for his response to the charges.

Subsequently, a trial by jury was set to commence, whereby Josie Bellamy and Rosina Wray were forced to testify at length about the treatment they'd had to endure and the effects this had had upon their lives. Josie Bellamy stood tall, looking directly at Day whilst she recalled each transgression, he had committed against her, describing in detail each act of sexual abuse and rape. A defiant Day stared right back at her, unmoved by the harm he had inflicted, and only displaying the contempt of superiority associated with the pleasure and gratification her testimony offered him.

Rosina Wray was not as confident, so kept her eyes fixed on the jury whenever she answered either the prosecution or defence solicitors' questions. A tip that was given to her by the court official, who had escorted her to the courtroom, had given her a primary focus that allowed her sufficient courage to stop her knees from buckling beneath her.

Sallyanne Peters testified on behalf of her sister, being able to give a firsthand account of the background of Amelia's relationship with Day. Although she had widespread professional experience of delivering what was often described as a rather stoic statement in court, she was far from able to omit her emotional expression during the proceedings. More importantly, Sallyanne was also able to humanise 'Meli', bringing her to life through their shared experiences both through childhood and in their adult life. Her descriptive insight regarding her sister's Olympic triumph, along with her knowledge of the pool at the Baztan apartments, determined the jury's belief that she would not have hit her head by mistakenly diving into the shallow end.

Subsequently, when then presented with foolproof evidence that Day had secretly made the trip to those apartments as stated in his tax returns, supported by his passport endorsements and satellite navigational data, there was no room for doubt. There were two surprises in the support of this evidence, one from Rosina Wray, who, when questioned when she had begun a relationship with Day, had replied, '5th December 2018.' The prosecution solicitor had then cleverly asked what they had done together on their first New Year's Eve, and she had innocently said that 'she had spent it with friends because Day had a preplanned trip to Spain to see an old friend, called Meli.' She had absolutely no idea who this person had been, she had never met them and assumed it was someone who lived in Spain. When he had returned from Spain, he had told her that it had been a 'great success' and that he had 'thoroughly enjoyed himself,' inviting her to go with him the next time.

The second surprise was during Demi Lee's testimony, when she recounted how she came by the diary, the publication of her column and the secret indentation of the message on the wrapping paper. Demi stated that after she had delivered the diary to the police station, she remembered picking up mail on the day she had moved into her property. On sifting through this, she had found a postcard from Spain that Amelia Jayne Peters had sent to herself. It read:

'Sallyanne, I might be paranoid, but I thought I saw Robert today, I just want someone to know in case anything happens to me. Love you, Meli xxx.'

Daniela Conway's statement was read to the court by her representative, which she nominated as Officer Anita Collins; she did not make a personal appearance.

The court was told about Day's tendency to initially flood his victims with immediate declarations of love and how he had used his high sexual appetite to make them feel desired and wanted. How his excessive affection through small gestures to make their lives easier, or gifts of flowers, would create a sense of being very special to him. The replication of mirroring their past experiences, hobbies, likes and dislikes gave the impression of being understood, heard and listened to. The closing speech insinuated that it was perhaps their vulnerability that stood out the most to him, recognising it as a means to be able to exploit and use it to coerce them into doing anything he wanted.

For the first time in his life, Robert Day Jr had to sit quietly whilst he was confronted about the damage he had caused. He was now unable to run away by dismissing them, rejecting them or cutting them off when their sell-by date had expired but was finally being challenged openly, exposed and disgraced in public. The Mr Nice Guy image had been obliterated to reveal his true identity, whilst he sat in the dock no longer being praised, bowed down to, admired or willingly showered with love. He was now despised, being vilified, challenged and made to face the monster of whom he really was—a predator who had continually homed in and carefully chosen the victims he knew he could overpower and control mentally.

Women who were good-natured, had been hurt in the past, were willing to give love another shot, and were honest, wholesome, loyal and genuine. Women who were looking for a deep, meaningful connection that they had probably always dreamt of and believed they had found through his fake demonstrations of love and adoration. What each of these women had expressed was that from literally nowhere, they had suddenly felt seen, heard and no longer invisible, so they had easily, naturally and quickly gravitated towards its source. The quick progression of ingratiating himself into their lives and homes only cemented their belief in a solid relationship and of him 'being the one.' Through his projection of a promising future, shared dreams and fantasies of marriage, he secured his position and was able to talk them into literally anything.

However, this blind trust had given him the ability to play mind games, causing confusion and destabilising their sense of security. For at least two of the women, the emotional and psychological damage had resulted in months of therapy, whereas for two others, they'd had their lives ended by his hands. Robert Day Jr did not like being told 'no'; it ignited a shift somewhere deep inside that created a need to regain control and make these women do what he wanted.

The court was reminded of the details gathered from the independent statements of Rosina Wray, and Daniela Conway, the diary of Amelia Jayne Peters, and the video interview of Josie Bellamy. Each one had depicted the exact same experience of their boundaries being persistently exploited, their lives taken over by him, cut off from friends and mercilessly stalked when they tried to leave the relationship. Much more damaging was their accounts of being woken to find him sexually abusing them, their defences broken down to the level that raping them had become a normal act. An abhorrent, heinous act of complete submission that, in messages, he had declared he was apparently disgusted with himself about, but nevertheless he would continue to commit the same acts repeatedly.

Each person who had testified described their confusion, disbelief and despair, but Robert Day Jr was no longer listening to their plight. He would simply turn away until the next time. He even tried to dismiss all responsibility for his actions by specifying that he suffered from a medical condition that he called Sexsomnia. However, evidence collected from his mobile showed that this was something that he had simply researched and used as an excuse.

Other evidence was submitted via some messages he had sent to Josie Bellamy admitting that other women had also accused him of abusing them in their sleep. This was used to identify culpability because it stipulated that he knew he had a problem. Therefore, as a whole, it was submitted as a premeditated act because he failed to seek any appropriate help to deal with his problem and continued to put women at risk by sharing a bed with them. It was also dismissed as an excuse because there was no evidence in his medical records that indicated a formal diagnosis. It was put to the court by the prosecution that it was simply a facade that Day had concocted, as he thought it would excuse his behaviour. It did not.

In her statement, Shona Williams was able to disclose that in Day's interview, he had simply discounted the act of molesting Josie Bellamy, describing it as him turning over and his hand accidentally brushing past or knocking her breast. Yet she described waking to 'being aggressively groped' and, on other occasions, being prodded and poked vaginally, or being forced into oral sex and taken from behind whilst settling down to sleep. Why? Because Robert Day Jr 'had to have her', whether she was a willing participant or not.

The jury heard how his victims were persistently manipulated through confusion because he forever denied that his intention was ever as they believed. Therefore, he was guilty of nothing. Yet he continued to take advantage of these women in what should have been the safety and security of their own beds, despite their continuous disapproval and firm acknowledgement that these were non-consensual acts of sexual abuse and rape. Robert Day Jr would then play the victim, neither able nor willing to absorb the truth of their complaints.

Evidence of deleted messages on his phone stated, 'his disgust of what he had become' with the recognition that 'it would be far better to lock himself away so that he could not hurt anyone else.' Robert Day Jr may have sat in court in his smart suit with his puppy dog eyes trying to represent a man who had been misunderstood, but the evidence presented showed the extent of his true nature and real intentions. That is, these women had been mercilessly chosen by him to maul and rape at leisure, using the exact same initial love-bombing techniques to develop trust so he could persistently manipulate to coerce them into quenching his insatiable, debauched need to control.

Not one, but at least three different women's accounts matched each other's. The defence tried to argue that Wray and Bellamy were friends who had committed a hate crime against Day, whilst dismissing Conway's validity because she hadn't even bothered to turn up. With regards to Peters', they put forward that the diary was simply a figment of her imagination, the ramblings of a book she might be writing, if at all it did belong to her.

However, both Anita Collins and Shona Williams were able to give evidence regarding their interview with Daniela Conway, and Sallyanne was able to positively identify Amelia's handwriting. The prosecution also used Rosina's time on the stand to gain valuable insight into Heather's relationship with Day or similar experiences, along with the revelation that, upon the night she mysteriously died, she was going to leave him. This was the only snippet of information submitted at the trial whereby Day was visibly seen to demonstrate any form of a reaction.

Day was condemned as having no right to share a bed with any woman if, by his own admission, he knew he had a problem. Yet, he replicated the same abuse towards each victim. He was described as having shown no remorse, guilt, compassion or any level of understanding for the damage that would stay with them for the rest of their lives.

With regards to the life of Karen Blakely, the evidence presented by the police was basically incontestable, so to Day's dismay, his defence lawyer washed over it with a ploy for a temporary lapse of control. However, the 999 call, the discrepancy in the time of the ambulances' arrival, the shoe print that matched the trainers he was wearing, the clothes found secreted in the wheelie bin smeared with Karen's blood, skull fragments and brain matter, the recorded voicemail of the murder taking place, the visual and audible dashcam footage, the fake ring and the estimated time for the bath to fill to when it overflowed proved it had been turned on after Karen had been killed. This overwhelming weight of proof left no room for any reasonable doubt that, whether Day had impulsively lashed out or not, the sequence of actions that followed demonstrated a methodical, calculated and deliberate effort to cover up what he had done. The conclusion was reached that he knew exactly what he was doing, and therefore he was guilty of her murder.

Karen's mother, Diana, spoke admirably about the pride she'd had in her daughters' achievements both academically, professionally and sociably. Her sister, Mabel, described her as the 'perfect role model,' 'a sister she looked up to' and a 'friend that she thought highly of.' Both recounted how Karen had changed since her relationship with Day, becoming withdrawn, always being exhausted and of never visiting unless he was with her. Mabel had said it was like there was an invisible chain that he held around her neck, like a dog's choker, that he was systematically yanking her back with whilst keeping her at his heel. They both gave impactful statements of the loss they felt and would feel every day of their lives.

Marcus St John was the most expressive witness, who detailed his friendship with Karen Blakely, describing her as a huge loss to the world in general but personally to himself as both a colleague and a true friend. Before leaving the witness box, he addressed Day and simply said, 'May God have mercy on your soul, but may the place you are going, Hell, burn you to a slow, very painful cinder.' This was purposefully left to sit in the air.

Against his solicitor's advice, Day chose to stand up in court to attempt to sway the jury with his usual Mr Nice Guy act giving his pathetic recount of the evidence that had been presented. His defence tried to create a picture of a loving father, a loyal son, a lifelong provider and an avid contributor to the economy. However, without even realising that he would be subject to cross-examination, it gave the prosecution the ability to directly submit evidence of his debts, thefts from the tax man, credit cards, his gambling and failure to disclose his wages and pay adequate child support.

Day continued to dig hole after hole until his final performance of a pitiful emotional outburst, when a photograph was distributed to the jurors, the judge and other key personnel. They were then invited to compare the images of each of the victims as their faces were simultaneously projected on the screen in the court. A woman who not only bore a stark resemblance but whose age, circumstances and death mimicked the savage attacks on Karen Blakely and

Amelia Jayne Peters. The lady in the photograph was introduced as Susannah Day, Robert Day Jr's mother.

In the conclusion of the case, the judge addressed Day and told him his performance had been nothing more than an act, whereby the evidence box was merely a stage for him to play a role, exactly as the police had described during his interviews. 'Who is Robert Day Jr?' he asked the court. 'The answer is not the character he has played, trying to save himself in court, but it lies in the desperate written words of Amelia Jayne Peters' book, the hopelessness of Josie Bellamy's video, and the anguish of Rosina Wray. These women have testified before you and gallantly described their experiences to step in the gap for other women, despite no one standing in that same gap for them. They have a right to be heard, and they have a right to justice therefore I thank the jury for coming to the only possible judgement of finding Robert Day Jr guilty of the rape and molestation of Rosina Wray, Josie Bellamy and Amelia Jayne Peters.

'In the case of Amelia Jayne Peters' murder, you heard her sister, Sallyanne Peters, a medical examiner, testify to raising her concerns that Robert Day Jr was 'too good to be true.' She witnessed the same methods of operation that we have not only already heard of, but of which Amelia herself has communicated to us through her secreted journal. Let us just absorb that for a moment.

'Amelia, or as Sallyanne affectionately called her, Meli,' was so terrified for her safety that she had left behind a message urging the finder of her journal to 'take the book to the police' and stressing 'it was not a hoax.' She had even gone to the trouble of naming him and giving her date of birth, because she was sure he was going to harm her. And she was right. The police presented documentary evidence detailing the specific, off-the-grid route that Robert Day Jr had taken to intentionally commit her murder in the hope he would not be detected.

'This was a cold-blooded, premeditated act that would possibly never have come to light had it not been for the ingenious detective abilities of DCI Shona Williams and her team. They have shown an unwavering determination to ensure Robert Day Jr is made accountable for his crimes by also seeking the cooperation of the Spanish government. By obtaining supplementary evidence and the inclusion of the initial autopsy, its re-examination has determined that the damage to Amelia Jayne Peters' head was in fact caused through blunt force trauma and not hitting the bottom of the pool, as previously thought. It has therefore been concluded that, on the evidence presented, you have been found guilty of the murder of Amelia Jayne Peters beyond any reasonable doubt.

'In the case of Karen Blakely, the compelling evidence that you were responsible for her murder has again been overwhelming, yet you still maintain your innocence. The red and black fibres discovered on Karen's person the night she died matched the clothing fibres preserved in the carrier bag pushed down into the rotting slops of your household bin. Again, if it had not been for the dash cam footage capturing you approaching her car wearing those garments, a search warrant wouldn't have been executed. The testimonies from her colleagues that Karen communicated to them about your relationship are contrary to the stories you told the police.'

'The defeated conversation outlined by her friend Marcus, of the phone call also captured through the audio of the dash cam the night of the murder, was again a complete contrast to the one you would have us all believing. Then there was the lack of explanation for the time difference detected between the severing of the 999 calls in conjunction with the ambulance arriving. The change of clothes, the shoe print in the bedroom matching the new trainers submitted into evidence on the night of her murder and the non-existent unqualified intruder. We then have a match for your handprint as you gripped the side of the island to ensure you brought the maximum force possible to Karen Blakely's head. Whereby this would not be sufficient to stand alone, it is supplementary to the rest of the compelling evidence.'

'You have done everything in your power to shirk any responsibility for your actions, but the truth has been demonstrated fully and without measure in the recorded voicemail Marcus St John found on his phone. If there was any doubt, which there is not, then the thousands of messages you not only bombarded her with, but each of the women clearly shows the character of who you are as a man. And I use that word loosely. Through those messages, we are privy to the personal demonstration of an inability to take no for an answer, something that we have heard multiple times throughout this trial. Your incessant desire to overpower and control is not a reflection of how gullible and weak these women are, but how needy, clingy and desperate you are for attention.'

'Karen Blakely was another woman who had succumbed to your wily ways under the guise and misbelief of a prosperous future together. However, her hopes were soon dashed when she became wise to your methods. We have no way of knowing whether she was subjected to the same degradation as Amelia Jayne Peters, Josie Bellamy, Rosina Wray or Daniela Conway. We may never know Heather Day's full story, or whether you were responsible for your own mother's death.'

'However, despite Daniela Conway only agreeing to let her statement be used to support this case and not to bring justice for the crimes you committed against her, it is my intention to leave it open for Daniela Conway to present her case to this court should she wish to at any time in the future. And I would personally urge her to do so, if only to raise herself from the ashes as these other women have been able to do so. All I can hope is that you, June Brown, have taken note of what has been said in this court and that your eyes have been fully opened. I trust that not only have the scales fallen from your eyes and you have recognised who this man really is, but that you will also acknowledge the women who have stepped in the gap to prevent you from succumbing to the same fate.'

'Robert Day Jr, you seem to uncharacteristically observe yourself as the victim within the circumstances only you have created. From what we have heard, it seems that the only voice you hear is the one inside your own head, and it is this alone that propels you forward to pursue those desires, even at the damaging expense of every other person. You have shown a callous disregard for human life, a cold, unsympathetic stance towards your victims, and have completely failed to take an ounce of responsibility. Therefore, I have no problem in giving you the maximum sentences possible for each crime, but this will not be a cumulo sentence, as each crime needs to be addressed independently to reflect the severity of the offences.'

'I find that with regards to rape, each will be deemed as a category 1 due to the severity of the psychological harm, the individual's vulnerability, their continued humiliation, threats that their treatment would be worse if they did not comply, and your uninvited presence within their homes. The culpability level for each of the cases presented I determine as being a level A due to the degree of planning that you have exercised to execute those acts, the compliance sought through alcohol, and the repetitiveness of those acts whilst abusing their trust. I hereby sentence you to a maximum of 15 years for the rape against Josie Bellamy, 15 years for the rape against Rosina Wray and 15 years for the rape against Amelia Jayne Peters. Unfortunately, I am unable to pass judgement with regard to the rape of Daniela Conway at her request; otherwise, that would have incurred a further 15 years.'

'In relation to the murder of Amelia Jayne Peters, the court delivers a whole life sentence, which means you will not be eligible for parole.'

'In relation to the murder of Karen Blakely, the court delivers a whole life sentence, which means you will not be eligible for parole.'

'I will reiterate that it is my intention to leave the crimes committed by Robert Day Jr against Daniela Conway on file, should she wish to pursue the matter at a later date.'

She slammed the hammer down and proceeded to push her chair back as the court clerk shouted for the final time, 'All rise.'